A
Doesn't Fall

A Sparrow
Doesn't Fall

June Francis

BANTAM BOOKS
NEW YORK · TORONTO · LONDON · SYDNEY · AUCKLAND

A SPARROW DOESN'T FALL

A BANTAM BOOK 0 553 40364 8

Originally published in Great Britain by Judy Piatkus
(Publishers) Ltd.

PRINTING HISTORY
Judy Piatkus edition published 1990
Bantam edition published 1992

Bantam Books are published by Transworld Publishers Ltd.,
61–63 Uxbridge Road, Ealing, London W5 5SA,
in Australia by Transworld Publishers (Australia) Pty. Ltd.,
15–23 Helles Avenue, Moorebank, NSW 2170, and in New
Zealand by Transworld Publishers (N.Z.) Ltd., Cnr. Moselle
and Waipareira Avenues, Henderson, Auckland.

Printed and bound in Great Britain by
BPCC Hazells Ltd
Member of BPCC Ltd

Acknowledgements

My thanks to my brother Ron Nelson for taking the time to write his boyhood memories of the war and its aftermath. Also I am grateful to the men and women of Merseyside who shared their often painful pasts with me and the Librarians of Litherland, Crosby and Liverpool Central Library who helped me with research material.

Dedicated to my husband John and sons Iain, Tim and Daniel with gratitude for their patience and the cups of tea and cocoa they brought me when slaving over a hot keyboard instead of the kitchen stove.

Are not two sparrows sold for a penny? And
not one of them will fall to the ground without
your Father's will. But even the hairs on your
head are numbered. Fear not, therefore;
you are of more value than many sparrows.

Matt. Ch.10, v29–35

Prologue

Flora Cooke had been dreaming again. She woke with a start, forcing her eyelids up. Dawn was pearling the bedroom wall, and for a moment she lay stiff with anxiety before making the effort to reach for the man who lay beside her.

Waking brought relief flowing to all her limbs, easing her fear. 'Tom,' she whispered, placing her arm across his naked chest. He stirred but made no answer. 'Tom!' Her fingers tugged one of the golden hairs on his chest.

'Watch it, Flo,' he murmured sleepily, slapping her hand. 'Or I'll do the same to you but harder.'

'I don't have curls on my chest.' There was a hint of laughter in her voice as she leaned over him, and her bare breasts brushed his chest tantalisingly before she took his face between her palms, and kissed him full on the mouth.

His arms wrapped round her. 'You should eat more crusts for curls,' he said softly, the moment he had breath. 'Then after the war we could make our fortune. I could paint you and exhibit your portrait all over Lancashire. Roll up, roll up! Come and see the carroty-haired double-breasted beauty.'

Her pale brow creased. 'My hair's not carroty. But I like the idea of making a fortune. Maybe then we could have that house I dream about.'

'You and your dreams,' he scoffed. 'They'll never get you anywhere, Flo. Our class has to work for everything.'

'Don't be so miserable. You should have more faith.' She stretched herself out on him and buffeted his chin with her head. 'You didn't really mean that about painting me half naked and selling my picture?' Her tone was

1

serious. 'I don't mind you looking at me, Tom, but other men – no.'

'If it was going to make us a fortune, I would,' he teased. 'Now there's my dream, Flo – painting. It beats soldiering or making door frames and windows for folk. But as for you, girl, you really have no shame. Look at the way you're behaving now – you hussy.' He caught her by the hair, dragging her head back so that he could the better nuzzle her breasts.

'What's the shame in it when we're man and wife?' she demanded. 'Doesn't it say in the Bible that a man leaves his mother and father to cleave to his wife? I'm making sure that you're happy with me. Then you're not likely to go seeking elsewhere for home comforts.' She nudged his head with her elbow and he looked up into her hazel eyes. 'I met this girl and her job was emptying the pockets of the uniforms sent back home to be cleaned. She said it was an eye opener to what soldiers got up to when away from home. So you do know what I mean? I'm making sure you don't roam.'

He laughed. 'So that's your recipe for any man who might want to stray.'

'I believe if you love a man, then you make sure he's well fed and well bedded – that's it almost in a nutshell.' She wriggled, brushing her stomach against his, and he caught his breath. She laughed, feeling the power swell in her. Then tears sparkled on her dark red lashes. 'It was you who told me they were the important things when we first got married. I was an innocent,' she whispered huskily. 'But it hasn't been easy, what with the war. Three years – that's all we had really, before you were called up. So now we have to make the most of our time together. But maybe after the war – you may scoff, Tom – then perhaps my recipe and my dream of us all being in that house will work together for us. Happy ever after we'll be.'

'You read too many books,' he muttered, a flame of desire igniting the depths of his brown eyes. 'Forget your dreams and think of right now!' He pulled her down on him, kissing her forcibly until her soft lips parted, and his tongue probed the sweetness of her mouth.

She responded enthusiastically, casting all cares aside as she offered herself unreservedly to him. Even after eight years of marriage she found him exciting, and desire soared.

They rolled over and he entered her, thrusting hard so that she gasped. Sometimes he was too rough but she coped and never complained. He moved slowly and she knew that he wanted to prolong the pleasure. It could be the last time for who knew how long? But his urgent need demanded instant gratification. Their bodies erupted into frenzied activity that had the rhythm of life in its beat. They were one giant heart pumping energy and pleasure. No other man had ever known her, and since girlhood she had willingly been his slave. She muffled a scream of delight against his shoulder, biting his flesh as he sent warm currents of pleasure through her.

He rubbed his cheek against hers. 'Flora Dora, you're a wanton.'

She was hurt. 'No, I'm not. You taught me to enjoy it.' And pulling his tawny head on to her breast, she said, 'I love you.' The words were only a thread of sound because tears were near. Soon they would part — him to his south coast camp and her home to Liverpool. She did not know how she was going to bear saying goodbye. In truth she decided that she would not. 'Tarrah!' or 'Cheerio!' would be better. They did not have the final feeling of a goodbye. She swallowed to ease her throat. 'When will I see you again?'

'I don't know,' he responded tersely, before kissing her breast. He lifted his head and gazed into her face. 'Don't start getting all maudlin on me, Flo. I'm hungry. Let's go and see what this place has in the way of breakfast.'

'If that's what you want.' She would have liked to have lain longer with him in her arms, but now she just stared at him, determined to impress on her memory every nuance of his countenance — the brown eyes fringed with golden lashes, the square, slightly bristly jaw; the aquiline nose which often gave a haughty cast to his face when he was vexed. Then she would have to coax and tease him until he was in a good mood again. She seldom failed.

His eyes crinkled at the corners. 'What are you thinking, staring at me like that?' he demanded, stretching and sticking

3

one hardened foot out of the blankets. 'You'd think I was a stranger.'

'I was thinking how glad I'll be when the war is over,' she murmured, not wanting, or even knowing how, to tell him that she was absorbing the way he looked in the flesh. Her dream had frightened her, and a photograph, posed and too often wooden-faced, was not the same to remember someone by. She felt as if a hand squeezed her heart. How she hated the war! The uncertainty and the fearing to hope that all would come right in the end.

'Perhaps it won't be as good when we're sleeping together every night.' His eyes scanned her rosy oval face as he reached for the cigarettes on the little table by the side of the bed. 'It wasn't always. At least this way we never get fed up of each other.'

Anxiety darkened her eyes, and she sat up abruptly. 'What a thing to say, Tom. I was happy doing whatever you wanted. Were you getting tired of me before the war?'

He made her wait for his answer as he lit up and exhaled his breath in a puff of smoke. 'Not that I remember. But who knows? If the war hadn't come ...' He grinned as she opened her mouth, her face expressing her pained indignation. 'Come on, girl, you know I still fancy you.' He kissed her bare shoulder. 'I've just made you happy, haven't I, you little whore?'

Her mouth drooped. 'Don't call me that, Tom. I'm your wife!'

He moved his shoulders. 'It doesn't mean anything. A joke because you're always so eager. Now shall we get up and have breakfast? Then it's heigh ho, back to messing about in boats I have to go.'

'Boats?' She leaned over to pick up her frock from the floor. Chill fear clutched her heart again. Not far away was the English Channel, and the other side of that – France and Hitler's soldiers.

'Don't be worrying.' He sat back against the headboard, watching her graceful movements as she dressed. No underwear, only a green and white flower-patterned old cotton frock. He hoped that she did have some knickers somewhere to put on later. He knew she knew he liked her going without

4

when she was with him, and she had almost always been amenable — in the beginning she had been shy about stripping off, but he had soon cured her of that. He had told her he loved her body and she had gradually lost all embarrassment. She looked quite lovely this morning, with the flush on her cheeks and her shoulder-length copper-coloured hair in a tangle. He would have liked to have taken her again, but there was no time if they were to eat. 'Tell me about the kids.' Tom inhaled luxuriously. 'How's our George behaving himself?'

'The same as usual,' she murmured, beginning to brush her hair. 'But he's too much like you. A mad Alec! He never seems to see danger.'

'You see enough of it for all of us.' He added lazily, 'Stop worrying, Flo. It might never happen.'

'But then again it might,' she said quietly, her hands trembling. Her dream was with her again. 'He plays soldiers or football most of the time. Soldiers! Tom, you've no idea what he gets up to playing war games.' Her voice was brittle.

'He's a lad and it's war time, so he's bound to play and pretend. Don't we all pretend at times?' he muttered tersely, apprehension tightening his stomach.

'So you think it's okay to collect shrapnel and shells, and lob them at each other over broken-down walls, pretending to kill each other? I get scared. He's only seven, and he's always in and out of bombed houses. I wish you were able to speak to him, love,' she said earnestly. 'Or write him a letter even, telling him it's dangerous. He'd listen to you.'

'You reckon? He hardly knows me.' A stream of smoke issued from his nostrils. 'Maybe I'll write. Is anything else bothering you?' he murmured absently. 'Are you managing on your allowance? I know it's not much.'

'I'm managing,' she said quickly, determined not to bother him with the difficulties that wives with young children faced every day. The one pound, two shillings and five pence army pay did not go far, and she had considered finding a part-time job. She had Rosie's name on a nursery waiting list, but it could be some time before she heard anything about that. Her father had lent her the money to come south, but she

5

would have to pay him back — even if it was only a couple of coppers a week. She had asked him about looking after Rosie for a couple of hours a day, but he had said that she was too much of handful. She looked at her husband. 'Rosie doesn't know you at all.'

'I know.' He got out of bed and went to wash in the china flower-sprigged basin on the stand in the corner. 'That's one of the annoying things about army life. I've got a daughter I've only seen once.' He pulled a face as he began to wash. 'I'll write her a letter too if you like. "To my darling daughter — are you as gorgeous as your mam?"'

'I could read it to her,' she said pensively, brushing her hair. Then she added shyly, 'Do you really think I'm gorgeous?'

'Would I say it if I didn't mean it?' He glanced at her, soapy hands resting on his hips. 'If I had to toss a coin between you and your sister, who would I want to come up heads?'

She smiled. 'You're teasing me. Our Hilda is lovely, and you could have had her. I couldn't believe my luck when she went out with Jimmy Martin, and you asked me out. Although her and Jimmy didn't last long. We've lasted, haven't we? We still love each other.'

His eyes flickered over her face, before dropping. 'Too true. If I'd stuck with your Hilda, it wouldn't have been like it is with us. She can't be trusted.' He began to lather his inner thighs. 'How long since last you saw her? I hope she doesn't come bothering you again.'

'A couple of years — she took the baby with her after a row with Father. I do worry about her sometimes.'

He gave a sharp laugh. 'You don't have to worry about your Hilda. She'll find somebody else to get round. She's a conniving bitch.'

'Tom!' There was almost a rebuke in her voice. 'She's my sister, and if she ever needs me I've got to be there. Aunt Beattie always preached that families should help each other. She looked after us when Mam died and Father was at sea. Hilda was all I had then. We slept together, ate together, even played together sometimes — remember?'

'She always thought you a nuisance, tagging on behind the gang. You and some of the other young ones.' He laughed.

'Old days, Flo. Times change. People change. Now shut up about your Hilda.'

She fell silent, watching him pull on his khaki shirt, hoping that she had not annoyed him. She hated being out of friends. Going over to him, she wrapped her arms round his waist. 'I love you. I wish you didn't have to go.'

He paused in the act of buttoning. 'Don't be daft,' he said impatiently. 'I have to. Besides we just might have Jerry on the run soon, and then I'll be home by Christmas.'

'I've heard something like that before.' A trickle of apprehension turned her legs weak. 'Have you heard anything?'

He shrugged. 'The big nobs are always going on about a Second Front. But don't you start worrying me. I've come through so far, haven't I?'

'Yes.' Her throat constricted, and she rested her cheek against his back. 'Don't take chances, Tom. I know what you're like – you don't think of the consequences. Don't play the hero.'

'Who, me?' He laughed. 'Don't be stupid. I'll keep my head down.'

'Good.' She didn't believe him, remembering his daredevilry when they were younger. He had always been a ring leader, daring the other boys into doing all sorts of dangerous tricks. 'Do be careful.' Her eyes pleaded with him through the round wooden-framed mirror.

He pulled away from her, a scowl on his face. 'Don't go on, Flo! You'll have me nervous.'

She smiled. 'You don't have a nerve in your body. I've never seen you scared of anything.'

He did not smile back. 'Shut up, Flo. And get a move on if I'm going to the station with you.'

'Don't be cross.' Her expressive hazel eyes clouded. 'Perhaps it would be better to say our farewells here. I hate the waiting about until the last second. Then we wave and wave as the train puffs and puffs. It drags out the pain and I hate it.'

'God, Flo!' he cried angrily. 'Don't go on, or I won't come to the station with you.'

'Oh no! Come!' She reached for his hands and clung to them. 'But just one long kiss and a tarrah – then go.'

7

'A tarrah, girl! How Liverpudlian.' He gave a twisted smile. 'Say hello to the Liver bird for me. Although I'm only half scouse, I've a feeling sometimes for the sight of the thing.'

'A home feeling,' she said huskily, her throat tight with tears as she went into his arms and hugged him. They kissed and went down to breakfast.

Part One

Chapter One

The summer day started well. It was a perfect morning of bright sun and polished blue sky. The pigeons cooed gently beneath the eaves of the terraced house, and the nasturtiums in the windowboxes in the backyard put forth orange and yellow flowers. There was lamb's liver at the butcher's, and Flora had enough money and coupons. For once Rosie, now three, was not screaming after her brother George, who had gone out to play, but instead laughing at the antics of the cat chasing a mouse.

Then the mouse scrabbled up the tablecloth with the cat in blazing pursuit, and the sugar basin was sent flying.

'You stupid moggy,' yelled Flora, daring to put a foot on the floor as she moved Rosie off her knee and on to the chair. Now the cat had the mouse pinned beneath his paw. Flora made a swipe at it but the cat only stared at her balefully, its ginger and black tail lashing furiously.

Flora decided to ignore it and turned instead to stare at the mixture of glass and sugar on the rag rug. The sugar was a whole week's ration. She could have wept. Perhaps it might not have seemed such a tragedy if she had not been reading over Tom's letter that morning. But then everything seemed too much to cope with since the invasion of Europe had begun a few weeks ago. What lay ahead for Tom? Her nerves were taut with the anticipation of bad news.

She went and found the brush to sweep up the mess. Rosie was kneeling up on the chair, tilting it dangerously backwards so that she could watch the cat toying with its prey behind it.

'Be careful!' exclaimed Flora, steadying the chair and glancing behind it. Why couldn't the cat just kill the mouse? she thought savagely. One swift blow and oblivion. Or what? Was there a heaven for dead mice? She pulled a face, wondering why she should be worrying about a mouse when there was so much else to be concerned about. Tom! Money! Tom!

On her knees she realised that brushing was not going to work, and had to lift the heavy rag rug and take it outside to tip the mess in the bin. That was still not enough and she had to hang the rug over the line and brush it until there was a fine layer of dust adhering to her sweaty face. She had just got sorted out when George came in. There was a tear six inches long in his grey flannel shorts and several bleeding grazes down his filthy legs. She fought to control her temper, asking unsteadily: 'What have you been up to?'

He shrugged. 'Nothing much.'

'Nothing, eh?' Her expression hardened and she forced him to strip off and stand in the stone sink in the back kitchen. With the threat of no jam on his bread hanging over him, he submitted to having blood and muck scrubbed off him. They were both near to tears by the time he was clean.

While Flora mended his trousers, George sat in front of the empty fireplace with a piece of sheeting wrapped round his middle. Then a thunderous wielding of the knocker sounded on the front door. She went to answer, not really in the mood for battle.

'I believe this is your George's,' accused Mrs Murphy, flourishing a football. She was the big Irish woman from three doors up, with a bosom like a bolster. She had six daughters and a small husband, known as Little Paddy, who had once been a jockey. They had moved into the street only a couple of years ago after being bombed out.

'Yes, it's my son's,' said Flora brightly, taking her by surprise by seizing it quickly and back-kicking it up the lobby. She folded her arms defensively across her breasts. 'What's your complaint?'

Carmel Murphy shook her head, almost sorrowfully it seemed. 'He's been on me lavatory roof watching our Kat'leen and Mary treading the blankets in the bath in their knickers. Not nice at all, I say, Mrs Cooke. You never know where these things may lead.'

Flora sighed heavily. 'I don't believe he thinks girls up to much yet.'

'They start young these days. It's the war! And the bad example her next door sets. Her and her Yanks!' She wriggled broad shoulders and leaned against the wall with all the appearance of being ready for a good gossip, but Flora was not in the mood.

'I don't think it's got to that stage with George, surely,' she said blandly. 'I'll tell him, though, that he's not even to speak to your girls − if you'll stop them frolicking half-naked, polluting young boys' thoughts.'

Mrs Murphy straightened up hurriedly. 'Now don't be taking offence, luv. We don't have to go as far as that. But I don't like him seeing them in their knickers, and that's the truth.'

'All right,' said Flora politely. 'We won't fall out over it. Good day to you, Mrs Murphy.' She closed the door and marched up the lobby to confront her son.

'What have you been doing, ogling young girls in baths?'

'They had their knickers on.' George rubbed his cheek on the sheeting and stared at her with Tom's eyes. 'They asked me to get in with them. But I heard her coming and moved quick. That's how I ripped me kecks − clambering down her back door.'

'Well, no more of it.' The smallest of smiles lifted her mouth. 'I don't know what to do with you sometimes, George Cooke. If your father was here −'

'But he isn't.' George smiled. 'He's killing the Jerries.' He swept his arm round and made a noise like a machine gun. Rosie joined in, and Flora put her hands over her ears. 'Shut up, the pair of you,' she yelled. Last night her dream had come to her again and left her feeling uneasy. 'I hate the noise of gunfire.'

'It's only a game, Mam.' George got up and dragged at her arm, only to have to reach down hurriedly for the sheeting. 'Let's go to Grandad's. He might have some pigeon eggs for us.'

'He'll probably make us pay for them, the way he's been lately.'

George grinned. 'You should stand up to him, Mam. He treats you like a little girl.'

She smiled. 'I think I still am to him. He's as bossy as ever he used to be. It's all those years on the sailing ships. He's had a tough life, your grandad, and he was always hellbent on making it tough for me and our Hilda when he was home. I got into the habit of saying nothing – sitting in a corner reading books that your great aunt Beattie lent me. That way he didn't notice me as much. But our Hilda! They used to go at it hammer and tongs. But we'll go and see him. The walk'll tire Rosie out. Now put them on.' She threw his pants at him.

He was dressing when the knocker sounded again. With an exaggerated sigh she went to answer its summons.

A telegraph boy stood before her, and immediately her heart leapt suffocatingly into her throat. He held out an envelope. 'Here ye'rrah, missus.' She took the flimsy offering and did not see him ride off speedily on his bicycle. Her trembling fingers tore the envelope open and her eyes fixed on the words in front of her.

'We regret to inform you that soldier' ... the number blurred as she read the rest ... 'missing presumed dead.' An icy blast of despair seemed to deprive her of all movement. Only her brain still functioned, repeating the words frantically, hammering them into her mind. 'It's a mistake,' she whispered, addressing the shining blue sky. 'You wouldn't let him die when I've prayed and prayed for him to be kept safe.' Her voice gained strength. 'He's not dead,' she yelled angrily.

George came flying up the lobby, buttoning his pants, and the door to the next house opened slowly. 'What's up, Mam?' He clutched her arm, and with his other hand plucked the telegram from her shaking fingers. He read it carefully. 'It says me dad's presumed dead,' he cried in an unbelieving voice. 'It's written here.'

'Bad news is it, luv?' Mrs Bryce, with her jet black hair

14

in curlers beneath a green turban, walked slowly towards her. 'It's hard to take these things in. A luv'ly man, yer husband. But they don't send telegrams if they think they're making a mistake.' She put a hand on Flora's shoulder, but she rounded on her neighbour angrily.

'Well, this time they have. It's a mistake, I tell you, and I'm going to make them realise it as well.' Her eyes were sparkling with tears.

'You do that, luv.' Mrs Bryce was undeterred. 'But I doubt it'll change things.' Her raddled cheeks quivered. 'He was a one, your husband — a luv'ly man. Go inside and have a cup of sweet hot tea. That'll make you feel better.'

'I don't want tea,' murmured Flora through stiff lips, her face white. 'Even if the cat hadn't spilt all the sugar, tea wouldn't do me any good right now!' She turned away with a swirl of skimpy skirts. 'I'm going to my father's. They won't be able to lie to him. He'll tell them.' The door was left wide as she marched up the lobby. George followed her, still holding the telegram.

'Mam!' His voice was uneasy. 'What'll I do with this?' He waved the telegram in the air. Flora, in the process of fastening Rosie's shoes, did not answer, and with a heavy sigh he shoved it in his pants' pocket. Finding his plimsolls, he put them on, and followed Flora and Rosie outside.

She barely noticed several of the neighbours standing in groups talking in low voices. Nor the familiar landmarks on the way to her father's — the icecream parlour, the drinking fountain in the centre of the cobbled road, the church, where she had taken her first communion. She came to the street of yellow brick houses and banged her father's heavy knocker.

'It's hard to take, girl, but you've got to accept it.' Jack Preston stared at Flora from beneath bristling greying brows as he picked up the old clay pipe from the mantelpiece. 'A pity. He wasn't a bad sort, your Tom, despite having some daft ideas.'

'It's a mistake, Father,' she responded calmly enough, her eyes fixed on his lined face. 'You'll write to them for me and they'll listen to you — you being a man.' Her hands lay still in her lap, the fingers interlocked so that the knuckles gleamed white.

'Don't be daft, lass,' he said gruffly. 'That'd likely be a waste of time.' He took a dead matchstick from a tin on the hob and lit it from the fire. 'Besides it's not me that's had fancy book learning. You had all that from your mam's sister.'

Flora's eyelashes flickered, and pain flashed in her face. 'But he might not be dead,' she said earnestly, spreading the telegram on her lap. She read the words yet again. Missing presumed dead. Dead! Her hopes dimmed but she persisted. 'If he's dead, Father, why do they say presumed?' she stammered. 'If they can't find his body, then − '

Her father bit hard on his pipe and rubbed his chin. 'Have you forgotten the May blitz, girl? And the mess a landmine caused? How many went missing in those days − some never to be found.'

Flora moistened her dry mouth; she felt sick and cold as her father's words conjured up pictures in her mind, so that she could almost smell brick and plaster dust, and the acrid smoke as the heart of Liverpool had collapsed and burnt. She remembered going past Mill Road Hospital with the newly born Rosie in a pram. That had been terrible − hit by a parachute mine, most of the mothers and babies in the maternity ward had been killed. Even so there had been places in the city where people had been dug out alive after being missing for several days. She sought to hold on to her previous hope. 'But it's still possible that he's just missing. He might still be alive!'

'It's not impossible, I suppose,' muttered her father grudgingly. 'But they don't send telegrams if there's a good chance of someone being alive, girl. You've just got to accept that he's gone, and get on with your life for the kids' sake. You're not the only one grieving, Flora.'

'I'm not grieving at all because he might be alive, Father. He'll come back, you'll see.' Her hands shook, and her thumbnails dug into her flesh. The pain was a distraction from the greater chilling dark ache that had her in its hold.

He shook his head slowly. 'We'll see, girl. But I think you'd be wiser accepting these things happen.'

Avoiding his eyes Flora rose from the straight-backed chair. 'You won't write then, Father?' He shook his head. 'Then I will,' she murmured, squaring her shoulders. 'I'll go home and do it now.'

She was halfway to the front door when her father called: 'What about George and the little lass?' His fierce blue eyes accused her. 'Don't be thinking just of yerself, girl.'

Her cheeks flushed, she went to get her children but her mind was filled with thoughts of Tom. They came without any fuss, George clutching a couple of small eggs. Her father told him he could have them.

They had only just got home when there was a knock on the door. George went to open it. On the doorstep stood Kathleen Murphy, skinny and dark with pinched features, who was of a similar age to him. She grinned and thrust a cup at him. 'Me mam sent this sugar. Said yer mam's gorra make 'erself a cuppa tea, sweet and 'ot. And if there's anything she can do, yer mam's only gorra ask.'

George took the half filled cup of sugar and shifted awkwardly. 'Thanks.' There was a pause as they stared at each other. 'Will you be playing out after?'

Her smile broadened. 'If you're not playin' with a ball and getting in the way of our rope, we could play duckin' under without touchin'.'

'Or stroke the bunny!' he retorted, almost enthusiastically.

'Yer'd 'ave to get some of the others to play,' said Kathleen. She liked the hide and seek game, especially when there was the chance of ending up behind a privet hedge with George.

'See you later then.' He winked and closed the door.

Flora was touched by the gift from Mrs Murphy, guessing that she could ill-afford it, and made them all a cup of sweet tea. Later she wrote off to the War Commissioners, pleading with them to find her husband, then she waited.

The next few weeks passed in a haze. Flora did all the normal tasks, but it was as if she was standing outside herself, watching someone else perform them. She could not eat and slept only fitfully. Sometimes she drifted into slumber and dreamed her old dream of the house by the sea. In that

17

period of half waking, half sleeping, she imagined that Tom was with her – that they were holding each other.

Fully awake, it was as if she was in a glass bubble looking out on a world of people going about their everyday lives, unaware that she existed. In a way that was what she wanted. When people attempted to intrude into her bubble, its protection grew wobbly and she feared it would collapse and her with it, because she could not bear the way they all felt sorry for her. They believed Tom dead, and that made him dead. They asked if there was anything they could do, but she always refused very politely, and so the weeks went by.

The day that the letter came telling her that no trace had been found of Tom – that he had been in an area where a shell had exploded, killing five other men and wounding two – her hopes were shattered. It was just as her father had said, and he was generally right.

She went to church, the children sitting on either side of her, and knelt throughout the whole of a morning service. Prayer was beyond her. All that she could do was to stare fixedly at the brass eagle with its soaring wings, holding the large Bible. 'They shall mount up like eagles – they shall run and not be weary –' The lines from Isaiah trickled through her thoughts, and she wondered whether Tom was existing in a heaven somewhere.

The day after, Mrs Murphy stopped her in the street. 'And how have you bin, Mrs Cooke?' she asked. 'Our Kat'leen's been telling me that George said there's no hope of your husband being alive now.'

'Yes,' said Flora in a voice that was calmer than she felt. 'I still find it hard to believe.'

There was compassion in the Irishwoman's face. 'I'll say a prayer for you, girlie,' she murmured. 'And for your good man's soul. I'm on my way to mass now.'

Flora did not believe in praying for the dead. Salvation was in Jesus, and only His forgiveness of confessed sins could save you. Still, her grief caused her to clutch at anything more that could be done for Tom. Later that day when she passed St Michael's, she caught a glimpse of a statue and the brightly decorated altar through the open door, and she thought of her father. He would have a fit if he ever got to

18

know that she had had prayers said in a Catholic church. Orange was the sash her father wore, he hated papists. But for once she did not care about religious differences. Mrs Murphy had wanted to help in the way she thought best.

Flora stared up at the sky, grey without a glimmer of sun. Where were all her dreams now? Vanished with Tom. She attempted to straighten drooping shoulders, but it was as if a weight pressed them down. Despair gripped her. How was she going to cope with life without hope of ever seeing him again?

As Flora went about her household tasks or stood in queues she was haunted by the past. So many places shrieked: Remember! When Tom paid a whole shilling to take you to the Paramount when it first opened and you saw Claudette Colbert in *Cleopatra*. When he taught you to swim in the baths in Stanley Park. When he kissed you for the first time on grass, lush green and sprinkled with daisies, and it felt like heaven.

And although Tom had barely slept in their double bed since the war began, now it seemed over-large and terribly empty. How now was it possible to rise in the world — to have that house by the sea for her and Tom and the kids? A large house with a bathroom and a garden big enough to grow lots of flowers. Her past dreams seemed to mock her.

Slowly all her interest in, and love of, life seeped out of her, and only caring for the children kept her going. Sleep was difficult, although she always felt tired. She could not eat, having no interest in food. Her father told her that she was losing her grip on things and that she must pull herself together.

Flora tried but one day she was so weary that she could not get out of bed. Instead she lay watching specks of dust caught in a beam of sunlight that came through the bay window. Slowly the conviction that Tom was standing at the edge of the ray's brightness filled her being. Only Rosie wandering round and round the room, dragging a well-worn knitted golliwog, distracted her momentarily. Eventually the little girl managed to open the bedroom door and shut it

19

behind her. The sun shifted round to the west and still Flora lay in bed.

When George came home he discovered Rosie sitting on the rag rug in the kitchen, her arms wrapped tightly about the cat. She smelt. He was sick with hunger but it was obvious to him that there was no tea. 'Where's Mam?' he demanded of his sister in an angry, worried voice.

She rubbed her nose against the cat's fur. 'Bed,' she muttered forlornly. 'Hasn't got up.' Then she released the cat and held out her arms to him. 'Carry, Georgie.'

He shook his head. 'You've dirtied yourself.' Suddenly panic seized him. It wasn't like Mam to let Rosie get in such a state. He turned and raced upstairs.

The room was filled with the shadows of early evening and for an instant he thought Flora dead. Then her eyelids slowly lifted. 'Tom?' Her voice was husky as she squinted at George.

'Mam, why aren't you up?' His voice cracked. 'Are you ill?' He sat nervously on the edge of the bed.

'Oh, it's you, son.' She smiled faintly. 'I thought I saw your dad.'

Fear held George motionless and speechless, and his mouth went dry. He swallowed. 'You can't have,' he said baldly.

Her head shifted slowly on the pillow. 'You're wrong, son. He was over there in the corner. Perhaps he wants me to go with him?'

'But he's dead!' Involuntarily his eyes searched the corners of the room and relief mingled with his panic. 'There's nobody there, Mam! You're seeing things. Come on – get up. You shouldn't be in bed at this time of day unless you're ill. And you're never ill.' His hands seized the covers and he twitched them right back, revealing her body in the blue cotton frock she had worn all week. He was even more frightened then. Why hadn't he noticed her getting thinner and thinner? She was bony, and that wasn't his mam. What if she died?

He took hold of her wrists, gripping them tightly, wanting her out of the bed and on her feet. Once upright he felt sure that she would be okay.

George pulled hard yet as gently as he could. Flora came

up to a sitting position abruptly, a surprised expression on her face. 'That's it, Mam.' He forced a smile. 'Now you've got to get out of bed.'

'I don't know if I can,' she murmured. 'I'm so tired, son.' The lines of her narrow-cheeked face drooped wearily, and her body sagged backwards.

'You've got to.' He felt quite desperate as he gripped her wrists the firmer. 'We need you, Mam.' He pulled, and suddenly they toppled over and his head hit the floor.

Rubbing the back of his head, he lay where he landed. 'That hurt!'

'Oh, George,' she said in a trembling voice, her hazel eyes catching the last of the daylight as she struggled to rise. 'You should have left me. Now you've hurt yourself.'

'I'll live.' He stared at her, and a sob rose in his throat. 'But you – you look awful, Mam! Your hair's all tatty and long, like a witch's in the stories you used to tell me.'

'Stories?' Flora's eyes rested on his anxious, young face, meeting the brown gaze so like Tom's, and she remembered the days of the blitz when she had taken the four-year-old George and baby Rosie down into the cellar when the bombs were falling. She had never felt safe in the air raid shelters since the Martin sisters and their mam had been killed in a direct hit. Now, staring at her son, she struggled with her emotions, thinking of the times she had found comfort in her children's company when danger had been close and Tom away at some training camp. She had sung lullabies and songs when fear had to be kept at bay.

'Remember the story about the dogs, the soldier and the tinder box?' demanded George eagerly. 'That was a favourite of mine.'

Unexpected tears pricked her eyes. 'That had a happy ending,' she whispered.

He smiled, wrapping his arms round his hunched knees, watching her shadowy face and noting the glistening tears. She had hardly cried since his dad had died, nor had he. Suddenly he wanted to weep, but boys were not supposed to cry. 'I like happy endings.' His voice was husky.

'Happy ever after,' she said unsteadily, reaching out for her son. Her arms went round him and she touched the

21

bump on his head with shaking fingers and then kissed it. At last she managed to swallow. 'Life's endings aren't always happy, son, but maybe that's because we don't go on believing and hoping long enough.' Her voice gained strength. 'I'll get up. You must be hungry.'

'Yeh!' George felt a surge of joy, knowing that in the last few minutes she had become his old mam again. He felt like he had won a battle. 'Let's go downstairs. There's not much to eat, Mam. You haven't been shopping today, and I couldn't find the ration books yesterday.'

'I've probably put them somewhere safe. In the meantime you'll have to have some butter on that bump.' She dragged his head down and kissed it again.

This time he struggled. 'I'd rather have it on bread if there is any.' He took hold of her hands and pulled her up.

Flora's legs felt wobbly and her feet as if glued to the floor, but she stumbled on to the dark landing and somehow they got down the stairs.

As they entered the kitchen Rosie was poking the paw of the struggling cat through the bars of the unlit fire, but as soon as she saw them she dropped the animal and it fled into the back kitchen. 'Mam!' She held up her arms, and her tiny white teeth gleamed in the dark. 'Cat scratched me.'

'You smell!' Flora fought down the wave of nausea, and summoning all her strength lifted her child. 'Poor little girl,' she whispered.

Rosie snuggled against her shoulder. 'Door locked, Mam. Take me the lav?'

Flora nodded wearily, before addressing her son. 'Get a chair and light the gas mantle, George.' He hurried to do as he was told while with cautious steps she carried her daughter down the back yard.

The cold air refreshed Flora and when they came back in the house she washed her daughter, standing her in the stone sink. Rosie was shivering by the time they went into the kitchen, lit by the glow of the gaslight.

George had raked out the ashes from the grate and was laying paper and wood. Flora found the shovel, and feeling her way carefully down the cellar steps in the dark she fetched coal. It was not long before the fire was burning and the kettle was on.

The children followed her out into the back kitchen to the food cupboard. 'Old Mother Hubbard went to the cupboard,' murmured Flora. 'Now what would Mrs Beeton do with what we've got?' She reached for the half packet of dried egg powder, the half bottle of milk, the hunk of bread, and the small block of salt.

'Who's Mrs Beeton?' George took the milk from beneath her arm, not wanting it to slip.

'She was a Victorian lady who wrote a book and used to give recipes for fancy meals. I found a copy, old and tatty, in the printing works where I once worked.'

Not interested in old Victorian ladies, George said nothing more, only leading the way into the kitchen. He took the frying pan from the oven at the side of the black leaded fireplace.

'We'll have omelettes.' Flora took off the steaming kettle and made tea. 'You can make toast, son.'

After their meal George went over to the wireless, and began to twiddle with the knobs to produce a cacophony that made Flora want to scream. Then on the air came Vera Lynn.

She could no longer sit still. She wanted to cry, but what good did crying do you? Better to try for a smile. Smile, darn you, smile! It would take a lot of time and effort to heat water to fill the tin bath just a few inches, but she'd do it. 'Keep smiling through,' she sang unevenly, and fanned the embers of hope in her heart.

Chapter Two

Shortly after a letter came with a warranty note telling Flora that she was entitled to a certain amount of money in accordance with the will soldier Tom Cooke had made. Her newfound hope almost died then, but she told herself that those in charge were only behaving properly. Besides they needed some new clothes for the winter and she had the coupons. So they went to T.J. Hughes and had a good old spend. She bought a two-tone coat in mustard and brown, some liberty bodices and warm knickers for Rosie, and flannel shorts and socks for George.

Having spent most of the money she knew that she would have to set about finding a part-time job. She went to her father's, hoping that he might have changed his mind about taking care of Rosie.

'You look different,' he grunted, as she entered the front room of the two-up, two-down terraced house not far from Liverpool football ground. He waved his old clay pipe in the air. 'Come to your senses, have you, girl?'

She tossed back her long, well-brushed hair, and smiled determinedly. 'You could say that. I've brought you some bread. I wasn't sure if you'd been able to get out with that bad leg of yours.' She placed her shopping bag on the drop leaf, dark oak table, noticing it had a veneer of dust over it.

'I managed,' he grunted, peering closely at her. 'That's a new coat! Where d'you get the money?'

She told him, proud that her voice did not tremble at all. Shrugging herself out of it, she placed the new coat carefully over the back of the rocking chair near the black leaded grate which took up most of one wall of the small dark room. Thankfully she sat down in the chair. Her feet were aching from standing in queues.

Rosie climbed on her knee, making herself comfortable by squirming for several seconds, before addressing her grandfather. 'Cup of tea, Grandpa? Cold outside.' She shivered expressively.

Jack Preston's grey brows drew together. 'That's fine manners, you've got,' he growled. 'Little girls should be seen and not heard. What's your mother teaching you – that's what I'd like to know.'

'Her letters, Father,' put in Flora, her tone light and amused although slightly on the defensive. 'Knowing them will help her to get on quicker when she goes to school. I did the same for George, remember?'

'George is a boy,' said Jack, scowling. 'All this learning isn't any use to a girl. What good did it do you having your mother's sister teach you? You had your head in a book half the time when teaching you to scrub a floor properly and cook a decent meal would have been more to the point.'

'I've scrubbed many a floor and cooked lots of meals since those days, Father,' retorted Flora with a touch of spirit. 'But if you think that's all I want for my daughter, then you're mistaken. The war's changed things and a woman's place in the future won't be just in the home. Look at Aunt Beattie, God rest her soul! It's a good job that she had some education or where would she have been when she had to earn a living for life? Being in service isn't a picnic.'

'And being a spinster school marm was, I suppose?' grunted Jack.

'Better than lots of jobs.' She met his gaze squarely. 'And it's a good thing she didn't marry, otherwise she mightn't have been able to look after me and our Hilda.'

Her father's face darkened. 'Don't mention your sister's name in this house. Shamed me, she did.'

'It was the war, Father.' Flora heaved herself out of the chair, still holding Rosie. 'She wasn't the only one to get caught because she loved a man.'

'Love,' muttered Jack. 'Carnal lust, that's what it was, girl. A daughter of mine! Your mother must have turned in her grave. I put some of the blame on that cattiwake next door. Your sister had the nerve to tell me years back that she'd spent the night in bed with three boys!' He bit hard on his pipe, staring into the fire.

Flora could not help laughing. 'There was nothing in it! We were only kids, and Mam died suddenly, and Aunt Beattie was trying to get in touch with you and make arrangements for the funeral. It was good of Mrs Kelly to take us in. I remember there were seven in the bed — all lined up like sardines in a tin.' No way would she tell him that one Kelly tearaway had stuck his foot up her nightie!

He grunted. 'All wrong — wouldn't have been allowed in the same house in my day. Never mind Orange and Green in the same bed.'

'Being Catholic isn't catching like whooping cough. It didn't rub off on us in the dark!' She put Rosie back on the rocking chair and going over to the fire, placed the kettle on the glowing coals. She fell silent, remembering that it was outside the Kellys' house that she had sat on the kerb, watching Tom and her sister talking to each other, before the rest of the older kids started a game of rounders. Tom had sent a ball way up the street and had broken a window. They had all run like mad to escape the scolding of old Mr Jones. They had fled to the park but soon Tom had them all laughing about being so scared of an old man whose bark was worse than his bite. A long low breath escaped her and there was an ache in her chest as she thought of that mad Alec Tom.

'Well, girl, are you making tea or dreaming?' rasped her father, bringing Flora out of her reverie.

She turned to face him. 'I was wondering, Father, if you've given any more thought to looking after Rosie for me? I'll have to get some kind of work. Money's tight and —'

'Why don't you try Mrs Kelly?' Her father's faded blue eyes gleamed with the faintest hint of malice. 'I mean, she might have gone a bit crackers in her old age, but she can't have forgotten how to handle kids. She had enough of them!'

Flora shook her head at him. 'Now be serious, Father. She

26

has enough on her plate, taking charge of her grandchildren while her two daughters are working.'

'Aye, well, I'm not so young, and Rosie is a handful of trouble. I reckon you'll just have to try and manage till she goes to school. Can't be long now.'

'September.' Flora supplied the answer in muted tones, as her hands busied themselves making tea. But she had made up her mind that she would not ask her father again. Somehow she would have to manage.

She had almost resigned herself to waiting until September before looking for a job, when Mrs Murphy, pushing a pram with two girls inside and two more hanging on to the sides, paused to pass the time of day as Flora scrubbed the step.

'I heard you were looking for a little part time job, girl.'

'That's right.' She looked up quickly, water dripping down her arm from the scrubbing brush. 'Have you heard of one going?'

'It's not much now. But Paddy was hearing from his brother, whose wife's a cleaner, that Smith's are wanting women. Just a couple of hours a day.' She paused for effect, and to drag one of the girls off the wet step. 'It's four till six in the mornin', sorting out the newspapers to go to the different newsagents round the town.' Flora pulled a face, and the other woman added quickly: 'I know it'd mean leavin' the kids alone in the house. But surely they'd be asleep, girl?'

Flora nodded. 'It's better than nothing,' she murmured, dropping the brush in the water and getting up from her knees. 'I'll have a go.'

Mrs Murphy beamed. 'Why not?' she said, and walked on in the wake of the two girls who had run on ahead.

Flora applied for and got the job. It gave her something else to occupy her mind.

Finances became slightly easier, and when in late spring the papers carried the news that Hitler had killed himself, Flora realised that the war would soon be over. It seemed wrong to her that Hitler should have escaped comparatively easily after causing so much suffering and death. She spent several minutes conjuring up ways in which she would have liked him to die. Even guillotining, which horrified her, and slow boiling in oil did not seem harsh enough, and she found herself hoping that there really was a fire and brimstone kind of hell. As well as a heaven fit for heroes. But no, she was not going to think about heroes and heaven — that would be like believing that Tom was no longer alive and she had to still cling on to the hope that he was, somewhere. Just where or how she did not think about. Her hope had no rational basis.

A few days after Flora had read the article about Hitler, she was in the city centre buying bacon from Cooper's stores — her father would have it from no other — when she decided to walk to the Pierhead and get the tram home. The river had always drawn her. Perhaps there was some truth in her father's claim that all true Liverpudlians had salt water in their veins. As she walked along the damp streets with Rosie, she wondered if she would ever become accustomed to the devastation that the bombs had caused — the familiar landmarks obliterated or damaged. Lewis's great store with its roof menagerie had been gutted. The Bluecoat School, Liverpool's oldest building, had been severely damaged. The city museum was roofless, its pillared portico exposing the walls inside — priceless collections had been destroyed. There were great expanses of derelict land about the Victoria Monument, and that more than anything grieved her. It was like No Man's land. She swallowed painfully and hurried Rosie on towards the Mersey.

She came to the Pierhead, and the salty tang of the sea was drawn deep into her lungs. She avoided the passengers disembarking from the ferry, and wondered how many times she had crossed the river with Tom — to Moreton, where they had spent a night under canvas or to New Brighton with its fair and beach. George had made his first sandcastle there, while Tom had done a pencil drawing of him.

Hurting and angry, she stared at the grey water slapping against the landing stage. Then a seagull keened overhead and swept gracefully up into the air, drawing her gaze to the building towering over three hundred feet into the sky. It was crowned by a huge bird. The building had been hit during the war. Suddenly she was remembering Tom's last words — 'Say hello to the Liver bird for me.' Tears welled in her eyes and the huge bird blurred. Her hand touched her trembling mouth and she threw a kiss in the direction of the Liver bird. Only half Scouse he had said he was — the other half was Welsh. The lilt in his voice had been something that had made him different from the other boys. He could sing too, just like his mother who had spoken the Welsh but was now dead. She smiled tremulously at the sudden memory. Then Rosie tugged her hand, and they started in the direction of the tram stop. It had begun to drizzle.

They had almost reached the stop when the ships' hooters began to bellow out an overwhelming cacophony of sound. Flora's pulses stirred and her breath quickened. Rosie's fingers tightened about hers, and her hazel eyes, so like her mother's, widened. They both stood rooted to the spot. Church bells began to clang somewhere in the distance.

A couple in the queue in front of the turned round, their faces alight with excitement. 'It sounds like it's come at last,' said the woman in a high, emotional voice. 'My son'll be coming home! He's been a prisoner in one of those camps.'

A driver came running towards them. 'The war in Europe's over,' he yelled. 'It's over! It's over!'

The next moment Flora's arm was seized, and both she and Rosie were pulled into a whirling group of cheering women, men and children. A Union Jack was produced from somewhere and waved madly. 'Rule Britannia!' was taken up by several people and sung discordantly but joyously.

'The boys will be coming home,' shouted a woman. 'When Johnny comes marching home again — hurrah! Hurrah!'

Flora managed to disentangle herself and Rosie, and began to run with the tears rolling down her cheeks. Soon her path was blocked by people pouring out of buildings here, there and all over the place. It took a long time to reach her own street. She had had to hoist Rosie in her arms, and her back was breaking. But there was to be no peace at home.

Houses must have been emptied of people because the street was alive with chattering women and men. Children skipped and hopped, singing songs or whistling when they could not remember the words. Escape from the festivities would be impossible. The children were too excited by it all. A party was being planned.

Flags soon appeared like so many lines of washing up and down the street. Next door to Flora, Mrs Bryce's upper window sprouted the Stars and Stripes. Flora was not really surprised. She only wondered what would happen when Mr Bryce came home from Egypt.

Tables were lined up in the middle of the road. Everybody was providing something. Flora opened a tin of sardines and mashed them to make butties. A feast was prepared as if by magic. Jam, spam, fish butties, cakes and jellies. There were even a few sweets and chocolates for the children, as well as lemonade.

Bonfires were lit and soon a piano was tinkling out tunes reminiscent of the Great War: 'Tipperary', 'Keep the Home Fires Burning'. Someone had an accordion, and Little Paddy produced a fiddle, to play tunes that set feet tapping. Then the piano took over again to play heart-tugging Vera Lynn songs. 'Yours', 'White Cliffs of Dover' and 'We'll meet Again'. A surge of hope bubbled inside her as she remembered what one of the women had said at the Pierhead – her son was a prisoner-of-war. Maybe Tom had escaped the shell somehow and been captured by the enemy?

She swayed in the firelight, nursing Rosie who was almost asleep, singing along softly.

Sleep did not come easy that night. There was the murmur of voices through the wall from next door and Flora felt angry, hearing the deeper tones of a man. How could Mrs Bryce do what she did?

Gradually she drifted off, only to wake with a start as the van's horn sounded beneath the bedroom window. She forced unwilling eyelids open. In the single bed against the wall, Rosie began to whimper. Flora's heart sank as she slid out of the double bed and made her way unsteadily across the darkened room. She had to struggle with the sash window before she could open it to stick out her tousled head. 'I won't be a mo',' she whispered.

'Okay, luv.' The capped head of Joe the driver withdrew.

Flora's groping fingers found her clothing and she hurriedly dressed, conscious of Rosie's eyes on her. 'Go back to sleep, love.' She slipped her feet into the well-worn shoes, easing the cardboard inner sole. 'Mammy's just going down to light the fire.'

'Don't want to sleep.' Rosie pushed back the covers, her round flushed face determined. 'Come and help Mam.'

'No!' Flora's voice was sharper than she intended. It was one thing leaving her children fast asleep and oblivious of her absence; another having them watch her leave. 'You'll do as you're told.'

Rosie's bottom lip quivered. 'I want to come with you.'

'No!' Flora knew that the clock was ten minutes fast but that still meant she was late, and she could not afford to lose her job. 'Mammy has to go,' she said gently. 'Stay here, Rosie.'

Her daughter silently watched her go out of the room.

When Flora came back from the lavatory Rosie was in the kitchen, curled up on the rug with the cat. Feeling flurried, Flora said nothing as she took her jacket from the hook on the door. Rosie got up hurriedly. 'Mam!'

Flora did not look at her as she opened the door. Guilt and panic were tearing her apart. A fine mother she was, leaving her child. Any moment now Rosie would start crying. The door opened behind her and her daughter's pattering feet followed after her. Flora hesitated and turned round. 'Go back to bed, Rosie,' she ordered quietly, then she opened the front door and closed it swiftly. It did not shut off Rosie's roar as the child flung herself against it.

The van's horn hooted again and Flora lifted her eyes. Joe beckoned her and she hurried down the step. As the vehicle raced up the street she could no longer hear Rosie's cries, yet they echoed in her ears, rebuking her. It isn't right, she thought fiercely. I shouldn't be leaving her! If only Tom ... But he was not there. The thought pained as much as did leaving her children. But she had to accept that she alone could provide for them now.

It was on her way back from work that Flora collided with the American coming out of Mrs Bryce's path. For a moment his gaze rested on her tired face, than he ran his eyes over her

31

slight figure, bringing an angry flush to her cheeks. She felt like saying, 'Was it you last night who disturbed my sleep? If it goes on I'll lose my job, and I've got kids to feed. I'm really fed up with you Yanks!' But she only stared at him coldly as he winked and raised his cap, and wished her a beautiful morning before strolling down the street. She wondered savagely if all Yanks were the same when away from home. They had a helluva reputation! Although she knew that it was not only American soldiers that behaved like this one. She turned the key in the lock and went into the house.

'Where've you been?' George's voice accused Flora of instant neglect. 'Our Rosie's been screaming the place down and Mrs Bryce banged on the wall.'

'Did she now!' Flora's eyes smouldered. 'Don't you mind her. If she says anything to you about this, I'll have a word or two to say to her about her keeping me awake nights. Now where's Rosie?'

'In bed.' He scratched his head and frowned. 'I made her get back in — but I was too wide awake so I lit the fire.'

Flora sank on to a chair. 'You're a good lad, I haven't told you before but I've got a job. Just two hours each morning, sorting papers out. There's a couple in my bag, and a comic if you'd like a read. I thought there was no point in worrying you about me being out of the house, but now the days are getting longer I don't think you'll be scared. I suppose I should have told you.'

'It's alright, Mam,' he said roughly, shrugging his shoulders impatiently. His mouth set in a way that caused her a pang of anguish. He was so young to shoulder responsibility, and so like Tom! The war had made him old beyond his years. He scuffed his shoe on the rug. 'I'll be able to look after Rosie while you're at work. Are we very hard up?'

'We'll manage if we're careful,' she responded brightly. 'There's nothing for you to worry about. If you can just keep Rosie happy in the mornings if she wakes — although you need your sleep. I don't want you nodding off in class and missing lessons.'

'I won't. Sir would throw something at me if I did, and I'd soon wake up then. Don't you worry, Mam.' He tilted his chin, his eyes bright. His hand stretched out for the papers she had brought and he walked stiffly over to the armchair that had been his dad's. He was the man of the house now and had to help his mam all he could. His eyes perused the picture of a crowded Trafalgar Square, and for a moment he thought of how his dad wouldn't be coming home, and then he put down the paper and picked up the comic and began to read that instead.

Some of the tension oozed out of Flora and she made tea and toast for them both. Upstairs she found Rosie sprawled across the bedcover fast asleep. Later she would take her to the park, certain that would tire her out. And tomorrow morning she hoped that she would be able to creep out without any fuss from her daughter.

Rosie was a monster! A lovable monster, but a monster nonetheless. For the last four nights she had refused to settle. Even now past midnight she was still awake, humming some tune to herself. Flora knew that if she got out of bed then her daughter would quieten immediately, but when she got back in again Rosie would begin to hum. Eventually her daughter would go to sleep but she was staying awake long enough for Flora not to go off till the early hours. Twice she had not heard the van horn being sounded and Joe had had to bang on the knocker. He had warned her that the third time would be the last. It was not that he was unsympathetic but the other women were complaining.

Flora determined to ignore her daughter, but once she did her thoughts were on Mrs Bryce next door, and the man whose laughter had prevented her from getting to sleep till late last night. She had not been able to stop herself from imagining what was taking place, and it caused such an ache inside her body. Was the man the one she had seen a few mornings ago? She had not seen him since and was glad of it.

Turning on her stomach Flora dragged a pillow over her head, praying that all would be quiet next door that night. Tom filled her thoughts and she remembered the nights they had spent in this bed making love, and of the years of war that had kept them apart. She began to cry softly.

33

Suddenly Flora realised that Rosie had quietened, but now she could hear the slightest murmur of voices. She tried to set her mind on sleep but pictures kept coming into her head. Heat seared her body and she lay there rigid, trying to empty her mind, but she was still awake when dawn came and with it the van.

All was quiet when she returned home later that morning, not even George was stirring. She lit the fire and put her feet up, and had a cup of tea before going to wake the children. She felt a little better if weary, but was hopeful that the peace signalled a change for the better in Rosie's behaviour.

The change was short-lived, lasting three days only. Flora had managed to grab some sleep but it was not undisturbed. A stranger had invaded her dreams. So far she had kept him at arm's length, shocked that she could dream of another man with Tom in her heart. She blamed the American and Mrs Bryce, and wished that she could have had another adult in the house to talk to about her problems.

The next day it rained. Flora's spirits sank even lower. When she heard a hammering on the door she thought it was someone coming to complain about George playing football in the street again. She was ready to defend him as she marched down the hall.

'Well! Aren't you going to ask me in?' demanded her sister crossly. 'I've had a terrible journey on the tram. I had to stand all the way, and then there was the walk up the lane in the rain. One of the strings on the bags snapped, and Viv was no use at all. Whinge, whinge, all the way up the lane.' She dumped the brown paper bags on the step and stared intently at Flora. 'You look terrible! What's happened?'

'Tom is missing presumed dead.' Her voice almost broke.

For a moment Hilda did not speak. Her blue eyes sparkled with tears. Then she shook herself. 'Well, don't you go letting yourself go to pieces! No man's worth it,' she said harshly. 'Can we come in?'

'Of course!' said Flora, squaring her shoulders. 'You just took me by surprise. You've never written and I haven't known where you were since you went off while I was away with the kids, seeing Tom.'

'It was Father's fault as usual. He came to visit you,

and found me and Viv.' Hilda's mouth tightened. 'The old swine! The things he said to me — not that I hadn't heard them all before. But to go on and on about Mother and how I'd besmirched the family's good name! Mother cared for me — she would never have thrown me out of the house in the first place.' Her eyes glinted with tears again.

'I'm sure she wouldn't have.' Flora did not remember their mother as well as Hilda, and her memories were mainly of a tired, pretty woman lying in bed most of the time with Aunt Beattie, or one of the neighbours, a constant visitor when her father was not there. 'But come in.' She held out a hand to Vivien. 'I haven't seen you for ages. You were only a babe when you left this house, pet.'

Hilda's red mouth pouted. 'She's no pet — she's a pest. But then, you've always liked kids. Crazy!'

Flora picked up one of the bags, and took Vivien's hand. 'Have you come to stay for a while?'

'I thought you might like some company.' Hilda dropped the bags just inside the kitchen and her eyes roamed the brown-painted walls of the shabby room. 'I'd forgotten how small this place was,' she murmured, frowning. 'But at least I won't have Doris moaning at me all the time.' She sank into an armchair near the fireplace, ignoring Rosie's presence on the rug. Dragging off the navy blue felt hat that had sat at an angle on her red-gold hair, she threw it in the direction of the hook on the door. It missed, and Flora picked it up to place it on the sideboard.

'Is that why you're here — because you've fallen out with your friend?'

'No.' Hilda lowered her eyes and toyed with her nails. 'I just wondered how you were getting on.' She lifted her head and their eyes met. 'What happened about Tom? I always believed him the kind to make it, somehow.'

'A shell exploded. They never found any traces of him but they're pretty sure he's dead.' A muscle quivered in Flora's cheek.

'Sod it.' Hilda put her head back and closed her eyes. 'What a way to go. But it'd be quick. He'd never know anything about it.'

'I suppose not.' Her voice was unsteady. 'I haven't thought

about it much. I keep thinking that he could still be alive — that maybe he escaped somehow.'

Hilda opened her eyes and looked at her. 'You always were a dreamer, Flo. It's no good fooling yourself by believing such things! Wake up, girl, and look at life as it really is,' she said bitterly. 'It often slaps you in the face, but you just have to keep on going.'

A sharp laugh escaped Flora. 'What d'you think I've been doing, sitting back and taking it easy? I've got two kids and I've had to get myself a job. I'm glad you're here because it means that I won't have to worry any more about leaving them alone early mornings.' She picked up the kettle and put it on the fire. 'Cup of tea?' she asked the silent Hilda.

'Thanks,' murmured her sister, taking out a packet of Players and lighting up. 'I'll get myself a job too. I'll try Ogden's. It should work out, the two of us together again. The girls will be company for each other — they're much of an age.' She gazed down at the glowing tip of her cigarette, eased off her shoes and held her toes to the fire. 'I'll give you something for my keep.' Her voice was carefully casual. 'But we can discuss that later.'

Flora nodded briefly, not allowing herself a moment of uncertainty. She had wished for another grown up in the house, and she had got what she wanted. Recalling the last time her sister stayed with her would do neither of them any good. Maybe Hilda had changed since she had been away. 'You've brought your ration books?' she murmured.

'Oh, aye! I'll give them to you, Flo. I don't really understand points and all that. But you tell me if there's anything you want me to do,' said Hilda absently, switching on the wireless. 'I'm always prepared to pull my weight.' She closed her eyes, jiggled a foot to the music that poured out, and began to hum tunelessly.

Flora stared at her before going into the back kitchen, her mind now busy with planning how to stretch tonight's meal to feed two more. It wasn't going to be easy and George would probably complain because there'd be less for him to eat. She could see a few difficulties ahead.

Chapter Three

Sorting out the practicalities of Hilda's moving in took no time at all, although her sister grouched at having to share the same room with Flora and the two girls. Afterwards she bounced into the little back room and threw up her arms. 'You have this perfectly good room going spare! You should get it sorted out, Flo. It'd be perfect for me!'

'There has been a war on and it'd take money to do it up,' said Flora fiercely. Her eyes darkened. 'Besides this was Tom's special place where he used to let himself go. He did some good painting and drawing.'

'He mucked about,' said Hilda disparagingly, picking up a canvas and narrowing her eyes as she looked at it. 'I'll give you that he could paint a pretty picture, but this doesn't look a bit like me when I was young.' She tossed it on the floor.

Flora snatched it up and gazed at it. 'That's because it isn't you,' she muttered. 'It's me.'

Hilda gazed at the delicate lines of water colour again. 'I should have known. You were real skinny.' She walked out of the room.

Flora ground her teeth, carefully placing the picture against the wall. She fingered a paint brush, a pencil; gazed at a sketch of a lamp post in Rodney Street and a couple of cartoons. She went out with tears wet on her cheeks. It had been hard to believe that the girl of eighteen with smiling eyes and rounded cheeks was herself, or that the artist might never return again.

The house settled into a new routine. Rosie welcomed the advent of a cousin, someone to play houses and shops with indoors, and to skip and throw balls at walls outside. She stopped keeping Flora awake nights.

But Hilda's coming provided Flora with different problems. A couple of weeks went by before her sister gave her any money and then it was barely enough to feed Hilda, never mind Vivien. But Flora took it with a word of thanks, not liking to ask just how much Hilda was earning. She guessed it was much more than she did, but thought that maybe Hilda had debts she might have had to pay off at this Doris's she had mentioned. Not everybody was as soft as herself. But when her sister started going out a couple of evenings she wondered whether her sister was taking her for a ride again. The two evenings out became three, then four, five, and the only time Hilda seemed to be in was when she was washing her hair.

Flora began to resent her sister using her as a child minder and chief cook, washer and cleaner. It had never been easy for her to stand up to Hilda. There was five years' difference in age between them, and in their younger days at Aunt Beattie's her sister had expected her to remain biddable at all times. And Flora, shy, insecure child that she was after her mother died, had done exactly what her sister wanted, adoring her because she was all that Flora was not – lovely and lively.

Thinking of their younger days made Flora feel less resentful, and besides it wasn't all bad. There were times when the two sisters got on well enough.

One day they were lying on the warmed stone roof of the outside lavatory, drying their hair in the sun and watching what appeared to be members of the League of Nations going in next door and sliding out again.

'Norwegian sailor, Polish soldier and American airman,' whispered Hilda with a giggle. 'I don't know how she does it. How does word get round? She doesn't have a lamp over her front door.'

'Nor over the back,' murmured Flora, closing her eyes against the sun. 'If Father only knew that I lived next door to a house of ill-repute, he'd be worrying in case it was catching! D'you think she actually speaks Polish or Norwegian?'

'She doesn't have to, does she?' said Hilda lazily. 'Sex transcends the language barrier, little sister. All she has to do is point them in the right direction, open her legs and think of the money.'

'Crudely put,' responded Flora, pulling a face. 'But I suppose that's exactly what she does do. But she must do more than that with some of them because I've heard them talking into the night.'

'They speak some English, soft pot.' Hilda gave her a light punch. 'But she can natter as much as she likes to the Yanks,' she yawned. 'Although in my book they like to do the talking.'

'You've met some, have you?'

'Who hasn't in Liverpool?' said Hilda casually. 'And they have a good opinion of themselves. But they're generous, and some are more than just mouths and trousers.'

September came in and Flora decided that maybe now was the time to make a few changes in the running of the household.

She watched Hilda putting on her coat the evening before the girls were due to start school, and said quietly, 'D'you think you could get up early in the morning and light the fire for me?'

Hilda's hand stilled as it reached for her handbag. 'Can't George do it?'

'They all start school in the morning. I'd like him to have a good rest. Besides he's often done it during the holidays. It would give me a headstart on the day, Hilda.' She watched her sister struggling for an excuse.

'All right,' she said finally with a heavy sigh. 'I'll do my best. Don't wait up for me. I'll probably be late in.' And with that she closed the door behind her. Flora could not believe that it had been so easy, and her spirits felt a little lighter. It was good to think that when she got back from work in the morning, there would be a cup of tea ready and waiting.

Flora turned the key in the latch and stepped into the lobby, but no sound of activity welcomed her. Anger stirred within her. It seemed that Hilda had forgotten her promise. Flora paused only to fling her coat over a chair before raking out the ashes. In a short time a fire was burning, and the kettle on. Seizing the piece of rag that served as a face cloth she went upstairs to the front room, illuminated by the early September light, and dragged back the covers on the double bed.

Her sister gasped as Flora dripped cold water on her face. 'You bitch!' She wrestled blindly for the bedclothes. 'I'll kill you when I get my eyes open.'

'You're a lazy cow! I felt like murdering you when I came in this morning. I asked you to light the fire, but of course with all the late nights you're keeping you can't get out of bed.' Flora's angry voice quivered slightly as she looked down at her sister's wet, sleepy face, and she had to swallow a giggle. 'Lordy, missy, you look like a drowned rat.'

Hilda pulled a face. 'Very funny. I forgot. And it's not just due to my coming in late. It's her next door – gosh, you wonder where she gets the strength from. I think I'd have felt hammered into the bed by now. She's no better than an old pro!'

'Hilda,' hissed Flora warningly, glancing in the direction of the girls' bed. 'Keep your voice down. And, anyway, it's no excuse. She's kept me awake many a night but I've got myself up. You've got to pull your weight. I'm tired when I come in.'

'You can rest during the day,' said her sister sullenly. 'I'm working full time.' She wiped her face with a corner of the pink bedspread.

Flora shook her head in disbelief. 'How much rest d'you think I get? It shows how little you know about taking care of kids and a home. How much time d'you think it takes to keep this place clean and do the washing, shopping, and look after the girls?'

Hilda shrugged and turned on her side, resting her pointed chin in one palm. 'You'll have more time now they're going to school,' she said sweetly.

'I was thinking of getting myself a different job,' said

Flora emphatically. 'It's no fun having to be at work at four in the morning.'

'Moan, moan,' responded Hilda, giving a yawn. 'You'll manage somehow, Flo.'

Exasperated, Flora stared at her. Hilda gazed back out of pale blue eyes that slanted up at the outer corners. She darkened her lashes with spit and soot, but now the soot was smudged. Her mouth curved in a bow-shape. 'It was such fun last night,' she said dreamily. 'The lights have gone on all over Britain now and there's as much fun to be had as during the war. I don't intend staying single all my life, Flo. I want a husband — tall and handsome — who'll take me away from all this.' She waved a hand.

'A husband, is it?' Flora's voice was disbelieving. 'What about Viv's father? Won't he be coming home?'

There was a silence, then Hilda laughed mirthlessly and gave her a glittering stare. 'Oh, him! I don't think I'll be seeing him again.'

'I thought you loved him,' said Flora doubtfully. 'The way you carried on.'

Her sister dropped her eyes. 'War does funny things to people, Flo. And time changes us all. Although it hasn't altered you that much yet. You're still so innocent in a way — so trusting. Sometimes I've wished I could be like you.' For a moment her mouth drooped unhappily and then she laughed again, this time more cheerfully. 'Now how about a cup of tea, Flo?'

'Alright,' said Flora slowly, wondering whether her sister had had news somehow that Viv's father was dead, or whether it was that she had just not heard from him again after getting pregnant. 'I should make you get it, but seeing as how I'm up ... But you've got to rise and shine now. The girls start school today.' She whipped back the covers so that they fell over the bottom of the bed. Her sister groaned but got up to search for her scattered clothing.

'Why couldn't Mam have waited?' asked Vivien, staring up at Flora with mournful brown eyes.

'She had to go to work, love.' Flora smoothed the child's wayward curls. 'But she said you looked smart.'

41

Vivien wrinkled her neat nose, and a smile lighted her face. With her golden curls, it caused her to appear altogether cherubic. 'It's nice having new clothes.'

'We're lucky, aren't we, Mam?' said Rosie, tossing her sandy pigtails.

'Yes.' Flora carefully licked a finger to wipe the jam from the corner of her daughter's mouth. 'The cardigans are courtesy of your dad.' Only dire necessity had led her to unpick Tom's blue jumper; it had pained her to do so. She had washed the wool and wound it round a bottle filled with hot water to uncrinkle the yarn. She felt as if she had closed a door on Tom and that upset her.

'It's lovely wool.' Rosie stroked the cardigan lovingly. 'I wish I'd known my dad.'

'He wished he'd known you better.' She forced a smile. 'There's a letter he wrote upstairs. When you're older you can read it. He wrote it especially for you.'

Rosie's face brightened, but Vivien's grew longer. 'My dad never wrote me a letter − nor saw me.'

Flora could think of nothing to say, so she just took their hands, wishing that she had never mentioned the letter. But she found herself wondering just who was Vivien's father. Hilda had been very secretive about the whole thing when she had come to Flora after their father had slung her out. It had been a bad moment. Flora had been expecting herself and felt ill, but she had been unable to turn her sister away. Soldier, sailor, airman? Hilda had said only that he was in the forces.

Flora placed the grey trousers she had been darning on the arm of the chair as the door opened to reveal Hilda. She focussed her tired eyes on her swaying figure. 'What time's this to be coming in?' she asked with assumed mildness.

'You shouldn't have waited up.' Hilda stumbled over her words and fell into the chair the other side of the fireplace.

'You're drunk,' accused Flora, getting up.

'Only tiddly.' Hilda giggled. 'Have you ever had a cock-tail, Flo?'

'No.' She whipped her sister's scarlet felt hat off her head as Hilda slid down the chair. 'How many have you had?'

'Two too many. But it was worth it.' Hilda closed her eyes. 'Mind you, it was a near thing. He wanted to put my garters on for me.' She stretched her legs towards the fire and lifted her skirts, revealing nylon clad thighs with home-made garters of elastic and pink rosettes. 'Nice, aren't they?'

'Yes, but –' Flora sat abruptly, her heart beating fast. 'Did he touch you?'

Hilda opened one eye wide and straightened herself. 'It depends what you mean by touched.' A slight smile curved her brightly painted mouth. 'He's a good kisser but there it stopped.' She sighed and stretched. 'I met a friend of his tonight, and he's so handsome and rich – you wouldn't believe it. And as there's no future with Mike – although he's fun – I just might take up Tony's invitation.' She dragged herself up and went to gaze in the mirror. She hummed a few bars of a dance tune as she blinked at her reflection. 'Hell! My hair's a mess.' A hand forced it back from her unwrinkled forehead before going to her mouth. 'And he's smudged my lipstick.' A smile lifted her lips. 'I'll miss him.'

Flora stared at her sister. 'D'you know what you're doing?' she demanded. 'Aren't you playing with fire going out with his friend?' She was thinking of the past.

Hilda wrinkled her nose and pouted at the mirror. 'Mike is married. Tony isn't.'

'But you let this Mike kiss you?'

Hilda laughed. 'It's hardly rape. You're turning stodgy, Flo. It would do you good to get out.'

'Chance would be a fine thing,' she said coolly. 'Who'd look after the kids if you're gallivanting every night?'

'All right, all right, forget it!' Hilda flopped into a chair. 'I suppose you wouldn't go if you could anyway. You're the type who thinks faithfulness goes beyond death, and all that.' She closed her eyes and rested her head against the back of the chair. 'You're a fool, Flo. Men aren't that true blue.' She yawned.

'And you're selfish. It would help if you stayed in more at nights.'

Hilda's answer was a snore. For several minutes Flora stared angrily at her, waiting for some other reaction, but her sister only snored again, so she walked out of the room and up to bed, feeling dissatisfied because there was something unfinished about the whole conversation they had just had. What was her sister up to, and why did she have to make being faithful sound like a sin? She hoped that Hilda would sleep downstairs all night because at that moment she did not want her sleeping in her bed. The bed where she and Tom ... She subdued the unsettling memories and feigned sleep as she heard Hilda's footfalls on the stairs.

Chapter Four

Flora sat watching Hilda apply lipstick, determined to say what was on her mind — although it would probably be a waste of time, like everything else she had tried to say to her sister lately. 'You and Father should settle your differences. It's not right for families to be divided — especially when it'll be Christmas soon.'

'There's plenty of time to Christmas yet.' Hilda twirled a dark gold curl round her little finger. 'But even so, who wants to spend Christmas across the table from Father? I'm planning something different — if my Yank pops the question.'

'Your what?' The sock she was darning fell from Flora's limp fingers.

Hilda's hand stilled. 'My Tony,' she murmured, her eyes bright and amused as she gazed into the mirror and met her sister's stare. 'He's so handsome and adoring, and not short of a bob or two. As I think I've mentioned to you before.' She frowned as she smoothed the padded shoulders of the blue-patterned rayon frock, and gave a perceptible shiver.

'You never mentioned no Yank before!' Flora folded her arms across her breasts, and frowned. 'You know what they're after — only one thing.'

'You know a few, do you?' Hilda laughed as she swung round to take her winter coat from the hook on the door.

'You know I don't — but we've seen plenty going in to her next door. And I bumped into one once, and — the way he stripped me with his eyes was nobody's business.'

'Lovely, isn't it?' Hilda's eyes danced. 'But they're not

all the same. Tony's different. I wouldn't be surprised if he was a virgin.' Hilda's smile vanished. 'I've never had one of them before. They've been inclined to be all hands and mouths – as well as other things! Even Tom knew a thing or two at sixteen.' She turned her head and looked at Flora. 'There's no need to look like that, dear sister. He was mine before he was yours. And one of you needed to know what it was all about. I've often wondered what it was like between you two. He was so alive and you were such a quiet little thing. But then, they say the quiet ones are the deep ones.' Her eyes narrowed. 'Are there hidden fires in you?'

'What Tom and I did in bed was solely between him and me. And, anyway, we were talking Yanks. You haven't been so clever in your life, big sister. D'you know what you're doing now? He might be leading you on.'

Hilda's expression hardened. 'You can guarantee there won't be anything doing again till there's a ring on my finger. I'm after a one way ticket to America, and tonight might be the night he pops the question. Then you won't see me for dust, little sister.'

'D'you love him at all?' Her voice was scornful.

'Love?' Hilda's smile was brittle. 'Only you would ask that. What's love to do with it? You pinched Tom while my back was turned.'

'You were going out with somebody else,' retorted Flora, dangerously sweet. 'Two timing isn't nice.'

'Don't preach morality to me, Flo.' Her sister's eyes flashed angrily as she opened the door. 'Or I'll tell you a thing or two that will shock the drawers off you. Don't wait up.'

'I don't intend to!' Flora swept past her, snatching up her coat as she went. She slammed the front door behind her and ran down the street.

She began to calm down as the chill foggy air made itself felt, and slowed to a walk. Why did Hilda have to go on about Tom the way she did? It made Flora mad. Matters weren't working out at all the way she had hoped when her sister came to stay, and at the moment Flora wished that Hilda would vanish into thin air. But she would have to go back and face her.

If she had some money then the pictures would have been just the place for her to cool off and take her mind off things, as well as giving her a reason for staying out longer, but she had not thought to pick up her purse. Instead she walked twice round the block before going home.

It was George who answered Flora's hammering on the door. He rubbed sleepy eyes. 'Where've you been, Mam?'

'On a message to your grandad's,' she lied. 'You should have let your aunty answer the door.'

He yawned, padding up the lobby in front of her. 'She's not in.'

'What!' Flora pushed open the kitchen door and saw that he was telling the truth. Anger stirred within her again. 'Go back to bed, son.' He nodded and left her.

She made herself a cup of tea and stoked up the fire, huddling close as tiny flames licked the coal, and tried to not care what her sister did. But she was still seething when she went to bed, and it was some time before sleep claimed her.

'D'you want to know how my evening went?' Hilda rested her chin on her hand.

Flora did not answer, but spoke to George as she handed him and the girls a penny each. 'Now straight to Sunday School, and don't lose the money down a grid.'

'Do I have to go?' asked George with a long suffering air, pocketing his penny which he intended spending on some broken crisps.

'Yes.' She frowned. 'You've got to take care of the girls. It's a brother's job.'

'Viv's my cousin.'

'You know what I mean,' she said quietly. He nodded and pushed the girls before him. Flora saw them out before returning to place the flat iron on the fire and spread a piece of sheeting on the table.

'I'll repeat my question,' said her sister impatiently. 'D'you want to know about my evening?'

'Why should I be interested?' asked Flora flatly. 'What you do is your own business.'

'You wouldn't think so the way you go on. I believe

you're jealous.' Hilda smiled. 'You're stuck in this place for life, and you're jealous because I'm going to get away from it.'

Flora gave her a look. 'I'm not jealous,' she murmured. 'You have your life. I have mine.'

'Yours isn't much of a life.'

'You could make it easier.' She placed one of the girls' frocks on the sheeting. 'You could try doing some work around here for once. It would be good practice for if you do get married.'

Hilda took out a packet of cigarettes and lit one with slow deliberation. 'When I get married there'll be no need for me to slave away like you. I'll have somebody to do the housework and washing and stuff.'

'Oh, aye? Tony's that rich is he? Or do you only think it'll be like that because of the movies?' She wrapped a cloth round the handle of the iron, and spat on the bottom of it to test if it was hot enough.

'Tony has money, dear sister.'

'So you've told me. But men can exaggerate about some things.'

Hilda frowned. 'Tony didn't tell me — Mike did. And why should he lie? You're only saying it to get on my nerves.' Flora smiled but remained silent. Hilda inhaled deeply. 'I suppose you think it's wrong to consider money important.'

'It's not everything.'

'You can't live just on love, Flo, and you damn well know it. Look at this place!' Hilda's disparaging glance swept the room.

Her sister's eyes glinted. 'You don't have to stay, but if you do I'd like the money you give me trebled. I can't keep you and Viv on five shillings a week and you damn well know it! This isn't a charity home.' She threw a frock over the back of a chair and picked up another.

Hilda flushed. 'Is that what this is all about? Money?'

'You've just said that it's important,' said Flora in honeyed tones. 'That people can't live on love. So how about it, dear sister?'

Hilda blew out a stream of smoke, her expression moody.

'All right, I'll give you some more. Anything else while we're at it?'

'Yes.' Flora would have felt more convinced by her sister's words if she had produced the money on the spot. 'You can do your own, and Viv's, washing and ironing. I'm not a skivvy.'

'I did tell you to ask me if there was anything you wanted me to do.' Her voice was irritable.

'I have, and you haven't done it. You've got cloth ears.' Flora's hand trembled on the iron. 'You've said I know nothing about life,' she said vehemently. 'Well, it's time you learnt a thing or two. Life's not about you being carried by people all the time.'

'Oh, I'm going out!' exclaimed Hilda loudly, stubbing out her cigarette. 'I'll iron the clothes I want to wear myself now. That'll save you.'

'Be my guest,' said Flora, putting the iron back on the fire, and walking over to the window to stare out at the yard with its empty windowboxes. The silence now was overwhelming. She turned and switched the wireless on. Martial music marched into the room. Her lips twitched as her sister thumped the iron in time to the music.

'I won't be in for dinner.' Hilda's voice was loud. 'Nor for tea neither – so that should save you some money.'

'Good,' murmured Flora, watching her place a scarlet jumper on a chair, and pick up a skirt. 'Will you be in for bed?' Her voice was light.

Hilda's eyes darkened. 'Are you being funny?'

'No,' said Flora with an innocent wide-eyed stare. 'I just don't want to lock you out all night.'

'I'm not going dancing, so I probably will be in fairly early. Unless it's that you want the pleasure of locking me out?' she said frostily.

'I wasn't planning on that.' Unexpectedly Flora felt like an old, old woman with a wayward daughter, and was chilled. I'm too young for this, she thought rebelliously.

'All right then.' Hilda put down the iron and began to change.

For once she did not take an age fiddling with powder, soot and rouge. It was only ten minutes before she was dragging on her coat. Her hand was on the door knob when she faced Flora, automatically picking up Hilda's nightdress from the floor. 'You should leave it for me when I come in,' she said with a touch of amused malice. 'I don't expect you to slave for me like you did for Tom. The original doormat, that's what you were, Flo, and I suppose that's what he saw in you. He was an arrogant sod but you could never see it.'

Flora drew in a hissing breath and flung the nightdress at her. 'Bitch!' Hilda caught it and threw it back but when Flora picked up a shoe she quickly shut the door and click-clacked up the lobby, slamming the front door behind her.

The shoe slipped from Flora's fingers and for a moment she just stood staring at the door, knotted up with hurt and frustration. Then she picked up the iron and rammed it on the fire.

Flora was curled up on the well worn couch reading a library book when Hilda returned just after nine. She did not look up as her sister entered the kitchen.

'Would you like a cuppa?' Hilda's voice was soft and hesitant. Flora glanced up at her and then down at her book. Her sister continued, 'Flo, I'm sorry. I shouldn't have said what I did. I suppose it was my guilty conscience that caused me to. I am grateful for what you do for me and Viv. You're a much better mother to her than I'll ever be.'

'She's a nice kid,' murmured Flora, surprise and warmth flooding her. 'If you're making that cuppa I'll have one.'

Hilda smiled. 'Right!'

The kettle was soon boiling and from her pocket Hilda produced a rather squashed bun. Hurriedly she picked a speck of red fluff from its top and handed it to her sister.

'Thanks.' Flora took a bite. It was slightly stale, but she accepted that it was a peace offering so knew that gratitude was in order.

Her sister passed her a cup of tea, then lit up a cigarette. 'Viv get to bed all right?'

'Of course.' Flora stared at her; it was not like Hilda to ask. 'Did you have a nice day?'

'Lovely.' Her face glowed. 'We went to Blackpool and had our dinner in a hotel.'

'Did you walk along the front?'

'For a little while.' She shivered. 'Tony likes that sort of thing. Wind and weather — seagulls and the sea all grey and stormy. He quite likes Liverpool.' She sounded surprised.

'Why shouldn't he?' said Flora indignantly. 'Where does he come from?'

'New Jersey. A place called Harrison, just over the river from Newark, which he says is their largest city.' She hesitated. 'Flo —'

There was something in her voice that caused Flora to still. 'What?' she asked warily.

'He's asked me to marry him.' Hilda sounded half excited, half frightened. 'He's really asked me to marry him!'

'And you said yes, of course,' murmured Flora, not sure exactly what her feelings were.

Hilda moved closer to the fire. She was trembling. 'What did you expect me to say? I'm going to America! Away from rationing — away from the sight of bombed buildings — from shortages and that boring job in the tobacco factory. Oh, I can't wait to leave this place. Wish me happy, Flo!'

Unable to keep still any longer, she stood up. 'Of course I wish you happy, only —'

'I can't go straightaway.' Hilda stared into the fire. 'There's all sorts of things to be done. Forms to fill in. I might have to wait a while. Tony says that some wives have been waiting ages to join their husbands. Some have waited over a year with visas, passports and everything. But I don't mind waiting now I know I'm going. The war's over so things are bound to move quicker.'

Flora forced herself to say, 'It's a pity you'll have to take Viv away from school just as she's settled.'

Some of the excitement faded from Hilda's face and she moistened her mouth. 'I've been thinking about Viv — and as you say it would be a shame to take her out of school.' She fiddled with her cigarette. There was a silence.

'You have told Tony about Viv, haven't you?' said Flora at last.

Hilda flung her arms wide. 'I couldn't! He thinks the

sun shines out of me! Calls me his angel. Thinks I'm won-
derful – that I'm a virgin!' She paused and lowered her
head. 'Don't look at me like that, Flo. I'm just not mother
material. It's not that I'm not fond of Viv. I am. But I just
couldn't tell Tony about her.'

Flora stared at her unbelievingly. 'You'll have to tell him.
If he loves you, he'll understand these things happen in
war.'

Hilda looked uncomfortable. 'Not Tony. He's religious.
He's Catholic!'

'Catholic!' Flora stared at her. 'Father'll have a fit.'

'It's got nothing to do with him,' said Hilda impatiently.
'I don't go to church so what does it matter? It's my life.'

Flora frowned. 'You said it! But doesn't your faith mean
anything to you?'

Hilda pulled a face. 'Father put me off it a long time
ago – he's so narrow and bigoted. And where's the love
in his kind of religion?'

'I know!' Flora let out a low breath. 'But just the same,
a Catholic. Doesn't Tony mind you being a Protestant?'

'I said I'd change.'

Flora bit back what she would have liked to have said,
and instead murmured, 'I hope you know what you're doing.
They believe in large families – lots of kids. But then maybe
because of that he might be inclined to understand what
happened to you better than you think.'

A sharp laugh escaped her sister. 'Don't be so naive, Flo.
You know men have one rule for them and another for us.
And to some, sex outside marriage is the big sin – bigger
than pride or greed.' She frowned. 'Viv will be happy with
you. But if you don't want her – then – I'll just have to
stick her in a home.'

'A home! Little Viv!' Her face dark with anger, Flora
slapped Hilda's face. 'You're cruel! Selfish!'

Her sister's hand went to her stinging cheek. 'Don't you
ever do that to me again,' she hissed.

Flora's eyes blazed green fire. 'What if when Mam died
Father had put us in a home? Would you have liked it?'

'I wouldn't have cared!' Tears sparkled in her eyes. 'Did
you believe that Aunt Beattie took mother's place for me? I

was older than you. I'd spent more years with Mam. I hated Aunt Beattie's for ages.'

'Aunt Beattie was good to us — she was family. You loved Mother. Don't you think Viv loves you?'

Hilda's eyes fell. 'I don't know. You're good with her. And I don't think it's fair to take Viv away now. She'd miss you and the others much more than she'll miss me.'

'You're making excuses,' snapped Flora. 'You're her mother and she should be with you.'

'You don't understand,' she muttered sullenly.

'I understand well enough.' Flora was suddenly weary. 'You want to go to America with Tony and Viv's in the way. But he has a right to know the truth about you, Hilda. If he can't understand' Her voice tailed off, but she drew breath again. 'Good lord, how many G.I. bastards are there in Liverpool?'

'But that's why,' cried Hilda earnestly, leaning towards her. 'It's because of Burtonwood, the G.I. airbase, and the sort of woman she is next door that I daren't tell Tony. Don't you think those men talk about the women they've slept with? He might think that I was like that, and I never went that far. It was just fun — slap and tickle, Flo.'

'Except the once,' she said quietly. 'Did you love him?'

Hilda stared at her and smiled wryly. 'There you go again, Flo.' She paused before adding, 'Yes, I believe I did — once. But love hurts and makes you behave stupidly. I don't want ever to feel like that again.'

'It has its good moments.'

'Yes.' Hilda's face crumpled. 'Oh, Flo, this is my chance — don't spoil it. I could work at loving Tony. I want to go! I need to escape! I'm thirty and if it wasn't for the war then maybe I wouldn't feel like this. But I can't bear Liverpool now. I acted rashly once — am I to pay for that mistake for the rest of my life?'

'Do I have to pay for your mistake for the rest of mine?' asked Flora fiercely. 'How will I manage for money? It's bad enough getting any out of you now.'

'I promise, Flo, that I'll see you're all right,' Hilda said fervently. 'Before I go I'll give you all the money I have, and when I get to America I'll be able to send you food parcels – that'll help.'

Flora slowly shook her head. 'I wish I could believe you.'

Hilda's hand fell and tears hung on the end of her eyelashes. 'We're sisters. Once you'd have done anything for me. I thought you cared for me.'

'That's blackmail,' said Flora stonily, moving away from her sister to pick up the old flower-sprigged pyjamas on a chair. 'But say for now that I'll keep Viv.' She turned away. 'I just hope you know what you're doing and don't live to regret it. I've had enough – I'm going to bed.'

'Flora!'

'What?' She did not bother looking at her sister.

'Thanks!' Hilda's tone was bright. 'And if there's anything I can do for you – I'll do it.'

'Thanks,' she said drily, before fleeing up the stairs.

That night she dreamed and was s.' ocked into consciousness. Her body felt boneless and her thumb wandered to the thin band on her left hand. What kind of woman was she to conjure up such a dream? She had lain with a man in the garden of her dream house and on her finger had flashed a bright shiny new wedding ring.

Dear Lord, what is wrong with me that I'm dreaming of sex? Will I be cast into utter darkness where there'll be wailing and gnashing of teeth? Or is it just Hilda's talk about sex and marriage invading my subconscious. Oh Tom, where are you? I have such needs!

There were tears on her cheeks when she slept again.

When Flora woke it was to remember her words to her sister about Viv, and she wondered if she had been quite crazy. What faith she had in her sister providing for her daughter was tiny. Then Hilda surprised her that evening by giving her a pound note. 'You'll get more, Flo,' she said with a smile. And Flora wanted to believe her, but for now she had other matters on her mind.

The first post-war Christmas happened without too much fuss. There were extra rations and her sister gave Flora some more money. Flora bought some colouring pencils, and lead animals for the farm George was trying to build up. The girls received paintboxes and picture books. On Christmas evening they gathered about the fire to listen to the radio exchange of carols and greetings among children of different countries. And Flora thought of Christmas past and Tom, and ached with longing.

A couple of weeks later Hilda came in after being out with Tony and sat opposite Flora by the fire. She fiddled with her fingers before looking up and saying, 'Tony would like to meet you.'

'Oh, would he now?' said Flora drily, putting down her darning.

'You don't have to sound like that! Mind you, I only want him meeting you. So we'll meet away from the house – in town, maybe? We can have a drink. I'll let you know when.'

'I can't wait,' murmured Flora.

Hilda pulled a face. 'Wake up, Flo. I thought you'd be glad of the opportunity to see him – to make sure I'm not throwing myself away on any old bloke!'

'All right, keep your hair on,' she said mildly. 'I would like to weigh him up and see if he's worth all the fuss you've made over catching him.'

'Good.' Hilda smiled. 'Put on your best bib and tucker. You can look quite nice when you try.'

'Thanks,' said Flora sarcastically, despite having made up her mind that perhaps meeting Tony was a step in the right direction. As her sister had said, at least she would be able to make up her own mind just what kind of man he was.

Chapter Five

Flora glanced at the clock and hoped that it was still fast. She had taken the children to her father's. He had made a bit of fuss as usual over Vivien's presence but in the end he had grudgingly said he would look after them all. She picked up the fur plantpot hat that she had made for Christmas out of a moth-eaten fur coat that she had bought at a jumble sale, and placed it carefully on her copper hair. She wasted a second or two licking her finger and running it over her eyebrows, before asking herself why she was bothering. Only to come back with the answer that her sister had put her on her mettle. She felt that she had to look good for her own sake, not for Hilda's or Tony's. She went out the backway and legged it up the entry in the direction of the main road.

She caught the tram just as it was about to depart and settled on a window seat. With the darned thumb of her glove she cleared a patch of the steamed up window and peered out at the grey cold muggy day. As they went down Low Hill into the city, she remembered that in days gone by, when she had been with Tom, she had crazily wished that the tram could sprout wings and fly away over the city across the river to the distant hills of Wales, to the sea and adventure. That had been when she was young and full of dreams. She felt old now and very alone.

There were two men in uniform waiting with Hilda as Flora reached the pub where they were meeting. Her heart seemed to jump into her throat as she recognised one of them. He was shorter than the other man, fair, snub-nosed and looked older. She thought there was a gleam of surprise in his eyes, then he smiled a large, wide and welcoming smile. But before he could speak Hilda pulled the other man forward, and to Flora's relief, said, 'Flo, this is Tony.'

Tony appeared nervous, clearing his throat as they shook hands, but he was good looking, Flora could agree with her sister over that. He introduced the other man. 'This is Mike, he's gonna be best man.'

Her hand was enveloped in a warm strong clasp. 'It sure is a pleasure meeting Hilda's little sister,' he drawled. 'But you ain't a bit like I imagined.'

'Aren't I?' she said coolly, her eyes sparkling slightly.

'No. The things I've heard about you.' He pursed his mouth and shook his head, but his eyes twinkled as they searched her features. She could not but admire his nerve, but it was a long time since a man had flirted with her so she felt a little out of her depth.

'Perhaps you thought I'd have horns and a tail?'

He laughed. 'Something like that.'

'Mike!' Hilda appeared half-annoyed, half-embarrassed. 'Take no notice of him, Flo.'

'Sure he's a terrible man,' said Tony smiling. 'He kissed the Blarney stone, I reckon.'

'My grandfather did.' Mike's glance lazily washed over Flora. 'Hilda made it sound like you were older than her so I had this picture of an old crone in a black shawl — you know, like you see in your market. Some of them sell flowers. I'd like to buy you flowers right now. Marigolds — golden petalled, with hearts to match.' His eyes were grey and gazed straight into hers. It took Flora all her self-control not to blush.

'It's winter,' she said coolly. 'You'd have a job finding them. Are we going in? It's cold out here.'

'Sure.' He took her arm before she could say anything else and led the way in.

'Now what are we having to drink?' he asked, once the women were seated. 'This isn't a wake, folks. This is a wedding we're gonna be celebrating soon. Although some would say where I come from that there's not much difference!' He smiled and rubbed his hands together.

'I'll have one of your specials,' said Hilda, frowning him

57

down. 'But our Flora's not used to drink and she'll probably think them nasty.'

'One of the port, sherry or lemon dash crowd is she?' Mike gave Flora a teasing glance. 'Have one of my specials. Go on, be a devil.'

Annoyed with her sister for speaking for her and making her appear frumpy, Flora answered in a bright voice: 'Why not? A special drink for a special occasion.'

'That's it,' said Tony, smiling and showing his shining teeth. Very like Cary Grant, thought Flora, understanding even more what had attracted her sister. Hilda had always been a film fan. Hadn't she named Viv after the female star of *Gone with the Wind*? Tony continued, 'Let's celebrate another union between the old country and the U.S. of A.'

'Yes, let's,' murmured Flora drily. 'I can honestly say that Hilda can't wait to go. She talks of nothing else but you and living in the States. Is it as much like heaven as she makes out?'

'I think so, but then I'm biased.'

She rested her elbows on the table and eyed him carefully. 'I've always wondered what heaven's like. Not in the clouds after all. Perhaps me and the kids should migrate there.'

'Well,' he began uneasily, 'it's taken some time for the wives of guys already home to get out there just now.'

'Oh, take no notice of her, sweetie,' said Hilda, forcing a smile. 'She's only joking. You'd never get our Flora out of Liverpool.'

'Yes, I love Liverpool,' she responded lightly, 'but who knows? If I lived in America I might love it there too.'

'Is that so?' Mike placed a glass in front of her. 'If I wasn't already married with six kids — I'd make you mine and take you home.'

Flora had realised that he must be the Mike that Hilda had mentioned months ago, and she was annoyed because he could so lightly mention a wife and six kids and yet go in to Mrs Bryce next door. She could not think of any remark that she could give voice to, so she downed her drink in one go and nearly choked.

He slapped her on the back. 'I've never seen one go down that quick,' he murmured. 'I'll get you another.'

'No,' she spluttered, but he was already making his way to the bar.

Hilda, who had been exchanging light-hearted banter with Tony, turned and looked after Mike, before staring at Flora through narrowed eyes. 'What are you up to?' she said impatiently. 'You'll be getting tiddly. Watch it!'

Flora felt her hackles rise, aware that Tony was looking at her as well. She was so irritated that when Mike brought her the next drink she downed that in one go too. She knew that in doing so she was acting childishly but something had got into her and she felt mildly reckless.

Mike stared at her and grinned. Hilda looked at him, and Tony gazed at Hilda. A giggle rose inside Flora. 'Have you set the date for the wedding?' she asked for something to say.

Tony switched his gaze to Flora and his face lit up. 'Hilda thought some time in June.' He hesitated before adding, 'She sure would like someone of her own there. Says her pa won't come, but we'd like you there.'

Flora took a deep breath. 'I don't know. It's in a Catholic church?' She felt – floaty. Probably because she had not eaten since breakfast.

'Yes.' There was a slight pucker between Tony's dark brows.

'There'll be incense and candles.' Flora was only vaguely aware of Mike rising again. Her thoughts were of the time she had looked through St Michael's doorway. The church had a sort of fascination for her. The lure of the forbidden perhaps? She cleared her throat. 'If you look at some of the statues long enough,' she murmured, 'you can imagine they can see into your soul.'

'She's not used to drink,' Hilda was excusing her.

Flora guessed that she was not making sense to them. 'Two drinks I've had. Drowning my sorrows.' She cleared her throat and blinked at them. Mike set another cocktail in front of her, and sat back.

'Forget the past, Flo,' said Hilda, her eyes sparkling angrily. 'Look to the future.'

Flora's hand curled round the stem of the glass and this time she drank more slowly. It tasted pretty nasty, she reckoned. 'Ha! Some future!' she exclaimed.

'The future's great! We're looking forward to the future,' murmured Tony, seizing Hilda's hands and gazing deeply into her eyes.

'No future without Tom.' Flora's words were slurred and she sniffed back sudden tears.

'Don't start crying now!' Hilda spared her a quick embarrassed glance. 'Pull yourself together, Flo.'

'Leave her alone,' said Mike, frowning at her.

'She's my sister! You're to blame for this,' whispered Hilda angrily, looking about them. 'You have to try it on with every woman, don't you?'

'I'm getting out of here.' Flora's words cut across theirs, and she rose. Mike looked at her and got up hurriedly.

'I'll come with you. Don't these lovebirds just make you sick?' He seized her hand and dragged her away from the table, hurrying her out of the pub. Hilda called something, but Flora did not catch the words. And besides she did not want to listen to what her sister had to say.

The cold hit her as Mike hurried her along Lime Street. It was trying to snow. Suddenly Flora realised that he still had hold of her hand and she dragged hers away and came to a halt. This man reminded her of sex and she was better not thinking of it. 'You can go back to them now. I'm all right. I've met Tony and I can go home.' Her tongue stumbled over the words.

Mike stared down at her and smiled. 'I have got you into a state, haven't I?' He took her arm. 'I'd best come with you.'

'Oh no!' Flora backed away from him. She knew that it wasn't only because she didn't trust him that he mustn't come home with her; Hilda would not like it, she was sure of that. 'I know just the kind of man you are, and I don't want anything to do with you,' she added for good measure.

'Sure you don't,' he said soothingly. 'But you need someone to take care of you.'

Her eyes blurred with tears again. 'I don't need anybody to take care of me — I have to do it myself. I know what you're after and you won't get it from me!' She wrenched her arm out of his hold and stepped off the kerb, taking several paces into the road as a tram came rattling towards her.

'You dumbo!' Mike seized Flora's arm, pulling her back as the tram rattled by. 'You're not safe to be let out.'

She swallowed hard, staring up at him with wide frightened eyes. 'Don't get out often.'

'I can believe it.'

'It shows? Not sophisticated enough! Not like Hilda. And I suppose her next door talked about me,' she stammered.

'I asked.' He smiled crookedly, and she could not think of a thing to say. Then he seized her hand as another tram went by, and ran her across the road. A yelp escaped her as her shoe caught in one of the tram lines but she managed to hook it back on again without stopping or falling. They just missed her tram on the other side.

Flora dragged her hand from Mike's and leaned against the plinth of one of the crouching blackened lions in front of St George's Hall. She focussed carefully on his face. 'You can go back to them now. I'm at the right stop − but I suppose you know that. Although I just might walk so I can sober up. Either way, you don't have to bother about me.'

'I'd like a walk.' He eased his shoulders under the service mackintosh.

'I didn't ask you to come.' She thrust herself away from the lion. Then she paused, and turning gave it a friendly pat before walking away.

Mike fell in step beside her. She looked at him and her stride lengthened. So did his. He took her arm and she attempted to shake his hand off, but he kept a firm hold of it. She gave up the fight as the drink wrapped her round, insulating her against the chill and the falling snow as well as his presence. She was home quicker than she would have believed possible.

Mike dropped her hand as she fumbled in her bag for her key. Carefully she placed it in the lock, turning it and pushing the door wide. Inside all was quiet. Facing her escort, she said, 'Thank you. You've done your duty. Goodbye.'

He put one foot on the brass threshold. 'Aren't you going to invite me in?'

Flora drew herself up to her full height of five feet two inches. 'Certainly not! You'll ruin my reputation − if you haven't done so already. The curtains will be twitching. "Flora

Cooke's come home with a Yank," they'll be saying.'

He shrugged. 'Is that why Hilda hasn't brought Tony here? You sure aren't very welcoming.'

Her brow wrinkled. 'D'you expect me to be – knowing what I know about you?'

'You're writing me off because of two visits to Lena next door? That's not fair.'

Her eyes flashed. 'Neither is carrying on when you're a married man. Even my kids know when you Yanks have been. There's fresh chewing gum from her kids. Sweet Sixteen is George's favourite. It's cinnamon-flavoured, and he thinks it's great when the Yanks come calling. He doesn't know the whole story!'

'Hell!' said Mike savagely. 'What's a guy to do when he's offered an open port in a strange country? You've no idea how a man needs that kind of comfort – a double bed and a soft woman, the getting away from all the other guys. Even your Tom – maybe he might have needed that when you weren't there. Would you have cast him away for sinning once or twice? When the rest of the time he –'

'Stop it!' She almost screamed the words. 'I think you've said enough.' She had paled. 'I don't want you here! I don't need you here!'

He stared at her meditatively. 'I think you do.' And somehow he managed to push past her and walk up the lobby into the kitchen.

Flora followed him hurriedly and saw him sitting on Tom's chair. Something inside her snapped. 'How dare you? You've got a nerve, you lousy Yank!' She ran over to him, and seizing his arms, attempted to pull him out of the chair. But Mike took hold of her hands and she fell on his knee. She struggled to rise but he twisted her round and kissed her.

At first she was so stunned that she could not move. His lips were cold from the wind and she was aware of the scent of cigarette smoke on his damp mackintosh. Then the smell triggered off a memory, reminding her intensely of Tom when they had last said goodbye. She struggled violently and getting an arm free, caught Mike a stinging blow across his chin. His head snapped back and he stared at her. She burst into tears.

'Hell,' he muttered, 'I'm sorry.' His pleasant features mirrored his regret. 'I was only trying to make you feel better. You looked so sad that time I saw you. All screwed up. I've never quite forgotten you.'

'You'd be all screwed up in my position,' she sobbed. 'I'd been kept awake by you and her next door, then Rosie woke up and I had to leave her crying. I don't know how you can live with yourself — if you knew how many men she'd had! And now you seem to think that you kissing me will make me feel better. How you work that out I don't know! I love Tom and no other man can make me feel better.'

'But he's dead,' murmured Mike uncomfortably. 'And you need someone, Flo.'

She lifted her head and stared at him from tear-drenched eyes. 'Missing presumed dead! D'you know what that does to a woman? The uncertainty is killing. You accept, then you start hoping again — then you lose hope — then something triggers your memory and you want what you've lost again so badly that you start hoping again. You so want to believe that somewhere — against all the odds — your man has survived. That he's out there — alive!' She got up from his knee and sat on another chair, wiping her face on her sleeve.

'What happened?' Mike leaned forward, his hands laced between his knees.

Flora dropped her arm and looked at him. 'A shell. They said he was in the vicinity when it exploded. Several men were missing presumed killed. My father said that there wouldn't be much left of them.' She sniffed.

Mike nodded, his grey eyes keen. 'If he escaped the explosion, what d'you think could have happened to him? Or haven't you thought of that?'

'Yes,' she said eagerly. 'Maybe he was thrown by the explosion and wandered off in a daze, and was captured by the enemy. He could have been put in a prisoner-of-war camp.'

'He'd have been freed by now.'

Her expression dulled. 'Yes. But he might have lost his memory.'

'He'd have identification on him. Unless the explosion blew off all his clothes. In that case he could have hardly escaped notice. Some peasant would have found him. And if the enemy were the ones to do so, the same thing goes as before. He'd have been freed and files checked.' He shook his head regretfully. There was one other reason for Tom still being missing if he was alive, but Mike had no intention of mentioning it.

'You think he's dead,' muttered Flora, staring at the fire that was almost out.

'It's the most rational explanation!' There was pity in his look.

'Yes.' She moistened her mouth. 'I'm not a very rational person. I just hoped.'

'That's natural. But there comes a point where you've got to face the truth.'

'Yes,' she reiterated, and shivered. Her heart felt like a lump of lead in her chest. She did not want to consider what he said but had to.

'You're cold.' He got up. 'Cellar in the same place as next door?'

Flora nodded, and looked at him. 'I suppose I should thank you,' she said with a touch of anger.

'For what?' He picked up the shovel.

'Making me think sensibly. Our Hilda says I'm too much of a dreamer and I suppose she's right.' She squared her shoulders. The lump was still there and seemed to drag at her. They exchanged glances.

'There's nothing wrong with dreaming,' he said softly, 'but if it takes the place of reality and messes up your life, that's when you have to call a halt. I'll get the coal and you can make us a cup of your English tea.' He disappeared down the cellar before she could protest.

Flora stood like a tired cabbage for several moments listening to him shovelling, before she went and filled the kettle. More to take her mind off her thoughts than anything.

Watching him place lumps of coal strategically on the fire, she knew it would be a little while before she could boil water, and wondered how she could get rid of him. His presence disturbed her because it seemed to fill the room and change its atmosphere.

64

Mike straightened, dusting his fingers. 'Why hasn't Hilda asked Tony here?'

The question took her by surprise. She glanced about her, avoiding his eyes. 'Surely it's obvious? This isn't exactly the Ritz.'

'Tony isn't Fred Astaire looking for Ginger Rogers,' he said. 'But it figures Hilda would be ashamed of this place. She wants to fly high, your sister.'

'She's not really a snob,' replied Flora defensively. 'And for all she goes on at me for being a dreamer, she has her own dreams. Gets her ideas from the pictures, so that she believes everywhere in America has big rooms with lace curtains — and satin bedcovers.' Her voice tailed off as their eyes met, transferred a message. She moved quickly to pick up the toasting fork from the hook on the wall. She felt more secure holding it.

Mike's mouth twisted lopsidedly. 'I knew she was on the make — that's why I told her I was married.'

Her gaze flew to his face. 'You make that sound as if —'

'I'm not?' He smiled. 'I've seen too many guys tie themselves in knots in the throes of going off to battle. And when some of them come back they wonder how the hell they got themselves into such a mess. There's plenty of girls round like Hilda who see a man as a ticket to the Promised Land. I don't like that.'

'Tony loves her,' she said quickly, 'and she —'

'— likes a good time and plenty of dough.' He eased his tie. 'Nothing wrong with that. But marriage — well, that's different. I just wonder if she knows just how seriously Tony takes the girl-boy stuff. She'll be bored with him within six months, and could hurt him a lot.'

'I'm sure Hilda will be faithful to him once they're married.' Her voice sounded defensive again.

'Sure.' His smile was disbelieving. 'But let's forget them and talk about us instead.' He rammed his hands in his pockets and scuffed the rug with the toe of his shoe. 'What say you and me go out together while I'm here?'

'What!' Although he did not make a move towards her, she was instantly nervous. Her tongue flickered out to lick her lips briefly. 'You must be joking! With what I know about you and her next door, I'd have to be daft!'

'That's over with ages ago, believe me.'

She did, but his presence a couple of feet away made her edgy. What if he came closer again? 'It's not on.' Her voice was firm. 'I just couldn't.'

'Because of Lena or because of Tom? You're a young woman, Flora. You can't grieve forever. I can tell you're lonely and need taking out of yourself. Going out with me would do you good.'

An incredulous laugh escaped her. 'You fancy your chances, don't you?'

'Nope! But I fancy we could have some fun together.' He moved and she instantly brandished the toasting fork. He grinned and moved the kettle from the hob onto the fire. 'You sure are jumpy. I'll be the perfect gentleman, honest.'

'So you say.' She experienced a sense of helplessness. 'You'd be wasting your time. I'm all dried up. I'm no fun.'

'You could be if you let go.'

'I can't! I can't forget. I hurt.' Tears pricked her eyes and she squeezed her lids together in an attempt to force them back.

Mike stepped towards her. His breath stirred her hair and his hands rested lightly on her shoulders. She stiffened and raised an arm. He plucked the toasting fork from her fingers. 'I don't know about you, Flo, but I'm hungry. How about me using this thing and making us some toast?' His lips pressed lightly against her cheek before he moved away.

Somehow that gentle caress undermined Flora's resistance. She went and fetched the bread. He had taken off his mackintosh and cap and no longer seemed the threat he had been a short while ago. Still she kept some space between them as he made toast and she infused the tea, not quite trusting him.

Mike whistled under his breath as he stretched out his legs to the blaze and crunched into a piece of toast. 'This is good,' he said cheerfully. 'Almost like home.'

'You have a family?' Flora's fingers curled tightly round the cup, finding comfort in its heat.

'I have five brothers and sisters. Two older brothers and a

sister, and two younger sisters. The big ones are married, so I have a handful of nieces and nephews. Sure miss them.' He grimaced. 'They'll have grown bigger and maybe the youngest will have forgotten who I am.'

'You'll be able to pick up where you left off with them, though,' she murmured.

He nodded. 'Too right.' His teeth bit into the last of his toast. 'Hilda said you had kids. That must comfort you?'

She took a sip of tea and swallowed, remembering. 'I don't know what I'd have done without them. I wanted to die at one time but George rid me of that nonsense. They need me and I love them and that's what keeps me going.'

'That's the stuff, Flo. You keep on fighting the miseries and you'll come through. Wanting what might have been don't do you any good.' He stared into the fire. 'I had a girl once. Met her at college, had a good thing going. Then she was killed in an automobile smash.' His expression was sombre. 'Don't pay to dwell on what might have been. Life's for the living and there has to be a reason why some cop it young while others get a fair old stretch. So go for it while you've got it, that's what I say.' He stretched out a hand towards her, but in that second the door knocker banged furiously.

Relief showed on Flora's face, but Mike stood and swore as she hurried to answer its summons. He picked up his mac and cap and followed her slowly, so that he was a couple of feet behind when she opened the door.

'Good! You're in,' said George. 'Grandad said —' His voice faded away as he caught sight of Mike.

'This is a friend of mine.' Flora could think of no other explanation. 'I wasn't feeling well so he saw me home. He was just leaving.'

'You don't have to go, chum, because of us,' said George, his face brightening as he weighed up the American.

'That's nice of you, kid, but —' He shot a glance at Flora and knew from her expression that she wanted him out. 'I reckon your mom's going to be busy now you've come home.' His smile flashed. 'But it was sure —'

He was interrupted by Rosie, who planted herself in front of him. 'You're a Yank! Have you got any gum, chum?'

George cuffed her head. 'Rosie, you don't ask!'

'Nothing wrong with asking.' Mike's smile grew broader. 'Haven't got any cinnamon-flavoured on me, but I'll sure get some and pass it on to your mom.'

'Thanks.' George grinned and thrust out his hand. 'I'm George — pleased to meet you.'

'Likewise.' They shook hands.

'I'm Rosie, his sister.' She shoved George aside. 'And this is my cousin Viv.' She dragged Vivien forward, and Hilda's daughter smiled shyly at Mike.

He stilled. 'Guess I'm pleased to meet you too,' he drawled, taking Vivien's small hand. He slanted another look at Flora standing rigidly in the doorway, and could not prevent an unholy grin. 'D'you all mind going in while I have a last word with your mother?'

'That's not necessary!' exclaimed Flora, her eyes involuntarily going to Vivien. 'We haven't anything else to say to each other.' Her hands reached for the girls. 'Goodbye, Mike.'

'I think we have,' he said cheerfully, his fingers busying themselves with buttons. 'Those girls sure look like their mothers.'

Flora swore silently. George looked at her. 'Mam, do we go in or stay here?' His gaze went to Mike, who indicated indoors with his head. George did not move but looked at his mother.

'Inside,' Flora said. 'I won't be long.' They went and she turned on Mike. 'Now what is it you've got to say to me?' Her tone was sharp.

'I think you know. Viv is Hilda's kid, isn't she?' He looked her straight in the eye.

'And if she is,' she said fiercely, 'are you going to tell Tony?'

'That depends.' He stepped up on to the step beside her. 'If you come out with me I can forget I ever saw her — although it goes against the grain with me.'

She stared over his shoulder. 'I don't think I like you. And now you've said what you wanted to say, you can go.' She turned back into the lobby but he took her arm.

'Flo, it could be good,' he said earnestly. 'Hilda's and

Tony's affairs are theirs. You and me now — let's have some fun. And I mean just that — no hanky panky. I understand how you feel about Tom.'

'Will you go?' she said furiously, aware that a curtain was twitching across the street. 'You're making a show of me.'

He tutted. 'The neighbours? Is all that respectability stuff that important to you?'

'Truth is. People say things about widows and Yanks! Now will you let go of my arm?'

'Sure.' He glanced up at the louring sky. 'Give it some thought, Flo. Why should it be only Hilda who gets to go out? You've had it tough — you need a break.' His hand brushed her cheek.

She stilled. His touch was somehow comforting, and unexpectedly some of the derogatory words Hilda had said about her rang in her head. For a moment she was tempted to agree to go out with him. It was gratifying to have a man taking notice of her, whatever his motives. Then she thought of Tom. 'Go, Mike,' she pleaded. 'There's nothing for you here.'

He shook his head slowly. 'I'm the best judge of that. But I'll give you time to think.' He raised her hand and kissed it. 'I'll be back, and I'll be hoping the answer is yes.' His fingers squeezed hers, and then he left her before she could say any more.

Flora watched him until he was out of sight, and then she went in, closing the door slowly. The sensible thing to do was to tell Hilda what had happened, so that she could tell Tony about Viv before Mike did. Her sister was not going to be best pleased but she had to tell her. Having decided what she was going to do, Flora tried to put disruptive thoughts out of her mind and settle to cooking the children dinner.

It seemed a long time before Hilda came in, and when she did she was on the bounce.

'What the hell did you mean by going off with Mike?' she demanded, her lovely face contorted with anger. 'It was Tony you came to meet and you left the pair of us hanging high and dry while you waltzed off.'

'Hold on now,' said Flora slowly. 'It wasn't my idea. It was Mike who took me in hand, and as soon as he gave me a chance to catch my breath at the tram stop in Lime Street, I told him to go back to you. I didn't want his company.'

'Ha! It didn't look like that to me. The way you were knocking the drinks back and then crying and working on his sympathy, I was ashamed of you.' She folded her arms and kicked at the slumbering coals.

'I'm sorry.' A small flame of anger started to burn deep inside Flora. 'You don't have to worry about it happening again. I'm hardly likely to – '

'Tony was embarrassed,' interrupted Hilda, frowning into the fire. 'We left the pub almost immediately after you and couldn't see any sign of either of you. Where did you go?'

'I came home, and – '

'Mike was away ages.' Hilda tapped her fingernails against the chimney-breast. 'He wouldn't say where he'd been. I suppose he met someone else. Another girl after he left you at the tram stop. He's a dreadful flirt.' A slight smile eased her mouth. 'He even flirts with me occasionally. It's only a bit of fun. Tony knows that, although he's a bit jealous. Mike likes a laugh.' She was silent a moment, staring at the wall. Then she switched her gaze to Flora. 'He'd hardly get that with you, Flo. I mean you're still so miserable. A man doesn't like that – you'd be no fun.'

'No. No fun at all.' Flora's voice was taut. 'I suppose you think that he wouldn't find me attractive either?'

Hilda studied her. 'I suppose he might – we do have a look of each other sometimes. But you're not really his type.' She sounded calmer now. 'What did you think of Tony? Isn't he handsome?'

'Gorgeous,' said Flora shortly. 'I'm going to bed now. Goodnight.' She went upstairs and undressed slowly. Afterwards she lay thinking over Mike's words about Tom, staring dry-eyed into the darkness with the leaden sensation in her insides. Then she thought about her sister and what she had said about her and Mike, and she came to a decision.

That night she dreamed that she was the Statue of Liberty and Mike was scaling her.

Chapter Six

Flora was tense over the next few days, half-expecting Mike to call or her sister to explode into fury because he had told Tony about Vivien. But neither thing happened and gradually she relaxed a little. She was still trying to come to terms with what Mike had said about Tom but she found it difficult to be rational and her emotions were almost as confused as they had been when the news had first come about him being missing presumed dead.

More than a week had passed when George came in just as Flora was putting some scones in the oven. 'Mam, I've got a message for you.'

She sniffed. 'I can smell chewing gum.'

He grinned. 'It's that Yank, Mam. He's waiting to see you round the corner. He said he wouldn't come to the door — something about your reputation.'

'Oh! What's he want?' She tried to appear casual and uncaring but her nerves were jangling. Now that Mike had actually come she found herself reversing the decision she had made before she had dreamed about him.

'He didn't say.' George stared at her with a look of feigned innocence in his brown eyes. 'But maybe he wants to take you out.'

'You can tell him the answer's the same as before — no.' She straightened up and wiped floury hands on her apron. George did not move. She raised interrogative eyebrows. 'Well? What are you waiting for?'

He rubbed his nose. 'He seems a nice bloke, Mam. And

it'd do you good to go out. Aunt Hilda's always gallivanting but you never go anywhere.'

'Well, I wouldn't be able to go anywhere now because she isn't in and I'm not leaving you kids on your own. So you can go and tell him that − if you're so worried about hurting his feelings with a direct no.'

George pulled a face but nodded and went out. He was back again within five minutes, smiling. 'Mike said that we can go with you as well. He suggested the pictures. What d'you say to yes, Mam?' he said persuasively. 'We haven't been to the pictures for a couple of weeks.'

Flora hesitated, then met his imploring gaze. Without giving herself more time to think or feel, she replied: 'All right. But tell him he'll have to wait a while. I've got scones in the oven and I'll have to change − and you lot'll have to wash,' she added in a rush, dragging off her apron.

George whooped: 'It's Sexton Blake!' and dashed out to fetch the girls. Flora's feelings towards Mike suddenly warmed and she went to get ready.

The girls and George washed and changed at top speed and disappeared before Flora was even half ready. She found them waiting with Mike round the corner in the doorway of the wool and babywear shop. His eyes showed surprised appreciation as she came to a halt in front of them, and she was glad she had made the effort to do the best to her face with what Hilda had in a drawer upstairs.

A grin lit up his pleasant features. 'It sure was worth the wait.'

A smile tugged at Flora's lips. 'I'm sorry to have kept you but I'd forgotten what you said last time and didn't expect to see you.'

'Didn't you?' His tone seemed to suggest that he knew she was lying.

'It's been over a week.'

'Yes. We've been busy.' He took her arm to cross the road. The children fell in each side of them. 'Some of us are moving out. So it's all systems go.'

She gave him a quick sidelong glance. 'Will you be leaving?'

'And Tony. Which means that the wedding might be

brought forward.' He frowned and added in a low voice, 'Did you know this guy Hilda went with? Was she engaged to him or something and he got killed.'

'I don't know,' she murmured, wishing he had not brought up the subject. 'She told me so little at the time and I got the impression that questions would be unwelcome. But she doesn't expect to see him again. Perhaps he's dead. He was in the forces.'

'Which one?'

'I don't know. Can we drop it? I take it you didn't tell Tony?'

'No, I didn't,' he said shortly. 'Did you tell Hilda about me?'

'No. I didn't think it was any of her business.' Her voice was terse.

They looked at each other and Mike smiled. 'Good.' It began to rain and he talked about the British weather. Flora was surprised at how good it felt listening to a man's voice and enjoyed the warm feel of his hand on her arm. They discussed films, arguing the merits of American against British.

She enjoyed the picture and not only because the children were obviously doing so. The brush of Mike's shoulder against hers and the look in his eyes when they exchanged glances gave an unexpected lift to her spirits. Nevertheless she almost turned him down when he suggested another date. Only he asked the children where they would like to go and that settled the matter.

Mike took them to the Pavillion and they saw Dorothy Ward in *Mother Goose*. Flora would have felt quite guilty at him spending so much money on them except that he appeared as much a child at heart as they did when it came to booing the villain.

It seemed to be expected when they parted under the lamp post at the corner of the street that there would be another meeting.

There was a cold snap and it was a Sunday afternoon when he next called, so they went to the park where George frightened the life out of Flora by sliding on the iced-over lake, which cracked. He made it to the bank but had wet feet and socks so they went home. Flora knew that she could not do anything else but invite Mike in. Fortunately Hilda was out. They had hot tea and shared a Polperro Pasty made from pilchards, leeks and mashed potatoes. Mike said that it was better than service food and asked her out again – this time without the kids. It would have been difficult to say no, so she agreed but warned him that she might not be able to make it if she could not persuade her father to mind the children.

'Tell your Hilda you're meeting an old friend and let her have the kids for once.'

So she did. Her sister frowned. 'What old friend? This is sudden, isn't it?'

'Yes. She's just come out of the Wrens.' And Flora left the kitchen quickly before Hilda could ask any more questions. She prayed that the children would not mention Mike, and was annoyed with herself for fearing her sister's reaction to the truth. More by luck than deceit Mike's name had not figured in any conversation in Hilda's presence.

It snowed and so Mike took her for a meal. As they talked he told her that Mrs Roosevelt had gotten involved in the affairs of the G.I. wives in Britain, and now things were bound to speed up. He covered her hand and added, 'What d'you think of us Yanks now that you know one a little better?'

'You shouldn't ask me questions like that,' she said in a light voice, trying to free her hand.

'Why?' His tone was serious. 'I want to know what you think. You English are experts at hiding your real feelings. D'you still think I'm the rake you first thought me?'

She lowered her eyes. 'You're much nicer than I thought you could be.'

'Nicer!' He sounded disgusted. '"Attractive" and "fascinating" were the words I was hoping for.' His eyes twinkled roguishly. Flora laughed. 'That's better.' His fingers squeezed hers. 'You're lovely when you forget and let yourself enjoy the moment.'

The laughter died in her face. 'Mike, I – haven't forgotten. Or at least, it is only for the moment. Then I remember again. Don't let's get –'

'Serious?' His expression was warm. 'Sure.' He stroked the back of her hand with his thumb. 'Let it be fun.'

She nodded and slipped her hand from beneath his, asking him where he came from.

'California — where it's hot and sunny. I'm in the fruit canning business.'

She smiled. 'Go west, young man! Where all the wagon trains went. San Francisco — the golden gates — sunshine — and earthquakes! That's as much as I know. New Jersey is where Tony comes from, so Hilda said, and that sounds a lot different. How did you two meet?'

'In the forces. But don't let's talk about that.' He stroked the back of her hand again. 'Let's talk about you.'

'Boring,' she said, deciding to ignore what he was doing.

'Tell me about your family and when you were a little girl,' he insisted.

So she told him about her father and his stories of life on the old sailing ships, and how her mother had died of rheumatic fever when Flora was nine. About Aunt Beattie who had taken care of them, and how Hilda had said she was like a witch because she had six cats and was a bit eccentric in her dress. Several times he laughed at the tales she told. Then she talked about Liverpool, and how she and Rosie might not be here still if the baby had come a week earlier. About the bomb that had torn into the hospital not far away and killed the mothers and children. And after that she fell silent because she was thinking of Tom.

When the evening was over Flora thought Mike might not want to go out with her again. She had not scintillated and she felt certain that he must have got bored with her. But he asked her out again despite her warning him that she might have to bring the children next time.

The weeks passed and Flora and Mike continued to see each other, although they were seldom alone again.

'Mam!' George's breath was warm on Flora's cheek as he leaned over her. 'I've got a message for you.'

Flora breathed in sharply. 'Mike! Didn't you tell him you weren't allowed any treats? Your sins have caught up with you George Cooke?' she said coolly.

'Oh, Mam! When are you going to forget?' he cried unhappily.

'Probably never.' But her lips twitched. 'You must go the park if you're going to play football. You're like your dad. I remember him breaking a window and – '

George brushed her recollections aside. 'I was going to the park and I just sort of dribbled. I've got to practise so as I can play for Liverpool one day!'

'Never mind Liverpool and football – they're not doing so good at the moment. You'd be better paying attention to your education. You've got a brain in that head, if you bothered to use it. So take note – less football and more reading.'

'Awww, Mam! Don't go on,' he muttered. 'Mike's waiting for you at the bottom under the lamp post. Why don't you go out and have a good time? I'll see to the girls.'

She looked at him and her heart ached. Tom had sometimes thought life a game as well. 'Never you mind Mike, it's *you* we're talking about. You go gallivanting and I don't know where you are half the time. I worry about you.'

'There's no need. I don't go far. Not like Aunty Hilda going to America.'

She hushed him quickly. 'Don't say that so loud. Viv might come in and hear you.'

'I wish she was going to America,' he said moodily. 'She's a right whinger. I don't know why we have to put up with her. Why, when I tied her to the lamp post, she – '

Flora stared at him fixedly. 'What were you playing at, tying her to the lamp post?'

George stepped back a pace. 'Playing cowboys and Indians – and our Rosie didn't cry. Not even when we lit a fire pretending to burn her at the stake.'

Her mouth gaped open. 'You what?'

'She was all right, Mam,' he replied hurriedly, taking several paces in the direction of the door. 'We put the fire out. The wood was damp and only the paper burnt.'

Flora ran at him, but he was too quick for her and had the door open and was halfway up the lobby before she reached it. She followed him out and stood on the step, gazing after him.

Rosie, who was making a house from bricks taken from

a bombed site, looked up at her. 'Mike'll catch him, Mam.' She turned to watch her brother. 'See.'

Flora saw and her cheeks warmed slightly as Mike waved a hand. Aware of the interest of Mrs Jones from over the road, who had paused in brushing her step, she lowered her eyes and scrutinised her daughter's bare legs, filthy socks and scuffed pumps instead. 'George said he lit a fire under you. You mustn't let him do these things, Rosie. It could have burnt you badly.'

'It was only a game,' she said carelessly. 'He put the fire out with his bare hands.'

'I don't care how he put it out.' Her tone was severe. 'If he does anything like that again, you must tell me.'

Immediately Rosie looked worried. 'But he mightn't let me play with him if I tell on him.' There was a forlorn note in her voice.

'You shouldn't be playing his games. He's a boy and you're a girl.'

Rosie shrugged thin shoulders. 'I like rough games.'

'They can be dangerous. You play with Viv.'

The girl sighed and went back to play. Flora watched her a moment then looked up, hiding a smile as Mike waved to Mrs Jones and said, 'Good day.' The elderly woman half-smiled, then hurriedly went inside. His face was alight with amusement. 'You wanted this guy?'

'Did he tell you what he's done?' She tried to sound severe.

Mike nodded. 'D'you want me to beat the living daylights out of him?'

George looked alarmed. 'You wouldn't!'

Mike stared at Flora. 'I would if your mom asked me to — but I reckon there's marshmallow beneath that frosty exterior.'

'Don't you believe it.' She seized George by the hair. 'You, George Cooke, are not to encourage your sister to be a tomboy.' She moved his head roughly. 'She is a young lady and you are to treat her as such. D'you hear?'

He nodded, wincing as she tugged his hair hard for a second before releasing him. Slowly he made for the house and went inside, rubbing his head.

Mike stared at Flora. 'Would you enjoy me tying you to a lamp post and setting fire to you?'

'Just try it.' Her lips twitched. 'Our Rosie didn't turn a hair though. Now she's tough beneath that skinny exterior,' she said proudly.

'She's a nice kid — like her mother.'

Flora blushed. 'I think you're trying to get round me?'

He grinned. 'What if you were tied to the lamp post and I came galloping up on my pinto and rescued you — would you open your arms to me then?'

She lowered her eyes demurely: 'I'm not looking for a celluloid hero. Just a sensible ordinary guy who could worship me and take care of my kids — and keep me in the style to which I'm not accustomed.'

'Shucks, m'dear, I'll do it!' He slapped his leg. 'I'm not that sensible, nor that ordinary, but life could be interesting if you'd let me take you away from all this to where the horizons are wide and the horses carry five.'

'Five! Now that's boasting!' There was a challenge in her eyes. 'You'd run a mile if I said yes.'

'You could be mistaken,' he said quietly, and there was a look in his eyes that caused her to fix her gaze on his well-polished shoes.

'I don't think so,' she murmured. 'Five's too many.'

'You could get rid of one if you told that sister of yours where to go. That would make room for one of our own.' He touched her shoulder and her head lifted.

Her eyes were worried. 'I thought this was just going to be fun, Mike. We said nothing serious. And if this is some game of yours, I don't play them very well. Wartime romances — you don't agree with them, remember?'

He gave a twisted smile and playfully batted at her chin with his fist. 'So I don't. How about the movies tonight?' She hesitated before asking where. 'The Lido. It's one of your British films. Stiff upper lip and all that.'

'What's wrong with stiff upper lips?' she asked seriously. 'It shows fortitude and strength.'

'Difficult to pucker.' He blew her a kiss and she could not prevent a smile.

'You're daft. But I haven't got anybody to look after the kids. Hilda's going out straight from work.'

He scowled. 'Doesn't that sister of yours ever think of you?'

'It's just one of those things and it won't last forever. She'll be getting married and leaving.'

'What about Viv? I bet she's still gonna stay quiet about her. It's not right, Flo, that you have the raising of her. Nor that Tony's being lied to,' he said irritably, thrusting his hands deep in his pockets.

'It's her decision. Mine too, if I'm honest.' Flora's brow creased in thought. 'I just can't believe how I've managed to go so long without her finding out about you. I mean the kids haven't said a word to her — but then she doesn't see much of them, and doesn't talk much when she does.'

Mike shook his head. 'Tony wants kids. She's got a rude awakening coming if they get married.'

'If?' She looked at him.

He shrugged. 'Nothing's final till it's done. What about tonight then?'

'I'll have to bring the kids, I told you.'

He sighed. 'What about your father?'

'It's too late in the day.'

'Okay, then. Bring them. I'll see you outside in half an hour.' She agreed and he went.

They sat close in the pictures, Mike's arm about Flora's shoulders. She had given up removing it half an hour ago. The children sat three rows in front near the screen. She tried to concentrate on the picture but her mind was on Mike and what he had said earlier that evening.

'Is this stiff upper lip and terribly British type your sorta guy?' he whispered.

'He's what helped us win the war,' murmured Flora, very conscious of his nearness.

'*We* helped you win the war. But that's not the answer I'm looking for. Do you go for the kind of guy on the screen?' There was a note in his voice that pleased her even as it caused trepidation.

She looked at him, thinking that his profile seemed that

of a stranger in the flickering half light. 'I don't think of them as real people,' she muttered. 'It's our Hilda who goes for the film star look-alikes — rich, conquering hero types. She's a dreamer for all she's supposed to be the one who knows all about life.'

'And you don't go for rich, conquering heroes?' He sounded slightly incredulous.

'I didn't say that — I've nothing against money. But my hero was Tom and I'm not looking for another.'

'But —'

'Sshh,' came a voice from in front. 'Some of us are trying to watch the film.'

They both fell silent, but their attention had wandered from the screen. Flora was thinking about Hilda and Tony, and herself being with Mike, and of his arm round her shoulder.

When they got outside the children ran on ahead, playing tig. Mike dragged Flora's hand through his arm, linking his fingers through hers. It would have been difficult to free herself short of causing a fuss before the crowds hurrying home. She must end it, she decided. When Mike spoke she jumped.

'I swore I wouldn't get carried away by a girl when I was over here, Flora, and I've kept to it so far. I told myself that there's girls at home who understand the kinda things I like doing. Who'd fit into my ordinary civvy life just fine. But now —'

'Don't Mike. We've been through this earlier. Maybe we should finish right now?'

He stopped in his tracks and turned her to face him. 'Flo, you can't mean that. Think again. I like you a lot. You're kinda vulnerable but gutsy with it. I'm thinking more and more of taking you home with me.'

'Don't!' There was a shadow in her eyes. 'What about the children? You couldn't take them on. It wouldn't be fair. Besides hasn't it sunk in over all these weeks, Mike? I can't give you anything. I'd be no rival to those girls at home.'

'I wouldn't say that.' His expression was gentle as he traced the line of her cheek with a finger. 'Nice eyes, good thick hair of a lovely colour. No make-up tonight —

I'm getting to like that.' He touched her mouth and it trembled.

'Stop it,' she stammered, removing his hand. 'This can't go on.'

'Let's give it a little longer while we can. Please, Flo. Are you really in such a rush to have me out of your life and be back to where you were again? You're more relaxed now and I like it when there's a smile in your eyes.' He pulled her into his arms and his face was bright. 'Shall we go dancing next time? I've never taken you dancing.' She gasped as he began to polka with her up the middle of the cobbled road, not seeming to care about the passing cinemagoers who shouted, 'Go it, Fred and Ginger!' Or the kids who gaped, or the lads who grabbed their giggling girlfriends and aped them.

Flora began to feel exhilarated and like a star in a musical. Her head was whirling. 'Stop it, Mike,' she cried, laughing. 'People are watching us.'

'Who cares?' He swung her off her feet before bringing her down to earth, gasping. 'Promise that you'll go dancing with me next time.'

She clung to him, staring into his face, and realised with a sense of shock that she would miss him quite a lot. 'Just one more time,' she whispered.

They swayed together and then they were kissing as if they could not get enough of each other. The crowds surged about them and several lads wolf whistled.

Gradually they drew apart. Mike smiled down at her and linked his fingers through hers.

The next moment the kids had caught up with them, and Rosie was dragging at Mike's jacket. He turned and seized her hand. 'Let's go, kids,' he cried. Then Vivien grabbed Flora's other hand and George seized hers, and they all raced like crazy to the bottom of the street. There Mike left them. 'Till the next time,' he called. They all waved before slowly weaving their way up the street and into the house.

Flora's emotions were confused as she hustled the children to bed. On a high she impulsively climbed on to the double bed. Standing on tiptoe, she took an old chocolate box from a high shelf. For a brief second she peered at the picture of a lupin-filled cottage garden on the lid before lifting it off.

She emptied out the letters, cards, photographs, dried flowers and ribbons on the bed. Fingering a dried daisy she remembered the sun glinting on the lake in Stanley Park and Tom rowing her in a boat, showing off his muscles. Picking up a yellow ribbon she recalled his proposal and how she had almost stopped breathing with the shock and the thrill of it coming only two months after them walking out together, although she had long been in love with him.

Almost instinctively her fingers reached for the letter written on a half sheet of old exercise book paper. It had come with the one for her shortly before the telegram arrived, and she had meant to show it to Rosie before now. Slowly she unfolded it to read the words that Tom had written. 'My darling daughter, I'm sure you're being a help to your mother, and growing —' The words blurred and she folded the letter swiftly.

She was in the middle of putting things away when she found the photograph. It was of a group of soldiers. Her fingers traced the lines of Tom's face; his lips, his nose. There was a lump in her throat as she gazed into his smiling eyes. 'Age shall not weary them nor the years condemn.' She tried to come to terms with her loss.

So wrapped up in her thoughts was she that she did not hear the front door open or the footsteps on the stairs.

'What are you doing sitting like that?' Hilda's sibilant whisper caused her to spin around. 'And what's all this mess on the bed? How can I get in? I'm tired with being on my feet.'

'I'll move it,' said Flora in a low voice, putting the photograph under her pillow. 'I was just looking for something.' She began to pile her memories back into the box. 'How was your evening?'

'Fine.' Hilda yawned. 'Will you be all right for the wedding in three weeks? It's all fixed at last.'

'I should be.' She hesitated. 'Have you thought any more about Viv? About telling Tony?'

Hilda paused in the middle of undoing the zip on her skirt. 'You're joking!' She frowned. 'You aren't changing your mind now, are you?'

Flora stood on the bed, glad to have her back turned. 'I

just thought you might. America's a long way and Viv's going to be upset. When are you going to tell her? I don't think you should leave it till the last minute.'

'Why not?' Hilda's voice was cool as she pulled the covers back. 'There'll be less time for her to go on about it. But if you think she should know — you tell her.'

Flora felt the familiar sense of frustration and anger. 'You're her mother! You're leaving her, so the least you can do is tell her yourself.'

'All right, all right! Keep your hair on.' Hilda heaved a long sigh as she lay down and closed her eyes. There was a brief silence before she spoke again. 'Tony was telling me that Mike's going out with some woman or other.'

'Oh!' Flora tried to make her voice sound disinterested, but her heart felt as if it missed several beats.

'He thinks he's quite serious about her.' She gave a sharp laugh. 'Who'd have thought old Mike would be so stupid — just when his stint over here is almost through too. It serves him right for playing around.' She turned over. 'Tony reckons it started that day we met you in town. I wonder if he's told her he's married? Probably not. He didn't tell me right away.' She yawned. 'Perhaps he'll bring her to the wedding. He's got that kind of nerve.'

Flora almost told Hilda the truth but she held back, in no mood for a fuss. Besides, it would wake the girls. Her hand reached beneath the pillow to touch the photograph of Tom. Tears pricked her eyes. She owed it to his memory to remain faithful to him, and that meant saying goodbye to Mike.

Chapter Seven

'Some of the G.I. brides are on the move,' Mike informed Flora as he whirled her round the dance floor of the Grafton. 'They're joining the *Queen Mary* in Southampton and sailing to New York.' He looked at her quizzically. 'Don't you find that idea exciting, Flo? Sailing off into a whole new life?'

'It could be,' she gasped, trying to keep her eyes on his face as he twisted her round again. 'But I'm not about to be swept off my feet by the thought of a bit of excitement.'

'I wasn't suggesting that.' He held her close a moment as he snatched her out of the path of a couple who seemed to believe that they owned the dance floor. Both of them were instantly aware of the effect such nearness had on the other. 'Honey, think what I could give you,' he whispered against her ear. 'I've got some money – we could build a house big enough for a family. Your George could do with a man about the place. He needs discipline.'

'I know.' She rubbed her cheek against his. 'He's very like his father. Got plenty of spirit.'

'Nothing wrong with spirit. All I'm saying is that it's hard for a woman alone to cope with a boy. I'd like to help. I sure am in love with you, Flo.' He brought her to a standstill beneath the glittering twisting ball overhead and stared down into her flushed face.

'Oh, Mike! I wish you hadn't said that. I'm really flattered, and if I was honest I'd have to admit I don't think straight about lots of things when I'm with you.'

'That's how I like you,' he muttered, his lips brushing her

ear. 'Let's get out of here.' He pulled her hand and she went with him through the gyrating couples.

It was dark outside with only the street lamps casting pools of light here and there. Mike pulled her arm through his and they were both silent as they began to walk. She was thinking of what it had been like a year ago when it was still wartime and the blackout. What a state she had been in over Tom! At least now she knew that she could cope with living, although it had not been, and she supposed it never would be, easy.

'Flo!' He squeezed her hand and she looked sidelong at him. Her heart misgave her. 'Please, Mike, don't ask me again.' Her voice was unsteady. 'Don't think that I'm not tempted, because I am. But it wouldn't be fair on you. You need the whole shebang from a woman and I couldn't give you that.'

He frowned. 'You haven't given yourself a chance, Flo. How d'you know you can't give me what I want? Just a few kisses we've had, and the last one gave off sparks.' He pulled her into his arms, Flora struggled but his grip tightened and his mouth came down over hers. She resisted, closing her lips tightly, telling herself that Mike could only be a friend. A good, good friend, because it was Tom who was still in her heart and it was impossible to love two men at the same time.

Mike lifted his head and gave a short laugh. 'Hell, Flora, you can do better than that. I think you don't give a damn about me,' he said crossly.

Unexpectedly she was reminded of a film that she had seen, and a giggle rose inside her. 'Frankly I do,' she murmured demurely, remembering how she had always wanted Rhett Butler to be terribly overbearing once more and to sweep the stubborn, stupid Scarlett into his arms and up the stairs.

'You do?' The anger in his face vanished to be replaced by a grin. 'Then you'll marry me?'

'No.' Her voice was uneven when she added, 'I'm terribly, terribly fond of you, and I've enjoyed terrifically our times together, but — I can't go to America, however pretty a picture you paint of it. And you Yanks can sure do that! Cherry blossom springs, white Christmases, hot summers and autumns that are so beautiful that folk take rides on Sundays

85

just to see the colour of the trees.' She took a breath. 'Oh, and I mustn't forget that there's also plenty of food and no rationing or bombed buildings.'

There was a faint smile on his face. 'Your Hilda's been listening to Tony. But it's a bit different where I come from. We have the sun all right but we also have the Pacific. I know you like the sea. Think of having a beach house and watching the rollers coming in. Think of me and you walking along a beach.' He was gripping her hand tightly now. 'Think of me and you making love and being happy ever after.'

She groaned and put an arm about his neck and pressed against him. Her voice was muffled when she spoke. 'I don't walk on clouds, love. *You* think hard. Of having the kids around all the time − of supporting them. And of me being homesick for Liverpool. Because, believe it or not, I would miss this battered old city. I do know how you feel because I care for you, and though it mightn't be wartime there's a sense of urgency, of not wanting to let go, of needing something that you might never have a chance at again.'

'You really feel like that and you can turn me down?' he said seriously, holding her gently.

She lifted her head. 'I think we'll get over what we feel right now.'

There was a short silence before he murmured, 'And what do you feel, right this moment?'

'I want you,' she said huskily, her face burning as she met his eyes squarely. 'And if you feel the same, then you'd better grab me while I'm offering because tomorrow I'll probably go all respectable again. Tonight's goodbye, Mike. A clean cut is better than a lingering farewell.' She paused and their fingers twisted and gripped tightly. 'What d'you say?' she whispered.

` He lifted her hand to his mouth and kissed her little finger. 'Oh, honey, I never thought you would,' he said in a low voice. 'So I'll grab you while the going's good.'

'Where do we go then?' A shiver of excitement raced through her and she determined not to allow feelings of guilt to spoil everything. Afterwards she would ask God and Tom to forgive her.

'I know a place.' He gripped her hand tightly and began to run her towards the tram stop.

'I hope you're prepared?' she gasped, blushing even as she said it.

'Nope, but I'll see to it.'

The place was a hotel near Lime Street. The proprietor asked no questions about their marital status and for that at least Flora was grateful, although she was less nervous now than when she had had a two day honeymoon in Rhyl.

Their room was clean and comfortable. She looked at Mike as he hung up her coat, feeling awkward, wondering how to get from fully dressed into the bed.

Mike smiled. Taking one of her hands he let out a whoop and twirled her round the room so that her short skimpy skirts fluttered madly. Then he caught her up against his chest and they kissed as if tomorrow was already upon them. His hands covered her breasts, his fingers stroking her nipples till they hardened and seemed to thrust through the fabric. His lips nuzzled her neck, her cheek, found her mouth again and moved over it hungrily.

Her lips opened beneath his and his tongue dallied with the tip of hers while he stroked the frock from her shoulders. Within seconds he held both her breasts in his hands and, lowering his head, his lips found first one rosy nipple and then the other. Her pulses beat in her ears and she swayed against him, as her frock fell about her feet. His fingers searched inside her underwear, caressing lower and lower, until he stopped, and clasped, then explored inside her. Her heart seemed to jump suffocatingly into her throat. She closed her eyes briefly before dragging at his arm. 'Mike, please.' The words came out in a throaty thread of sound.

He looked into her dazed face and without speaking, stripped her and carried her over to the bed. She lay naked, watching him undress. Then he was beside her, fingering her shining copper hair spread on the pillow. Reaching up, she let her hand run slowly over the light brown hair on his chest. Then the movement stilled as she remembered how she had tugged at the golden hair on Tom's chest the last time they had been together, and she could have wept because already her body was trembling in anticipation of what might happen next and she so wanted Mike to make love to her but now it was impossible. She was flooded with guilt, and rolled over and buried her face in the pillow.

'Honey, what's wrong?' Mike's voice was urgent. Flora made no answer, struggling with her emotions. There was a short silence, then he shocked her into forgetting everything else but the moment by straddling her. His mouth touched the nape of her neck and nibbled before nuzzling down her spine. A shiver raced through her, and as his tongue licked her tail bone a low murmur of pleasure escaped her.

He dropped on top of her, reaching beneath to seize her breasts and kissing between her shoulder blades.

'Mike, please,' she whispered, unable to move when every fibre of her was yearning to respond.

'Please what?' he retorted in a slightly mocking voice against her ear.

'Let me turn over.' His body lifted slightly, just enough.

They looked at each other and then he kissed the corner of her mouth gently and her muscles seemed to turn to marshmallow. She put her arms around his neck and pulled him down on top of her. Desire was suddenly a whirlwind, carrying them along to do whatever they wished. One kiss merged with the next and the next. He caressed her all over, even touching her bare toes, rousing her to a trembling state of sensitivity. She nuzzled his face, his throat, his broad shoulders – and thrust her hands between their torsoes so that he would lift off her and she could kiss his chest and his quivering stomach muscles. He groaned and stilled her hand, covered it and pressed it hard over him. His grey eyes were dark with emotion. 'You do believe I love you, Flora?'

In that moment she believed it. High with anticipation she did not want to cheapen the moment by thinking of the other women he had had, and that she just might after all be one in a line. She watched in a fever of impatience as he pulled on a sheath.

His sigh was swallowed up as they kissed, and he stroked her trembling hips with unsteady hands as she strained the lower part of her body up to him. It had been so long and her need was so great that she could not wait for him to enter her. Her nails dug into his shoulder blades and she moaned as his fingers prepared her for his entry. He was so gentle but aroused her beautifully. Whispered words of love escaped her as they joined, their bodies pulsating jerkily at first before quickly catching a rhythm. She could barely credit the pleasure he dispelled to all her limbs before he climaxed.

Afterwards they drowsed, holding hands, and she pondered over how Mike had been able to satisfy her the first time. She had thought that only Tom, who had known her body intimately, could bring such satisfaction. Perhaps she was a wanton as he had said. The thought disturbed her almost as much as her desire for Mike. It was not going to be easy parting from him.

They made love again, and again he asked her to marry him and was turned down. 'I can't love you enough,' she cried in distress, ruffling her hair with an unsteady hand, and avoided his eyes. 'Tom's still in my heart.'

He frowned at her. 'Dammit, Flora, I think you do love me. After the time we've just had. It was so good!'

'As good as all the other times with other women?' She didn't know why she said it.

His generous mouth tightened. 'They were before I met you. And never as good. And not once since −'

'I believe you,' she interrupted quickly, and put her arms round him. 'Forgive me, Mike, but accept the inevitable. I have to go. I've got work in the morning.'

'Give it a miss.' The words were muffled against her hair.

'I can't,' she said, pulling away from him.

Despite her protestations he got up, and they walked through a Liverpool that seemed unreal to her in her new determined but melancholy mood. They halted under the lamp on the corner of her street, and for a moment neither of them made a move to part. Then she took a step away, only to have him pull her back. 'I'm going to miss you like hell,' he muttered, hugging her tightly to him.

'And I'll miss you.' She was near to tears but she drew away from him determinedly. 'There's the wedding, of course,' she said unevenly, kicking the bottom of the iron lamp post.

'We'll have to pretend we barely know each other. It won't be easy. Our Hilda –'

'She isn't a patch on you and doesn't deserve Tony, but she'd never have given the way you have tonight,' he said roughly.

'Don't let's talk about her now.' Flora clutched at his lapels. 'Tarrah, Mike.' She kissed him hard and he responded just as forcefully. She had to tear herself out of his arms. There was a great ache in her chest and she ran up the street as if all the hounds of hell were on her heels. She wanted to look back for a final glimpse of him, but did not dare because ending it was hurting far more than she had thought it would.

She let herself into a darkened house, allowing the tears to course down her cheeks. The fire was not quite out and the kettle was still warm. She drank a cup of warm water with sugar in it, great sobs wracking her body as she gazed with blurred vision at the grey embers of the fire.

Eventually she regained control of herself but where her heart had been, it felt like there was an enormous stone. A shuddering sigh passed through her and she closed her eyes. It was over and that was that. Going to America with Mike was an impossible dream. They had had to say goodbye. The pain would pass. It wasn't as if she had loved him to the same extent that she had Tom.

She forced herself to think of Tom and gradually she dozed off – to dream that she and Mike were in a garden, and he was saying, 'Frankly, I don't think you give a damn about me, Flora.'

'No, yes,' she stammered, 'maybe I'll make up my mind tomorrow,' But he had vanished in a swirling grey mist, leaving her lost and alone. And it was in her mind that something like this had happened before – in a film – and when she had seen it, she had known that Scarlett was making a terrible mistake in turning Rhett Butler away. And she woke up and cried again, knowing that breaking up with Mike was one of the worst things that she had had to do in her life.

Chapter Eight

Hilda entered Flora's house in a whirl of slamming doors and clattering heels. Her expression was thunderous as she threw her handbag on a chair, and her coat at the hook on the door — only to miss it. She let it lie where it fell as she faced Flora, who was reading a story to the girls. 'You sneaky, conniving bitch!' Her fingers tore the book from her sister's hand to fling it to the other side of the room. 'You always were jealous of me, but I didn't think that you were that evil that you'd spoil my chance of going to America!'

Flora's heart beat quickened in alarm. She pushed the girls away and sat up straighter. 'Don't call me names in front of the children,' she said, determinedly calm. 'If you've got anything to say you can wait until they've gone to bed.'

Hilda's face was dark with fury. 'Is that what you did when you brought Mike to this house? You got rid of the kids upstairs? How could you see him without telling me?' She almost choked on the words.

Flora rose slowly, her expression wary. 'I didn't *bring* him here. He wouldn't take no for an answer and insisted on coming to see me.'

'I don't believe you.' Hilda's fists clenched. 'I suppose you'll deny it's you that he's been seeing for weeks?'

'No.' Flora tilted her chin. 'I was going to tell you that first day — only you went on about me not being any fun, and that he wouldn't want my company. Well, you were wrong. He did!'

'Ha!' The exclamation came out like a pistol shot. 'You

expect me to believe that? You chased him, I bet!' She slammed her fist down on the arm of the chair, causing Vivien and Rosie, staring wide-eyed at them both, to shoot under the table and crouch on the crossbars beneath. 'I'm not such an idiot that I didn't see you working on his sympathy as soon as you met him. But I thought him being married would put you off. It appears that I don't know my own sister after all.'

'He's not married,' murmured Flora, moving back against the table.

Hilda gazed at her wildly. 'What d'you mean — he's not married? Of course he's married. He told me so himself.'

Flora bit on her lower lip hard. 'He says that to put off the girls he thinks just see him as a ticket to America.'

'You mean — he lied to me?' Her face went scarlet. 'The swine! The sneaky swine! How dare he lie to me and not you — and then do what he's done! I wish I had his face in front of me right now — I'd smash it!' She pulled off her shoe and flung it across the room. It bounced off the door. 'I could do murder where he's concerned. I hate him and I hate you. You!' She whirled round. 'What did he see in you? Maybe a little of me, and because I turned him down he went after you. It was the same with Tom — can't you get a man of your own?' she sneered. 'Is it that you've always got to have my cast-offs? I bet he was talking about me all the time, wasn't he?'

'Like hell he was!' Flora's control snapped, her hands gripping the table behind her. She spoke in a furious voice. 'The only time he spoke of you was in connection with Tony. He didn't like what you were doing. He'd read you right and knew what you were after. He asked me to marry him — was prepared to take on the kids too! So why is it, dear sister, that you reckon men think I'm second best? Tom and I were really happy, but you're always trying to undermine my confidence where he's concerned. He found me perfectly satisfactory — for all you seem to hint that you were the expert when it came to being with a man in bed. And Mike found me just as satisfactory too!'

'You and Mike!' Hilda was now deathly white. 'And you say Tom — Tom found you —' She paused. 'It shows how much you know!' She slapped herself in the chest. '*I* slept with him! Even though he was married to you he wanted sex with me!'

Flora felt as if she had been punched in the stomach. 'I don't believe you,' she gasped. 'You're only saying that to hurt me!'

'Am I?' There was a gleam of triumph in Hilda's eyes and a flush had darkened her cheeks again. 'You'll never know, will you, Flo? The dead don't tell tales.'

'Get out of my house.' The colour had drained from Flora's face.

'Don't worry, I'm going. You don't think I'd stay here now after what you've done?' Hilda's voice was harsh. 'I'll never forgive you for spoiling my chances. Call yourself a sister — I wouldn't own you for one! I'm leaving and I'm never coming back.' She swept up her shoe, bag and coat, and wrenching the door open went out. Her footsteps sounded angrily on the linoleum, and then the front door slammed shut.

For several seconds all was silent in the kitchen, and then a cinder fell on the hearth. Flora stirred. At the same time the girls crept out of their hiding place. Vivien's brown eyes were anxious. 'Where's Mam gone? She's forgotten me.' Flora made no answer, only reaching for both girls and pulling them close.

Vivien was trembling. 'Mam was very angry,' she blurted out. 'Is she cross with me?'

'No, lamb. Only me.' Flora hugged her tightly.

'What's sex, Mam?' asked Rosie, looking at her curiously.

Flora flushed. 'Never you mind.' She rubbed her chin against her daughter's hair, determined not to allow herself to brood over what Hilda had said about her and Tom. But what had got into Mike to tell Tony after all this time?

'I want my mam.' Vivien's eyes suddenly filled with tears.

'She said she wasn't coming back,' murmured Rosie, leaning against her mother and watching Vivien's face. 'And if she does maybe she'll be a murderer, because she said she wanted to kill Mike.'

A howl escaped Vivien that set Flora's teeth on edge. She

lifted the child off her feet and carried her to the sofa. 'Hush, Viv, that won't bring her back. You can have some cocoa, and then I'll take you to bed and tell you another story. And when you wake — well, tomorrow's another day.'

'Will Mam come?' sobbed Vivien, rubbing her face against Flora's cardigan.

'She might.' Flora did not want Hilda returning and doubted she would. If her sister could consider going all the way to America without Viv, then she was not going to worry about her now. There was a hard core of cold anger inside her as she soothed Vivien. Eventually the child calmed down and they went to bed. George banged on the door just as Flora came downstairs. She did not have the heart to scold him but sent him straight to bed. The morning would be soon enough to tell him what had happened.

The early hours brought the van but Flora did not need its tooting to wake her. She had lain unsleeping the whole night. Her head ached as she went out into the cool morning, and she realised that her situation was now worse than it had been before she had wished for someone she could leave the children with, and to talk to. Having your wishes come true was not all that it was cracked up to be, she decided, climbing into the van with a heavy heart.

A couple of days after Hilda had left Flora came back from her father's to find George playing hopscotch on the pavement in front of the house with a group of kids that included Kathleen Murphy. 'Me mam said could yeh give 'er a knock 'cos she's got summat to tell yeh.'

'Oh, okay,' murmured Flora, hoping that it was not something about George and Kathleen. The girl seemed to have taken a shine to her son and haunted their front step.

She went into the house first to leave her shopping, and discovered that her sister had been there. All her clothes were gone and so was her savings book from the sideboard. There was no note mentioning Vivien, and Flora was furious to think of her sister coming and taking but not sparing a word for her own daughter. Bursting to talk to someone, she went to Carmel Murphy's.

The older woman took one look at her face and placed

94

the yard brush she was wielding in the lobby. 'Come in, Flo girl. I'll make you a cuppa.'

'Thanks,' said Flora, tight-lipped, following her in.

She had never been invited inside the Murphys' home before but was not surprised to see that it was as untidy and poorly furnished as one could expect of a bombed out household that contained six kids. She experienced a stirring of compassion for the other woman that blotted out the depression she had felt since parting with Mike and her anger over the argument with her sister.

Perching herself on a rickety dining chair, she smiled down at the youngest of the Murphys. One-year-old Bernadette was playing on the oilcloth with a battered black pan and a clump of plaster. She was clad in a mucky blue frock that was too large for her, and little else, but her toothy smile was a delight.

'You'll perhaps know that your Hilda's been,' said Mrs Murphy, pouring tea from a chipped brown pot into two odd cups, one flowered, one plain white.

'Yes,' said Flora as calmly as she could, her feet shifting restlessly on the torn oilcloth. 'You saw her, I take it?'

Mrs Murphy nodded. 'On your step. Arguing she was, with that nice Yank you've been seeing. Slapped his face!'

Flora's head shot up. 'She hit Mike!'

'Going at it hell for leather she was — shouting at him fit for the whole street to hear. That was, until he walked away.' She spooned sugar into the flowered cup and handed it to Flora. 'He stopped to talk to me in that nice accent he has. And smiled luv'ly — and sez to tell you that he's after leavin' Liverpool in the morning and that he'll never forget you.'

Flora put a hand to her mouth and her eyes glistened. 'Oh, hell,' she cried in a muffled voice, and her shoulders shook with the effort of trying to hold back the tears. Some of the tea spilt over and almost scalded her knee.

'There now, girlie,' said Mrs Murphy in a comforting voice, leaning forward to wipe up the tea with the edge of her pinafore. Bernadette looked at Flora curiously as she banged a chunk of plaster against the pan and sent a small puff of pinkish dust over the floor.

She swallowed the enormous lump in her throat. 'I'm okay,' she said painfully. 'It's not that I really loved him. But he was so kind and nice, and —'

'— he took yer out of yerself.' Mrs Murphy's voice contained a wistful note.

'Yes.' Flora forced a smile and there was a friendly silence while both sipped their tea. Then she said, 'My sister — did she say anything to you?'

Mrs Murphy shook her head. 'As fidgetty as a flea on a cat by the fire while he talks to me. And then has a face as hard as sandstone, and just as pink, when she comes out of your house with bags of stuff and marches past me.'

Flora pulled a face. 'Ah, well, that's that!' She squared her shoulders. 'But I'm going to have to find myself another job. Now the girls are at school, I've been meaning to, anyway.'

'What was yer job before you were married?' Mrs Murphy glanced up briefly as she managed to squeeze another cup each out of the pot.

'I worked in a printer's.' She sipped the strong brew thoughtfully, before saying slowly, 'I suppose it might be worth going and asking if there's anything doing.'

Mrs Murphy nodded vigorously. 'That's the ticket, girl. Now them's fighting words. Don't you be letting life get yer down.'

'I won't.' Flora drained her cup and stood up. 'Thanks for the chat and the tea. If there's anything I can do for you — anytime.'

'I'll remember.' Mrs Murphy smiled, showing teeth that needed attention. 'Just send our Kathleen back when you've had enough of her.'

Flora nodded, and was escorted up the lobby and out.

That evening she told Vivien that her mam might be gone for some time, but that she was to be a brave girl, and not to cry — they would all look after her. A few tears oozed from beneath the girl's lids, but they soon dried after a jam buttie, a cup of milk, and a story.

Once the children were in bed, Flora washed her hair in Amami shampoo. She had decided that in the morning she would go down to the old firm and ask Mr Martin for a job.

The smell of ink was strong even in the small lobby, and the whole building seemed to vibrate as belts slapped and machinery clanged rhythmically. Memories flooded back, giving Flora an unexpected lift.

On her left was a partition constructed of dark wood and leaded stained glass windows. She rang the bell there, and a few moments later a man came to the counter. 'Good morning, Mr Foy.' She smiled, slightly nervously at the elderly man with a pencil stuck behind his right ear.

Johnny Foy stared at her intently over his Woolworth glasses and down along his large nose. His cheeks and throat moved, and she knew that he was struggling to gather a huge amount of tabacco juice for ejection before he spoke. He turned and spat in a corner, then scrubbed at his greying gingery moustache. 'It's little Flossie Preston, if I'm not mistaken,' he commented in his rumbling voice.

'Flossie Cooke now. Remember I left when I got married?' At fourteen she had been terrified of him, but had eventually discovered that he was not the bogey man she had considered him. 'How are you, Mr Foy?'

'Well enough, lass. And yourself?' The brown eyes were kindly as they focussed on her face.

'All right.' She cleared her throat. 'How is everybody? The Old Man?'

'Ken's away in the Navy. Bill's in the army, but should be out soon. One of the apprentices, young Joey, just got his call up papers. You heard about Jimmy Martin, I suppose?' Resting dun-coloured overalled elbows on the counter, he leaned towards her. 'He copped it at El Alamein.'

Flora's heart lurched uncomfortably. Another bright spark gone. She wondered if Hilda knew. They had been close once. 'I'm sorry to hear that. The Old Man'll be upset.'

'Taken it hard. Had it all worked out that he would take over the business. Now it's down to his brother if he can pull himself together. He's in hospital somewhere down south — been there for ages.'

'Stephen has? The war was it?' Flora and Stephen Martin had been in the same class as infants.

'Shot and blown up he was — not at the same time, of course.' He shook his head slowly. 'Nerves all to pieces, the Old Man said. To be expected really. Lost not only his brother, but his mam and sisters in the blitz as well.'

'Tough,' she murmured, feeling sorry for the absent Stephen.

'Aye,' he rasped. 'But I'm thinking you didn't come in here just to ask how we all are, lass. What can I do for you?'

She cleared her throat. 'I'm looking for a job, I'm – widowed now – have kids.'

'Heard about that. Pity. So it's a job you need.' He made a clicking noise with his tongue, then he lifted the counter flap. 'Come in, lass, and see the Old Man. Maybe he'll be after taking you on. We've been short of workers because of the war, and experience counts.'

'Once learnt never forgotten,' she said brightly, quelling her apprehension as she followed him through a couple of machine rooms and up a narrow wooden staircase.

They came to the Composing Room where she would work if she got a job. An elderly man with a composing stick in his left hand was picking up lead letters from various boxes with his right. He gave a cheery grin. 'Hello, Flossie, long time no see.'

'Yes.' She paused and looked about her. How long ago it seemed since last she was here. Over by the window was a wooden bench cluttered with pots of glue, gauze, thread, and several piles of printed paper. Someone was in the middle of collating, although there was nobody there at the moment.

As they went towards the Guillotine Room where the paper was cut, a woman in her fifties came through the doorway carrying a tray of steaming cups. They narrowly missed a collision.

'Hell's bells!' exclaimed Molly, her bushy dark brows coming together. 'It's you, Flossie. A little thinner but definitely you. What are you after?'

'A job,' replied Flora with a wry smile.

'Well, I hope you remember that it's slave labour.' She smiled and went in the direction of the stairs. While Flora followed Mr Foy into the Old Man's presence.

He put his cup on a crowded table and stared intently at

her. 'Good morning, Flora,' he said in his quiet voice, 'I believe you're in need of a job.'

'Yes, Mr Martin.' She stood straight-backed, her hands by her side, a sad smile barely lifting her mouth as she remembered the past. He was not really an old man, but had turned prematurely grey after his wife had been killed in a tram crash. They had no children, and he had never quite recovered from his loss.

'You think that you can cope with it? I believe you have a couple of youngsters.'

'A boy and a girl, but they're both at school,' she informed him quickly.

He nodded. 'You're a widow.' His voice was calm enough but his eyes were bleak. 'The war's been unkind to us both, Flora. But I think I can take you on. Start on Monday. We'll be having a big job coming in next week and will be glad of your help. It's the wood catalogue – you must remember it, so you know that there's a lot of competition in these matters, and speed is of the essence.'

'Yes, Mr Martin.' She did not betray by a flicker of an eyelash her apprehension. Speed took practice and she was out of that.

'See you Monday then.'

Flora thanked him and left with a feeling of exhilaration mingled with trepidation. Would she be able to do it? Of course she could! It would help her to stop missing Mike and constantly dwell on what her sister had said about Tom.

Chapter Nine

'I must say, Flossie, that it's nice seeing an old face,' said Mollie, collating pages of the wood catalogue with a swiftness that was difficult to keep up with. The book had a hundred pages so that meant twenty-five piles of sheets to gather up and staple on the treadle machine. 'So many have gone and not come back. When I think of our poor Jimmy and Mabel and the girls, I could weep still.' The lines of her plump face drooped. 'Still there's Stephen, although he's not Jimmy. Sam had it all planned for him to run the business. He would have brought it out of the doldrums.'

'Business been bad then?' Flora lined up pages and knocked them up.

Molly pursed her lips. 'Chronic at times.' She lowered her voice. 'But then, what can you expect when all the able-bodied men went off to fight, leaving you with old men, boys and a cripple?'

'That's hardly fair,' protested Flora. 'They all seem to work hard to me.'

'They could work harder if our Sam would push them,' said Molly in a brisk voice.

'But Stephen will be returning.' Flora glanced at her taut expression. 'He was a good worker.'

The older woman nodded. 'Aye. He was always reliable and steady was Stephen. Although all he does at the moment is stare at the wall in that place down south.'

'He's been through a lot, by the sound of it.'

'Maybe,' said Molly grudgingly. 'But we've all had a hard war, and it's time he snapped out of it.' She banged the sheets of paper on the bench. 'Our Sam needs him.' She changed the subject abruptly. 'D'you want to have a go at stapling now – to give us a bit more room on the bench?'

Flora nodded, showing no sign of her nervousness. She messed up the first few and her hands grew sweaty. Then suddenly the staples started going in the right places. Her anxiety subsided as her hands and mind co-ordinated, and she wondered why she had been so bothered. Even so she was glad when the job was finished and packed, and one of the apprentices took it away for delivery.

She soon settled into a routine of packing leaflets, billheads, and rounding the corners of invitation cards for weddings or birthdays. There were church magazines, booklets and ledgers. Some of these had to be sewn, bound up in sections before being glued. Ledgers were bound in cloth with a leather spine, or were all leather. She began to take a pride in turning out a good job. But she was no match for the expert bookbinders next door.

Flora enjoyed going in there, and often paused to look about her when on some errand. The place was a shambles with shelves and tables crammed with materials – gauze, linen, cloth, and leather. Books were hand-backed, so there was a laying press, wooden backing boards and the round-faced bookbinders' hammer which battered the books into shape in sections – that had to be done carefully or the paper could be badly creased.

She loved the smell of the leather, calf and sheepskin as she handled the books with care. She had always loved books and reading but now there was little time for that or for dwelling on the past or the future. There was much to do in a day and time passed swifter that way, with little time to brood.

It was the evening before Victory Day which was also Flora's birthday, and a street party was being planned to celebrate not only the victory but the homecoming of so many husbands and sweethearts. She was making raspberry jelly when there was a hammering on her door.

She opened it to find a large man with a shock of ginger hair and an irritated expression on his red freckled face.

He wore a pin-striped demob suit. With a sinking heart she recognised him immediately and held out a hand. 'Mr Bryce! It's — lovely to see you home.'

'Thanks.' He squeezed her fingers briefly. 'D'you know where Lena and the kids are?'

'No.' She did not like telling a lie but could hardly say that Lena had gone down the entry with a Yank, while the kids had gone up the entry an hour earlier. 'Can't you get in?'

He did not give her a straight answer. 'I thought I'd surprise her,' he muttered, 'and she's not in. Have you any idea where she's gone?'

'You could try the top pictures — the Royal,' she said weakly, not wanting to be the one to tell him the truth.

His face brightened. 'Thanks.' He half-lifted a hand and then legged it up the street.

Flora was just about to go in when her name was called. Mrs Jones was putting the finishing touches to the decoration round the photograph of the King and Queen in her fanlight. She got off her chair and waved to Flora. There was supressed excitement in her voice when she shouted: 'I bet there'll be high jinks tonight once he finds out what she's been up to. You'll have a front row seat!'

'I'd rather not,' yelled back Flora.

'She deserves everything she gets, bringing down the tone of the neighbourhood with her comings and goings,' said Mrs Jones, sticking her nose in the air. 'At least you only had the one. She's no better than a whore.'

Flora did not want to get involved in slagging her neighbour off, so she made her jellymaking a quick excuse to get inside the house. Once there she finished the job off but could not settle to anything else because Mrs Jones had reminded her of Mike. The children had gone to the park with a gang of other kids to play rounders, so she decided to walk that way to meet them.

It was when they were returning that they met Mr Bryce and his children. They looked like they had been crying and his face was set. He walked past them without saying a word. But Mavis, his daughter, called, 'It's me dad and he's takin us to me gran's, and we didn't even see the end of the picture!'

-'Shut up!' growled her father, clouting her over the ear. She howled and he hit her again, dragging her along behind him.

George exchanged a quick glance with Flora, devilish glee in his face. 'There's going to be a fight next door tonight, isn't there, Mam?'

'I hope there's going to be nothing of the sort,' she said tartly. 'You and the girls'll be in bed anyway. You'll have a late night tomorrow.'

George said nothing. He was certain that being in bed, wouldn't stop them from listening to the goings on next door.

All their near neighbours seemed to be of the opinion that there was going to be something worth watching later that evening. An awful lot of steps were getting swept and scrubbed. Privets at the bottom of tiny gardens received a late trim. Some washed windows with a leisurely sweep of cloths. Even the priest who had been visiting the Murphys stood on their step, lingering. The less daring sat in their front parlours, peering round the curtains.

Only a few knew the moment when Mrs Bryce, slightly aglow with drink, went up the back entry with her Yank. But the news was soon passed on. Flora wondered whether she should knock and warn her, but was only thinking about it as she sat in the dark in the front parlour when she heard Mr Bryce's light tread on the front step. Instinctively she ducked her head as he glanced in the direction of her house, and the next moment she heard a key in next door's lock and realised that he must have got it from the kids. There was going to be no escape for the couple in bed.

It was the roar of Mr Bryce's voice and the sound of smashing glass that drew her to the front door. A boot lay in the middle of the street, to be joined the next moment by another. There were raised male voices and a high-pitched screech. Then the noise of an overturned chair. Clothes came flying through the broken window. Soon everybody was out in the street, including George, and the girls in their nighties.

'He's thrown the Yank's uniform out,' said one man with glee, picking up a jacket and flinging it in his garden.

'I like the Yanks,' commented Kathleen Murphy, sneaking up behind Flora to stand next to George. 'Me dad said that it's her that should be thrown out.'

'She'd fly through the air with the greatest of ease,' sang George, swinging Kathleen round by one arm.

She giggled and Flora could not help a smile.

They heard gusty sobs from upstairs and a few minutes later the front door was opened with such violence that several pigeons sitting on the roof took to the air in alarm. A scuffle started in the doorway and some of the neighbours crowded round quickly to conceal the sight of the naked American from their children's eyes. But George had already seen him. 'Here comes Bare Bum the Bandit!' he yelled.

A ripple of laughter ran through the crowd and Flora made a swipe at his head. He danced away with Kathleen in pursuit.

Meanwhile one of the men laughingly offered his shears to Mr Bryce. 'Cut it off, mate.'

Mr Bryce took them, and the Yank, much smaller than the other man, stared around him in dismay. 'You guys have to be joking!'

'I don't think it's a bloody joke to find you in my bloody bed with my bloody wife,' said Mr Bryce through gritted teeth, working the shears as he approached.

The American swore and backed away hurriedly. Several of the neighbours were convulsed with laughter, but Flora realised that Mr Bryce was deadly serious. She darted forward in front of the Yank and smiled at her neighbour's husband. 'Is such a little thing worth chopping off? A big gorgeous hunk like you would be better off showing Lena what she's being missing all these years.'

He hesitated before saying, 'Get out of the way, luv. I've got no argument with you but I have with that Yank.'

'What about Lena?' shouted someone. 'It's not just this Yank. She's had hundreds of them.'

'Not hundreds,' came a quick laughing retort. 'Maybe fifty.'

'She's had more Yanks than I've had hot dinners,' said the first voice.

'Don't be exaggerating,' said Flora, watching a dull flush

run under Mr Bryce's skin. He threw down the shears and dragged the belt from his trousers. Then he turned and ran up the lobby.

'Oh, hell! Someone stop him,' cried Flora, glancing up at the front window.

'In a minute, girlie,' said Little Paddy, appearing out of nowhere to stand beside her. 'Let her be havin' a taste of his belt first. She's had it coming for a long time.' He scrubbed at his droopy moustache.

'But –' Flora winced as a scream sounded from the bedroom.

'No buts. You be after finding that Yank his pants and get him out of here.' He patted her bottom and she stared at him in astonishment before withdrawing from the scene.

Someone had given the American a pinafore to cover himself, but George came skipping over with his underpants on the end of a stick. They were dragged on hurriedly, while their owner avoided the eyes of the curious. Kathleen brought his vest, and Rosie his trousers. Two other kids appeared with the rest of his clothes and his boots.

By the time he had gone and Flora had managed to get hold of her children, the crowd had dispersed and Mr Bryce had been persuaded to spend the night at his mother's. His wife had slammed the door in their faces, and now next door was shrouded in an unfamiliar silence.

The next morning Flora heard Mrs Bryce going out and looked out of the window to see her lugging two carrier bags up the street. She experienced some relief that her neighbour had gone. Otherwise there might have been more trouble that day.

She was not sure how she felt about Victory Day and the street party. Thinking of the returning servicemen reminded her of Tom and caused a surge of frustrated anger at the sheer waste of his life. But the children were all excited about it.

'I wish I'd known my dad,' said Rosie, stroking the cat as they sat on the front step. 'You never gave me that letter, Mam.'

'Didn't I, love? I meant to.' Flora patted her shoulder. 'Maybe later I'll find it for you.'

Rosie nodded in a satisfied manner. 'I can show our class. I bet none of them have a letter from a dead dad.'

Flora had not looked at it quite like that, and was about to say so when Vivien spoke. 'I haven't even got a mam now.' She gazed unwaveringly at Flora. 'George said that she doesn't want me — that she was going to America without me.' Her bottom lip trembled. 'Is it true, Aunty Flo?'

'Of course not,' retorted Flora without hesitation. 'You take no notice of George. Now go and play all of you. The party will be starting soon.' They took the hint and she wandered through the house and into the backyard.

She sat on the back step and held her face up to the sun, her thoughts a million miles away, so that she did not hear the knocker go or footsteps up the lobby and through the kitchen. Not until a man's deep voice said, 'Hello, Floss!' did she start and her eyes flew wide open.

'Who is it?' He had moved so that he was dark against the sun.

'Don't you know me, Flossie?' He lowered himself to her level, sitting back on his haunches so that she could see his face more easily.

'Stephen Martin?' He had changed — grown up — there were scars on the side of his face up near his left eye, and lines of suffering about his mouth and nose. 'It's been a long time.' She held out her hand and he took it.

They were both silent as they remained handfast. So many years had passed since the last time they had seen each other, and their worlds had been vastly different places then. The sight of him caused memories to tumble helter skelter into her consciousness so that she experienced unexpected grief. She dropped his hands but still continued to stare at him.

'I was so sorry about your family, Steve,' she blurted out, noticing how his dark brown hair still curled vigorously, and remembering how his brother had teased him, saying that only girls had such curly hair and that he should put a ribbon in it. Once she had found him in the works yard, trying to get it to lie flat with the shoe polish.

'Yes! It was terrible.' Pain shadowed his face. 'In this street where there's no damage I find it hard to believe that it's happened. But in the city centre — hell!'

Now the silence had a waiting feel to it. 'Tom,' he said abruptly.

'I'd rather not talk about it.' Her voice was strained. 'Please!' There was another silence and neither of them could think how to break it. It was Flora who spoke in the end. 'I heard you were wounded.'

'Aye. Twice.' He leaned against the wall that needed white washing, and his mouth twisted into a semblance of a smile. 'Careless of me, wasn't it?'

'You're still alive, that's the important thing.' She noted the hollows beneath his cheekbones, and the jaw that looked as though it had not seen a razor that day. His nose was still slightly crooked from when Tom had hit him with a cricket bat playing on the sands at Waterloo! She had almost forgotten about that but now she remembered how pale, bloody and angry Stephen had been. His nose had been broken, and he and Tom had never had much to do with each other after that. It was a pity. She added sympathetically, 'It must have been awful.'

'Awful both times.' A sharp laugh escaped him. 'But no worse a hell than that which took Mam and the girls!' He broke off abruptly and the silence this time seemed to stretch endlessly.

'Stephen!' Flora's clear voice was worried. 'You look miles away. I'm sorry if I've brought back bad memories.'

His throat moved and he swallowed. 'I was thinking of Tom and Jimmy. I can't help it! Seeing you —'

'I know,' she said quickly. 'Especially today they must be in our thoughts. You know what happened to Tom?'

Stephen drew a breath. 'I know you're a widow.'

'A widow. I suppose so.' Flora tested the word. 'Missing presumed dead,' she murmured, and wondered why he tensed and fumbled for words.

'My Uncle seems glad to see me.'

Flora smiled. 'I'm sure he is. He has high hopes of you taking Jimmy's place.'

'He was the favourite.' Stephen's blue eyes were dark when he lifted his head. 'Now he expects all sorts of things from me, and I don't know if I can, or want to, live up to his expectations.'

107

'Want to?' Her voice rebuked him. 'Surely you owe him a lot.'

'I know I do — moneywise.' He tore petals from one of the nasturtiums in the windowbox. 'When Dad died — when I got the scholarship to the Institute — he was always there with an open hand.'

'He was proud of you.'

'Only because I went to college. He preferred Jimmy.' He smiled tightly. 'Now our Jimmy had a way with him — just like Tom did.' He glanced at her and away again. 'They could wheedle blood out of a stone.'

'Yes,' she murmured. 'They had charm.'

'The gift of the gab,' Stephen said softly, his face pensive. 'Are you thinking, Floss, that life is unfair?' He paused, staring down at his hands. 'There's Tom and Jimmy with all that going for them — no longer here. And here's me. The girls and Mam would have mourned for me if I'd been killed and them still living. But I've no wife or sweetheart — only good old Uncle Sam, glad that I've survived for the firm's sake.'

'You sound sorry for yourself,' she said, disturbed by his words. 'What's the point?' She scrambled to her feet, her face quivering. 'Maybe there's some reason why it's you that's alive — I don't know' She turned away. 'I'm going to make a cuppa. You'll have one, I suppose?' Not waiting for his answer she went indoors.

When Flora returned with her composure a little more intact, Stephen was sitting on the dustbin with his eyes closed. For a second she noted the way the dark lashes fanned into the sunken sockets, then she nudged him with her foot. 'Wake up, Stephen. I don't know how you can doze off with all that racket going on outside.'

'It's easy when you've slept in some of the places I have. This is peaceful in comparison.' His eyelashes fluttered and his gaze flickered over her slight figure before he pushed himself up. 'It's fun outside for some. Wouldn't you like to go and see what's going on?' Not only could a barrel organ be heard now, but the faint sounds of an accordion.

'I don't think so,' she replied calmly, handing his tea to

him. 'I'm glad the war's over and that I have a roof over my head –'

'But you don't feel as grateful as you really should,' he muttered. 'You don't consider the victory involves you.'

'We've had parties already,' she said unevenly. 'Enough's enough. Let the victorious march in London by all means. I like a parade – but my British Tommy isn't going to come marching home.' She put a hand to her eyes, forcing back the tears.

'Floss!' His voice was harsh and his fingers wandered to the scar on his face. 'About Tom –'

'No! I've told you. I don't want to discuss it,' she murmured in a wobbly voice. 'The past is the past, and you know – it's my birthday today!' She scrubbed at her eyes. 'I didn't tell anybody. What's the point of making a fuss. It can't be a happy birthday.' A sob shook her. Stephen's coming had somehow unlocked the floodgates. She had already cried in the house but still she wanted to weep for Tom, and all those soldiers, sailors and airmen who had suffered or died and wouldn't be coming home. And she resented Stephen for causing her to break down, even though looking at his scarred face made her want to cry for him too. He had once had such a nice face.

'Hell,' he said, putting down his cup. 'What if I wished you a happy birthday – birthdays should be taken note off, Floss. How old are you? Only months younger than me, I remember – that makes you twenty-eight.'

'Don't remind me,' she said baldly, tears rolling down her cheeks.

'It's not old! You've got years and years ahead.'

'That should make me feel better?' There was a note of anger in her voice. 'Years and years of being alone. Now you're making me sorry for myself.'

'I'm a fool.' He rifled his hand through his hair. 'I wasn't thinking. I'll go – that'll be the best thing. I'm not doing you any good here, am I?' There was a touch of irritation in his tones. 'Besides, Uncle Sam will be missing me. I didn't mean to upset you.'

'I suppose not. It's just your choice of words.' She lifted her cup to her lips but her teeth chattered against the rim.

Stephen stood watching her, his face unhappy. 'Why don't you come out with me?'

'No thanks,' she said coolly in an attempt to gain control of herself again. 'You go and be a conquering hero. You deserve some fun.'

His face was suddenly angry. 'Don't I just! You've no idea what it's been like! Before I even left Britain, when I was in Scotland, the news came about Mam and the girls. It was lousy. I was the soldier but they were killed, it seemed so crazy! But at least it helped me to know what I was fighting for besides King and country. Then Jimmy was killed, and you know, that was almost the worst moment of my life. We used to argue like hell! The last time I saw him we argued about Mam. But he was my brother, Floss.' His eyes glistened and his mouth tightened. 'I just didn't care after that what happened to me. I did all kinds of crazy things! But then suddenly, at the point where death was pretty close, I cared about being alive again.' His fists curled. 'You said about me not feeling sorry for myself – how about you? Come out in the road with me. You might feel a lot better.'

Her head lifted and her face was taut. 'I'm sorry, Steve. I'm not good company. Leave me.'

He scowled. 'I always thought you had guts, Floss, but it seems I was wrong.'

'Shut up!' Her bottom lip quivered.

His anger seemed to drain out of him as quickly as it had flared up. 'Floss, don't you think it's hard for me?' His voice was quiet now. 'They're all so bloody happy! I want you to come so that I don't have to walk out there all on my own. It scares me to death.'

Unexpectedly his words struck a chord. Flora remembered how she had felt on VE Day, and she understood. 'Why shouldn't they be happy?' she whispered. 'We shouldn't take that away from them.'

'I don't want to.' He suddenly looked tired. 'Come on, Floss – for old times' sake, let's be friends and see if it's catching.' He held out a hand. She hesitated and then took it.

They walked silently side by side until they came out

110

into the street which was noisy with activity. Then Flora wondered why she had allowed him to persuade her. Envy was an emotion she did not want to experience — it was like a knife twisting in her breast watching the newly demobbed men with their wives and sweethearts. But she pinned a smile on her face and they went over to where the girls were laughing at the organ grinder's monkey's tricks. Stephen stuck to her side. She sensed the loneliness in him and sympathy stirred inside her.

It was getting dusk and Flora considered it time to get the children to bed, but then people started dancing and the girls dragged them both into a circle. Flora was reluctant to ape them, but when others were kicking their legs as high as they could in a 'Knees up, Mother Brown' she felt compelled to join in. Then a twisting, wriggling, laughing serpent of a line was formed to do the Conga up and down the street. Stephen's hands gripped her waist, manipulating her this way and that, until the line collapsed and people staggered away to fall exhausted into the well-worn chairs grouped on the pavement.

The accordion player drifted into a waltz. Flora would have sought out the children then, but Stephen gripped her hand tightly and said in a muffled voice against her hair: 'Come on, Floss, for old times' sake.' And she could not resist the pleading note in his voice.

Weariness rippled over her in languorous waves. Her head drooped against his blue shirt-clad shoulder. She forced it up and looked into his face, searching for something to say. Then she realised there was no need for polite conversation because his thoughts were somewhere else, just as hers had been most of the evening. She relaxed and her head drooped again. Up early, she was tired.

Stephen's hand moved up her back and pressed her head against his shoulder. His arm tightened about her waist. It felt comforting and they danced on and on.

The next morning she arrived at Martin's ten minutes late with no thought of seeing Stephen, only to be brought up short by the sight of him in one of the machine rooms.

'Hello, Floss,' he said quietly.

'Morning! I overslept for once,' she said in a rush. 'I'm not used to late nights.' She made to pass him but he grabbed her arm, bringing her to a halt. 'Hey! D'you mind? I'm late!' She attempted to pull herself free.

'Not that late,' he said slowly, releasing her. 'What are your hours here, Floss.'

She rubbed her arm, considering that he was stronger than he looked. 'The same as the men's,' she murmured. 'Half eight to half five.'

'That means those girls are home from school a good hour and a half before you.'

'Yes. But a neighbour keeps her eye on them,' she said defensively. 'And sometimes they go to my father's. They aren't just left to roam.' A long breath escaped her. 'Can I go now, Mr Martin?'

He raised both eyebrows. 'What's with the "Mr Martin"? It was Stephen last night.'

'Last night we were old acquaintances meeting again. This morning you're one of the bosses,' she said promptly.

'Not yet I'm not!' He laughed shortly. 'And I mightn't be. I just came to see what the old place felt like after all these years.' He glanced about him. 'Nothing much has changed. The old type is still gathering dust over there against the wall — and Mr Foy's still here.' He smiled slightly. 'He used to terrify the life out of me when I was like the lad over there, learning the trade from the bottom up.'

'He frightened me too.' She hesitated before asking, 'But what d'you mean you mightn't be a boss?'

'What I say.' His dark brows drew together. 'I don't know if I want to step into my brother's shoes even if it's what everybody expects of me. They'll always be comparing us.'

She frowned. 'Maybe they will for a while — but it's more likely they'll compare your ways with the old man's.'

'You think so?'

'I'm sure of it. Things have changed, Steve. There's been a war, remember? The apprentices are different, and they only know Jimmy as a name. As for the rest, it's a long time since they've worked with either of you, and I think they'll remember what a good worker you were.'

'So you think I should give it a go?'

'Yes,' she said definitely, before adding, 'what else could you do anyway?'

His hand went to his hair, his fingers threading through its tangled mass. 'I had something in mind. But maybe I should give things here some time.'

'It makes sense.' Her eyes went to the clock on the far wall. 'I'd better get moving or Molly will have something to say.'

'Let her!' He pulled a face. 'She's somebody who hasn't changed − still doesn't have a high opinion of my talents.'

'Change her mind for her then,' she murmured, seeing no point in denying what he said. 'You were always a good reliable worker, that's what's important.'

'I had no chance to be anything else.' He scowled. 'We needed the money at home. And any ideas I might have had of doing something different were dismissed. Although Mam would have liked me to have been a teacher.' There was only the slightest hint in his voice that the memory still rankled. He smiled at her. 'Have you thought of asking my uncle if you can go home earlier to be there when the kids get home? It would mean a slight drop in pay but not that much.'

'I have − but I need the money.'

'I see.' He dug his hand in his pockets. 'It must be difficult for you.'

'Of course it is.' Unconsciously she squared her shoulders. 'But then life's difficult for a lot of people.'

'You must hate not being there for them when they get out of school,' he murmured thoughtfully. 'A mother should be at home with her children.'

'If she can,' she said with a touch of impatience. 'Now can I start work?'

A flush crept into his cheeks. 'Sure. Maybe I'll see you around.' He walked over to the apprentice and started talking to him.

Flora stared after him, then hurried across the floor, not looking at him as she passed.

Molly looked up as Flora entered the Comp Room. 'You're late. Overslept, did you?'

'Like thousands of others.' Flora hung her coat on the stand in the corner. She was in no mood for conversation.

'The Old Man said Stephen told him he went to your street party.'

Flora stared at her. There had been a curious note in Molly's voice. 'Is that a crime?' she said quietly.

The older woman shrugged. 'He just mentioned it.'

'So you thought it worth mentioning to me.' Her tone was deceptively mild. 'Why?'

Molly promptly veered the conversation down another path. 'Did you see our Stephen on your way up?' She eyed Flora carefully. 'Sam says he hasn't made up his mind about working here – did he mention anything to you about staying?'

'Why should he?' asked Flora, picking up the worksheet.

'He must have said something to you?' Molly could not conceal her curiosity.

'I was late. Now let me get down to work.' She moved to pick up some cards and began to hum a waltz tune.

'Dancing all night says something,' said Molly, determined not to be frustrated. 'Stephen was never one much for girls. Not like Jimmy.'

Flora sighed, knowing that the older woman would go on and on. 'We've known each other most of our lives and it was a pretty upsetting day for both of us – so we kept each other company. Now are you satisfied?' Her voice was sharp.

Molly tossed her head. 'There's no need to get huffy. I was only asking!'

'Well, I've only answered you.' She got to her feet and went to fetch some gauze, considering it ridiculous that she could not dance with Stephen without Molly seeing something in it. Probably just because she was a young widow! Stupid woman! She put it out of her mind.

On Saturday afternoon Flora took the children to the park. They galloped on ahead of her to the swings. She took her time walking the short distance, her mind idling over the last week. Nothing had felt normal with Stephen at work, although most of the time he had been closeted with his uncle, poring over the books. Molly thought that a good enough reason to believe that he would be staying on.

After the swings, monkey ladder and maypole, they went to feed the ducks. They were standing on the bridge, tearing up a stale crust, when a whispering voice spoke in Flora's ear: 'You're not supposed to feed the ducks, missus. Haven't you heard that bread's going on the ration? I'll have the police on you!'

She jumped and turned, then relaxed. 'Stephen! You gave me a fright.'

He smiled. 'Is that the effect I have on you? If I could have frightened the enemy that easy, I'd have had no problems.'

She could not help smiling. 'It's the way you crept up on me.'

'That's my training. Surprise is half the battle.' He leaned against the railings, looking about him. 'This takes me back.'

'Yes. And George is doing just what his father used to do.'

She moved quickly to drag her son down from the railings. He struggled but she cuffed him across the shoulder before presenting him to Stephen. 'George, this is Mr Martin. Say how do you do.'

'Hi,' said George, pulling his arm out of his mother's hold, and staring up at Stephen with something akin to admiration. 'Are you the one who was a commando? My dad was a commando. Have you got any medals?'

'One.'

'Can I see it?'

'If you want,' said Stephen slowly, a nerve beating at his temple. 'Perhaps next time you're passing.' George smiled and whooped as he ran down the bridge. The two girls followed him.

Stephen turned to Flora. 'There's a photo of Tom with our Jimmy in Uncle Sam's somewhere — George is very like him at that age.'

'Everybody says he's like him,' said Flora proudly. 'I'd like to see that photograph.'

'Sure,' he said mildly. 'I'll look it out.'

'And bring it into work?' she said eagerly.

He nodded. 'George must be a handful at times.'

Flora shrugged. 'Sometimes he's a real worry. But as Tom used to say, he's a boy.'

115

'That's obvious. But it's no excuse for behaving badly,' said Stephen.

A flush coloured Flora's cheeks, seeing what he said as an implied criticism not only of George but Tom as well. 'He's not a bad boy, just a dare devil. He's got no nerves, just like Tom.'

He stared at her. 'We all have nerves, Floss. They just don't show until we're really up against it.'

She frowned. 'What are you saying?'

He was silent a moment. 'Only that kids don't recognise danger, that's why they aren't scared. I'm not saying that George is a bad kid.'

'No?' she said quietly, almost unemotionally.

'No,' he said firmly 'How could I pass judgement? I don't know him. I only knew Tom.'

'So you were hinting that he behaved badly.' Her voice was cool. 'I suppose because he broke your nose? But that was an accident.'

'I wasn't even thinking about that,' he said in a flat voice. 'But now you've brought it up – it was no accident. I got him out at cricket and he didn't like it.'

'Maybe not but he wouldn't have meant really to hurt you.' Her eyes sparkled. 'Fancy having a grudge against someone all these years! I'm surprised at you, Stephen.'

'Surprised at me! Why are you so sure it was an accident? Just because it was Tom? If our Jimmy was here – or even your Hilda – they'd tell you. He liked his own way, Floss, and if he didn't get it, then he worked against the ones who got in his way.'

Flora paled, not at all liking the way the conversation was going. 'I don't know how you can speak like this to me!' Her hands curled into tight fists. 'I was married to Tom. I knew him better than anybody. He wasn't the way you say.'

'I'm glad if he wasn't with you,' said Stephen. 'You probably brought out the best in him. Just don't give him a halo.'

Flora moistened her dry lips. 'I didn't know you hated him so much.'

'I don't now,' he said quietly.

116

'You sound like you do.' She felt sick. 'It's easy to attack a dead man, Stephen.'

'I'm sorry if I've offended you.' He walked away before she could say anything else.

Flora ran down the bridge in the wake of the children, determined not to let Stephen's words hurt her. But he had attacked Tom and she considered that utterly unfair. She had thought better of him and felt as if he had let her down.

'Good morning, Floss.'

'Good morning.' She had almost decided not to speak to him.

'Here's that photograph I promised you.' He dropped an envelope on the bench in front of her and walked on into the Guillotine Room. She stared at it.

'What's this about a photograph?' Molly peered curiously at the buff envelope.

Flora made no answer, but snatched up the envelope and opened it. There was more than one photograph. She rifled through them. Jimmy was on them all, but Tom or Hilda were on most. There was even a couple with Stephen and herself. He serious and straight-nosed — until after the cricket incident.

She went through them a second time more slowly, her heart racing. Tom at eight, ten — he was like George — twelve, fifteen, nineteen, twenty. At twenty-one he had stopped going out with Hilda and his friendship with Jimmy had ended. She knew that she was being a fool to herself staring at the young faces of her husband and her sister laughing at each other, but she could not stop. Hilda's parting words repeated themselves in her head but Flora firmly refused to give them credence. Tom had been handsome and charming, and jealousy was a terrible emotion.

She put the photographs back in the envelope, placing it on the corner of the bench. Molly promptly picked it up. She made a leisurely perusal of the contents, giving a running commentary as she did so. 'What a mousey little thing you look, Flora! Your sister's dress was far too short there but you can see the boys like it. She had style despite her being

117

a madam! And she doesn't look that much different to when I saw her in town with a soldier during the war.'

Flora's hands stilled. 'You saw our Hilda with a soldier?'

'Only saw the back of him. She was seeing him off at Lime Street. Winter it was − not long after they dropped the first lot of bombs on us, and our Mabel and the girls were killed.'

'I was pregnant then and feeling pretty rotten,' murmured Flora. 'I wanted to go up to Scotland to see Tom but he managed to get a couple of days and come down. He could only stay one night and I wasn't much fun.'

Molly put the photographs back in the envelope. 'I've wondered since if that soldier with your Hilda was our Jimmy. He never quite got over your sister, despite our Stephen telling him he was a fool in that quiet way of speaking he has.' She shook her head slowly. 'Not that he's so quiet now. Him and our Sam have had a few set to's. Stephen seems to think that the men coming back will be dissatisfied with what Sam's paying here. He says that there's a lot of reds around − that's why Atlee defeated Churchill. He reckons that there's going to be a shortage of manpower − as if we didn't know − and that it'll be a workers' market. They'll be able to shop around for the highest wages and the unions will see that they get them.'

'And what does the Old Man say to that?' asked Flora with interest.

'That Stephen doesn't know what he's talking about. That no way is he going to allow the unions in his shop to tell him what to do. Stephen wasn't too pleased I can tell you! But that's for them to sort out and nothing to do with us. We women don't get enough money, but do we complain?'

Flora smiled. Molly, the greatest complainer going, could really be a tonic at times. She decided that she would thank Stephen when he came out again and give him the photographs back.

But when he came out Flora did not have a chance to say anything. With a face set like granite, he strode swiftly across the room without looking to left or right. Half an hour later she discovered that he had quit. She was disappointed, having believed that Stephen would give the job a fair trial. She wondered what to do with the photographs and decided to take them into the office.

The Old Man looked downcast and was sitting not doing anything when she entered. Suddenly she felt angry with Stephen. He had erupted into both their lives and disturbed their peace.

She put down the cup of tea and a couple of biscuits, and said in a rush: 'Stephen loaned these photographs to me. I wonder if you could take them back?'

He nodded slowly, and took the envelope she held out. To her surprise he opened it, slid out the pictures and began to look at them, murmuring, 'He says that his mother wanted him to teach but he was persuaded to work here instead.'

He fell silent and Flora wondered if she should slip away. Somehow she stayed. He seemed such a sad, lonely figure.

'So many memories, Flora,' he muttered, 'He was starting to shape up quite well. I told him that he could be as good as Jimmy if he worked hard. He didn't like that. He wanted me to consider raising the men's wages. I told him that they weren't worth the sort of money he was talking about — but he said I'd have to do it once the other men were demobbed. I didn't agree with him and he called me short-sighted.' His mouth tightened. 'The wars changed a lot of people, Flora, and I don't think it's a good thing. He would never have talked to me like that in the old days.'

'Jimmy did, though! He used to argue with you but in such a way that you took it,' blurted out Flora. 'If you really wanted Stephen here, you should have accepted that he'd have his own opinions. He's been mixing with men of his own age. Working men, who'll have talked about the kind of life they wanted or expected after the war.'

He stared at her and for a moment she thought he was going to tell her to get out of his office.

Unexpectedly a slow smile softened his features. 'You wouldn't have spoken to me like that before the war either, Flora.' He paused. 'I can't understand the lad but you obviously do. Talked to you about his plans, has he?'

'Not really.' Flora's cheeks suddenly burned. 'But I've gathered from conversations we've had that he believes you think him second best to Jimmy. I think that hurt him, and perhaps because of it he'll try harder to get over his own point of view.'

'I see.' He tapped his forefinger against a lean cheek. 'Maybe I should ask him to reconsider – to have a bit more patience with an old man?'

Flora kept silent and picked up her tray. He seemed to be talking more to himself than her now. She went out of the office, wondering if Stephen would come back.

It was Molly who told Flora that Stephen had turned down the Old Man's offer of another stab at the job. 'He said that he'd already put wheels in motion and had applied to do teacher training at a college in Wrexham. There's an emergency training scheme – one year instead of two. Apparently the country is crying out for teachers because school leaving age is going up to fifteen next year.'

'The Old Man must be upset,' Flora murmured, feeling annoyed with Stephen. 'What's going to happen?'

Molly shrugged. 'We'll carry on like we have for the last six or so years. Bill Turner's out of the army, anyway, so I don't doubt he'll be around in a day or so asking for his job back. Maybe things'll buck up.'

Flora thought maybe they wouldn't. But she was determined not to worry. She felt comfortable in her job but there were always others. At the moment she was more concerned about what to do with the children in the school holidays, although Mrs Murphy had promised to keep an eye on them, and her father would have them a couple of days a week now that they were getting older and more sensible. And there was the Sunday School outing for them to look forward to.

Mothers and grandmothers bustled around the charabanc waiting outside the Mission Hall, giving last minute instructions, and in Flora's case several little bags of sweets that the apprentice had passed on to her. He had been given them from one of the sweet factories for which they did printing.

'We're off, we're off, we're off in a motor car,' sang George, kneeling up and dangling his hands out of the window. 'Sixty coppers are after us, and they don't know where we are!'

Rosie, her face bright with laughter, said, 'I wish you could come with us, Mam.' She hugged Flora for the third time, before her mother hustled her up the steps of the charabanc.

'I'll have a nice time getting the house sorted out,' she said, stepping back as more children jostled to get on, and Sunday School teachers tried to count heads and tick off names on lists.

There was a concerted chorus of farewells and wishes for a nice day and then a great sigh of relief passed through the women as the vehicle drove off and they broke up to go their separate ways.

It felt odd to enter the empty house which was in a mess due to the rush in which they had left it earlier. She cleaned it from top to bottom, thinking that there was nobody to untidy it again till about eight that evening. She washed and changed then took a cup of tea and, on impulse, her copy of Mrs Beeton's *All About Cookery* into the backyard. She settled on the back step in pale sunshine and opened the book to August's Bills of Fare. Hungry after the housework, she wanted something different, while doubting the ingredients for many of the recipes would be to hand. Still, she would enjoy reading them.

Dinner for eighteen persons. The page showed a plan of how the table should be set and listed first course, second course, entrées ... (What was an Entrée?) Some of the dishes had French names. *Fricandeau de Veau á la Jardinière* – whatever that meant! Stephen might have known because he had been in France. Stephen ... She shrugged. Ah, this sounded more like it! Fillets of Duck and Peas.

'First catch your duck,' she murmured to the cat, which mewed and rubbed its head against her ankle. 'There's always the park, I suppose.' She read on. Third Course – Grouse removed by Cabinet Pudding. What was Cabinet Pudding? She looked it up under C. Cabinet or Chancellor's Pudding. Ingredients: candied peel, currants, sultanas – obviously there had been no rationing in Mrs B's day! She noticed that there was another Cabinet Pudding – or Boiled Bread and Butter Pudding, plain. She smiled, remembering how Aunt Beattie used to make ordinary bread and butter pudding.

121

Still this was more like it! Although raisins were needed, this recipe was not beyond her means. Time — one hour — average cost ninepence. Sufficient for five or six persons. What was a Victorian ninepence worth today? It was beyond her working out. It needed three eggs — well, that was out, but there was dried egg. She would have a go because there was plenty of bread, and there would be enough for the children when they came home.

Flora rubbed her nose. For firsts there was sardines on toast, and that would have to be it. Closing the book she jumped up and went to find a pudding bowl.

Feeling a little lonely she put on the wireless, forcing herself to hum along. Acting impulsively again she covered the scratched table top with her best tablecloth. Going outside she cut several orange and yellow nasturtiums from the windowbox in the yard and placed them in an egg cup in the centre of the table. The pudding was on the boil and she was really hungry. Her only wish was that she could have had someone to share the meal with. A man. Tom. Her hand stopped halfway to the cutlery drawer. What was she thinking of? She knew that she could not have him. A tear rolled slowly down her cheek. Stupid woman! She sniffed away her tears and hurried over to the oven.

Her cheeks were flushed from the heat of the fire as the plate was placed on the table. Music fluted from the wireless and she was suddenly restless. She thought of Mike and how he had danced her up the road. He would have enjoyed the food and made her laugh. Stephen had danced with her too. It had been rather comforting in a way. They had known each other so long that she had not had to worry about his arm round her. Tom had never liked dancing, which was strange because it could be so sexy. She felt warm at the thought, and filled her mind with football, cricket — Tom had like them — films, the music hall, and painting. Maybe he was in heaven talking to da Vinci right now!

The tears were tight in her throat as she spooned the nutmeg-scented golden pudding into a bowl and propped her library book against the blue sugar bag. Again she brushed a tear away, determined not to give in to self-pity, but she could not help thinking that if she had been in a film, a handsome stranger would have knocked on her door right now, and dined with her. Maybe he would not have revealed that he was really a prince in disguise, who was ready to take her away from the cinders and make her dreams come true, but he would have been her lover.

Mike had been a good lover! Mike ... oh lord, forgive her. She shook her head as if by doing so she could rid herself of all memory of that night, and told herself that real life didn't have much room for romance and dreaming. Real life was a recipe not going quite right, not enough moisture because of the dried egg. Real life was loneliness and heartache. Flora reached for her cup of tea and wished the children home soon.

Chapter Ten

Flora was tired. The thought of Christmas coming made her groan because there was so much to do. There were threats of power cuts, and so many shortages, worse than during the war, that she viewed the next few months with dismay.

As was her custom on the Sunday before Christmas, she went to Anfield Cemetery to visit her mother's grave and place a holly wreath there. She thought of Hilda and how much she had loved their mother. No word had come for Vivien or herself and that hurt for Viv's sake. Where was Hilda? They were sisters and should have been friends.

Brushing the dampness from her knees Flora got up and gazed in the direction of Stanley Park. How sinister the trees looked, so black and stark against the sky. She began the walk past white angels and black and white marble stones. In Memory Of. Words ran into one another, as did names and dates. Some had died so young — but the texts from the Bible seemed to indicate faith in the after-life.

'"There's a friend for little children above the bright blue sky!" Jesus, are your there?' she called, sadness gripping her.

'Floss!'

Startled at the sound of the voice, she whirled to confront Stephen in a tweed overcoat a size too big for him. For several moments she just stared at him, considering that he looked much thinner and paler. To cover her surprise at his appearance she felt that she had to make a joke. 'Here we are, here we are, here we are again! You seem to have a habit of creeping up on me, Steve. Your training, you once said.

You weren't planning on doing something nasty to me here among the gravestones, were you?'

He smiled. 'I've no intentions of doing you foully to death if that's what you mean. Not you, Floss.' His blue eyes rested on her rosy face. 'How have you been?'

She shrugged. 'All right. No point in complaining. It's a tough life for everybody at the moment.' She deliberately did not mention his uncle. 'And you?'

'Flu! But I'm okay now.' He turned up his coat collar against the chill. 'I could hardly believe it when I caught sight of you back there.'

'I was visiting Mam's grave.' Flora began to walk, hunching inside her mustard and brown coat. She glanced at him and thought that he should have stayed home. Her maternal feelings made her want to tuck him up snugly with a hot water bottle, and give him drinks of lemon and honey with Aspro. 'What are you doing here?' she asked abruptly.

He came to a halt and faced her. 'Same as you. Mam used always to visit Dad's grave around Christmas. I suddenly decided that traditions like that shouldn't die. I was in Liverpool, so –' He gave a twisted smile.

The wind buffetted them and she put a hand on his arm and squeezed it gently. 'You are nice sometimes, Steve. But you should have stayed at home instead of coming all this way in the cold.'

'I have a car. I'll run you home.'

'That's nice.'

'That's an understatement.' He smiled and Flora smiled back. For a second neither of them spoke. Then he cleared his throat.

'Well? Do you want a lift or not, Floss? I don't know about you, but I'm starting to feel the cold.' He stressed each word heavily.

'A car – that's something new, isn't it?' Her voice was bright.

'Yes,' he said briefly, hurrying ahead of her, so that she had to almost run to keep up with him. They crossed the road and came to the black car outside the park. 'It's an Austin 10,' he muttered, patting the front bumper. 'You get inside while I crank her up.' He reached for the handle.

Flora had never been in a car before. The seat was leathery and cold to the touch, and she clutched it tightly when after several minutes the car jolted. It coughed and spluttered and then there was a pause in activity before the engine coughed again, and then suddenly roared into life. Stephen flung the handle on the floor, reached for the controls, and she shut her eyes.

When she opened them again they were travelling quite smoothly past the other side of the park. Stephen smiled at her. 'It's fun, isn't it? I was mad at Uncle Sam for buying me it, especially when he said that he thought it would be useful for business. But I must admit if it wasn't for petrol rationing, she'd prove her weight in gold.'

'She?' Flora relaxed and settled herself more comfortably.

'The car. I call her Daisy.' He began to sing snatches of a song about being crazy for the love of Daisy.

Flora was amused. 'It's a lovely present.'

'Lovely.' He frowned. 'It's secondhand and a good few years old — and I wish he hadn't given me it. I love it! But, hell, Floss! It makes me beholden to him, and I don't want to feel like that.'

There was a short silence and her mind searched for something to fill it, but she knew that it was not up to her to say the words that needing saying. The moment passed, and then he spoke. 'D'you remember when you were sixteen and the old King hadn't officially opened the tunnel to the public — but for the price of sixpence we were allowed to walk through.'

'The money went to charity.' She smiled reminiscently. 'I would have panicked if it hadn't been for you. Did you think me quite daft when I kept glancing up at the roof?'

'No, I was thinking the same. What if it cracked and the Mersey poured in?' A muscle tightened in his neck. 'Tom and your Hilda thought we were both crazy.'

'And your Jimmy. None of them ever seemed to be scared of anything.' She glanced at him, and added quickly: 'But

126

they probably were. Everybody's scared of something.'

'I hate tight places and caves,' muttered Stephen, his hands curling on the steering wheel. 'And the thought of what happened to Mam and the girls still gives me nightmares. I see them choking in dust and bricks and I can never reach them.'

'Don't!' She shuddered. 'You shouldn't think about it because it won't do you any good. Let's talk about something more cheerful.'

He nodded. 'Sorry, Floss. Do you remember that was the year *King Kong* was on the pictures?'

'It was the year Prince George opened the Walker Art Gallery. Our Hilda and Tom took me with –' Her voice tailed off, remembering what her sister had said about Tom. She forced the thought aside. Would Stephen always be reminding her of the past?

'Uncle Sam bought a Marconi radiogram that year and allowed me to listen to his records of Gilbert and Sullivan. Light opera was something we both enjoyed that our Jimmy didn't.'

Flora was silent a moment, then she said roughly, 'He still needs you, Steve. Bill Turner's back but he isn't a patch on you, and he's a troublemaker. The Old Man doesn't know how to take him. You could handle him, though!'

He let out a long breath. 'Don't let's talk about it now, Floss,' he said heavily. 'I know the situation and I might come back if Uncle Sam was prepared to bend a little more. We'll see.' She nodded, and settled for just enjoying the ride.

The car drew up outside her house. Stephen got out but left the engine running. 'Are you getting out, Floss?' He held the door open for her.

She had almost nodded off and had to blink her eyes open wide to focus on his face. He looked tired and again she felt that spurt of maternalism. 'You really should be in bed. You look awful.'

'I feel awful.' He took off his trilby and wiped a hand across his brow.

'Would you like to come in for a cuppa?'

'I'd better not. Uncle Sam will be expecting me.'

127

'Of course.' She smiled and held out her hand. 'Thanks for the lift. Perhaps I'll see you around.'

He clasped her hand and squeezed it. 'Maybe.'

She stepped back, waving as he drove off.

Flora did not see him again over the Christmas period and Molly told her that he would be returning to Wales in the New Year.

The worst weather in a long time bit deep, causing Flora constant worry. The outside lavatory froze – icicles eighteen inches long hung from window sills and eaves. Power cuts affected them at work to such an extent that she had to help operate the foot treadles. The cold meant that the ink did not dry as quickly as it should and tempers got frayed.

Because of the coal shortages George had to take time off school to queue for hours on end.

'I hate going there,' he told Kathleen Murphy when she was walking with him, pushing her mam's pram with her coal as well as the baby.'

'I hate *her*,' said Kathleen, referring to the woman who owned the coal yard. 'She's like a fat spider the way she sits by them scales making sure nobody gets the teeniest ounce more than they should. A quarter of a hundred weight! How far will that go?'

'Not far,' muttered George, shifting the hessian sack on his back. 'What I can't stand about her is her having no teeth, and the way she sucks at that clay pipe. She's not a spider – she's a black toothless slug sucking the life out of the poor,' he said with relish. 'I'd like to put some coal beneath her and set her alight! Imagine being a cannonball and having her for dinner.'

Kathleen giggled. 'I think y'mean a cannibal.'

'I know.' He grinned.

'Are you going to try and get some wood for your mam?'

'Probably.' George moved the sack to the other shoulder as they came to the bottom of their street. 'But don't go telling your mam – she just might tell mine, and *she* goes on enough about me missing school and sitting the eleven plus.' He sighed and Kathleen gave him a sympathetic look. They parted amicably at the bottom of his step.

The coal soon ran out and sometimes they could not get any more. George came in with wood, and Flora worried about him, guessing that he had been in bombed derelict houses.

Once darkness fell it was miserable in the house. Every room except the kitchen was like an ice box, and their coats were heaped on to George's and Flora's beds. The girls slept with her and she would tell them stories till they forgot the cold and drifted into sleep.

Flora herself slept fitfully and her dreams were a jumble of past events and fairy tales. She hated her dreams; hated the snow and the cold, even though the children made the most of it.

The roads were slippery with the slides they made and the air resounded with their cries of delight and laughter when some of them fell and slid on their bottoms down the shiny passage of ice. They built snowmen and played snowballs until their hands lost all feelings and dusk shadowed the streets.

George manufactured heat and light in the shape of winter warmers made from holed tin cans and lengths of wire. He filled them with paper and wood and then they were lit.

Often Flora would come home to be met by the children running in the dark, twirling the lighted cans over their heads, and she wished that she could regain some of the magic of being young and carefree. Instead she had to cope with wet clothes, and George's long face after the exam, and chilblains which itched unbearably so that she sought help from an old crone in the next street, who gave her a foul-looking brown ointment called Snowfire which she swore would help.

Flora kept a check on her father when she could, and one Saturday afternoon trudged through the snow only to find him out. She was in no mood to be pleasant to anybody on the return journey.

There was a car parked outside her house and as she approached Stephen got out and came slowly towards her. 'Hello, Floss.' He shoved his hands deep in his pockets. 'Terrible weather we're having.'

She halted and looked at him. 'Is that what made you come home? Worried about your uncle because of the weather?' Her voice was hard.

'In part.' He frowned as his gaze passed swiftly over her face. 'But I was also wondering how you were coping with everything.'

'That's nice of you,' she said tartly, lifting the heavy shopping bag in both her arms and holding it against her chest. 'I've coped fine, thanks! Did you expect me suddenly to fall to pieces because of the snow? I've got up every morning and gone out to do my job. I've stood in queues till my feet froze. I've washed but can't get the clothes dry quick enough. I've somehow seen to the kids. I've got damn chilblains that drive me crazy.' Her voice suddenly broke. 'But, *yes*, I've coped.' She would have brushed past him but he seized hold of her shoulder and put his arm round her.

'Poor Floss.' His voice was concerned.

'Don't be sorry for me,' she said fiercely. 'Don't be nice to me.' She attempted to control her tears but could not, and tried to pull away but he forced her against him. Exhaustion flooded over her and she buried her face against his coat and sobbed her heart out.

He patted her soothingly until at last Flora gained control of herself and lifted her head to look at him through wet eyelashes. 'I'm sorry, Steve. I don't generally make a fool of myself like that.' She sniffed and rubbed at her face.

'Poor ol' girl. I suppose that things have been tough in work too?'

'You shouldn't have gone away. Nothing would have been so bad if you'd have been there.'

'Wouldn't it?' The tip of his index finger wiped away a tear.

She let her cheek rest against his hand. It was comforting having someone to lean on.

'I'm thinking of coming back. What d'you think, Floss?'

'About time too.' A watery smile lifted her mouth. 'I'd ask you in for a cup of tea, only the fire's not lit. We save the little coal we've got till evening.'

'Some other time.' He slowly released her. 'I'll probably see you in work in the morning.'

'Good.' Her smile widened. 'Your uncle'll be pleased.'

'Aye.' He moved away. 'Put your feet up for a while. It'll do you good.'

'I will.' Flora stood in the snow, watching him get into the car and drive off. Then she went into the house.

The thaw came, bringing with it the constant drip, drip of water. The children built dams with stones and broken bricks in the rushing water-filled gutters, floating sticks in the pools created. The air was warmer, and clothes could be washed and dried the easier.

In the Works the atmosphere changed, not quite overnight but within weeks. All the men received a rise but were told to speed things up. The more the firm prospered the more money there would be for all. Everybody saw the sense in that and knuckled down under Stephen's authority. Sometimes he came to watch Flora, standing behind her so that for several seconds her fingers lost all rhythm and she would stop and say, 'How am I doing?'

'Fine.' He would smile before moving on.

One afternoon he paused longer, and added, 'What about me coming round this evening and we could go for a walk?'

She was taken by surprise. 'I don't know if that's on. I've got the girls.'

He hesitated. 'I suppose they could come with us.'

'Okay then,' she said cheerfully, considering it would be quite pleasant to have a man's company.

He came earlier than she expected and she was scrubbing the front step. 'Why did you have to be doing that now?' he asked with a touch of impatience.

'Because it has to be done — and I didn't think you'd arrive so soon.' She paused to glance at him. He looked tidy and cool and she was instantly aware of feeling sweaty, and dirty from the water dripping down her arm from the scrubbing brush.

'It could have been done some other time.'

'When?' she asked bluntly, dropping the brush into the bucket and getting up from her knees. 'I'm at work all day, and I don't have a char at home to do for me.' Her hazel eyes challenged him.

He grimaced. 'Sorry. I'll wait.'

'Good.' She picked up the bucket and called the girls who were playing ball, and went inside the house.

Stephen whistled when she reappeared and she was glad that he had come. It seemed a long time since she had dressed in a pretty frock for a man. Not since Mike ... A slight crease appeared between her brows. She fluffed the skimpy skirts of the yellow and white frock, wishing that she could afford the New Look with its petticoats and yards of material. The style had not reached their shops at all. Still one day, maybe.

The girls ran on ahead and she and Stephen talked about work and the weather, the Government's introduction of whale meat and the forthcoming wedding of Princess Elizabeth and the Duke of Edinburgh.

It was pleasant in the park. There were flowers and the branching trees showed burgeoning leaves. They lingered by the bandstand on the way back, Flora's foot tapping to the rhythm of the brass band.

She continued to see Stephen outside working hours. Often they had to take the girls with them and she wondered how fair she was being to him. Sometimes she worried about leaving George out of things and insisted on his going with them too.

On one such outing they went by tram to Kirkby wood. It was pleasant and green, and a relief to be away from the clatter of machines and the smokey atmosphere of the city. The girls picked bluebells while George dug up an ant hill, climbed trees and fished for tiddlers, wading in the brook in his wellies.

All seemed well but on the way home, George, with a glint in his eye, kicked off his wellies in the girls' direction, and said, 'They're snowing with ants!'

Vivien screamed and both girls quickly removed themselves as several insects scurried out. George laughed, hanging over the back of the seat. 'Scaredy pusses!'

'That's enough,' snapped Stephen, getting up and going over to him. 'Get those wellies on and sit down. You're making a show of us.' He seized him by the shoulders and forced him down.

George scowled at him. 'You're not my dad. You've got no right to tell me what to do!'

'That's enough, George,' said Flora sternly, although she had found the incident amusing.

Most outings with George were only a qualified success. They went by train to Waterloo, a few miles along the coast from Liverpool, and he got stuck in black treacly sand. Flora, fearing it was quicksand, had to be forcibly prevented from going in after him. Instead Stephen went to get him out and clipped him over the earhole. 'That's for being stupid.'

George resented his action, sulked, and was missing when they were ready for the next outing on a crowded ferry to New Brighton.

'This is more like it,' said Stephen, lying next to Flora on a packed beach, stroking her bare arm with the tips of his fingers while she watched the girls paddling. She had to admit that it was much more peaceful without George although she felt disloyal saying so.

They were seldom alone and in a way Flora was glad of that. Only once did her father stay with the children while they went to see *Pirates of Penzance*. On the way home Stephen drew her into a doorway and kissed her. No bells rang but it was pleasant enough and she did not pull away. 'If only we could be alone like this more often,' he muttered, before he kissed her again, a bit more passionately this time. And again. This time his fingers began to explore the roundness of her breasts.

After a couple of seconds she removed his hand, slightly disturbed. 'It's time I was getting home,' she said in a low voice. 'Father will be wanting to leave.'

'I suppose so,' he said resignedly. 'If it's not the kids, it's your father coming between us.'

'You wish they weren't around.' Her voice was controlled.

'Don't you, at times?' He smiled.

She could not say no, so instead murmured, 'That's not a question to ask a mother. I'm responsible for them.' He pulled her arm through his.

'I know and hear. I can't have you without them.'

She stilled. 'What d'you mean — have me?'

'I mean our future together. You and me.' He sighed, then nibbled her ear. 'It could work, Floss.'

'Could it?' A nerve twitched in her cheek. 'I don't know — there's the kids.' Meaning George because the girls liked Stephen. 'And I'm somebody who still has her dead husband haunting her,' she added.

He lifted his head and looked into her face. 'He haunts me as well,' he said seriously. 'Perhaps together we can lay his ghost.'

'Why should he haunt you?' she asked with a puzzled expression.

He glanced away from her. 'Probably it's because me and him never got on, and you were married to him. But we could try it and see.'

'I don't know,' she said unhappily, a shadow in her eyes. 'Saying things and doing them are very different. I promised myself that I would never marry again. I would feel unfaithful to his memory — that's something you can't understand.'

'I can! I've always been fond of you, Floss. Now I'm in love with you. But perhaps you don't want to hear that kind of declaration from me?' he said humbly.

She felt suddenly sorry for him. 'Don't I? I'd be a funny woman if I didn't want to be told that I was loved. Life can be very lonely without a companion. I'm fond of you and I've enjoyed going out with you, Stephen. But I can't tell you that I love you.'

He pulled a face. 'Not yet you can't. But in time you might. Shall we give it more time?'

She could not refuse him. 'All right.'

Gently he kissed her and she hated herself for suddenly thinking of Mike and passion. Then they walked the rest of the way home, hand in hand.

The summer blazed in. One day at work Flora was standing, fanning herself with a sheet of paper, waiting for the kettle to boil. At this time of year business went slack so that the men were glad of other jobs to do. Some were painting the walls downstairs in the lobby and Stephen was in the yard with Bill. The kettle boiled and she made the tea and took it downstairs to the men.

The sun dazzled on the newly white-washed wall, causing Flora to blink. 'Tea up!'

Stephen, in shorts and vest, put down his brush and came over to her. 'I'll have finished here soon,' he said in a low voice, 'and as there's not much work and the Old Man's left me in charge, we'll pack up early and go and enjoy the sun.'

She smiled. 'For how long? The children —'

He pulled a face. 'The girls won't be home for a while yet — and anyway George'll keep an eye on them if we're back a little bit late. But isn't it the evening they go to your father's?'

She nodded. 'All right. Where will we go?'

'We'll decide that on the way.' He smiled. 'Wash the cups then spruce yourself up.'

They went to Southport, which Flora did not expect. 'We won't be able to stay long,' she said, as they walked along Lord Street, looking in the shop windows.

'Stop worrying about your kids all the time.' He screwed up his craggy face. 'You're like a mother hen, Floss, the way you go on. Let's go and have tea.' He pulled her hand and she had no choice but to go with him.

The cafe was busy and they were kept waiting for their order. Eventually it came and Flora ate just one cake and gulped her tea down. Stephen took his time.

She was on flinders all the way home, worrying about George. He had been awkward lately, wandering off without letting her know where he had been, and sometimes staying out way past his bedtime.

They called in on her father who was in a grumpy mood. 'The kids didn't turn up,' he growled, biting on his pipe. 'I could have been in the park watching the bowls instead of waiting in.'

'Sorry, Father.' She aimed a kiss at his cheek and left hurriedly, concerned about the children not being at his house, but not over-anxious. The weather was lovely but hot, and it could be that they might have felt too lazy to walk to their grandfather's.

135

As they drove down her street Flora noticed that it was not as busy with children playing street games as usual. But it was not until she saw the crowd gathered at the bottom of the step that her nerves tensed.

Stephen exchanged glances with her. 'Don't start working yourself up – it could just be a cut knee, another broken window.'

Flora said nothing. Her heart was pounding and she had the car door open as soon as it stopped. She slammed the door shut with hands that shook, and the hubbub of sound that assailed her ears hushed as she became the focus of all eyes. 'What's happened? George! Is it George?' she demanded in a rising voice.

'Not the lad, luv,' called Mrs Murphy out of the crowd. 'It's Rosie! It's bad, girl.'

For a moment Flora could not move, then her feet seemed to fly up the step of their own volition as a babble of sound broke out behind her, hushing briefly as Stephen elbowed his way through to follow her inside the house.

Chapter Eleven

A policeman turned as Flora entered the kitchen, his helmet under his arm.

'What happened?' Her fingers shook on the door panel as her eyes went beyond him to George. His clothes were wet and his fair hair dripped moisture down his face and neck. For a second he did not move or speak.

'It was awful, Mam. I thought I could save her – but she was under by the time I got there,' he stammered. 'I caught her by her knicker elastic but she was too heavy in the water – she slipped out of my hand.' His eyes brimmed with tears and he hung his head, his whole body trembling. 'I went in then but I still couldn't lift her out.'

Flora stared at him wide-eyed, unable to take in what he was trying to tell her. 'George! What are you saying exactly? I – tell me that Rosie's all right!' she pleaded, moving towards him to wrap her arms about him. A sob burst from him and he buried his head against her shoulder. 'She's drowned, Mam! Our Rosie's drowned!'

'Oh God!' A feeling of cold dread seized her stomach. She felt as if she had been hit. She clutched her son convulsively, unable to believe what he was saying. 'She can't be dead.' Her eyes met the policeman's over George's head.

'I'm sorry, luv.' His voice was almost flat. 'I presume you are the mother?'

'Dammit! Of course she's the mother,' said Stephen, coming further into the room. 'Isn't that obvious?'

The policeman, a man of middle years, gazed stolidly at him. 'I'm just establishing the facts, sir. And who might you be?' He flicked over a page of a notebook.

'I'm Mrs Cooke's employer,' answered Stephen harshly, ramming his hands in his pockets. 'We finished early so I took her to Southport.'

'Where's Rosie?' Flora's quivering voice drew both their attention.

The policeman's tone softened. 'The ambulance took her away. We tried out best to save her.'

She swallowed. 'How could she drown?' Her voice seemed to be coming from a distance. 'I don't understand.'

'In an E.W.S. tank. Used an old iron bedhead like a ladder. Some of the lads had been sailing wooden boats and sticks in the water. The other little girl told me that your daughter went up after they came down. It was her that found me up the lane in time to pull your lad out.'

'Viv did! Where is she?' She gazed wildly about her.

'I'm here, Aunty Flo.' Vivien got up from under the table, bringing the cat she was nursing with her. 'I'm sorry.' She sniffed. 'I told our Rosie not to go up, but she wouldn't take any notice of me. Then I saw her topple over and I was frightened and screamed and I ran –'

'She came for me, Mam,' interrupted George, pulling a little away from Flora and staring up at her. 'I sent her to the Works, thinking you must still be there.' His eyes brimmed again. 'Why did you have to go to Southport, Mam?'

The colour drained from her face. 'It was such a nice day.' She stared blankly at Stephen, who moved forward quickly with a chair and lowered her on to it. George fell at her feet and Vivien came to lean against her knee.

The policeman cleared his throat. His voice was husky when he spoke. 'Maybe a cup of tea – sweet and hot – might help, sir?'

It was several moments before Stephen moved to put a match to the neatly laid fire in the grate.

'You'll want to see her,' said the policeman to Flora.

'Yes. Where is she?' Her eyes focussed painfully on his face. He told her which hospital and she nodded.

'I'll take you,' said Stephen, and she nodded again. The policeman said something else but she could not take it in, and just went on nodding. The policeman stopped talking to her and instead spoke to Stephen, then he went out. Vivien whispered something to George that she could not catch and he got up and left the kitchen. When he came back he was dressed in dry clothes. The kettle whistled and what seemed an age later Stephen placed a cup of tea in her hand. She sipped obediently. Then he spoke to her of the hospital and the car — of Mrs Murphy keeping her eye on George and Viv — and then he led her out.

They did not speak as Stephen drove her through the streets. He kept glancing at her, his expression anxious. She wanted to reassure him that she was perfectly all right; that she wasn't going to break down. They came to the hospital.

The nurse led them through what seemed miles of corridors until they entered the room where Rosie lay. Stephen's hand tightened about Flora's but she pulled it loose and went to stand alone by her daughter. 'Her hair's still wet,' she said through trembling lips, touching the rats' tails that hung about her daughter's blank face. 'She'll catch her death if it's not dried. Can I have a towel?'

The doctor exchanged glances with Stephen. 'We'll see to it, Mrs Cooke,' he said gently. 'Got other children at home, I hear. Perhaps it would be best if you saw to them first.'

Flora tried to swallow the tightness in her throat. She was having trouble breathing properly. 'But she's my daughter. Why should you see to her? I know — what you're thinking — but I know that — that —' A long shiver shuddered through her body, strangling her voice. Stephen moved forward and put his arm around her.

'Come on, Floss. You can't do anything here.'

'I want to stay a little while.' Her eyes filled with tears and she put a hand to her mouth, biting hard on her knuckles.

Stephen stayed with her until the doctor nodded to him and he made to lead her away. She refused to move, clutching at him with her other hand and still staring down at Rosie. Gaining control of her voice, she said, 'I want — Rosie brought home. It's only right that my daughter should be — laid out — in the front parlour.'

'I'll see that it's done, Floss.' Stephen squeezed her

shoulder, and this time, although her feet dragged, she went with him.

They did not speak all the way home but Stephen held one of her limp hands tightly most of the journey. Flora felt numb and wondered how she was going to cope. The image of Rosie, unbelievably still and silent, refused to be torn from her mind.

When they arrived at Flora's house her father was waiting there with Viv, Kathleen and George, who had escaped Mrs Murphy's to go and inform his grandad about what had happened. 'Well, girl, this is a sad day for us all.' His fierce blue eyes showed compassion. 'No one's to blame. These things happen and Rosie was always a tomboy.'

'It was my fault, Father.' Her voice was almost inaudible as she sat in a straight-backed dining chair. 'I should have been here with her.'

Stephen went to speak but her father was before him. 'You can't be in two places, girl.'

'I could have been here at that time − if −' She looked at Stephen and there was a huge angry hurt inside her.

'We weren't to know!' Stephen's voice was rough.

Tears filled her eyes and she lowered her head, shaking it. George came and stood at her shoulder, resting his head against hers, while Vivien sat against her legs. 'She wouldn't listen,' the little girl said sadly. 'It wasn't your fault, Aunty Flo.'

George glanced down at her, and was angry. 'Mam's right! If she'd have been here, Rosie would have listened to her! Why should she listen to you? You're younger!'

Vivien reddened and her mouth trembled. 'If you hadn't have gone up that bedstead, Rosie wouldn't have gone up.'

The boy paled. 'I told her not to be following me all the time. You know I did.'

'Stop it!' rasped Flora. 'You heard your grandad − nobody's to blame.' She wiped a hand across her damp face. 'Viv, it's time you were in bed. George, it wouldn't do you any harm to go either. You've both had a shock. I'll make you a drink and you can have it upstairs.'

'But, Mam,' cried George, clutching at her arm, 'I don't want to go to bed. I won't be able to sleep.'

'You heard your mother,' put in Stephen. 'Just do as you're told.'

The boy glared at him. 'It's not fair for you to be telling me what to do. If Mam hadn't been with you our Rosie would be here.'

'That's enough of that, lad,' growled his grandfather, poking him with his pipe. 'Your mother's weary to the bone, and upset — don't you go making matters worse.'

George's mouth trembled. 'She was my sister. I should have —' He got no further, and dashing a hand across his eyes he rushed out of the room and up the stairs. Flora felt as if her heart was going to burst and she would have followed him, only her father held her back. 'He'll get it out of his system the better, girl, without you there. Leave him be.' She stared at him, then nodded, and without another word began to busy herself making cocoa.

She took hers with Viv's, upstairs, and the girl poured out the whole sorry story as she sat on the bed, painting such vivid pictures that it was as if it was happening before Flora's eyes. She wanted to scream at the girl to stop, but guessed that this was Viv's way of getting it out of her system.

When she went downstairs Stephen was still sitting there. 'I wonder if you could take Father home?' she said in a controlled polite voice. 'I'd like to go to bed myself. It's been a long day and it'll probably be even longer tomorrow. So I must get some sleep.'

'You don't want me to come back after I've dropped your father off?' he said in a low voice, trying to take her hand. She put it behind her.

'No thank you.'

'Tomorrow then?' he insisted. 'Uncle Sam'll understand why you can't come into work.'

'Work? I won't be able to go into work.' She felt that spurt of anger again. 'Surely you understand that I can't leave the children?'

He stared at her, then said awkwardly, 'Of course. I'll come as soon as I can tomorrow.'

She wanted to say 'Don't', but changed her mind. It wasn't fair to blame him.

Flora saw them to the car, waving a hand as it drove off,

before turning and slowly walking back inside the house. She stood with her back to the closed door, trying to think what to do next. Her mind seemed unable to work properly. Still in her imagination she could see Rosie — so still, so silent — and herself helpless to do anything to bring her back to life. If only she had come back home in time, she would have saved Rosie. But it was too late now. Horror gripped her and she buried her face in her hands. God, make it not be true, she prayed, even as she knew such a prayer was foolish — and that this evening had to be the worst of her life.

The days that followed seemed unreal to Flora. During the short June nights she lay, staring wide-eyed into the darkness, tortured by memories and thoughts. The hours when Rosie would have been at school were the easiest to get through because her not being there was normal. She forced herself to be active — washing, scrubbing, cleaning, walking. She must have walked miles without a thought to her destination. Her feet often led her to the Pierhead where her eyes would stare out over the river. Then, turning, she would gaze up at the Liver buildings and remember how she had come here with Rosie on VE Day, and then her mind was not only filled with memories of Rosie but of Tom also.

The evenings were difficult because, on the face of it, most of her actions were everyday. Several times she automatically laid a place for Rosie, and Viv would remind her that she was not there. Somehow she managed to maintain her self-control.

When she saw Stephen her emotions were mixed. The sight of him increased her remorse and she found it difficult to feel anything when he took her in his arms. She did not rebuff him but she could not respond at all to his gentle kisses. Yet she listened to him and in a way was glad that he was there because he was dealing with all the arrangements for her.

It was Stephen who attended the inquest where a verdict of accidental death was declared. There was a report of the incident in the local paper, the *Echo*. He made all the funeral arrangements and had Rosie's body brought home in a pale oak coffin, which was placed in the parlour the day before the funeral.

Going into the parlour and gazing on her daughter's dead face increased Flora's feeling of unreality. She felt as if she were two people – one living in the normal world, and the other dwelling in a shadowy world on the edge of the unknown. She had to believe that Rosie's spirit did live on in Heaven, otherwise she could not have coped. It was now that thoughts of Tom being missing presumed dead started to haunt her once again. His voice seemed to speak in her head. Even in her dreams, when she managed to drift off the night before the funeral, he seemed to be calling her. Then she woke and realised that there was no Tom and no Rosie with her, and she wanted to cry but no tears would come.

Stephen arrived early the morning of the funeral and George opened the door to him. They gazed at each other assessingly. 'I thought you'd be at school,' muttered Stephen.

George's eyes smouldered. 'Viv's gone. But she's not as old as me – and besides Rosie was my sister. I should go to the funeral and I told Mam so.' He squared his shoulders and jutted out his chin.

'It won't be fun, you know,' said Stephen, frowning at him.

'I'm not daft,' said George, shoving his hands in his pockets. 'If you want to see Mam, she's in the parlour.' He led the way in. 'It's full of flowers. The street collected for her – and the school. And there's flowers from people I don't even know.' Pausing in the doorway of the sunlit parlour he breathed in the fragrance of roses, carnations and lilies. He liked flowers but now they only made him feel slightly sick.

He watched Stephen go over and kiss his mam's cheek and was irritated. She sat by the open coffin, looking thin and severe in a plain black frock. Suddenly he was remembering Rosie asking Mike whether he had any gum, chum, and a huge lump filled his throat. He turned and walked out.

Flora did not look at Stephen, only saying quietly, 'I've just been combing her hair. She looks beautiful, don't you think?'

'Lovely. But I think it's time you left her now.'

She glanced up at him and her smile was brittle. 'Beautiful

is a better word. Tom thinks her beautiful. He only saw her once, you know.' Her voice wobbled and she swallowed several times, before adding, 'You do believe that Tom's dead, don't you, Steve? You do, don't you?'

Some of the colour ebbed from his face. 'Of course. Do you doubt it?'

'Missing presumed dead,' she said slowly. 'I can't help thinking of that now. They never found his body.'

He stared at her, and moistened his lips. 'Why don't you come and sit in the kitchen before the cars arrive? Have a glass of sherry. It'll put a bit of strength in you.'

'In a minute,' she said vaguely, putting a hand in her pocket and bringing out an envelope which she placed in the coffin.

'What's that?' he asked, startled.

'A letter that Tom wrote to her. She treasured it.' Her voice was unsteady as she gazed at Rosie's face for the last time. She and Mrs Murphy had dressed her in the frock she had worn in the Rose Queen procession. Tears slid unheeded down her cheeks.

It was five more long minutes before she allowed Stephen to lead her from the room.

The vicar, who had christened Rosemary Flora Cooke and had known her all her life, gave a sermon that caused most to shed a tear in the church, but not Flora. She had herself determinedly in control now and knew that she had to keep it up until the whole thing was over. Even so she was glad of George's arm to cling to as they followed the coffin out of the church and into a sunlit day.

The sky was a deep blue beyond the trees in the cemetery and in Flora's head the hymn they had sung at the service was running over and over. 'There's a friend for little children above the bright blue sky.' Her vision blurred and through a veil of tears she searched the vicar's face as he said the words of committal. Did he really believe in what he said?

She tried to keep her mind concentrating on Rosie being in Heaven, but as she picked up a handful of red-brown earth, part of her mind was seeing and taking in what was before her eyes as she dropped the earth on the coffin. 'Tarrah,

Rosie,' she whispered. Then icy shudders rippled through her and her head felt as if it was going to burst and her knees gave way.

The doctor gave Flora a sedative, which she had to take because he insisted on her doing so while he was there. If anything everything seemed even more unreal as she floated between sleeping and waking.

The next morning she still felt terrible but determined to get up and see to George and Vivien, only to discover that her father had stayed the night, sleeping in George's bed. He took one look at her and shook his head. 'Back to bed for you, girl,' he grunted, from his place in Tom's chair. 'George, make your mam a cup of tea. I'd better stay a few days till she's feeling better.'

She wanted to say, 'I'll never feel better. Are you going to stay forever?' but instead she thanked him. Such action was unprecedented and she was gratified.

Once back in bed her thoughts ran on and on until she could not bear them any longer and sought relief in taking one of the sedatives the doctor had left. She drifted into sleep.

That evening Stephen called. The door was opened by Flora's father, with Vivien just behind him, her head peeping through his crooked arm. She smiled shyly up. 'Hi, Uncle Steve.'

He nodded absently. 'I've come to see Flora. Can I come in?'

'She's sleeping.' Jack Preston cleared his throat. 'And I won't have you disturbing her. It's a terrible shock she's had.'

'I know.' Stephen forced a smile. 'I want to look after her. I want to marry her.'

Jack stared at him. 'Give her time. Come back tomorrow.' He closed the door, and heaved himself up the stairs to Flora's bedroom.

She was awake and dressed. 'I was just on my way down. Was that Stephen at the door?'

'Aye.' He gazed at her from lowering brows. 'Why didn't you knock on the window? It would have saved me the climb up them stairs.'

'I didn't want to see him.' She moved away from him and over to the window, gazing out. Some sparrows were squabbling over some crumbs in the gutter.

'He wants to marry you.'

'I can't marry him,' she said wearily. 'Not the way I'm feeling. I'm too miserable to marry anyone. I just want to be left alone and to look after George and Viv like I should have taken care of Rosie. D'you know that I left her for the first time when she was four years old? She screamed after me and I had to close the door on her. I felt terrible doing that then and I feel even worse about it now.'

'It'll pass, girl.' He patted her shoulder. 'Don't be reproaching yourself all the time. I felt the same when your mother died. I should have given up the sea — should have realised sooner how sick she was. You can never get the time back — you just have to accept that you can't change anything. Remember when Tom was killed you almost went to pieces then? Don't let yourself get into that state again. You marry Stephen. He's got money and he'll look after you.'

Flora said nothing. It would be so easy to do what he said — to let Stephen take the everyday cares from her shoulders. What did it matter if she didn't love him? Love only brought pain. Her sister had been right saying that. 'I'll think about it,' she murmured.

'Okay, girl.' He squeezed her arm. 'Come on down now and have a cuppa. You'll feel much better after that.'

She went, smiling slightly because so many seemed to believe that a cup of tea was the cure for everything.

When Stephen called the next day she was sitting in the parlour in a patch of sunlight, her hands on the darning in her lap.

'Hello, Floss.' He sat down on the shiny horsehair sofa next to her. 'You look miles away.'

'I was thinking about Tom,' she said in a dull voice.

'Tom?' His dark eyebrows rose and for a moment he looked annoyed. 'Not Rosie?' he asked with a little laugh. She gave him a look but said nothing, and he added, 'I mean — Tom's been dead for three years now. You should have been over him by now.'

'I loved him.' Her expression was vague. 'You don't ever forget people you love.'

'I know that.' He looked angry. 'But three years, Floss. Time to put the past behind you and to look towards the future.'

'I do try.' There was a sudden sparkle in her eyes. 'But the war's not so far in the past, and Rosie's death reminded me of Tom. She was a tom boy!' Her hands clenched in her lap. 'Why do we say that? Tom boy? Why not tom girl?' Her throat moved. 'She was Tom's girl,' she said unsteadily. 'And she was just as brave as he was.'

'Still making him out a hero, are you?' burst out Stephen. 'He wasn't, you know. You went on about him being missing presumed dead on the day of the funeral. Well, he went missing all right!' He gulped. 'He was a deserter, not a hero!'

The room was suddenly very still and silent but for the meter ticking in the gas cupboard. She gazed at him in disbelief. 'Take that back,' she cried hotly, jumping to her feet. 'How dare you! I know you hate him.'

'So I do.' He stood, his face twisted with annoyance. 'But I can't take it back because it's true. It's true!'

Flora put a hand to her mouth. 'This isn't real,' she said in a muffled voice.

'It's true, I tell you,' he insisted.

'Then – then Tom's alive?' The words came out in a whisper.

'No, he's not,' he said slowly, his blue eyes dark. 'He came back but did not know the password and was shot as an enemy.'

The room spun round her. She sat down hurriedly. 'How? Why? How d'you know all this? Tom never mentioned you being in his company?'

He sat on the sofa, leaving a foot between them. 'It was weeks after the D-Day landings. We lost a lot of men and so did the company he was with. They put us together. I was wounded in the explosion. He ran away just before it hit. I saw him, but was too confused to take it in,' he said heavily, his hands clasped on his knees. 'I only found out about him being dead months later.'

'Why didn't they tell me?' Her voice was hard, her face set.

'What was the use? You'd already been informed that he was presumed dead. Why hurt you further?'

'Why indeed?' A bitter laugh escaped her. 'Instead, you've done it for them. How could you when you know the way I've been over Rosie?'

'I'm sorry, Floss,' he mumbled. 'I would never have told you if you hadn't have gone on about him being some great hero.'

'No, I suppose you wouldn't have,' she said, suddenly exhausted. 'I think you'd better go.'

'Floss, please.' The lines of his face were dragged down. 'I didn't want to hurt you. Forgive me. I want to take care of you.'

She tilted her head. 'I can take care of myself. I'll see you out.' She moved over to the parlour door and opened it. He followed her slowly. 'What about your job? You'll be coming back?' he said anxiously.

She lowered her eyes. 'It's the school holidays soon. I'll be staying at home with the children.'

'But how'll you manage?'

'That's my problem.' She forced a smile. 'Please go, Steve. I've got things to do.'

He hesitated, opened his mouth to speak, but she shook her head. He turned on his heel and left.

As the car drove off, she sagged against the door jamb, shivering uncontrollably.

'Are you all right, Flo?' Mrs Murphy's voice pierced her frozen isolation.

Somehow Flora managed to focus on her broad features and to answer brightly, 'Fine. Just taking a breath of fresh air. I'll be going in. I've — got the tea to make.' She closed the door, not wanting to talk. Carmel Murphy had an intuitive grasp of some things. Although she knew that it was stupid, Flora feared her neighbour being able to read her thoughts. There was no way she could talk to anyone about Tom being a deserter.

She made her trembling way back into the parlour, not yet able to face her father. She sank on to the sofa, dropping her

148

head into her hands. Tom couldn't be a coward! Not Tom! Not *her* Tom! Stephen was cruel, cruel! For a long time she stayed like that, forcing the words into her mind, but in the end they carried no conviction because suddenly she was remembering the last time with Tom. He had been nervous, jumpy. Anguish darted through her when she considered her words about him not having a nerve in his body. He had shut her up. Poor, poor Tom! He had been scared. But then who hadn't been at some time during the war? She could understand fear but the Tom she had believed in had always been big and bold. How well had she really known him?

Her head lifted, she stared unseeingly at the far wall with its charcoal and chalk drawing of George as a toddler. Tom had had talent despite what Hilda had said about him messing about with art. But what about the other things she had said about him?

Flora shook her aching head vehemently, not wanting to think any more but desperately needing to be up and doing – something – anything! She went through the kitchen, ignoring her father and the two children who were listening to *Dick Barton – Special Agent*, and filled a bucket with water. Then she began to scrub the back yard as if her life depended on it; while all the time gripped by despair, thinking of Tom returning to his own lines only to be shot as an enemy. Dear God, why couldn't you have looked after him better? What was the sense in hoping and praying? Why couldn't you have looked after Rosie for me? Or is it really all down to us to take care of ourselves and each other? Is that what bearing each others' burdens about? What if we fail?

For a second she stilled and rested her sweating forehead on the back of her wet hand. Then the cat startled her by leaping off the step and pit-pattering over the wet ground. Her eyes followed it to the bin, from whence it clawed its way up to the yard wall. What a life, she thought. Cats never seemed to care about anything but their own comfort. It didn't matter to it that one of its playmates had gone. Tears brimmed in her eyes. She rubbed them away and carried on working down the yard.

Then unexpectedly the air was ripped apart by the

squawking of a bird and the low growling of the cat. Flora looked up and saw the slow movement of the animal's tail and the bird pinned down under its paw on the lavatory roof. Anger suddenly erupted inside her. She threw the scrubbing brush at the cat. It yelped and stared at her with indignant eyes. The bird's wings fluttered momentarily.

Flora scrambled up the lavatory door, crying, 'Beat it, you horrible moggy!' She aimed a slap at it as she heaved herself on to the stone roof. The cat fled, leaving its prey behind. Slowly she slid her hand under the bird, feeling the quick flurried movement of its breast. She feared that its close encounter with death would kill it. Death! She'd had enough of it. Suddenly it seemed terribly important that the sparrow should not die. She stroked its head gently, and it struck her that she had not really accepted Tom's death till today. Missing presumed dead. Now she knew the truth and it made a difference to her thinking. Rosie and Tom — she hoped that they were together.

Flora looked down at the bird. 'Well, are you going to go for life or give up on it?' she said softly.

Its wings fluttered and the tiny claws sought a hold. A smile started inside her as slowly she slid her hand from beneath it and backed away.

The sparrow took flight, soaring up into the air for a short while before fluttering down on to the roof amongst its fellows.

Flora sat and stared at them a moment, and then she climbed down the door and finished scrubbing the yard.

150

Part Two

Chapter Twelve

Flora knelt on the hassock and buried her face on her folded arms, resting them on the dark wood ledge of the pew in front of her. It was over a year since Rosie had died. One year, nine weeks, three days of living without her lively presence in the house. It had not been easy and she had almost lost her faith.

She lifted her head and glanced about the empty church. The door had been open and on impulse she had come inside. The sun had been shining through the stained glass windows beyond the communion table, casting shafts of red, blue, green, yellow, and purple over the tiled floor and the linen on the table. The blaze of colour had drawn her further in.

She raised her eyes to gaze at the window depicting Jesus and the apostles at the last supper. Underneath were painted the words 'Till He Comes'.

'Lord, I have sinned and fallen short of the glory of God. Forgive me.' The words seemed to come from deep inside her and stole around the church. She found herself listening to the silence that followed. Peace in her mind — that was what she needed, not voices and pictures of her dear dead, and a burden of guilt, and a keening cry that seemed to go on and on inside, hurting.

The last year had been a difficult time for all of them and George seemed to have grown wilder than ever. She accepted that he was grieving for Rosie but his behaviour had tired her beyond belief. Even Kathleen Murphy, his faithful slave, had given up on him and gone home howling one day when he had pushed her over while playing rounders. The girl had

153

grazed both knees and her mam had come down. Only Carmel had not complained. Instead she had suggested that they all walked to the Pierhead to watch the ships and have a picnic of jam butties and watered-down orange juice. The salt air had done them all good and the walk had tired them out.

But while George had been difficult, Vivien had grown more sensible – had helped her in the house and gone shopping as far as the corner shop. It was her niece who had brought Mike to mind because there had been no money for treats and she had reminded Flora of how generous he had been. That, and the fact that trouble was brewing in Europe because of the Russians. It would be terrible if there was another war so soon.

At first she had stayed home with the children but at last she had realised the impossibility of keeping check on them all of the time. Financial necessity had caused her in the end to get a job in another printer's in Islington. It had finished last week because the owner had died and his middle-aged brother and sister had not wanted to keep the business on.

She had thought of returning to Martin's because Stephen had continued to come and see her every now and again despite her coolness towards him. For a long time she had found it difficult to forgive him for the hurt he had caused her. Stephen and Hilda ... Both had borne grudges against Tom and that surely had affected their judgement of him. She wished that her sister had never said the things that she had, and that she and Hilda could both forgive and forget. Sisters should stick together.

Yesterday the children had gone back to school. George had started at the Secondary Modern last year, having failed the eleven plus. Flora blamed the bad winter and his lost schooling.

Her main problem now was finding another job. Any job! Her father had spoken of seeing an advertisement in one of his local shops – perhaps it would be worth having a look?

She lifted her head and became aware of the pain in her elbows, resting on the pew. She would have tried praying then, but a carefully modulated voice speaking her name brought her head round. She felt slightly embarrassed at being caught on her knees. She, who only went to church on high days and holidays. 'Hello, Vicar,' she murmured, getting awkwardly to her feet and facing him. 'I hope you — don't mind me coming in?'

'That's what the church is for.' His expression was concerned. 'How are you? I called a while ago but your father said —'

She flushed. 'I can imagine what he said.' Her father had no time for the clergy for all he was strongly Protestant. 'I'm sorry I didn't see you but I wasn't up to talking to anybody.' She began to edge towards the entrance.

'And now?' He walked with her, smiling gravely. 'I presume you came here for spiritual help.'

'I suppose I did,' she murmured.

'Did you get any?' He was still smiling, and suddenly she smiled back.

'I didn't hear any heavenly voices speaking out loud if that's what you mean.'

He laughed. 'Now that would be something! Sometimes I think we'd all like our religion to be a bit more dramatic — miraculous even.'

'A few miracles would come in handy.' She gazed about her. 'A church is a good place to think, though.'

'Yes.' He followed her eyes a moment. 'You're welcome to come and think any time you like.' His voice was gentle. 'Sometimes it's easier when it's quiet like this. People can get in the way when we deeply need to communicate with the Lord.'

She nodded, not liking to say that she had hardly been doing that. And yet she was feeling more at peace and more positive about the future. 'I'll have to go.' She held out her hand automatically. He took it, holding it for a moment between both his own.

'I'll continue to pray for you, Mrs Cooke. We all miss Rosie. But I'm sure she's delighting the angels with her high spirits, just as she did us.'

Flora stared at him, feeling pleasure because he suddenly painted a different picture of Rosie for her. 'Thank you,' she whispered. 'God bless you.'

'And you.' He released her hand and saw her to the door.

She waved briefly as she walked away, her shoulders back and her head high, tears in her eyes.

Flora walked a couple of miles, not taking note of where she was going until she realised that she had automatically continued along the road and up in the direction of her father's house. Now she was outside one of the local bakeries. She paused to blow her nose and wipe her eyes, and as her vision cleared the large card in the window became readable. It was advertising for a shop assistant. It seemed an answer to a prayer, she thought with a hint of a smile, and must be the one that her father had mentioned. Pausing only to smoothe her hair and dab at her eyes again, she pushed open the door, setting a bell jangling.

A woman, tall and thin and possibly younger than the fortyish that Flora instantly decided on, pinned a smile on her thin lips and came forward. 'Canna help yer, madam?'

'Yes please,' she said positively with a smile. 'I've come about the job. I'm honest, hard-working and I need it.'

For a moment the woman stared at her and then she laughed. 'Self-praise is no recommendation.' She rolled her Rs slightly.

'I can give you the names of two past employers if you want them,' said Flora, and promptly did.

The woman's greying brows hooded her eyes. 'Yer don't have to convince me, dearie. It's the boss that yer'll have to be doing that to and he's in the bakeroom. Newly back from serving in His Majesty's forces and determined to expand against all the odds.' She paused, eyeing Flora carefully. 'Are yer in mourning, or do yer like black? It always looks smart, I think.'

Flora was taken aback but she answered the question and gave a couple of extra details, thinking that they might make the woman more sympathetic towards her.

The woman's face looked interested. 'Yer man killed in the war?' Flora nodded. 'That's sad.' She smoothed her white overall. 'I lost me fiancé in the war as well.'

'Oh, I'm sorry.' Flora did not really know what to say, not wanting to be drawn into talking about Tom and the war.

'Aye,' murmured the woman, staring at a point somewhere above Flora's head. 'Real weird, it was.' She shook her head.

156

'I'll get Mr Brown. The shop was his mam's but her nerves went when the bombs came and she killed herself. So I've been in charge while he's been away. Wait here now while I go and tell him someone's come for Norma's job.' She disappeared through a door into the back.

Flora glanced about the shop, wondering at the things people said to complete strangers, and hoping that Mr Brown wouldn't ask her too many personal questions. It was quiet in the shop but she realised that was probably because it was nearly lunch time and they would be closing soon. The sound of footsteps and voices caused her to turn.

She was completely unprepared for the man who came into the shop and her eyes widened. He was incredibly handsome with strongly angled bones to his face and eyes that appeared almost black. He had a perfectly straight nose and a dimpled chin, and his hair was dark and fell in a deep wave above finely drawn browns. His gaze met hers unblinkingly. 'So you've come about the job?' His voice was light and rapid. 'Maggie says that you're a widow. When can you start? The last girl left in rather a hurry — said her boyfriend had come home and they were getting married right away.'

'I can start now if that's what you want,' said Flora, slightly dazed by the flood of information. 'But I have no experience.'

He eyed her up and down and a slight smile eased his mouth. 'You'll soon learn.' He brought out a packet of cigarettes. 'Maggie'll tell you the pay and hours. What's your name?'

'Flora Cooke.' She felt uncomfortable beneath his scrutiny but decided she might as well say what was on her mind, and squared her shoulders. 'I was hoping my hours could be just till four. I have kids.'

His eyes narrowed. 'You stay till six unless everything is sold,' he rasped. 'I want a full-timer.'

'I couldn't do that today.' Her voice was steady, concealing her dismay. 'The children won't know where I am.'

He stared at her a moment longer, then nodded. 'Tonight you can go.' He lit his cigarette. 'Tomorrow you stay — Wednesday afternoons off. You work all day Saturdays.'

She nodded, although working all day Saturday did not really suit her at all. But her father's house was not far away

157

and he might be prepared to put up with the children, knowing she was just round the corner. The job would do her until she got the chance of another.

'Good!' He blew out a stream of smoke. 'Maggie'll show you the ropes. I live over the shop and I'm going for lunch now.' He left them, dragging off his white overall as he went.

Flora exchanged glances with Maggie, who wiggled both eyebrows. 'He's a looker, isn't he?' she whispered. 'But don't let those gorgeous eyes deceive yer. He's hard. But do yer job properly and yer won't have any trouble.'

Flora nodded. 'Do I start now? Where do I put my coat?'

Maggie shook her head. 'Didn't yer hear him now? It's lunch time.' She began to unbutton her overall. 'Come back in three quarters of an hour and then yer can get started.'

Flora nodded and left the shop, deciding that she might as well go and visit her father and ask him about Saturdays.

She was back at the shop exactly on time, relieved that her father had agreed to keep his eye on the children, although she guessed that George would play in the street. Maggie came along a couple of minutes after her and opened up. A white overall and cap was found for Flora. 'It was Norma's,' said the older woman. 'She was a wee bit shorter than yer and fatter but it should fit.' It did, and Flora set about learning the price of the different cakes and bread and pies — as well as how to work the big brass till — in what felt like a very brief quarter of an hour. 'What yer don't remember, yer'll learn as yer go along,' said Maggie, glancing at the clock on the wall before unbolting the door. 'Yer only have to ask.'

'I hope I don't muck everything up,' Flora said breathlessly, rushing behind the counter.

'We're never as busy in the afternoons as the mornings, so don't yer be worryin',' said Maggie. 'Yer'll cope.'

To Flora's relief she did, but being on her feet all the time was something that took some getting used to. They had a cup of tea halfway through the afternoon and it was then that Maggie surprised Flora by asking her how Tom had been killed.

'He was declared missing presumed dead,' she said shortly, sipping her tea. 'It was a shell — blew several of them up.'

Maggie stared at her with something akin to pleasure. 'Now isn't that strange? My Alf was declared missing and I couldn't bear the suspense — so I asked this friend, who knew this man who could see things if he could see anything for me.'

Flora felt slightly confused and her brow creased. 'What kind of thing?'

'Anything about Alf! It was real weird, I can tell yer. I told him about Alf and 'e said 'e were dead.' Maggie sighed. 'In a way it was a relief, knowing. Not long after I got a letter confirming 'is death. They found 'is body. It was frightening in a way — it's strange the way some people 'ave powers to see things.'

'The odds were that your fiancé was dead, surely?' said Flora sceptically.

Maggie smiled. 'I would have thought that meself but me friend had 'er fortune read by him. She was engaged to an airman at the time but he told 'er that 'e was not the man she would marry. And sure enough a couple of days later she met this other fella and she ended up marrying him.'

'He could have just put the idea in her head,' insisted Flora. 'She wouldn't be the only one to change partners during the war.'

Maggie frowned. 'You're an unbeliever, Flo. I can see tha'. But if yer'd only give it a go! This man I've been talking about can get in touch with the Other Side.'

'The other side of what?' asked Flora, unable to resist teasing her.

'You know,' hissed Maggie, nudging her, and taking her cup as a customer entered. 'I'll tell yer another time and maybe you'll laugh on the other side of yer face then.'

Flora just smiled and went to serve the customer, dismissing what Maggie said while considering it strange that both of them should have had their men missing presumed dead. But at least Maggie was friendly enough and that was a good thing.

It was busy in the shop the next morning, which suited Flora because it gave her less time to think. She enjoyed dealing with the customers. They were all different. She addressed the first woman in the queue. 'Can I help you, love?'

'A Vienna and two eccles, queen. Yer're new here, aren't

159

yer?' Flora nodded, smiling. 'Yer'll soon get used to us.' The customer's voice was cheerful as she counted out money along the counter, coin by coin. Flora hurried to pick it up because already an elderly man was rustling a ten shilling note and flourishing his bread units.

'Hurry up, girl! I haven't got all day.' He glared at her. 'Where's the other one gone? I'd just got used to her. Changes all the time. I don't know what the world's coming to.' Flora only smiled and rushed to get what he wanted.

'Any custards?' The twin girls' heads barely reached the counter. 'Me gran's fancyin' custards,' said one. 'And me Aunty Ethel's comin' for tea,' said the other.

So it went on most of the morning with few lulls in which to take a break. Flora's feet and back began to ache.

Mr Brown came sauntering in just as Maggie turned the 'Closed' sign. He leaned against the counter and tossed his cap on it, before pulling out his cigarettes. 'How's Mrs Cooke coped, Maggie?'

'Fine,' responded the older woman briskly. 'She's quick and polite and never lost her smile.'

'Good.' He stared at Flora. 'But it's early days — will you still be smiling at the end of the month, I wonder?' He lit his cigarette and walked out again.

Flora pulled a face but said nothing, shrugging herself out of her overall and getting her coat. If she rushed she would just make it home in time to stoke up the fire and put a hot pot in the oven. She hurried out.

That night she was really tired and for the first time in a long time she fell asleep as soon as her head touched the pillow.

'D'yer enjoy this job?' asked Maggie, watching Flora slide a tray of hot tin loaves along the counter a couple of weeks later. 'It must be quite differ'int from yer last two.'

'It is, but I don't mind that. It keeps my mind occupied and that's the main thing.'

'It must have been really sad for yer, losing yer little girl.' Maggie wiped crumbs off the counter. 'Alf would have liked kids.' She paused. 'Have yer given any more thought to what I said about the Other Side? I mean, yer husband and yer little

160

girl, they've passed over, haven't they? Yer could get in touch with them.'

Flora stared at her, feeling uncomfortable. She did not want any prying into her affairs. What if there was something in it and they found out about Tom being a deserter? There was part of her that still found that truth difficult to come to terms with. 'I don't really believe in that sort of thing, Maggie,' she said gently. 'I think it's all just wishful thinking.'

Maggie stilled, her toffee-coloured eyes round. 'You can't really believe that, Flo. Why the messages that 'ave been passed on to me! A real comfort, they've been. That's why I can stay so cheerful.'

Flora did not know whether to take her seriously or to smile. 'What kind of messages?' she asked with a certain reluctance.

Maggie's mouth split into a smile. 'Nice messages. Since Alf went on the other side he's a much better person. Sometimes he used to get real frisky, like after a couple of ports on a New Year's Eve.' Her fingers fidgetted with the keys of the till. 'But of course on the other side there's none of *that*.'

'That?' Flora stared at her with a strange kind of fascination.

'You know,' articulated Maggie carefully, glancing furtively at the bakeroom door. 'Sex.' Her finger pressed a key accidentally and the till tray shot out.

'Oh, sex!' Flora was pretty certain that Maggie knew little about it — so she was curious.

'You don't need it in Heaven,' informed the older woman. 'Men like it down here, but for us women it only means having babies to populate the earth. But in Heaven they'll have enough people. I mean all the children that have died like your little girl will be in 'eaven — they won't need any more.'

Flora could not take her eyes off Maggie's face. She could see that the woman was perfectly serious and felt a sudden affection for her. She smiled. 'I've never looked at birth, death and sex just like that. Thanks.'

Maggie smiled back. 'I worked it all out from things I've seen an' heard. I mean, it makes sense, doesn't it? It's love that's important, isn't it, an' caring? If yer're interested in getting in touch, Flo,' she said eagerly, 'I could take yer along to a gatherin'.'

Flora hesitated, not wanting to hurt her feelings. 'I might find it too painful, Maggie. And I have so little time to spare,' she said softly.

Maggie tried to hide her disappointment and persisted. 'I could try for you.'

Flora did not know what to say, not wanting to hurt her feelings. The whole idea of getting in touch with the dead gave her the creeps. But there was Rosie — she yearned after her child still. 'Please yourself,' she said. Then picking up the tray of bread she took it outside to the delivery van.

When she came back Maggie was serving a customer and there was another waiting. She was relieved that their conversation could not be continued and hoped that Maggie would forget all about getting in touch with the Other Side.

'I got news for yer, Flo.' Maggie's face was brimming with excitement as she pulled on her overall a couple of mornings later.

'Oh, aye!' Flora's nerves gave a peculiar kind of jump as she set a plate of buns in the window.

'Yer'll be 'alf pleased with wha' I've gotta tell yer.'

'Will I?' She turned and faced Maggie, unexpectedly apprehensive. 'I don't know if I want to hear. I mean, I don't really believe in all this.'

The older woman smirked. 'Yer will now. Your Rosie is perfectly happy. In a garden picking flowers.'

'Is she?' said Flora wistfully, her hands trembling as she picked up another plate. 'I wonder what she's going to do with them.'

'Wha'?' Maggie stared at her as if she had gone mad.

'The flowers. What would she do with flowers? What kind of flowers were they?'

'Roses, I suppose.' Maggie looked bewildered. 'What does it matter? Yer know I've never 'eard anybody ask a question like tha' before. I don't suppose it's important really. The important thing is that she's sorry for what she did.'

'She's sorry!' Flora stared at her unbelievingly, barely

noticing that Mr Brown had come into the shop. She cleared her throat. 'Anything else?'

Maggie pulled her face. 'We couldn't get yer husband. Pity! But there it is. Perraps if yer came with me?'

Flora was relieved but hoped it did not show — but how to put Maggie off? 'I don't know,' she said softly. 'Let me think about it.'

'Think on your own time, Mrs Cooke, and let's see you moving.' Mr Brown's voice caused them both to jump. Maggie hurried away into the back and Flora nearly dropped the plate of cakes. She glanced at him involuntarily and he stared back at her, unsmiling. 'You should have more sense than to take notice of Maggie. She's a bit screwy. She even wanted me to get in touch with Mam. Daft, I call it.'

'Yes, I suppose so,' murmured Flora. 'But if it helps her ...'

'Helps her!' he sneered, leaning against the counter. 'You must be as daft as she is. She pays that man and he tells her just what she wants to hear.'

'Pays him? She said nothing to me about paying him.' Her voice was low. She moved to put the cakes in the window.

'She wouldn't, would she? Not yet.' He gave a bark of laughter. 'Surely you aren't believing her! I can understand an old crow like her allowing herself to be deceived but you're only young. You could get another man.' He folded his arms and his eyes gleamed. 'So what's the point of Maggie getting her fella to call up the spooks? They won't bring him back. What you need, Mrs Cooke, is another man to help you forget.' His voice was silky. 'If you're in need I'm on call anytime — day or night.'

For a second Flora thought she had not heard him aright, then as she continued to stare at him, there was something in his expression that caused an angry blush to colour her face. 'No, thank you,' she said as calmly as she could before turning and going after Maggie into the back room.

She leaned against a table a moment, feeling like the day was already hours old. Was it because she was a widow that men thought that she was willing for a romp in the hay any old time? Or did she look like that kind of woman? Even Little Paddy had become a mite too familiar, putting his arm round her and calling her 'Poor girlie'. Squeezing her arm as well as patting her bottom. All this since Rosie had died. It was embarrassing and irritating, especially since Carmel had told her that she was having another baby. Well, if that short Irishman thought that she was ready for a bit of slap and tickle because his wife was expecting, he was in for a rude awakening one day. She smiled wryly. But perhaps she was getting things all out of proportion and taking it all too seriously.

Even so when it came to going home time Flora was out of the door quicker than Maggie for once and striding out along the road. Although why she should think that Mr Brown should follow her home when he had not taken any notice of her for the rest of the day was stupid. Besides, what had the man really said? For now she would forget him and look forward to seeing the children and putting her feet up once she had done the tea and tidied round.

Flora picked up Vivien at Mrs Murphy's and handed over a loaf, which she herself had paid for. It was the unasked for payment that she gave for Carmel's keeping an eye on the children. She was told that George had gone to the park to play football, and was relieved that at least she knew where he was and that he wasn't doing anything worse. She took Vivien's hand and they idled down the street, the girl telling her about her day in school.

Pushing the front door open, they walked up the lobby. Then Flora sniffed — Californian Poppy! With an over-whelming sense of shock she recognised the scent and for a moment she could not move. Then her hand went to the kitchen door, only to have it opened from the other side before she could turn the handle.

'At last!' exclaimed her sister, a cigarette dangling from her scarlet mouth. 'I thought you were never coming home. This is a fine welcome for the prodigal. Where's the fatted calf?' She took the cigarette from between her lips and smiled. 'Well, Flo, try and look pleased to see me!'

Chapter Thirteen

Uncertain what exactly she was feeling, Flora said nothing for a moment, nor did Vivien, and neither of them made a move towards Hilda. Then Flora freed a long breath. 'So you've decided to come and see us at last. It would have been a good idea to let me know instead of just walking in.'

Hilda pulled a face. 'I was up this way so I thought I'd call in. But if I'm not welcome then I can turn round and go back out again.'

'You could,' said Flora calmly, shrugging off her coat. 'What have you come for after all this time? To see your daughter, I hope.'

A frown creased Hilda's forehead. 'Partly. But I suppose you won't believe that. Just as you won't believe that I was worried about you when I heard about Rosie. I know the way you feel about your kids.'

'It's over a year ago! How did you find out?' Flora put a match to the fire, before sitting down and kicking off her shoes.

'Doris. She saw it in the *Echo* when it happened, but I only learnt about it the other day when I came back to Liverpool.'

'So you immediately came round to see me. How nice!'

Hilda walked over to her. 'I do have feelings, Flo! I was sorry to hear about the kid. How have you been?'

Flora closed her eyes and rested her head wearily against the back of the chair. Seeing her sister had brought to mind their last meeting and she was really in no mood for emotional turmoil. 'How do you think I've been?'

Her sister took a deep drag at her cigarette. 'Lousy, I suppose.'

A harsh laugh escaped Flora. 'Hardly describes my feelings. But it's nice to have you caring about me for once.'

'There's no need for sarcasm.'

Flora opened her eyes briefly. 'I wasn't being sarcastic. But knowing you — why have you come, Hilda? There's always something other than family feeling behind your visits.'

Hilda fiddled with her cigarette, not looking directly at her. 'I met Mike in town a few days ago.'

Flora's heart seemed to jerk and her eyelashes flew open. 'You can't have! He went back to America!'

'Well, he's at Burtonwood base again. Something to do with the Russians blockading Berlin.'

'How did he look?' Flora tried to calm the unexpected surge of feeling inside her. Hilda's eyes narrowed as she stared down at her painted fingernails through a haze of smoke.

'Just the same. You know Mike. Perhaps he's a little thinner.' She shrugged. 'Anyway, me and him sorted out our differences and we had a night out on the town.'

Flora straightened up, her fingers trembling on the arm of the chair. She felt slightly sick. 'Why bother to come and tell me?'

Hilda took another drag on her cigarette. 'It's funny, but I thought it might annoy you — me and Mike. I was almost sure you and him had something real going once.' She laughed mirthlessly. 'But he did tell me that it was all over.'

No way could Flora allow her sister to see how much the words hurt. 'Of course it's over. Mike was fun,' she said lightly. 'But I never kidded myself that it could work. I'm not the dreamer you always accused me of being.'

'No?' said Hilda, scrutinising her carefully. 'Perhaps that's your trouble, Flo. You've let life shake the stardust from your eyes.'

'How poetic,' said Flora with a false brightness. 'But you helped by loading me with your problems.'

'I'm about to help you out with one.' Hilda gazed down at the glowing tip of her cigarette, then lifting her eyes she stared at her daughter. 'She's grown. She's looking well.' She held out a hand. 'Come over here, kid.' Vivien returned her regard and moved slowly towards her, but instead of taking the hand or stopping in front of her, she brushed past and sat on the rug at Flora's feet. For a moment Hilda looked disconcerted and then she laughed. 'That's put me in my place! Okay, Viv, I admit I'm not much of a mother. But perhaps Mike's idea of me taking the role of being your mam more seriously isn't a bad one.'

'Mike said that?' said Flora. It should not really have surprised her because it was what he had said many times.

'Yes.'

'It would mean you staying in Liverpool,' she said in a mocking voice that concealed the hurt deep inside. 'After all you said about this dirty old city, dear sister, could you really stick living here?'

Hilda scanned her sister's face and smiled sweetly. 'I'm prepared to give it another go if it means catching Mike.' Her eyes gleamed as she flicked ash into the blazing fire. 'I always did have a soft spot for him. I know he's not devastatingly handsome — but he's got something, and it's just possible that it could be love that I feel for him.'

'It's never shown before,' said Flora, determinedly cheerful. 'Last time we spoke of him, you were going to murder him.'

'And you,' said Hilda pensively, blowing out smoke and watching it curl in the air.

There was a silence and Flora moved her shoulders, wanting to believe that by doing so it would ease the ache in her chest. Why couldn't Mike and Hilda have stayed out of her life?

'Could this sudden feeling of love for Mike, have anything to do with you still wanting to go to America?' she drawled. 'Mike's no fool.'

'All men are fools at times,' murmured Hilda. 'And of course I still want to go to Yankee land.'

'With or without Viv? Have you thought of her at all in the last few years?' she asked under her breath so that the girl could not hear. 'What's your excuse for not sending anything or getting in touch? She was terribly upset when you walked out.'

Hilda stubbed out her cigarette and smiled. 'Don't let's start an argument by bringing up old quarrels. So I left Viv with you and didn't get in touch! In the circumstances I reckon I had every reason for not speaking to you ever again. But — I'm not one to bear grudges, little sister, even though what you did made me really mad.'

'What you said about Tom made me more than mad,' blurted out Flora. 'It was cruel! You and Stephen both seem to want to get your knife into Tom, and it's not right. A dead man can't answer back, as you said.'

Hilda bit her bottom lip for a second, then said, 'Stephen who?'

'Never you mind,' said Flora, frowning and folding her arms. 'It's what you said that really bothered me.'

Hilda stared at her, her expression thoughtful. 'You're a dark one. Tell me — Stephen who?'

Flora smiled grimly. 'Mind your own business.'

'It is my business.' Her brow knitted. 'You're my sister and if there's a man in your life I want to know about it. The way you go on about Tom makes me laugh. First it's Mike and now it's a Stephen. You really get around, sister.'

'You're talking rubbish.' Flora cleared her throat. 'So I'm getting over Tom now — that's natural. It doesn't mean I'll ever forget him — or that I found it easy to take your nasty insinuations.'

Hilda shrugged. 'Truth, Flo. Now how about me taking Viv off your hands one day?'

'I suppose you think you'll fool Mike into believing that you've turned over a new leaf,' said Flora acidly. 'Viv's not a toy to be used in your games.'

'She's my daughter.' Hilda's smile was predatory. 'And I could take her from you.' Flora shot a glance at Vivien, who looked at her and shifted closer. Hilda laughed. 'There's no need for you both to worry yet. I haven't gone all maternal overnight. Just name one day a week for now I can see her.'

'There's times when I hate you,' said Flora quietly. 'But I accept that you have a right to see Viv. I just wish you realised what you're missing, not being a proper mother to her.'

Hilda grimaced. 'Face facts, Flo. Sentiment doesn't sway me. Name your day.'

Flora did not hesitate. 'Saturday. I have another job and

I have to work then. At the moment Father looks after the kids. It's not easy for him — he's getting old and I think he finds all day too much.'

'Saturday!' Hilda frowned. 'I was looking forward to dancing on Saturday.'

'Forget I mentioned it.' Flora's voice was bland. 'You'll never fool Mike into believing that you take your responsibilities seriously. Although I wasn't asking you to give up your dancing.'

Hilda's mouth twitched. 'That's a good job — because I wouldn't! So you want me to look after her during the day?'

Flora nodded and Hilda pursed her lips. 'Why don't you give her and George the money to go to the kids' matinée?'

Flora's eyebrows rose. 'Why don't you? You owe Viv.'

'I'll see.' Hilda threw the butt of her cigarette into the fire. 'What is your new job, by the way?'

'I work in a bakery.'

'Where is it?' Hilda yawned and stood up.

'Round the corner from Father's,' she said shortly. 'Are you going now?'

Hilda nodded. 'I know you can't wait to get rid of me.' She reached for a coat. 'I'll see you on Saturday then.'

'I doubt it,' said Flora. 'I'll be at work. But George will wait in till you come.'

'All right.' She stared at Flora. 'We should be prepared to forget and forgive each other everything, Flo,' she said dreamily. 'Isn't that what the Good Book says? But forgetting and forgiving doesn't come easy, does it?' She pulled on her gloves and swayed out of the room.

Flora and Vivien heard the door slam behind her. The girl's sharp eyes met her aunt's. 'I'm glad she didn't stay long.' She struggled to her feet, the cat in her arms. 'Do I have to go out with her?'

'She's your mother,' said Flora absently, wondering which one of them her sister's parting shot was intended for. Herself or Hilda? or both perhaps?

'She's not much of a mother,' muttered Vivien.

'That's enough of that,' murmured Flora.

The girl sighed heavily. 'It's nice that Mike's back. I wonder if we'll see him.'

Flora touched the fair curls. 'I wonder,' she said, struggling with conflicting emotions where Mike was concerned. It was stupid to be so pleased that he was back this side of the Atlantic. It would be because they needed more planes for air-lifting supplies into the Western sectors of Berlin. During the war Burtonwood had been one of the biggest American air bases in Britain. After the war they had handed it over to the R.A.F. but now it seemed the Yanks were back. But what had possessed Mike to go out with Hilda, knowing what she was like? But then, Hilda was the beauty of the family and men were susceptible to that kind of thing. Even Mike whom she had believed had a good head on his shoulders, for all he acted crazy at times.

She did not sleep well. The next morning Mike and Hilda and Tom were still in her thoughts.

Flora spent her lunchtime at her father's, telling him about Hilda's return.

'No good'll come of it,' he said gruffly, as they stood in his tiny yard, feeding his pigeons. 'She's a flibbertigibbet.'

'I wouldn't argue the fact, Father,' she murmured, stroking one of the bird's heads with the tip of a finger. 'But she's family.'

Her father gave her a look. 'And there's a black sheep in every one,' he snorted. 'Don't you be bringing her round to see me.'

'I doubt she'd come,' Flora said, putting the pigeon back.

'Suits me.' And on that note she left him and went back to work.

Flora felt keyed up that evening although she would not admit the reason to herself. She washed and changed into a clean frock. George had gone out with a Guy, in the hope of collecting money for fireworks for Bonfire Night. She was glad to have him out of the way, despite his having been unusually friendly with Vivien earlier. That was probably due to the girl's having stuffed some old clothes of Flora's father's with newspaper, providing a decent body for the cabbage head fronted with a Guy Fawkes mask which George had drawn.

She put the wireless on low, and picked up some darning. Vivien, instead of sitting like she usually did, reading a book or crayoning, prowled in and out of the kitchen, going up the lobby several times and opening the door. In the end Flora could stand it no longer and said, 'What's the matter with you? Have you got ants in your pants?'

Vivien sighed. 'I wish I was a boy. If I was you'd let me go out and collect bommie wood and ask for pennies for the Guy.'

'Not at your age I wouldn't and you know it,' she murmured. 'I understand how you feel, though. Boys and men,' she said with a certain tautness, 'seem to have all the fun. But is that what's really wrong with you?'

Vivien shrugged. 'I thought Mike might come.'

'Mike?' Flora's nerves jumped and she gave a tinkling laugh. 'Why should he come and see us?'

The girl gave her a look. 'He liked us – I know he liked us.'

'Well, perhaps you'll see him when you go out with your mam,' she said lightly. 'She seems to believe that she has him on a string.'

'Mam doesn't really want me,' said Vivien in a clear tight voice. 'She never has.'

Flora said nothing. What was the point in trying to deny it? The child wasn't an idiot. She pushed the darning needle in and out of George's sock, her ears attuned, despite herself, for the sound of the door knocker.

'It's true,' muttered Vivien, curling up on the rug. 'When I was little – before I came here. She never took me anywhere with her but left me with Aunty Doris's gran.'

'It wasn't easy for her, having no husband,' excused Flora, seeking a way to change the subject.

'You've got no husband,' countered Vivien quickly. 'I did think that you might marry Uncle Steve.'

'No,' said Flora shortly, putting down the sock and glancing at the clock. There would be no visit from Mike at this time of night. 'Shall I make us a cup of char?' Her expression was cheerful. 'And then how about Hans Christian Andersen?'

Vivien nodded. The tea was made; 'The Little Matchgirl'

read. George came in. They all went upstairs. And Flora had an overwhelming desire to burst into tears as she lay in her lonely bed.

The next day at work the hours seemed to drag, and having Mr Brown constantly watching her did not ease Flora's jumpy mood.

As she strode home, the shopping bag swung in her hand and her footsteps click-clacked rapidly. She wished she could go to the moon — that she could pull the stars down. Crazy, but she wanted the impossible — she wanted a man she could rely on. Or did she? Damn! Men confused all sensible thinking.

She exchanged a few words with Little Paddy as she picked up Vivien. 'And how are you feeling now, girlie?' he asked, stroking her shoulder and chucking her under the chin.

'Fine thanks,' said Flora, moving away quickly, thinking that he'd be kissing her next and she would have to say something then.

She fumbled for her latch key as she approached her doorstep, and jumped when a figure loomed up out of the darkness.

'Hi, Flora.' The man in an olive drab raincoat and eagle cap badge straightened up from the door jamb and thrust a bunch of flowers at her.

She stared at Mike, and for a moment she could not speak for the huge lump in her throat. It was ten seconds after she took the flowers that she remembered Hilda's visit. 'And what are these for?' she murmured, managing to keep her voice steady but unable to resist burying her nose in the russet-coloured chrysanthemums.

'I would have bought marigolds, but you once told me it's the wrong time of year,' he said quietly.

She was touched, and annoyed that he could make her feel the way she did. 'Fancy you remembering that,' she said drily. 'Where have you sprung from? Just got off the boat from New York?'

'No.' His brow puckered slightly. 'Came in September but wasn't sure you'd want to see me.' There was a short silence, of which Vivien quickly took advantage. 'You haven't said hello to me, Mike.' She put herself in front of him. 'I haven't gone invisible, have I?'

He smiled his heart-turning smile. 'No, chick. How've you been?'

'Very well, thank you. But Rosie died.'

'What?' His head snapped up and he stared at Flora, who had winced at her niece's blunt statement.

'Didn't you know?' Her voice was suddenly uneven. 'I thought our Hilda might have told you.'

'Hilda?' he said blankly. 'No, she didn't. How — did it happen?'

'She drowned in a water tank.' She averted her face and rammed her key into the lock.

He came to life and pushed open the door. 'Hell, Flora, what a thing to happen. You poor kid.'

'Don't pity me,' she said vehemently. 'I don't need pity.'

'Who said anything about pity?' His tone was serious. 'But sympathy, honey, surely I can give you that?' He took her arm and walked up the dark lobby with Vivien behind them.

'Perhaps. But you've been out of my life for a while and maybe it would be better if you stayed out of it,' she muttered. 'You and our Hilda both.'

'What the hell has Hilda been saying to you?'

'I don't want to talk about her.' She pulled away from him as they came into the unlit kitchen. 'Now where did I leave the matches?' Her trembling hands searched the lace runner on the sideboard and found the box of Swan Vestas. She struck a match, instantly casting a pool of light.

Mike's hand caught hers. 'I'll light the mantle,' he said. 'You sit down and rest. And take it from me, your sister can't be trusted.'

A slight laugh escaped her. 'D'you think I need you to tell me that? The thing is, we haven't seen each other for a long time.'

'A helluva long time. A hundred times I've been going to write to you but each time I kept thinking about what you said about Tom and a clean break — so I didn't do it.'

'It proves something,' she said, sitting and thinking inconsequentially how useful it would be to be tall enough to light the gas without getting on a chair every time.

'It proves that I respected your wishes.' He flashed her a glance as he pulled the chains to adjust the gaslight. 'And I've thought of you. How have you been? Apart from losing Rosie, that is?'

'I've survived,' she said brightly.

'Only survived?' Mike turned and placed his hands on her shoulders. His grey eyes gazed into hers. 'Then you missed me?' he said quietly.

For a moment she said nothing, thinking of Hilda and the two and a half years since they last saw each other. 'I missed you.' Her voice was light as she pulled away from him. 'But it would be strange if I hadn't. It was fun with you.'

His expression was suddenly uncertain. 'It was more than that between us. Why d'you think I'm here, Flo?'

She moistened her lips. 'You tell me! I presume I'm supposed to believe that you must have missed me.'

'Supposed? Flora, believe it.' He would have pulled her close but she placed her hands against his chest.

'Whoa! Not so fast.' She decided to carry on playing it frothy and light. 'I haven't exactly been in hibernation while you've been away. You can't expect to take up where we left off, just like that, after me believing you in California and gone for good.'

'You mean that we have to go back to the beginning,' he said quietly. 'Get to know each other all over again. It won't work – we already know each other and what we want.' And without any further preamble he kissed her. She fought him but the feel of his mouth on hers and the sheer brute strength of him momentarily subdued the fight in her.

'I'm cold,' said Vivien forlornly. 'Will you two stop canoodling and light the fire?'

Flora pulled away instantly, her heart thumping like any adolescent's after a first kiss. 'Priorities. Let's get our priorities right and light the fire,' she said, a touch breathless, impatient with herself for allowing him to have such an effect on her. 'We haven't had any tea. And where's George?'

'Wood hunting.' Vivien crouched close to the fireplace as Flora moved away from Mike to riddle the dead cinders with sudden energy before shovelling out the ashes.

174

'Here, woman,' said Mike, taking the shovel from her.

'Thanks.' She determinedly avoided his twinkling gaze, scrunching paper and laid it in the grate.

'I remember the first cup of tea you made me,' he said, coming in from the yard where he had emptied the ashes into the bin.

Flora glanced up at him from her kneeling position. 'I remember you coming out of her next door's,' she said in a low voice so that Vivien, who had moved out of the way, could not hear.

'That was the first time we set eyes on each other. I think I fell in love with you then.'

'I don't believe it,' she whispered, trying to concentrate on getting the fire going. 'How could you? We didn't even know each other.'

'I wanted to look after you. To protect you.'

'You didn't come back.'

'I didn't believe that you'd want me to. If looks could kill, I'd have been dead at your feet.'

'You'd kept me awake. I was mad at you. And that's what I really meant about remembering you coming from next door.'

'I thought you understood about all that,' he said in a low voice. 'How is Lena, by the way?' He leaned back on his heels as the fire began to burn.

'I don't know how you dare ask,' said Flora, suddenly cross. 'But she's left. Her husband came home and found her in bed with a Yank. There was all hell let loose. I have new neighbours now. Quieter.'

'Oh?' He did not look a mite embarrassed, much to her annoyance. 'I bet she's not as half as interesting to the neighbours.'

Flora gave him a hard stare. 'I should think not,' she said, emphasising each word. 'Mrs Bryce brought down the tone of the neighbourhood.'

'Who said that to you?' he said lightly. 'Her over the road.'

She bit her lower lip. 'Oh, shut up, Mike. She was a whore and you know it.'

'Who? Her over the road?'

She had to force herself not to smile. 'Stop it. I don't want you making me laugh.'

'Why? You need to laugh. The light's gone out of your eyes, and your bloom's all gone.'

'You sure know how to make a girl feel good,' she muttered, getting off her knees. He took her elbow, helping her up, and for a moment his lips touched the tip of her nose. 'Don't,' she whispered fiercely. 'There's no point in starting it all over again. Sooner or later you'll go home again. Anyway, you've got our Hilda chasing you now.'

'Hilda again,' he said impatiently. 'What has she said to you?'

'Enough!' Suddenly there was anger in her voice. 'You've had fun with her, so I presume you fancy her. She still wants to go to America and she's always had a soft spot for you — so she says!'

He stared at her; then a slight smile lifted his mouth. 'I believe you're jealous.'

'No, I'm not,' she lied, tilting her head to one side. 'I think that possibly you might — might, I say — be a good influence on her.'

He jingled the coins in his pocket. 'Perhaps I might. It might atone for my many sins.'

'Hmmph!' She scowled at him and went into the back kitchen, lit the gas mantle, shut the door and began to search for the potatoes, determined to ignore his existence.

She had peeled two when Mike came up behind her. 'I'd rather you tried reforming me,' he said in her ear. 'Your Hilda's as tough as a buffalo. I don't know if I've got the stamina to crack her hide.'

'You've made a start,' she responded promptly. 'At least she's going to take Viv out on Saturday. The evening, of course, was too much. She's going dancing on Saturday night as you probably already know.'

'Not with me she isn't.'

Flora turned and stared at him. 'Not?'

'No.' He dug his hands in his pockets and leaned against the draining board. 'It's a helluva mess back at the base — most of the buildings have fallen into disrepair and there's grass growing on the runways. We're up to our eyes in mud and there's an emergency on. I can't come and go as I please. Saturday night is out for me this week — but maybe next Saturday ...' His eyes teased hers. 'I might ask her out next week.'

She threw a potato at him which he hurriedly fielded. 'Unless you could come out with me?' His grey eyes flickered over her.

'I don't know if I want to,' she said, determinedly firm.

His voice was quiet. 'It would sure annoy Hilda.' He raised his eyebrows questioningly.

'So what?' she said slowly.

There was a silence. Then he murmured, 'I didn't think you'd give me up to her devious ways without some kind of fight.'

She could not prevent a laugh. 'You believe that you're worth fighting over?'

He laughed. 'Hell, yeah! Why let her have it all her own way? She's damned nice-looking, Flo, but you're not so bad yourself. In fact, you can be almost perfect when you make the effort.'

'Thanks.' Her voice was quiet. 'You've a nerve. D'you know that?'

'Sure. How about it?'

'I'll think about it.'

'Good girl.' He leaned forward and kissed the corner of her right eyebrow. She knew that she was being completely stupid allowing him into her life again. 'Now what's for chow?' he murmured.

'You weren't asked.' He voice was mild.

'No.' He kept on staring at her and she stared back. Then she laughed. He was back and life could be brighter for a while, as long as she did not take him serious.

She peeled several more potatoes.

177

Chapter Fourteen

Flora shortened the stems of the chrysanthemums and bashed their ends before putting them in a glass vase. She breathed in their earthy fragrance. Never, ever, had a man bought her flowers before; Tom had thought them a waste of money.

As she spread the table with the best linen cloth and placed the flowers in the middle of it she was aware of Mike watching her. Suddenly she remembered that day when the children had gone to Hoylake on the Sunday School outing, and her wishing for a man to come through the door to lighten her lonely meal. Mike had wanted to take her away from all this. For a second she pondered on a Cinderella-after-the-ball existence, and decided that glass slippers could hardly be called practical for work.

She stirred the scouse to stop it from catching, half listening to Vivien as she read a poem about autumn to Mike. It was one that Rosie had loved to hear Flora read to them. Her daughter had enjoyed this time of year – scuffing her feet through masses of fallen leaves in the park. And the preparations for Christmas had filled her with excitement, despite her never receiving much in her stocking. The Christmas story was pure magic to her and she had lived in hope of one day getting a doll with eyes that opened and shut.

Last Christmas had been terrible. Flora's throat was suddenly tight and she wanted to cry.

'What is it?' said Mike quietly.

She glanced up at him, her cheeks flushed from the heat of the fire, and shook her head wordlessly. He reached out a hand and caught her free one, holding it firmly in his strong clasp.

She was comforted and was able to raise a smile minutes later when George, with a dirty face and cut knees, arrived home with a tale of Mad Hewey who came round selling Aunt Sally, a red disinfectant, from a handcart. He was a huge man and not quite right in the head.

'You should have seen him, Mam,' said the boy, hardly noticing Mike in his rush to get the story out. 'He went crazy! There were these two gangs of lads hurling bricks and stones at each other. One gang said the other lot had been pinching their bommie wood.'

'You didn't join in, I hope,' interrupted Flora in a worried voice.

'Nah!' He avoided her eyes. 'We were only watching. But one of the bricks hit Hewey's cart and smashed a bottle. The next thing he was pulling corks out and laying into them with a bottle in each hand. There were gobsful of Aunt Sally going everywhere. You should have seen the gangs scatter.' He laughed.

'Sounds fun,' said Mike drily. 'He would have been useful in the war.'

George looked at him and grinned. 'Germans drowned in a swamp of Aunt Sally. We could always use him against the Russians. Mad Hewey turns Reds redder. Hi, Mike! I thought you'd gone back to America.'

'He did – but he's back,' said Flora, looking at her son with a faint smile. 'And if you want any tea, my lad, then you'd better go and wash your hands and face.'

George grimaced but obeyed.

'Was anybody hurt?' asked Flora as she dished out the food.

Her son paused in cramming half a round of bread in his mouth. 'One bloke had his head split open – but he didn't go unconscious or anything.'

Flora shook her head at him. 'Who needs another war when you can kill each other off over here!'

'Ma-am! Nobody's *dead*!'

'It sounds like it's more by luck than anything else,' said Mike wryly. 'What was this fight all about, did you say?'

'Bommie wood.' George picked up a fork and stabbed it in the dish of purple beetroot. 'It's for Guy Fawkes Night. We burn a Guy on a bonfire,' he said with relish. 'He was a Cattywack who tried to blow up the Houses of Parliament in King James' time. That was before *our* civil war,' he added in a kindly tone to Mike. 'You had your own, didn't you? The Confederates against the Yankees. Me grandad told me all about it. *His* grandfather used to sail on a ship that brought cotton from the South for the mills up Lancashire.'

'That would be before my family's time,' said Mike. 'My grandfather went to America from Ireland in the late 1880s.'

'So your grandfather really did kiss the Blarney stone,' interpolated Flora.

'Sure.' He smiled. 'I keep promising myself that I'll go and do the same one day.'

'D'you think that's necessary,' she said demurely, sitting on his right hand side and taking up her spoon. 'I think you can blether on all right as it is.'

'Is that a back-handed compliment?' He moved the flowers slightly so he could see her face the better.

Her eyes gleamed. 'I'm sure you could charm the birds off the trees.'

He raised an eyebrow. 'Can I persuade you to go out with me — that's what I want to know?'

She placed a spoonful of food in her mouth. 'Perhaps.'

'Great. Let the good times roll.' He smiled and she was suddenly unsure of him, and of herself.

'Some things haven't changed,' she said quickly. 'As long as we both realise that.'

'Sure we do.' He picked up his fork again, still smiling. And she wondered just what was in his mind and if it was the same as in hers. If so she was going to have to watch her step with him.

There was a spring in Flora's walk as she went to work the next morning despite the chilling smog that shrouded privets and houses and caused lamp posts to become unexpected hazards. Mike had not stayed late because he had to return to the base. She would not see him again till next Saturday

180

which was perhaps just as well because it would give her time to get her senses in order. She still felt a little like she was walking in a dream.

When she arrived at the bakery it was to discover that Maggie had raging toothache. 'It's real agony,' groaned the older woman, nursing her jaw.

'You shouldn't have come in,' said Flora sympathetically. 'There's nothing worse than toothache.'

'Going the dentist's is worse,' said Maggie. 'But I'll have to go this afternoon.'

The news didn't exactly make Flora's day but she was happier in her own shoes than poor Maggie's.

Flora was placing some cakes on a plate just before opening time after lunch when Mr Brown sauntered in. She ignored him and carried on with her work.

'Starting early to impress me, are you?' he said in his light rapid voice, a cigarette burning between his fingers as he walked along the other side of the counter.

'No, Mr Brown.' She drew back slightly as he leaned across the counter towards her. 'I'm just doing my job.'

His dark eyes surveyed her carefully. 'You're a good worker, Mrs Cooke, if a little prim and proper.' He lifted the counter flap and came her side.

Flora spared him a quick glance and made to brush past him with the empty tray in her hand, but he prevented her by blocking her path. She tried to go round him but he sidestepped and they collided. 'Say, "Excuse me, Mr Brown." His eyes gleamed with amusement.

She drew a quick breath. 'Excuse me, Mr Brown, but I haven't time to play games.'

'Haven't you? What a pity, Mrs Cooke, because you know what they say. All work and no play – '

'I know. Makes Jack a dull boy – or, I suppose, in this case you mean me a dull girl.' She stared at him. 'I am here to work.' She tried to get past him again but he pressed his body against hers and edged her against the counter.

'How about a kiss?' he whispered against her cheek.

She sighed heavily and was about to tell him to grow up when the doorbell jangled and he released her quickly.

Smoothing down her overall she turned towards the counter, hurriedly assuming a smile.

'Hello, Flo, you look flustered,' said Hilda, staring at her hard before her gaze fluttered to Mr Brown.

Flora wondered just how long her sister had been standing outside and whether she had been looking through the window. 'Can I help you, madam?' she asked politely.

'How nice and posh!' Hilda's gaze came to rest on Flora briefly. 'I'll have a jam tart.' She nudged her sister's arm as her eyes went back to Mr Brown, who was watching them. 'Introduce me, Flo.'

'No,' said Flora shortly, turning away to take a jam tart from a plate and putting it in a bag.

'Dog in the manger,' breathed Hilda, leaning on the counter. 'Who is he?'

'Mr Brown, my boss.' Flora's voice was emotionless. 'And you're better having nothing to do with him.'

Hilda's eyes glittered. 'Just because you were in a clinch with him? You must be joking! What a gorgeous-looking man.'

'Isn't he just!' Flora raised her eyebrows. 'Are you fancying him now, as well as Mike?'

'Always have more than one string to your bow, Flo.' Hilda's hand went to her hair, smoothing it. 'Does he come into the shop often? What's his first name?'

'Who?'

'Your boss, funny face.'

'Kevin,' said Flora. 'And you're paying for that jam tart.'

Hilda threw a shilling on the counter. 'Kevin,' she murmured. 'I quite like that.' Her teeth bit into the tart. 'Not Stephen,' she said with her mouth full.

'No.'

Hilda gazed at her thoughtfully. 'You are a dark horse. I'll find out who this Stephen is, you know.'

Flora shrugged and gave the change to Hilda. 'Forget it.'

'You'd like me to — but I sense a mystery, Flo. And I've always loved a good thriller.' A smile of anticipation lit her face.

'There's nothing thrilling about Stephen,' she said promptly, suddenly amused by her sister's persistence. 'You're wasting your time.'

Hilda frowned and was silent a moment. 'You could be lying to me, of course,' she said at last. 'Kevin could really be called Stephen.'

'He could,' said Flora with her tongue in her cheek, deciding to play her sister along. 'But then, he could be just one of many men in my life.'

'More than two? You?' Hilda put the last of the jam tart in her mouth. 'You're kidding me,' she mumbled, staring.

Flora's eyes widened. 'Of course I am. You know me — true blue.'

Hilda began to say something else but the shop bell jangled and several customers came in. Flora began to serve them and Hilda moved away, nearer to where Mr Brown stood, still leaning on the counter.

Out of the corner of her eye Flora watched them, wondering what her sister was getting up to this time, but to her relief it was not long before she heard Hilda saying 'Bye!' and Mr Brown went into the back room.

He came back in when the shop had emptied again. 'Your sister,' he said, fidgeting with a doily on a plate. 'She looks a bit like you.'

'A bit,' said Flora calmly. 'But we're not alike in personality.' She wondered what was coming next.

'No,' he murmured, staring at her with his brows puckered. 'She's switched on and you're not.' Another customer came in. He walked away, and did not trouble her for the rest of that Friday. She was glad after all that Hilda had come in.

Vivien was difficult to get out of bed the next morning. 'Your mam's coming to take you out, remember?' said Flora as she shrugged herself into her coat.

'Oh, goody gumdrops.' Vivien gave a wide yawn.

Flora glanced at George who was reading the *Wizard* comic. 'I'm going to work now. You'll see Viv out?'

He nodded and Flora left.

'I wish you were coming,' said Vivien to George, moodily

tracing a pattern on the tablecloth with her spoon. 'Or Rosie was still here.'

'You'll be all right without us,' muttered George, not looking up from his comic. He still found it difficult to talk about his sister, but Viv seemed to have no trouble.

'It'd be better with you,' she said with conviction. 'I wished it was Mike or Uncle Steve taking us all out. I wish I had a dad.' She stirred her porridge slowly. 'I feel safer when there's a man around.'

'You just like men,' drawled George, crossing his ankles as he put his feet up on one of the dining chairs. 'You're like your mother.'

'I am not!' Vivien scowled and made a swipe at his foot.

'Oh yes you are!' snapped George, aiming a kick at her. 'Your mam's a flirt. She's always been a flirt.'

'Aunty Flo has boyfriends.' said Vivien. 'There's nothing wrong with that.' She was smiling now. 'There's Mike – and Uncle Steve.'

George grunted. 'They're only friends. She won't marry either of them.' He gazed unseeingly at a far wall, suddenly uneasy.

'How d'you know?' said Vivien. 'They both fancy her and Mike kissed her when he was here.'

George looked down at his comic. 'I've kissed Kathleen Murphy but it doesn't mean I'm going to marry her. And Mam'd never go to America.' He lifted his head. 'Although I prefer Mike to Stephen. I wonder if he can get me some American comics? I should have asked.'

Vivien swallowed a mouthful of porridge and licked the spoon. 'Maybe he'll just bring some next Saturday.'

'Who's bringing what next Saturday?' They both turned as they heard a noise at the door and saw Hilda standing there. 'Not ready yet, Viv?' she drawled, taking the cigarette from her lips. 'I thought you'd be champing at the bit.'

'I've nearly finished,' said Vivien, exchanging a quick look with her cousin.

'Well, hurry up, because I want to get to town. I thought we'd look round the shops.'

Vivien swallowed a groan. She knew that nothing would be bought for her. She would be kept hanging around while Mam tried on this frock and that. She wished that her mam had never come back — because sooner or later there was bound to be trouble.

Flora was thinking much the same thing — but about next Saturday — as she walked home from work. What if Mike came just as Hilda was dropping Viv off? She'd explode. And what would Mike do? She pondered the question and decided that he'd somehow manage to bluff his way out. Was she an idiot going out with him, knowing that he had the power to disturb her? Probably. She grimaced. There was no backing out. Hadn't she determined not to let her sister have things all her own way for once?

Opening her front door, Flora was surprised to hear a man's voice. Then she caught Hilda's laugh, heard the voice again and knew that her sister had the solution to the mystery of Stephen. She did not feel too pleased about that, but there was nothing for it but to go in.

Four pairs of eyes turned to her. George's were bored but Vivien's showed undisguised pleasure as she came to take her shopping bag from her aunt. Hilda's expression was definitely mischievous — while Stephen looked guilty.

He rose from his seat by the fire. 'Hello, Floss. Your Hilda's just been telling me about her trip to Paris.'

Flora raised her eyebrows. 'Paris?' She turned her scrutiny on her sister. 'Nice for some — and there's me believing you were existing on the breadline.'

Hilda pulled a face at her, before smiling and saying, 'Steve's being bringing me up to date on what's been happening to him. Exciting to be his own boss, don't you agree, Flo? We'll see him living in Blundellsands one day with all the posh nobs.'

Flora crossed the room to the fire. 'I didn't know the Old Man had retired?'

'I persuaded him,' said Stephen. 'He was getting past it.'

'So what does he do with himself?' She held her hands out to the fire. 'I thought the firm was his life.'

Stephen shrugged. 'He's going to take up bowling.'

185

'In winter?'

'He needs a rest.' He shifted uncomfortably and ran a hand through his dark curling hair. 'It'll do him good to have nothing to do but be waited on. It's what he wanted — one of his nephews in the driving seat.'

'He wanted Jimmy,' said Hilda. She sighed. 'Poor Jimmy! He thought he'd be doing your job.' She stretched out nylon clad legs, and her gaze flickered over Vivien before returning to Stephen. 'He was so upset that November I saw him. Now he's dead as well as Tom. Poor Tom. Hitler has a lot to answer for.'

'Why are they poor?' said Vivien. 'D'you say that because they're dead?'

'Well — yes, of course,' said Hilda impatiently. 'Who wants to be dead.'

'Don't you believe in Heaven?' Vivien fixed her with an unblinking stare. 'You'll go to Hell if you don't.' She turned her attention on Flora. 'They're all happy, aren't they, Aunty Flo? Just like the little match girl in the story, who kept lighting the matches to keep warm and saw pictures in the flames. And then she saw her granny who'd gone to Heaven, and she went with her like a shooting star through the sky. They were happy because they were together, and she wasn't cold any more, and they were with God,' she finished with supreme confidence. 'And God looks after us all, doesn't he, Aunty Flo?'

'Yes, love,' she said lightly. This was no time for doubts.

There was a short silence which Hilda broke in a tight voice. 'Very nice idea, Viv, but I'd still rather be here.' She got to her feet. 'Anyway I'm going out so I'd better get cracking. You can see me to the door, Flo.' She faced Stephen and oozed effusiveness, holding out her hand to him. 'It was lovely seeing you again.' She patted his arm. 'Take care of yourself now and make a success of everything. I'm sure you can, and probably we'll see each other again sometime.'

'Sure,' said Stephen, flushing slightly and dropping her hand as he glanced at Flora.

She did not know whether to be amused or annoyed as she followed her sister out. 'What is it you want to say?' she murmured, her hand on the latch.

Hilda smiled. 'How well you know me, little sister.' She leaned against the lobby wall. 'Me and Stephen had a nice chat.'

'Oh aye,' said Flora drily. 'About you, I suppose.'

'My favourite subject,' murmured Hilda. 'But we did touch upon you. Why didn't you tell me it was *that* Stephen? He's not what you'd call good-looking now but he's got plenty of dough.'

'Tons of it, I suppose,' said Flora, instantly alert to the way her sister's mind worked. She leaned against the other wall and folded her arms.

'I suppose the woman who married him would have no money worries.' Hilda's voice sounded loud in the confined space and Flora wanted to hush her.

'Probably.' She almost laughed. Was her sister considering Stephen now as a target for marriage? 'He's got a car,' she said mischievously. 'Quite comfortable.'

Hilda looked at her sharply. 'You've been in it?'

'Loads of times. He's asked me to marry him.'

Hilda stared at her. 'And?'

'I haven't made up my mind yet but he's prepared to wait until I do.'

'Hmmm! He's got that awful scar on his face but the other side's all right.' She shivered slightly. 'From that side he looks a bit like Jimmy. In fact, he talks like him. It's like listening to a ghost.'

'They *were* brothers. And I hope you're not thinking what I think you're thinking.' She straightened up from the wall.

'If you don't grab him, then someone else will,' said Hilda, opening the door.

'I think he only wants me,' retorted Flora, smiling.

'Sez you.' Hilda rammed her hands in her pockets, shivering in the cold wind. 'I wonder if he'd like to give me a lift now?'

'On your bike,' said Flora. 'He came to see me.' And she closed the door with a gusty sigh of relief. Sisters! She almost laughed. It would be interesting if Hilda did make a play at Stephen but for now she had to go in and be nice to him, when all she wanted was her tea and to put her feet up.

187

He stood immediately Flora entered the room. 'It was a surprise seeing your Hilda,' he said quickly. 'The war doesn't seem to have changed her much.'

'No.' said Flora, beginning to empty her shopping bag. 'She was on munitions for a while, and of course she had Viv, but I think she actually enjoyed most of the war.'

'Yanks, I suppose,' muttered Stephen. 'I saw she was wearing nylons.'

Flora's hand, holding half a pound of mince, halted in mid-air. 'Yes,' she said slowly. 'But she's got nice legs for them, as you probably noticed.'

Stephen flushed. 'Your legs are nicer.'

'Thank you.' She smiled. 'What have you come for, Steve?'

He leaned against the table. 'I thought you might like to go to the pictures. There's a good film on at the Majestic.'

'It's kind of you but I'm tired and I've things to do.'

'Couldn't you do them some other time?' He stared at her moodily.

'When? I work all day, remember?'

'Is tea going to be long, Mam?' said George, getting up from his chair and going over to the wireless.

'About half an hour.' Flora looked at Stephen. 'Have you had yours?'

He shook his head. 'There'll be something ready for me at home.'

'You'll be going then?'

'I suppose so.' Reluctantly he moved towards the door.

She saw him up the lobby. Away from the children he tried to draw her into his arms but she resisted. 'I haven't time, Steve. I've got a meal to get ready.'

'You never seem to have time for me,' he muttered, holding her hand. 'I suppose you're still blaming me for Rosie and not liking me for telling you about Tom.'

She suddenly felt sorry for him. 'Not any more.' She aimed a peck at his cheek but he turned his head quickly and kissed her on the mouth, putting his arms round her far too tightly. 'Ste-phen!' she said against his mouth. 'Let me go!'

'Marry me, Floss.' He sounded quite desperate. 'I really want you.'

'I've told you, I'm not ready to marry anybody at the moment.'

'You were always too good for Tom. He used you, Floss, to get back at your Hilda for going out with our Jimmy.'

She was irritated, although over the last year she had wondered about that herself. 'Thanks very much,' she murmured. 'That doesn't make me feel any better about it all.'

'I'm sorry,' he said quickly. 'Forgive me.' And he kissed her again before she could say anything.

Inwardly she sighed but she allowed him his kiss, which went on far too long before she pushed him away.

She closed the door on him with relief. Then a giggle rose inside her. Tinker, tailor, soldier, sailor — rich man, poor man, beggar man, thief? It was a game that Hilda had played with plum stones as a girl. She had always cheated if it had not worked out the way she wanted; pinching Flora's stones to make them up to rich man.

Which man did her sister really have her eye on? She suspected that Hilda did not know herself yet — and only time would tell.

Chapter Fifteen

The following week she arrived just as Flora was making her way out. She smiled like a child who'd found a bar of chocolate. 'Hello, sister, on your way to work?'

'Well, I'm not heading for a slow boat to China,' said Flora drily.

'What a pity.' Hilda's eyes danced. 'Remember how we used to go in the Chinese laundry with the sheets and you'd avoid that bit in front of the counter?'

Flora could not prevent a smile. 'That was because you told me there was a trap door there – and if I fell in I'd end up as a white slave girl for a Chinese emperor.'

'Alas, neither of us ever did!' Hilda gazed at her fingernails. 'Life's been rather dull. But it's brightening up again now.'

'Oh aye? Going out with Mike tonight, are you?' she said sweetly.

'Mike!' Hilda's head lifted abruptly, and she paused, before saying, 'Oh, yeah. Mike's fun.' She stared across the street. 'I was talking to your boss the other evening. I met him by Anfield football ground.'

'Oh?'

'He was telling me about his war experiences. And about being in India till we gave them their country back. You know he's strangled men with his bare hands,' she said with relish.

'I can see him doing it,' said Flora drily.

'He's a bit younger than me but tough and strong.' A small smile played about Hilda's mouth. 'But I quite like men like that. I find them exciting. Kevin reminds me of

James Mason in that film with Margaret Lockwood.'

'*The Wicked Lady*.'

'That's right.'

'You're daft if you like men treating you like that,' said Flora.

Her sister shrugged. 'We're different types, Flo. Now Stephen would probably suit you better.' She frowned. 'He's so hard-working and dependable. He'll probably go far.'

'Probably be very rich eventually,' said Flora with a serious air. 'And lots of money can't be sneezed at.'

'You've changed your tune,' said Hilda, wrinkling her dainty nose.

Flora opened her eyes wide. 'Well, life's been hard for me the last few years – and I don't want to be going out to work forever. I'd like some comfort.' Her smile was honeyed. 'Anyway, enough about men. I have to get to work. Don't be late bringing Viv back. I'm going out, and Mrs Murphy's going to have her.'

'With Stephen?' called Hilda.

'Mind your own business.' Flora flung the words over her shoulder and ran up the street.

'D'you think Princess Elizabeth will 'ave a boy or a girl?' said Maggie, putting a plate of scones in the window.

Flora looked up from wiping the counter and smiled. 'I should imagine they want a boy, just like Carmel Murphy who's expecting in the spring.'

'I wonder what they'll call it,' muttered Maggie, taking a well-earned rest and sitting on a stool. 'Philip after its father or George after the King? It's due soon, isn't it?'

'A couple of weeks,' said Flora. 'And then there'll be jars out, I bet. Champagne and caviar! Then it'll probably be roast lamb and mint sauce – new potatoes – no, they'll be out of season. Make it roast potatoes or Purée de Pommes de Terre!' She waved a cloth with a flourish.

'What's them?' asked Maggie with a laugh. 'Yer're sounding in a cheerful mood, Flo.'

'Very thin mashed potatoes,' replied Flora, knowing that she could not tell Maggie why she was in a good mood. Maggie probably would not approve of the Yanks. 'We'll probably have potatoes done in the embers on Bonfire Night next week. Nice and black and burnt! You should see the wood that our George and his mates have been collecting. It's in our yard and I keep falling over it. I don't doubt they'll be out again getting more.'

'Lads!' exclaimed Maggie. 'Where d'yer get yer patience from, Flo?'

'I often lose it,' she said ruefully, stemming the slight anxiety she always experienced lately when thinking of George. 'Here's a couple of customers.' And she turned to the first one, hoping the day would go quickly.

Flora could not prevent a feeling of excitement as she made her way home from work. Perhaps Mike would already be there waiting for her as he had been last week? But maybe Hilda would be there as well? Hopefully not.

She had barely reached the top of her street when she heard her name being called, and to her surprise she saw Kathleen Murphy speeding towards her in the dark. 'What is it? What's the panic?' She seized the girl's hands before they collided against her chest.

'It's George,' cried the girl in a tearful voice. 'The floor's collapsed upstairs an' he's trapped.'

'What?' For a moment Flora could not move. This was something she had always feared.

'Yer'd better hurry. That Yank who used to come here has gone to help.'

'Mike,' said Flora in a dazed voice. 'Show me!' she ordered, taking the girl's hand and beginning to run down the street.

'George was collecting bommie wood,' panted Kathleen. 'In that bombed house round the corner. The Yank told me to get somebody to phone the fire brigade an' an ambulance. But I didn't know where to go and I knew it was time for yer to come home so I ran for yer.'

Flora made no reply as they came to an abrupt halt in front of a row of houses. Some were lit up, but several had been damaged in a landmine explosion, and although parts of their roofs existed as well as walls, the windows were unglazed and like dark empty eyesockets gazing out on the long front gardens and the road. She and Kathleen clambered over broken clumps of sandstone that cluttered the path and went towards the glimmer of wavering light they could see.

A couple of boys looked up as they approached, and despite their filthy faces and clothes Flora recognised them as regular mates of George. 'Why?' she demanded in an angry breathy voice. 'We've got a yard full of wood.' They made no answer, just staring at her, their eyes gleaming in their mucky faces. Kathleen pushed one of them aside and climbed over more rubble in the direction of a large bay window. Flora left the boys to follow her. She hoisted herself up on to the window ledge but before she could climb in, a voice said, 'Don't come in.'

'Mike! It's me!' Her hands shook so much that she almost fell inside.

'All right, Flora.' He sounded tired. 'But you still don't come in. Is the fire brigade on it's way?'

'No!' She moistened her mouth. 'Kathleen came for me. Where's George? Is he — ?' Fear suddenly suspended her voice.

'He's knocked out but he's okay,' Mike's voice quickly reassured her. 'But don't waste time talking, honey — go and phone. I need help to free him.'

'Can't I help? We could dig together and —'

'Hell, Flo! If it was that easy I could have had the guys digging,' he rasped. 'Just do as you're told and go, for Jesus' sake. Or the rest of the house might come down and we'll both be buried, and I don't fancy that!'

Without another word Flora went to the nearby newsagent's where there was a telephone. On the way Kathleen told her how George had got up on the roof by a drainpipe to take some slates off and make a hole. Apparently the stairs inside the house had already been removed but the boys had had their eye to the wood upstairs. 'He's not gonna die is he?' she demanded of Flora in a trembling voice.

'Don't even think it,' said Flora fiercely, fearing that the thought might foster reality. They came to the shop and went inside.

Flora and Kathleen had just got back to the ruined house when they heard the fire engine's bell come clanging on the air.

The news about George had spread and a crowd had gathered at the bottom of the garden. Stephen suddenly pushed his way towards her, his face taut. 'I heard that George is trapped in there. God, Floss! What made him go in? The whole place could come tumbling down!'

She stared at him, her mouth trembling. 'He's a boy,' she said unsteadily, and turning from him she ran towards the house.

She straddled the window sill. 'Mike! The firemen are here. Where are you?' Her eyes tried to pierce the darkness.'

'We're in the back room.' His voice was husky. 'Don't worry, he's still breathing. I've managed to shift some of the beams and rubble but there's a great big cast iron bath wedged over part of him. It's protected him a bit from some of the stuff that came down with it.' He paused. 'You're all right, aren't you, honey?'

She swallowed. 'I'm not going to pieces if that's what you mean. You! Are you hurt?'

'A few scratches. Don't you come in, whatever happens.'

'No, I won't,' she said. 'Here comes the cavalry.' She thought she heard him laugh as she got quickly out of the way.

It seemed an age to Flora before they brought George out. She gazed anxiously down into his filthy face before her eyes went beyond him to where Mike stood in his shirt sleeves, his jacket slung over his shoulder. He was as mucky as George. 'Thanks,' she whispered, just as she felt a hand close round her arm.

'Is he all right, Floss?' said Stephen.

'I'm not a doctor,' she said impatiently. Turning, she saw one of the stretcher bearers. She had not heard the ambulance arrive. Within minutes George was wrapped in a red blanket and was in the vehicle. Flora followed him and as she did, Stephen caught her arm again. 'I'll follow you in the car. You'll be wanting a lift back,' he called as she climbed into the ambulance. She made no reply, and the next moment the ambulance roared off up the road.

Kathleen stared at it in dismay and her bottom lip quivered. She looked over at Mike. 'They've left us be'ind.'

'It's okay, kid.' His eyes were on Stephen running down the road. Kathleen pulled on his sleeve.

'What'll we do?'

'Do?' Slowly he brought his attention to bear on her. She looked so worried that he put his arm round her. 'You're one of the Murphy girls, aren't you?'

'Aye. What'll we do?' She looked up at him.

Mike smiled. 'Go and ask your mom for a cup of tea.'

'Yer think George'll be all right?'

'Sure.'

He began to push his way through the dispersing crowds. Several people slapped him on the back as he passed. 'Well done, Yank.' He winced but smiled crookedly as he sucked blood off his knuckles. Then they collided with Hilda and Vivien.

'They told us our George had had an accident,' cried the girl. 'Was that him going off in the ambulance?' Mike nodded.

'You look a mess,' said Hilda, frowning at him. 'Our Viv said that you were seeing our Flo. Did she go in the ambulance? Was that her fiancé I saw speaking to her?'

Mike opened his mouth to say something but Vivien tugged on his sleeve. 'Mike! Mike! George isn't dead, is he?'

'No, Viv.' His expression was serious. 'Your aunt Flo's gone in the ambulance with him. He's roughed up and unconscious but I'm sure he'll be okay.'

'Good.' She let out a great sigh of relief. 'I was worried.'

'I told you there was nothing to be worried about,' said Hilda brightly. 'Now what do we do? I was going out but I suppose I'll have to stay with you.'

'Was?' Mike raised his eyebrows. 'You mean you mightn't go now?' he drawled.

Her eyes widened. 'I can't leave Viv on her own.' She hesitated. 'Although our Flo did say something about a Mrs Murphy looking after her.'

'I'll take care of it,' said Mike, his expression tight. 'You go off on your date.'

'Are you sure?' Hilda's voice was concerned. 'I don't want to leave you in the lurch. I could break my date.'

Mike shook his head. 'That's okay. I've got nothing better to do,' he said quietly.

'Thanks, Mike.' She leaned forward and kissed him lightly on the cheek. 'You are kind.' She turned to Vivien, who was staring at her with a calculating expression.

'Bye, Mam,' she said, waving a hand slowly.

'Bye, sweetheart.' Hilda blew Vivien a kiss, and brushing past her went on down the road.

Mike, aching and sore, with the girls either side of him, came to the Murphy's house. Carmel was standing in the doorway with Bernadette in her arms. 'Why, if it isn't Flo's Yank,' she said with a welcoming smile. 'You look wild. Come on inside and have a cup of tea.'

'He saved George, Mam,' said Kathleen in a tired voice. 'And now he's gone to the hossie.'

'Is that right now,' said Carmel, slanting her eldest daughter a slightly anxious look. 'I'm just glad that yer weren't with him.' She led the way in, saying in an aside to Mike. 'Follows that boy here, there and everywhere. Even though he's quite rough with her since Rosie went. I understand that it's been hard on the boy, but I wish that she wasn't so fond of him because he's a Protestant and we're gonna have to split them up sooner or later. I wish she'd gone to be a nun now instead of Mary.'

Mike made no answer, sinking on to a chair as she dumped Bernadette on the kitchen floor. Several other girls turned and looked at him, then at their mother as she lifted the steaming kettle from the hob.

Carmel gave him a speculative glance. 'George was telling our Kat'leen yer were back. Still fond of Flo, are yer, Yank? Cried her eyes out here, she did, when you left last time.'

'Did she?' His smile was the slightest bit grim. 'I've been told that there's someone else on the scene.'

There was a brief silence before Carmel said, 'Aye, I've seen him. A war hero by all accounts. Was wounded and got himself a medal. Has a car and a few bob. It could turn a woman's head — especially when life is hard.'

'Flora doesn't get her head turned easily,' he muttered, ramming his hands in his pockets. 'The Flora I used to know didn't, anyway.'

'She's had a tough time and a woman gets weary of coping alone.' She handed him a cup of tea and his dust begrimed hands curled round its warmth as their eyes met. 'But I'll tell you this, Yank —'

'Mike.'

'Mike.' She smiled. 'George doesn't like him.'

'Their Hilda said that they were engaged.'

'Well now, I wouldn't know about that. Flo hasn't mentioned it to me and she doesn't wear a ring.'

Mike stared at her thoughtfully, nodded and drank his tea, half listening to Kathleen telling Vivien, in a breathless whisper, what had happened to George. He drained his cup and got to his feet just as Mr Murphy came in.

The little man gave him a belligerent look. 'What's this now, woman? You entertaining the Yanks while me back's turned?'

'Don't be a bigger idjit than yer normally are, Joseph. He's Flo's Yank and he's just been after saving George's life.' Quickly she told him what had happened.

'Is that right now?' He nodded his head vigorously several times as he stared at Mike. 'You'll be needing a drink, Yank.' He lowered his voice. 'I've got a drop of whiskey.'

'I wouldn't like to deprive you,' said Mike, restlessly turning his cap between his fingers.

'No trouble, laddie.' Little Paddy winked at him. 'I'm not short. The Little People see me all right.' He went up the lobby and into the parlour, coming back with a full bottle of Irish whiskey. He proceeded to pour two generous measures into cups. His wife gave him a frown and he dropped a short measure into her tea.

Mr Murphy gave a toast. 'To the lad's recovery — but not too quick. It'll be a mite more peaceful around here without him.'

'Da — ad!' Kathleen's tone rebuked him.

'Aye, well, girlie. It's true. But I wish him well. He's a sore trial to his mam. Here's to her.' They all drank.

It was good whiskey, thought Mike, enjoying the warmth spreading inside him. Black Market probably. Fell off the back of a ship from the Emerald Isle. The thought made him smile and Little Paddy put another tot in his and Mike's cup.

The Irishman told him how he was labouring on the building now but soon passed on to former glories, telling about his racing experiences and how he had nearly won the Grand National before the war.

Mike sat, only half listening, his thoughts of Flora and a man called Stephen over-ridden by Paddy's voice, which had gone on now to speak of Ireland. He reminded him of his own grandfather with his tales of giants and monsters in bogs, of banshees and Saint Patrick and the high king of Tara. In later years it had been tales of the English — the old enemy — and the fight for independence.

He lost track of time. The fire was stoked up and Mrs Murphy vanished upstairs with several of the kids. The bottle went round again, and he heard Vivien ask whether she should go and see if her aunt Flo had come back yet. Flo, lovely Flora, who'd gone and got herself another fella while he'd been away and hadn't told him.

'She'll come looking for yer here, girlie,' said Little Paddy in a slurred voice, getting up and searching for his fiddle. 'Don't you be aworrin' now.' He'd hardly got into his stride with a dancing tune when the knocker sounded.

Vivien and Kathleen went to answer it and a few moments later Flora entered, pale but composed. 'Hello, Mr Murphy.' Her face brightened. 'Hi, Mike. I wasn't sure if you'd still be around.'

'Faithful, that's me.' He rose hurriedly, only to sway slightly when he was up. 'How's George?' he said carefully.

For several seconds she stared at him without speaking, then quietly she told him: 'He's got a fractured skull and a tiny crack in one of his vertebrae. He's got to stay flat on his back for several weeks while it knits. And —' she paused and her throat moved '— if he's sensible, then he should be able to walk again.'

He let out a long breath. 'That must be a relief to you.' The words were skilfully articulated. 'Did he come — round at all?'

'Yes.' She grimaced. 'He was sick in the ambulance and talking gibberish. But before I left, he seemed to know who I was. Although he kept going on about God punishing him and that he was sorry. I don't know what he was talking about.'

Little Paddy decided to take part in the conversation. 'As long as he's all right, girlie.' He lifted the bottle. 'Will you be having a drink to calm yer nerves?'

'Whiskey?' She smiled slightly. 'No thanks. It's not my cup of <u>tea</u>. I think I'd best be getting Viv to bed.'

He nodded. 'Perhaps it's just as well. You probably haven't got the head for it.'

'I doubt I have.' She switched her gaze to Mike. 'Are you staying here?' Her tone was hesitant.

'I was coming with you,' he said slowly. 'But I wasn't sure if you'd have the boyfriend with you.'

She stared at him and there was a shadow in her eyes. 'I take it you mean Steve?'

'Yeah, that's his name. I haven't met him, have I?' There was a sneering note in his voice which she was not accustomed to.

'No,' Flora said wearily. She turned her back on him and thanked Carmel, who had just come into the room, for looking after Vivien.

'No trouble, Flo,' she answered, her brown eyes going from Flora to Mike. 'How's George?'

Flora told her and then spoke to Vivien. The girl came and took her hand. They both looked at Mike. 'Are you coming?' said Flora.

'Why not?' he rasped and followed them out.

It was chilly and dark inside Flora's house and for a moment the three of them huddled together in the doorway of the kitchen. Flora was wondering just how much whiskey Mike had drank and what time he had to get back to the base. 'You sit down,' she murmured, deciding not to worry about him, and set about bringing a little light and warmth to the scene.

Vivien was fed and escorted to bed and when Flora came down Mike seemed to be asleep in the chair by the fire. She poked the fire noisily and his eyes opened to focus on her face. 'Drunkard,' she said softly.

'Not that drunk.' He winced as he eased himself up in the chair and looked about him. 'Where's Viv?'

'Bed.' She hoped he was drunk enough to forget about Stephen for the moment. She leaned forward and took one of his hands. 'You need some ointment on these.'

'They'll heal.' His fingers curled about hers. 'You okay?'

Her throat moved and for a moment she did not speak, then she nodded. 'You're filthy,' she said huskily. 'You could do with a wash.'

'I need a bath.'

'It'd take too long to fill. I'll bring you a bowl and you can strip off here in front of the fire.'

He studied her face carefully. 'Strip? I'm not that dirty,' he drawled. 'You aren't planning on having your wicked way with me, are you?'

A corner of her mouth lifted. 'Perish the thought – I'm only asking for your shirt.'

His fair brows rose. 'You'll have to help me. I'm a mite stiff.' He pulled her down on his knee and she did not resist. It made it easier to undo his shirt buttons.

'You'll get yourself as mucky as me,' he muttered, rubbing his cheek against hers.

'I don't mind.' She took a deep breath. 'I'm really grateful for what you did for George.'

He stared at her through narrowed eyes. 'He's a mate. And you're a very forward lady, taking my clothes off.'

'One shirt,' she said, pulling it off him. 'And you're drunk.'

He quirked a tawny eyebrow. 'My trousers could do with brushing.'

Flora said nothing, only smiling as she got to her feet and went into the back kitchen. When she came back he was sitting in his underwear. She stopped abruptly in the doorway. 'Are you crazy? You'll catch a chill like that.'

He waved an arm. 'Not if you come and keep me warm,' he said unevenly.

'You're indecent,' she scolded, half-filling the bowl from the steaming kettle.

'You didn't think what we did two years ago indecent.' His eyes were on her face. 'We were both naked as Adam and Eve without their fig leaves.'

'That was two years and I didn't think I would ever see

you again.' She attempted to stem the wave of desire that was washing over her in a hot tide. 'Times change,' she added in a voice that quivered as she straightened up.

'It's this Stephen,' he muttered. 'Stiff upper lip and all that, I bet.'

'You're jealous,' she mocked, going over to him, and holding out the flannel.

'Hilda said he's your fiancé.' He scowled.

'Did she now?' She smiled. His arm reached up and pulled her down on to his knee. 'He wants to marry me and I could so easily be engaged to him,' she whispered. 'But I'm not.' Their faces were so close that she could have counted his long light brown lashes. 'I don't love him.'

He seized the flannel and tossed it aside. Then he kissed her with a hunger that took her breath away so that she had to hammer against his chest. He lifted his head and breathed whiskey fumes all over her face. 'Take your clothes off,' he said, so quietly that if she had not been so close she would not have heard him.

'You're joking!' Her voice was flurried.

'No, I'm not. I love you, Flora. I'd marry you at the drop of a hat.'

She flushed and avoided looking into his eyes. 'I don't want to marry anyone at the moment. I want just to float through life without any ties because I'm still hurting from Rosie. And because —' she moistened her lips '— I found out that Tom was a deserter.'

'You mean he's still alive?' Mike's face paled.

'No, no.' She grimaced. 'He returned to his own lines but they thought him an enemy because he didn't know the password and he was shot.'

Some of the colour returned to his face. 'Hell! How did you find it out after all this time?'

'Stephen. He's from the old days — he knew Tom and me and Hilda.' Her voice quivered slightly. 'I had a bit of rough time of it after you told Tony about Viv. Me and Hilda had a big row and she flung at me that she and Tom had slept together.'

He stared at her and swore softly.

'They did go around a lot when they were young,' she

stammered. 'But even then she messed about and two-timed him with Steve's brother. Even so I could hardly believe that Tom and her – ' She swallowed. 'But since Stephen told me about Tom, I've wondered just how well I knew him.'

'When did this Steve tell you all this?' he said softly.

'After Rosie had died. Oh, Mike, there's been so much pain! And now there's George flat on his back. They say he'll walk again, but will he? Football's so important to him. And I couldn't bear it if he was crippled for life.' Her voice broke on a sob, and she buried her head against his bare shoulder. 'I feel that I need help to forget everything just for a while, Mike. Don't ask me to make decisions.'

'Sure, honey. Anything you want.' His voice soothed her. He kissed her gently, then hugged her to him and kissed her again and again. She responded passionately, and they eased down on the floor in front of the fire on the rug. The cat, who had been warming its flanks, protested with loud miaowings at being dispossessed of its comfortable spot and attempted to wriggle between them.

Flora pushed it away. 'Make love to me, Mike,' she whispered. 'I want to forget everything, to feel good.'

His grey eyes gazed into hers. 'Are you certain?'

'Yes,' she said unsteadily. 'If you've got a contraceptive.'

'Hell, Flo.' He laughed weakly. 'You sure take a guy unawares.'

'I don't want a baby. I have enough problems.' She blushed as she returned his regard. 'I've heard about how you fellas are issued with them because of V.D. before you're let loose on the local female population.'

'Yes, but – ' he ran a hand through his untidy light brown hair. ' – did you think I came expecting to make love to you?'

'I don't know!' She put her palms to her burning cheeks. 'Perhaps we'd better forget it.'

'No. You never fail to surprise me, Flora.' His eyes twinkled slightly as he picked up the cat and shut it in the back kitchen. 'I don't fancy having my butt or my front bitten,' he murmured.

'Then you – ?'

'Shhhh! Try to be a bit more romantic. Take your clothes off.'

She stared at him and then stood motionless for a moment. Then abruptly she went over to the lobby door, undoing her cardigan. She listened at the open door for any sound of Vivien waking, then closed the door quietly and walked over to the fire to undress.

He pulled her close again and his hands wandered down her spine, to hug her buttocks and then explore her front. He kissed her in most places. She shivered and began to caress him, before her hands slid upwards and pushed him down with some strength. Her lips roamed the skin of his chest, his nipples, his chin, his mouth. Then he pulled her down on top of him, pressing her length against him, before rolling over and over. Her senses were on fire as their legs entwined and the lower part of their bodies made sensuous contact. For an instant she thought of Rosie and Tom, experienced the keening grief that had pained for so long. Now George was in her mind as she had last seen him — but he was alive, thanks to Mike. Lovely Mike.

He drew away a moment and then he entered her and she gave herself utterly to the physical sensations washing over her, believing that the dispelling of her bitter memories could begin from this moment on. She was not going to allow herself to think about what it would be like when Mike left ... as eventually he would.

That did not bear thinking about.

Chapter Sixteen

'I want to go home, Mam.' George's brown eyes pleaded with her. 'I could lie in bed just as easily there.' Not if he was given the F.A. Cup to drink from would he tell her how embarrassing it was being confined to bed.

'No, you couldn't! This is a special bed,' she said. 'It's got a board underneath to keep your back straight. You know how the one at home sags in the middle.'

George frowned. 'I like my bed, and we could put our own board underneath.'

Flora looked at Mike who looked at George and said, 'It would be a lot of work and worry for your mom – and you know she can't afford to give up her job to look after you.'

George was silent, conflicting emotions flickering across his face.

'The main thing is that you get to walk again, son,' said Flora quietly. 'With a bit of good behaviour on your part you should be home for Christmas.'

'Christmas!' His face clouded with dismay. 'I'll die of boredom if I'm to stay here that long. There's nothing to do.' He made to fling back the covers but Flora's hand prevented him. 'Mam, let me out!'

'You're being stupid. Use your commonsense.' She squeezed his hand.

He subsided, staring at the cage that kept the blankets off his legs. 'I'm being punished,' he muttered. 'It serves me right.'

'If you're talking about taking daft risks, then that's

probably true,' said Flora, exasperated. 'We all pay for our mistakes.'

George shook his head vehemently. 'For letting Rosie die! I should have looked after her better.'

She and Mike stared at him. 'It's over. In the past,' she said in a firm voice. 'You must forget about it.'

'But if I'd only thought –'

'We can't be thinking for other people all the time,' put in Mike, leaning towards him. 'Forgive yourself, kid. And if you believe that you're paying for your mistake – perhaps that's not such a bad thing. Learn from it, and I doubt you'll go climbing into bombed houses again.'

'Too true,' muttered George. 'I won't go climbing anything. But what am I going to do with myself here?'

'I can get you some comics,' said Mike cheerfully.

Flora gave him a look. 'I don't want him wasting all his time reading comics.'

Mike shrugged. 'Come on, Flo. The lad needs some relaxation. Maybe a few good books, as well, and some drawing stuff.' He addressed George. 'Your mam was showing me the mask you did of Guy Fawkes. It's good. If you practised your drawing, there could be a career of some kind in it, George.'

'I want to be a footballer,' he said, moving his head restlessly on the pillow. 'To play for Liverpool. We were top of the League last season.'

'Perhaps you still will, one day,' said Flora, smiling. 'But it won't do you any harm to spend your time here, drawing and reading. It'll stand you in good stead when you go back to school.'

George pulled a face but said he'd be glad of the comics and a couple of good adventure stories. As well as the football *Echo*. Then he tried lifting his head to glance about the cream-painted orthopaedic ward with its large windows overlooking a stretch of lawn surrounded by shrubs. 'That boy over there, with the ginger hair, will never walk again, Mam,' he whispered. 'He's spastic. But you want to see him throw himself from bed to bed. And there's another kid who's had polio and one of his legs is a weird shape.' His brows drew together. 'I'm lucky really.

But I feel so far from home here on the other side of the Mersey.'

'I could wish you nearer but there was no room for you in one hospital and the other was in quarantine because of an outbreak of chicken pox, and you never did catch that. Besides the cleaner air here is better for you.' She smiled encouragingly, relieved that this had not happened a year ago before the National Health Service had come into being. 'You're not that far from Wales. If you could get up and walk outside, the River Dee's really close.'

'I wish I could sit up. It's going to be dead awkward reading and drawing flat on me back.' He added quickly, 'I'm not really complaining.'

'No,' said Mike and Flora in unison with a smile.

Shortly after, visiting time came to an end and they left to get the train.

'It's going to be tough on him,' said Flora with a sigh as she watched the tired-looking countryside go by through the carriage window. They had the compartment to themselves on that slate grey, cold November day.

'He'll cope,' said Mike, squeezing her hand.

'I will too,' she said quietly. 'But I wish you didn't have to go back to the base so soon.'

'So do I,' he responded in heartfelt tones. 'We've got bare concrete floors and not enough stoves to heat the huts. The wind comes whipping in the rain as thick as mist across the Mersey over those flat lands near Warrington. I could do with you in my bed to keep me warm.'

'I'm sorry about last night,' she blurted out. He had slept in George's room. She had felt a hypocrite asking him to do so, but had not wanted Vivien to wake up and find them in bed together.

He shrugged. 'I'm not complaining, Flora. I understand.'

She knew that he did because it had been him who had suggested his leaving by the back way and waiting for her at the tram stop.It reminded her altogether too much of Lena Bryce's antics, and knowing her neighbours she did not doubt that if she kept on sinning with Mike then it would not be long before the whole neighbourhood knew about it. The idea bothered her but she knew that right

206

now she desperately needed him in her life. 'It's not that I'm really worried about my reputation,' she said quickly.

'No.' He smiled.

'You think I am,' she said indignantly.

His smile deepened. 'I think you want to have your cake and eat it, honey. You'd be better marrying me.'

'That's a no go area at the moment and I've told you so.' She rested her chin on her hand. 'I never thought I'd have double standards. I'm a pharisee! I might as well have a whole shipload of lovers! And be hung for a sheep as a lamb,' she said woefully.

'Your house would be a bit crowded,' he said drily. 'And I'd object. Having this Stephen as a rival is bad enough.'

'I haven't slept with him,' she said, frowning. 'It's only you that's made me a fallen woman.'

'It takes two to jitterbug,' he murmured. 'And hopefully we'll have time for another dance when we get back.'

'Is sex all you think about?' she said in feigned disapproval.

'Not where you're concerned.' His voice was emotionless. 'But it'll do till something better comes along.'

'You're thinking of marriage again,' she accused, folding her arms across her breast. 'I've told you –'

'Sure, I know it's a No Man's Land,' he said, staring out of the window. 'But all's fair in love and war.'

She would have liked to have asked him what weapons he'd bring into play but they had come into a station and an elderly woman got into their compartment. She began to talk about the weather and was soon in full flood concerning its awfulness.

They had only been in Flora's house five minutes when Kathleen arrived with Vivien. 'Is he all right?' demanded Kathleen, her thin face anxious.

'He'll survive.' Flora smiled to reassure her.

'Mam's been,' said Vivien gloomily. 'She was with a man.'

'Who was it?' Flora exchanged a quick glance with Mike. 'What did she want?'

'She didn't tell *me*,' said Vivien, pulling a face. 'But he was tall, dark and handsome and she seemed made up with herself.' She rubbed her gloves over the oven door to warm them and then she and Kathleen went out again, slamming the front door behind them.

Mike and Flora looked at each other.

'I wonder — ' began Flora quickly, then shook her head, not wanting to believe that the man could be Kevin Brown.

'It couldn't be Stephen?' said Mike, raising an eyebrow.

'Steve's scarred. They had to dig shrapnel out of his face,' informed Flora absently. 'Besides, Viv knows him well. I was wondering whether it could be my boss.'

'You've got a tall, dark, handsome boss and you never told me about him *either*?' he said, his grey eyes flint-like.

'Only because I didn't think him worth mentioning.' She went over to him, putting her arms about his waist and rubbing her body against his. 'It was almost instant dislike on my part. Just one of those feelings you get sometimes about people.' She kissed him and was aware of a slight resistance. She was suddenly fearful. 'Why don't we dance?' she whispered against his mouth, swaying in his arms. 'Viv shouldn't be back for at least half an hour.'

'Suits me,' he drawled. 'A waltz or a quick step?'

Her mouth lifted at the corners. 'With only half an hour it'll have to be a quick step.' She went over to the window and drew the curtains, and began to undo buttons.

'Have you time for a cuppa and a slice of that savoury mince pie I made this morning?' said Flora, ushering Mike into the chair closest to the fire.

He glanced at his watch. 'Just about. But don't spoil me. I just might get used to this domesticity.'

'I like spoiling you.' She handed him the Sunday paper.

'But not on a permanent basis,' he said soberly.

'Mike! You said you understood.'

'Sorry.' He didn't sound the least apologetic.

She let it go, not wanting to spend the short time they had together in disagreement.

Maggie was shocked when Flora told her what had happened to George the next morning. 'Lads!' she exclaimed. 'There's never any knowing what they'll be up to next. But as long as he's going to be okay, that's the main thing.' She squeezed past Flora with an empty wooden tray and collided with the boss who had come quietly into the shop, carrying more bread. One of the cobs was sent flying out of the tray. 'Sorry, Mr Brown. Did I hurt yer?' Her voice was flustered. 'I'm all fingers and thumbs this morning.' She bent to pick up the loaf.

'You can't sell that now it's been on the floor,' he said irascibly. 'You're a fool, Maggie, not looking where you're going. You'll pay for that.'

'Yes, Mr Brown,' she said, looking dismayed as she brushed the loaf with her sleeve. 'But it isn't dirty.'

'You can't sell it,' he repeated. 'Your trouble, woman, is that you spend far too much time gossiping instead of paying attention to your job.'

'Yes, Mr Brown,' she stammered.

'Maggie's a hard worker,' intervened Flora quietly. 'And it was me that started her talking. I was telling her about my son's accident.'

'Don't interfere, Mrs Cooke. This is a disciplinary matter and I don't want you putting your oar in.' He turned away then twisted round again, looking at her with a faintly malicious gleam in his dark eyes. 'Your sister was telling me that you're going out with a Yank. I thought you'd have had more sense than to be in their company.'

For a moment she was taken aback, then irritation coloured her voice. 'What I do outside work is none of your business, Mr Brown. I'm a big girl now and my sister is no longer my keeper.'

He shrugged and said sarcastically, 'You're a member of my staff. I like to take a friendly interest.' There was a brief pause before he added: 'How is your son, anyroad?'

Her tone was less angry. 'George is going to be flat on his back for the next six weeks. So you can tell Hilda that if you see her before me.'

'I'll be seeing her tomorrow. She's washing her hair tonight.' A smile lit his handsome features. 'She knows how to have a good time, your Hilda.'

'I'm sure,' said Flora dispassionately.

'Right.' He smiled and placed the tray on the counter.

'Get on with your work. I won't have any slacking.' And he walked into the back room.

Flora exchanged looks with Maggie, whose brow was furrowed. 'Are yer really going out with a Yank?'

She nodded and folded her arms, realising that Maggie's opinion of her mattered. 'You're not going to tell me that you're prejudiced against every Yankee soldier, sailor and airman because of a few?' she said lightly.

'No,' said Maggie, shaking her head vigorously, a faraway look in her eyes. 'I met an American soldier once. He was a darkie an' had lost a leg. It was during the Great War an' there was quite a lot of them convalescing near our school. I think I was around ten years old an' I used to get to walk past where they used to sit out an' get fresh air. He gave me sum candy an' would ask me how I was.' She busied herself as she talked. 'An' then one day he was just not there any more. An' I wus real upset. I always prayed, though, that he got back to his own country.'

His own country, Flora thought uneasily. Mike's home, America. Huge, and thousands of miles away. Land of gangsters, home on the range, and musicals! Of Harold Lloyd, Bing Crosby and Bette Davis! Of popcorn, chewing gum and doughnuts! What was real life like there? Did they have scouse and bread and butter pudding as well? Could she fit in? Would she feel at home ever?

She shook her head. What was she thinking about? Going to America was impossible. And there were other things to worry her now — such as getting to the hospital that evening.

It was sleeting on the way home and Flora was not sure whether she felt dismay or relief when she found Stephen waiting in his car outside her house. 'I thought you might like a lift to the hospital,' he said.

She hesitated before saying, 'Thanks.'

He smiled. 'I won't be able to do it every day. You know there's petrol rationing?' She nodded. Who didn't! 'But this evening I thought I'd save your feet.'

Getting into the car she felt slightly guilty, knowing that Mike would not like the idea of her being with him. But the thought of the long journey in the dark made her feel tired just thinking about it.

Stephen asked her whether she had seen George yesterday and she told him how he had been.

'I can get him some scrap paper if he wants to draw,' he said, his eyes on the road. She thanked him and fell silent.

The silence stretched until they came to the Mersey tunnel. Then he broke it. 'Have you ever thought of coming back to the old firm, Floss?' He glanced at her, his craggy face eager. 'We're really busy now and I'd pay you a decent wage.'

It was the first time he had asked her to go back since the day he had told her about Tom being a deserter, and she did not know what to say. The money would be better than it was working in the bakery and that was tempting — but she would see too much of him.

'Let me think about it,' she said slowly. 'It's coming up to Christmas and Maggie said it can be real busy. It wouldn't be fair on my boss,' she excused herself.

He looked disappointed but only said, 'I can understand that. You think about it then — but don't keep me waiting too long or I'll have to find somebody else.' She nodded, glad of the reprieve in making a decision.

The car came out of the Mersey tunnel and passed Cammell Laird the shipbuilder's on the other side, heading towards the Wirral.

The visit to George started fairly well, although his eyebrows nearly disappeared into his darkening tawny hair when he saw Stephen. Flora had brought him his only classic book, *Treasure Island*, bought by his grandfather, which he had never managed to read to the end. He seemed glad to have it. 'Nurse Connelly said that she'll fix me up with this contraption with a mirror above that reflects the page of the book lying flat on the bed,' said George.

'That sounds a handy gadget,' said Stephen in a jocular voice. 'But what a pity that you had to act so damn silly as to go climbing into bombed houses and giving your mother the fright of her life.'

George went red. 'I've told Mam I'm sorry,' he said in a strangled voice. 'And she know I am.' The sight of Stephen with his mam worried him. 'Anyway, I don't see what it's got to do with you. I don't know why you've come because you've never liked me.'

'George!' rebuked Flora.

'That's not true.' Stephen's ears had turned red.

'You don't have to lie,' said George, stubbornly determined not to have this particular visitor coming to see him again. 'I'm not a kid like Viv. I know you'd have *me* out of the way if you could. At least Mike likes me.'

'That's enough, George.' His mam's voice sounded embarrassed. 'I know you're frustrated, being stuck in bed, but there's no need to be rude to Stephen. Say you're sorry.'

George hesitated, his brown eyes gleaming moistly. He did not want his mam getting too annoyed with him. He stretched his arms behind him to clasp the iron bars of the bedstead. It was a little bit of exercise and loosened the tight feeling in his chest. 'Sorry,' he said.

But Stephen had already got to his feet. 'I'll leave you with him, Flora. I've seen for myself that there's nothing much wrong with him that rest won't cure.'

'He has said he's sorry,' she said quickly, looking up at him. 'You could make allowances for him. He could have been killed.'

Stephen's mouth tightened and he rammed his hands in his pockets. 'His own fault, Floss. I'll wait for you in the car.' He turned on his heel and walked away.

Flora stared hard at George. 'See what you've done now! He probably won't bring me again.'

'Sorry, Mam,' he said cheerfully, easing his arms down and searching with his hand for the chocolate on the cover.

'You said all that on purpose,' she said strongly. 'It was wrong of you.'

'But it's true, Mam.' He broke off two squares of chocolate and held them out to her.

'No, you eat it — your grandfather gave me the money for it.'

'Okay.' He smiled at her and said in a coaxing voice: 'You aren't going to marry Stephen, are you, Mam?'

'Is that what this is all about?' she asked, frowning, and shifting on the hard chair close to the bed.

He shrugged. 'We're all right as we are. And it's his fault that Rosie —'

'Yesterday you blamed yourself, and we agreed that it's

best forgotten now. Stephen wasn't to know what would happen.'

George said nothing, but he was worried again as he broke off some more chocolate. She was defending Stephen. An uneasy silence fell.

'Kathleen Murphy gave me a letter for you,' said Flora.

He twisted his mouth wryly but watched with a certain amount of anticipation as she took the closely written sheet out of her handbag and gave it to him. He read it carefully. Kathy's handwriting was all over the place and she couldn't spell, but it appeared that she was missing him — loved him. This she had written in her own blood, and he must swear not to tell his mam 'cos she'd tell *her* mam, who'd belt her for doing such a thing. He grinned and read on. Mike had called at their house after his accident before going on to George's house and staying in his bed. His smile vanished and he read that last line again. He liked Mike but he hadn't lived next door to Mrs Bryce for nothing. Not that he thought his mam was really like Lena Bryce. His mam was decent which meant getting married, and if it was Mike she married that meant — America!

George slowly folded the letter.

'Any message?' Flora said, smiling.

'Tell her I'll write,' he said, screwing up his face and slipping the letter into *Treasure Island*. 'And *if* you'll be seeing Mike again, could you ask him about me comics?'

'I'll be seeing him,' she murmured, and suddenly there was a new softness in her voice and a warmth in her eyes.

George was worried and angry. Viv had been right about his mam having boyfriends. For the rest of the visit he answered her only in monosyllables.

Flora left the hospital, not looking forward to the drive home with Stephen. Even from a distance she could see him pacing up and down beside the car, a definite sign of his unrest.

'Your George — ' he began.

'No,' she interrupted, shivering slightly in the frosty air, and seeing her breath turn into vapour. 'I'm not going to discuss my son all the way home. We've had this out before, Steve, and it gets us nowhere.'

213

'He's too like Tom,' he continued as if she had not spoken.

'No, he's not,' she said defensively. 'He's my son as well and I don't think I'm without some fighting spirit.'

'I didn't mean that he's a coward,' he said with every sign of discomfiture.

She stared at him, muffled up in his navy blue overcoat, scarf and trilby, and was annoyed because she was cold and in no mood for such a discussion. 'I accept that you didn't mean that,' she said abruptly. 'So you'd better accept that if we're to carry on being friends then you'll have to stop bringing Tom into nearly every conversation we have.'

'I'm sorry,' he said heavily. 'It's just that I can't forget that you and he – '

'Forget it.' Her voice was hard. 'You killed my memories of him. I've never felt the same about him since you and our Hilda had a go. I accept that he wasn't a hero, or even faithful to me. Now can we get in the car?'

He gazed at her, his mouth gaping, before hurrying to open the door for her.

They drove for some time before speaking, then suddenly he said, 'Who's Mike?'

'A friend.' She had been waiting for him to ask ever since George had mentioned the name.

He glanced at her. 'Anybody I know?'

'No,' she said shortly.

'Known him long?'

'A few years.'

'You've never mentioned him.'

'Why should I? I hadn't seen him for a while.'

'And now you're seeing him again.' He sounded annoyed.

'I'm a free agent, Steve. I'm grateful for this lift but I can have what friends I like.' She turned her head abruptly and stared out of the darkened window.

'It's because I'm jealous of any man you go out with,' he muttered.

'Don't say any more,' she said emphatically. 'Talk about work – or the Russians – or the Lease and Lend Agreement. Anything that's not personal.'

There was a silence, then he said sulkily, 'All right. What

214

d'you think of the Lease and Lend Agreement? Bloody Americans! They'll have us in debt to them for years.'

'There wouldn't be so many houses getting built without their help,' she said calmly. 'And rations would have been cut even worse. As it is, they're below the wartime average.'

'At least the paper shortage has eased up.' He went on to talk about work, and the rest of the journey passed amicably enough on the surface.

He dropped Flora off outside her house without mentioning coming in, and she knew then that he was still annoyed. She thanked him once again and hurried inside, intending to light the fire before going for Vivien.

But the light was on and the fire already lit.

'You've been long enough,' said Hilda, putting down the *Red Letter* magazine. 'I was just thinking of going.'

'How was I to know you were here?' Frowning, Flora hung her coat on the back of the door. 'You should give me your key back. It's not right your coming and going when you feel like it in my house.'

'Have you something to hide?'

'Don't be daft.'

Hilda leaned back against the back of the cut moquette chair. 'Would you rather I climbed through the coal hole and arrived all mucky in your kitchen? Just when I'm showing an interest in my nephew's welfare. I thought you'd appreciate that.' Flora gave her a look and her sister smiled. 'How is George?'

'He's flat on his back and likely to stay that way till Christmas — as Mr Brown would have told you tomorrow. You and him going out together is all very sudden, isn't it?'

Hilda's smile barely lifted her mouth. 'None of your business, Flo. But, yes, we're both quick workers.' She flicked ash into the flames. 'How's your love life? Mike looked done in when I saw him on Saturday.'

'He'd just help save George's life! What do you expect? That he'd look like he'd come out of a band box?'

Her smile widened. 'Don't get shirty. You're as sly as ever, Flo. You didn't tell me that you'd seen each other.'

Flora folded her arms and leaned against the table. 'Why

215

should I? You were wrong about its being over, by the way. But it shouldn't matter to you,' she said softly. 'We're not really in competition, are we? You have Mr Brown now.'

Hilda's eyes narrowed and she flicked ash into the fire again. 'What does Mike feel about Stephen?'

Flora was silent a moment then murmured, 'What did you expect him to feel when you told him he was my fiancé? Troublemaker.'

Hilda grinned. 'Didn't like it, did he?'

Flora smiled sweetly. 'Which proves that he cares. Fortunately he trusts me more than he does you.'

Hilda pulled a face. 'And you trust him? More fool you! Think of his past. For a long-term prospect, Stephen's a much better bet.'

Flora's eyes narrowed. 'Why is it that you want to throw me into Stephen's arms all of a sudden?'

'You're thirty and it's unlikely that you'll go off to America with Mike, so why don't you plump for money and comfort. It's what we both should be looking for.'

'Is that why you have your eye to Mr Brown?'

Hilda wiggled her darkened eyebrows. 'He's not short of a bob or two and he certainly likes his comfort *and* he's gorgeous-looking. As well as knowing how to give a girl a good time. I had steak on Saturday. Thick steak! What did you have for your dinner that night?'

Flora felt like saying 'Love in front of the fire' but instead said, 'Spam butties.'

'There you are,' said Hilda with a touch of triumph. 'Wake up to reality, Flo. I wanted to go to America, as you know, but I've accepted that things are different than during the war and just after — a lot of this batch of Yanks are years younger than me for a start.'

Flora straightened up from the table. 'I'm not in a rush to make any decisions about the future. I've got enough on my mind at the moment, worrying about George.'

Hilda reached for her coat, her mouth pursed. 'When will he be home, did you say?'

'By Christmas hopefully.'

Hilda smiled as she opened the door. 'Roll on Christmas then — who knows what will have happened by then!'

Chapter Seventeen

'Now be careful, George,' said Flora, stumbling in her son's wake as he walked stiffly up the step.

'Don't fuss, Mam.' He scowled as she took his arm. 'Let me go! I'm all right.'

She moved away. 'I'm just concerned about this one high step. You might leap up it like a Red Indian on the warpath,' she joked.

'Don't be daft, Mam.' He stared at the front door, feeling quite emotional. 'Hurry up and open it,' he said roughly. 'It's cold out here.'

'Sorry!' She hastened to put her key in the lock and led the way in.

Vivien and her grandfather looked up as they entered and both stared intently at George as he entered the kitchen. 'You've put weight on, lad,' said Jack gruffly. 'You'll have to run that off.'

'I will, Grandad.' His voice was subdued. 'Soon be playing for the team again.'

'Sit down, son. You must be tired.' Flora brought forward one of the straight-backed dining chairs.

'I'm not,' he muttered. 'I've been doing nothing for weeks, haven't I? I'm hungry, though.'

'I'll get you something to eat.' She went into the back kitchen.

George glanced about him.

'D'you like our decorations?' Vivien approached him, her eyes shining. 'Me and Grandad did all the paper chains this morning.'

217

'It's great,' said George, rubbing his nose. 'Although everything looks strange at the moment.'

'Mike's coming later,' said Vivien. Her grandfather grunted and muttered something under his breath. She ignored him. 'Did you know he's still in England?'

'Of course, I do, stoopid! I haven't been to the moon.' He sat down, easing his back against the chair. 'And he's been sending me comics, hasn't he? And candy.'

Vivien's smile faded. 'You don't look very grateful. He saved your life, you know. You should be happy.'

'God saved me life,' he muttered. 'I don't know what for, though, if I can't play for Liverpool.'

'And why shouldn't you be able to play for them, lad?' His grandfather's gaze was fierce as he pressed tobacco into the bowl of his pipe.

'Yes, why shouldn't you?' said Vivien pertly, tossing her curls. 'You're just feeling sorry for yourself. At least you're alive! That's what Uncle Steve said.'

'Uncle Steve,' muttered George. 'Is he still around? I was hoping Mam had got rid of him.'

'Well, no, he's not,' said Vivien with a gusty sigh. 'We haven't seen him for ages.'

'Don't be so grumpy, lad,' said his grandfather, waving his pipe. 'I know how you feel, but you've got to think of your mother. She's only a young woman and you could do with a new dad to keep you in order. Stephen would make a good job of that. Although he seems to have given up since that Yank came on the scene.' His face clouded over.

'I'd prefer Mike if I had any say in it,' George said irritably. 'Although I don't want to go to America. They don't play proper football there.'

'There'll be no chance of that,' rasped his grandfather, his gnarled old fingers trembling slightly as he lit his pipe. 'I won't be having your mam marrying any Yank. Especially one called Mike. You can bet your last ha'penny that he's Catholic with that name.'

'His grandfather was Irish,' said Vivien promptly. 'He kissed the Blarney Stone.'

'Dammit!' exclaimed her grandfather, drawing on his pipe and thumping on the arm of the chair. 'He is a bloody Catholic! And he's been in this house and taken my daughter out.'

'What are you going on about, Father?' Flora had come into the kitchen without any of them hearing her.

He glowered at her. 'This Yank of yours — he's a bloody Catholic, isn't he?'

'And if he is?' murmured Flora, flushing slightly. 'Does it really matter, Father?'

'Don't talk stupid, girl. Of course it matters. I won't have any papists in my house.'

Her expression tightened. 'I'll remind you, Father, that Mike saved George's life,' she said in a vibrant voice, pushing back a handful of hair. 'And besides, this isn't *your* house.'

'Don't be speaking to me in that tone, girl. You know what I mean,' he grunted, his brows twitching. 'We've had no mixed marriages in our family.'

She folded her arms and stared at him. 'Who's mentioned marriage? Not me.'

'You mean — you're not getting married, Mam?' demanded George quickly.

'I haven't said so, have I?' she retorted. 'Can't a woman have a man friend without everybody jumping to conclusions?'

George let out a long breath. 'Then you're not going to America?'

'Not that I know of,' she said briskly, filling the teapot from the kettle and avoiding his eyes. She had thought a lot about going to America. Mike had been painting pictures of it that made her feel as she had when she was young and romantic, and wanting to find an enchanted land. So far she had resisted saying yes.

George began to whistle. Relieved, she gave her father the first cup of tea.

He fixed his fierce eyes on her. 'Stephen would make you a good husband as I've said before,' he growled. 'I don't know why you don't see him any more. George needs a man who can keep him in hand and share his interests.'

'He has friends for sharing. And he's not so bad that I can't control him.' She handed Vivien a milky tea.

219

The girl thanked her, then said casually, 'Mam's getting married.'

Flora's eyes dilated. 'Since when?' She had known Hilda was still seeing Mr Brown, but it was sudden for a wedding.

'Since this morning.' Vivien stared at her over the rim of her cup. 'She called after you'd gone the hospital but wouldn't come in. She said to tell you.'

Flora exchanged glances with her father. 'It'll be Mr Brown, of course.'

'He told me to call him Uncle Kevin,' said Vivien, wrinkling her nose. 'They're getting married in the New Year. The banns are getting read this week. We're all invited. Even Grandad, she said.'

'I won't be going.' Her father glared at Flora. 'Does she think to get round me to give her away?'

'It's what you've been wanting to do for years,' said Flora, her eyes twinkling. 'Do it if she asks you, Father. You'll never get a better chance.'

'Hmmph,' he said, and lapsed into silence.

Flora decided to change the subject and turned to George, 'I hope you don't mind, son, but we've put some of your dad's painting equipment in your room. Mike thought it might be of some use to you. He's helped me to clear out the back room, and we're doing it up for Viv, now she's getting bigger.'

'It's okay by me,' said George, twiddling his thumbs. 'I think I might have a bit of his knack with a pencil and paintbrush.'

'Mike's coming tonight so you'll be able to give him a hand decorating.'

His face brightened. 'I don't mind. I'm quite looking forward to seeing old Mike.'

'Good.' Flora's smile was forced. Obviously it was one thing for her to have Mike as a friend, another for a husband.

'I think it's going to look lovely,' said Vivien, watching Mike painting the window frame in the back bedroom.

'Loverly,' mocked George. He was having a go at painting the door pink.

'Everything's lovely.' Vivien swung her legs as she sat on a box. 'Uncle Mike, do you have Father Christmas in America?'

He flashed his wide smile. 'Sure, we have old Santa Claus.'

Vivien put her chin in her hand. 'That makes it even harder to believe that he's real,' she said with a deep sigh.

Flora looked up from the curtain she was sewing. 'What's this, Viv? I thought you believed in Father Christmas?'

Vivien wrinkled her nose. 'I don't know any more. A girl at school saw her dad sneaking presents on to the bottom of her bed last year. Why should he do that if there's a real one?

'Giving the real one a helping hand, young lady,' said Mike, smiling. 'You can bet your bottom dollar if you don't believe in him then you won't get any presents in your stocking.'

'I do want to believe,' said Vivien quickly, her expression changing. 'Honest, Mike. I'd really like there to be a Father Christmas. But why should I have had so little over the last few years if there is?'

'You're not the only child in the world,' put in Flora. 'So is it that you want Father Christmas's elves on even more overtime?' she teased.

Vivien's brow puckered. 'They wouldn't need to do overtime. It'd be all done by magic. Just like Father Christmas would need magic to get round the world.'

'Maybe he could conjure up some jet propelled reindeers,' said Mike, his face deadpan. 'They could wear little red fur-trimmed boots on all their hooves with wing-shaped jets. And the sleigh could have rocket boosters on its runners.' He glanced at Flora and winked.

Her lips twitched. 'That's all right if he doesn't over-shoot roofs and lands in our backyard.'

Vivien's eyes shone. 'Imagine finding Father Christmas with a sack of toys in your backyard on Christmas morning! It would be as good as finding the baby Jesus in a shed down the yard.'

'With angels and a cow and everything else, I suppose,' murmured George, eyeing the door for runs in the paint.

'There might be shepherds,' said Flora.

'They could bring their sheep,' suggested Mike.

'They'd make a mess but it would be good for the flowers,' she said.

'Marigolds in December?' drawled Mike.

'Why not — if there's magic in the air?' Their eyes caught.

'Magic me up three wishes,' he said quietly. 'It's deadly real in the bleak mid-winter at the camp.'

'Where would you like to be magicked to instead? The North Pole with Father Christmas perhaps?'

'I could think of warmer places,' he said softly, and her cheeks burned as he continued to look at her. She knew exactly what he was thinking and she would have liked it too. She was suddenly depressed and looked away. Mike got on with his painting.

Later when they were alone in front of the fire with Flora sitting on Mike's knee, trying to rub away a streak of pink paint in his fair hair, she said, 'I do hate you having to go back to the camp the way things are.'

'There's gonna be improvements. Rumours are rife that the top brass are on their way to have a look at us.' He paused. 'We had Jean Simmons, the film star, come to visit,' he muttered, stroking Flora's thigh. 'Very English.'

'You sound like you don't like that.' She pulled a little away from him and gazed into his frowning grey eyes. 'I'm very English, Mike. Even if I said yes to your proposal and went to America, I doubt if I could ever be real American.'

'It's not your Englishness that I object to,' he said seriously, forcing her against him again. 'It's your bulldog spirit that makes you hold out against all that I'd give you. We could have a real good life together, Flo.'

'I don't have only myself to think about.' Her voice was quiet.

'I know,' he drawled. 'There's your father and he doesn't like me.'

'He's old and set in his ways. He only has me and he doesn't really know you. He only sees the uniform. And now — '

'And now what?' His lean face wore an impatient look.

She let out a low breath. 'He's twigged on to your being

a Catholic. And you know he's Orange.'

They stared at each other. 'How much does it matter to you, the differences?' asked Mike.

There was a pause before she answered: 'I'm not bigotted. Mrs Murphy's a Catholic and I'm fond of her — and of the whole family. But I've been brought up to worship God differently. Although at times I think it's a sin that Christians should be at such odds with each other. Like on the twelfth of July.'

'We could agree to differ,' he murmured, kissing her neck.

'And if we had children — what then?'

He was silent, rubbing his cheek slowly against hers.

'See,' she said sadly. 'It matters to both of us, and one of us would have to give in. I don't know if I could agree to let you have it your way.'

'I'm the man.'

'And I'm a woman who's been used to making her own decisions and ruling the roost for quite a while,' she said strongly. Then suddenly she smiled. 'See what you want to take on, Mike. A bulldog bitch!' She kissed him lightly. 'We'd always be scrapping.'

'I like a good scrap now and then,' he said. Their lips met and this time they clung. The kiss deepened and her arms went round his neck. Differences were set aside as their need for each other took over.

Later over a cup of tea Flora said, 'Our Hilda's getting married.'

'Nice for some,' he said lightly. She gave him a look and he shrugged. 'The tall, dark handsome guy, is it?' He dunked a cookie in his tea.

She nodded, her eyes on the long strong fingers. 'In the New Year so Viv says. I haven't seen her myself to have it first hand.'

'It'll be interesting to see what kind of job she makes of it,' he said. 'I can't see her in a Mrs Miniver role. Is Viv going to live with her?'

Flora stilled. 'I hadn't even thought of it,' she said slowly and fell silent. She could not imagine her sister wanting her daughter permanently. And it was hard to picture Hilda and

Kevin Brown wanting her living with them. Still it was a possibility that made her feel slightly depressed.

'I know you'll miss her,' said Mike, 'but maybe having Viv with her would help Hilda settle down. And it would be one less problem for us to worry about.'

'Yes,' murmured Flora. 'I'll have to wait and see our Hilda to find out.' She switched the conversation into different channels, not wanting to consider losing Vivien, and soon after Mike went.

Flora did not have long to wait to see her sister.

The next morning she was rushed off her feet, despite two new girls having been taken on over the last few weeks. Mr Brown stayed in the back, which made it easier for her in a way. She found it difficult to accept that he would be her brother-in-law. Family!

She popped into her father's as usual at lunchtime, only to find him out. She made herself a cup of tea and sat in the rocking chair, biting into a sausage roll. Her father mightn't be long. The door knocker sounded and she went to answer the door.

'I thought you might be here,' said Hilda, looking relieved. 'Is he in?'

'Father?' Flora inspected her sister, face scrubbed clean of make-up for once and wearing a plain brown coat. She smiled. 'Can it be true? You've come to kiss and make up – and ask him to give you away?'

Hilda frowned. 'You can mock all you like, Flo, but if I'm going to have a big wedding, I want to do the whole thing properly. Is he in?'

'No, but come in and wait.'

'I can't stay long,' said Hilda hurriedly, following her in.

She stopped in the middle of the room and looked about her. 'Good God! It's unbelievable that nothing's changed at all since I left. No, since Mother died. That awful cream and brown paint.' She whirled round, scanning every wall with the pictures of the King and Queen on one and a plaque of William of Orange crossing the Boyne on another. 'How did she put up with living in this crummy place?'

'You moving into a palace, are you?' said Flora drily.

Her sister smiled. 'Jealous, Flo? It's some size the flat above the shop, I can tell you. Two floors and the rooms are huge. Nice tiled fireplaces and lovely high windows.'

'Take you sometime to clean them, then,' murmured Flora, sitting down in the rocking chair.

Hilda pulled a face. 'I've already mentioned to Kevin that I could do with some help upstairs.' She held out her hand, gazing admiringly at it. 'D'you like my ring? The diamond's not a bad size, is it?'

Flora admired the ring. 'Beautiful. And you really think he'll give you some help?'

Hilda sat and stretched lovely legs towards the fire. 'If he doesn't, he's in for a rude awakening. I'm not going to be a skivvy for any man. But don't you go telling him that.'

Flora could see trouble ahead, but she smiled. 'Why should I spoil the wedding? I really hope you'll make it this time. You'll make a lovely bride.'

'Thanks.' Hilda fluffed out her hair and taking out a compact she stared at herself in the tiny mirror and made a kissing sound at her reflection. 'I'm quite good for thirty, aren't I?'

'You're quite good for thirty-five too,' said Flora, amused.

Hilda snapped the gold compact closed. 'I've told him I'm twenty-nine — he's twenty-eight.'

'You're daft. He's bound to find out. Have you got your dress yet?'

'I'm having it made. White brocade and lace with a heart-shaped neck and long tight sleeves,' Hilda murmured in a dreamy voice.

'White?' said Flora.

Hilda flashed her a warning look. 'Don't say it, Flo. I always wanted a big white wedding, so why shouldn't I have one?'

'Very virginal. What about Viv?'

Hilda frowned. 'I know about Viv but I don't want everybody else knowing.'

'Does Kevin?'

She nodded. 'I thought it best. So I told him I had a fiancé who was killed in the desert.' She lit a cigarette, gazing into the fire.

'And is it true?' asked Flora, her fingers tightening about her cup.

Hilda grimaced. 'It's near enough to the truth. We were going to get married.'

'You and who?'

There was a silence before Hilda replied, 'Me and Jimmy Martin. Viv's his child.'

Flora stared at her and for a moment she could not speak. The news was such a relief. 'You had me almost believing that she was Tom's child,' she said slowly.

'That's what I wanted you to believe.' Hilda stared at glowing tip of her cigarette.

'Does this mean that you and Tom never did sleep together?'

Hilda hesitated, then sang softly, 'Cross my heart and hope to die, if I ever tell a lie.' She shrugged. 'You know what a liar I am, Flo.'

Flora was silent, not quite convinced which was the lie.

Hilda blew out a stream of smoke. 'Let's forget it. Life has moved on for both of us.'

'Yes,' said Flora. 'But what about Viv? Will you tell her who her father is one day?'

Hilda squared her shoulders. 'That's up to you, little sister,' she said, her expression altering to a more cheerful one. 'You've had the keeping of her. You do realise that makes Stephen her uncle? It would be fitting somehow if you did marry him.'

'More fitting if you did,' said Flora, getting up and going to look out of the window to see if there was any sign of their father. 'I take it that you won't be having Viv living with you and your future husband then?'

Hilda looked surprised. 'I didn't think I'd be able to pry her away from you! It's obvious that she looks upon you as her mother now, Flo. But I'll still take her off your hands once a week. She can come with you to the shop every Saturday.' She got up from her chair. 'I don't think I'm going to have the big reunion scene with dear Father. I'll have to go back to work. Anyway, I suppose my idea of having him giving me away is a bit daft.' Her brows puckered. 'He'd probably shame me by turning up in his old overcoat and a flat cap.'

'He has a best bowler and a suit.' Flora stared at her pensively. 'It would be a good thing, you two making friends. Why don't you call at our house on Christmas day? Father will be there and you can play the prodigal in earnest — ask his forgiveness and about giving you away. Sometimes being on neutral ground makes a job easier.'

Hilda pulled a face. 'I don't know. Kevin and me planned on having our Christmas dinner in a restaurant and then going to see Doris — her mam always throws a big party for all the family.'

'Forget it,' said Flora with a shrug. 'I take it that Doris'll be your bridesmaid?'

Her sister nodded. 'She is my best friend despite the occasional fights we've had.' On those words she opened the front door and went out.

Flora watched her go, thinking how much Vivien would have enjoyed being a bridesmaid. Then she closed the door and sat in the rocking chair to wait a while longer for her father, but he did not come. She left for work, considering all that Hilda had said, especially about Jimmy Martin being Viv's dad, and wondering whether she should do anything about it.

227

Chapter Eighteen

'"Away in a manger, no crib for a bed. The little Lord — "'
Vivien stopped singing to gaze at Flora as they walked side
by side down the street. 'What's the matter, Aunty Flo? You
aren't joining in. I thought you liked Christmas carols.'

Flora smiled. 'I do, pet. It's just that I've a lot to think
about.'

'About Christmas and Mam's wedding?' asked the girl
eagerly. 'I really like my new frock.'

'Those and other things.'

'What other things?' Vivien squeezed her hand as they
came to the front path. 'Or shouldn't I ask? Is it secret —
is it presents?'

Flora's smile was real this time. 'No. Although that has
been on my mind.' How could she say that she was thinking
about Viv's father?

'Are you thinking of Rosie?' she surprised Flora by saying.
'I'm always thinking of Rosie. Not right in front of my mind
all the time. But she's there at the back.'

'It's like that with me,' said Flora, staring down into the
pretty face surrounded by blonde curls. She sought traces of
Jimmy, or even Stephen, in its features but she could only see
Hilda. She mentally shook herself. Forget it. Christmas was
coming and decision making could wait till another time.

'You won't be too sad this Christmas?' Vivien sounded
worried. 'I mean, I know we'll be a little sad still — but
you won't be a lot, will you?'

'Of course not.' She touched the girl's head. 'I've got you,
haven't I? You'll cheer me up.'

Vivien nodded. 'And Mike will, if he can come. And George!'

Flora laughed. 'Too right they will!'

She turned her key in the lock and immediately heard voices, male voices — George's and Mike's — coming from the parlour.

They went in and her nose was assailed by the resiny smell of the fir tree placed in a bucket and set in the bay window. George was in the act of attaching tiny candles to its spiny branches while Mike was depositing parcels around the trunk.

'Oh, lovely!' cried Vivien, dancing over to them.

'What are you two up to?' said Flora softly, placing her shopping on the floor.

Mike glanced over his shoulder and smiled. 'Go out again. We haven't finished.'

'Too cold.' She returned his smile. 'You managed to get away then?'

'Looks like it.' He straightened up and kissed her. 'Can't be with you on Christmas Day, though. Sorry, honey.'

She swallowed her disappointment. 'Can't have everything,' she said lightly. 'Is the fire lit? Would you like a cuppa and something to eat?'

'Sure. We'll be finished here soon. Didn't want you coming in, really, till we'd lit the candles.'

'We'll go out again.' She grabbed Vivien's hand and dragged her away to go and prepare food.

When George shouted they went back into the parlour.

Mike had turned off the gas mantle and the mellow glow of the tiny candles glistened on tinsel. For a moment Flora felt like a child again, recalling a Christmas before her mother had taken to her bed and her father had managed to get home from sea. 'It's beautiful,' she breathed, hugging Mike's arm. 'Thanks.'

'Are some of the presents for me?' asked Vivien, working her way round the tree. There were some gifts tied to the tree that had not been wrapped — a trumpet, a small jigsaw, crayons, a mouth organ, a bottle of 'Evening in Paris' scent and a paper fan, to name a few.

229

'Sure are.' Mike drawled. 'And two special ones for your Aunt Flora, that aren't to be opened till Christmas.'

'You are a love,' said Flora, anticipating the pleasure of opening presents on Christmas morning. There had been nothing the last few years. 'I wish I could give you more than I've got.'

He murmured. 'You know the best present you could give me.'

She squeezed his arm. It seemed so ungrateful not to say yes when he set out to please her so much. 'You tempt me to say to hell with everything.' Her voice was low. 'But I can't, Mike. The problems are still there.'

'You are one hell of a stubborn lady, Flo.' His soft tone did not quite conceal his impatience. 'But then I always knew that – and that I couldn't buy you.'

'It's not that I'm stubborn.' Her voice was as quiet as his. 'But I made it clear from the beginning how it was. And I did ask you not to push it.'

'Sure you did.' His face was taut as he freed his arm from her hold. 'Let's go and have tea.' He moved nearer to the children, his expression lightening. 'How about the movies later, kids?' he said cheerfully.

'Yeah!' said Vivien and George in unison.

Flora knew that she had hurt him and hated doing so because it created a barrier between them.

It could have been like old times in the picture house except Flora did not have to keep removing Mike's arm from about her shoulder. His aloofness disturbed her even as it annoyed and it was difficult concentrating on the screen. It was a relief when the main film finished and it was time to go.

They jostled their way outside with the crowd, only to be met by a seemingly solid grey wall of fog which the adults regarded with dismay.

'Damn!' exclaimed Mike savagely. 'I'll never find my way back to base tonight.'

'You'll have to stay with us,' said Vivien, squeezing his hand. 'You can have my room. Can't he, Aunty Flo?'

'He'll have to, I suppose,' said Flora calmly, the fog muffling her voice. 'Unless he'd like to walk all the way to Warrington.'

230

'Nothing I'd like better,' rasped Mike. 'Which is south?'

'You'd get lost,' cried Vivien anxiously. 'He couldn't do it, could he, Aunty Flo?'

'Men think they can do anything,' responded Flora promptly, still feeling a little put out by Mike's behaviour. She pulled the collar of her coat up, burying her chin into it. 'They think they're God's gift to womenkind, and that we can't resist them.'

'It's the other way around,' said Mike with emphasis, glancing in her direction. 'Women think we're made of clockwork and they can wind us up and point us where they want us to go.'

She pulled a face. 'Men treat women either like dolls or slaves. They like us to pretty ourselves up for them and kowtow to their every need.'

There was the slightest pause, and Vivien's and George's heads slewed round in Mike's direction. They didn't have long to wait. 'Eve was made for Adam. So women are subordinate to men. But most of them, these days, don't know their place. They dress like men; they think they're as good as men.'

'Those women aren't setting their sights high enough,' said Flora, frowning slightly and searching with her fingers for the garden wall that should have been on her right. She stopped abruptly. 'I think we're lost. It's your fault.'

'How can it be my fault?' demanded Mike, his face looming close in the fog. 'You're the one who lives round here. I'm only a visitor.'

'Typical male excuse,' muttered Flora, looking away from him and attempting to pierce the darkness ahead with narrowed vision. 'We took the left turning and there was a garden wall on my left. It's gone.'

'It's come to an end, probably.'

'There's another wall after that.'

'You're right,' murmured Mike, frowning. He stamped his feet and she jumped.

'What are you doing?' Her voice was vexed. 'This is no time for a clog dance.'

'Cobbles,' he said.

'What?'

'We've wandered into the middle of the road,' he said

slowly and distinctly. 'That's why there's no wall, and if you look ahead you'll see a faint glow from a lamp to the left.'

'All right, I can see it.' Her voice had lightened. 'Let's head for home.'

She started to walk more briskly, Mike and George easily keeping up with her. Vivien was dragged along at a run, until Mike paused to lift her up on to his shoulders.

They were home in no time, and after a warm and hot drinks George and Vivien went up to bed.

Mike and Flora were unusually silent as they sat in separate chairs, pulled close to the fire.

What now? thought Flora. Who makes the first move towards the other or to bed? One of us has to do something! Or are we going to sit here all night expecting the other to move? She was tired yet wide-awake at the same time. The back of her neck was stiff and aching, and she would have enjoyed Mike massaging it. Damn! She hated being at outs with him.

She drained her cup to the dregs. 'I'm going to bed.' Her voice sounded so jolly it disgusted her. This was what living a lie was. 'You know where to find Viv's room.' Her eyes avoided his.

'You'll be waiting for me there?' he drawled.

'What?' She could not resist looking at him.

He pulled a face. 'You were right. I was wrong. You told me how it was and I decided to try and overrule you. Before we acted a bit like kids, but it's time to kiss and make up, I reckon.'

'To what end? Nothing's changed,' she said slowly, toying with a button on her cardigan.

'I don't like being out of friends,' he said ruefully, putting down his cup.

Warmth filtered through her and she smiled. 'Give me your little finger.'

'Why?' He stared at her, uncomprehendingly.

'Just do as you're told.'

He shook his head slowly but held out his right hand with the little finger cocked. She fastened her finger around his. 'Best friends?'

'Best friends.' He grinned.

'Shake on it,' she ordered. They shook hands and then he pulled her into his arms.

They rose before dawn from the cramped single bed and had breakfast together. The fog had dispersed before George and Vivien woke, and Flora had to leave for work. Mike and Flora left by the back door.

'I don't know when I'll see you again,' he said as they came to a halt by the tram stop into town. 'It's frantic at the base, trying to maintain the planes at the rate they need them. It mightn't be until the New Year.'

'Come when you can.' She thrust a small parcel at him, a tiny crease between her brows. 'Happy Christmas, Mike.' Stretching up, she kissed him then walked away, not looking back.

Christmas came, bringing present opening time in the parlour where a fire had been lit for the occasion. The children tore the paper from Mike's presents to reveal a leather football for George, as well as a baseball bat. His expression was thoughtful as he said, 'It'll do for rounders, I suppose.' And picking up the ball he kicked it across the room before Flora could stop him.

'I've got a doll and a book,' cried Vivien, her face alight with pleasure as she hugged the doll to her. Its eyes opened and closed and it had long eyelashes. Flora could not help thinking of Rosie, and remembered that she had not visited the family grave and must do so soon.

'What's yours?' Vivien's hands reached for Flora's presents and handed them to her. One was large and square.

Flora opened the box to reveal cookies, chocolates, tins of peaches, salmon and spam. There were red, luscious-looking apples, nuts and popcorn, a bottle of champagne and several brown containers of ginger ale.

George spared a moment to look at the goodies and reached for the champagne. He let out a low whistle. 'Good ol' Mike. Can I have a taste?'

'Not now, you can't!' Flora snatched the bottle back

and clutched it to her chest. 'Champagne's only for special occasions.'

'Christmas is special,' he countered. 'Can we have it with our dinner?'

'Champagne and rabbit stew!' A smile lit her face. 'You'll have ginger ale and like it. I'm saving that champagne.'

He shrugged and went back to improving his footwork.

Flora closed the box and reached for her other gift, hesitating as she fingered it once more.

'Open it,' said Vivien eagerly.

The green tissue paper fell apart and the girl gave a loud 'Oooh!' as a lemon satin and cream lace négligée was revealed. There was a note. "Wear it for me on our wedding night." Of course he had written it before their last meeting, thought Flora, so she could not be cross with him. She could not have been anyway for she had never had anything so luxurious in her life. Her cheeks colouring, she bundled the beautiful garments in their tissue paper and got up from her knees. 'It's time I checked that rabbit,' she said hurriedly, and left the parlour with both presents.

Her father arrived for dinner, dressed in his best suit and with a starched white collar cutting his neck. He presented George with a half crown; Vivien received a shilling. There was a china teapot patterned with dark crimson roses for Flora. She recognised it as having belonged to her mother. 'I noticed your teapot was chipped, girl,' he muttered, 'and you won't get one better than that in the shops today.'

She agreed and gave him the baccy she had bought. She was determined to make the best of the day despite Mike's absence. At least she wasn't at work and there was plenty of food to eat.

The rabbit stew, rich with carrots, onions and rice, flavoured with thyme and thickened with seasoned flour, was a gift to the taste buds. They washed it down with the ginger beer. Her father wasn't pleased when Vivien dropped the information that Mike had bought the beer — but it didn't prevent him from drinking it, nor from scoffing Mike's chocolates.

George disappeared with his football outside, and Flora was overwhelmed by restlessness as she cleared the table and washed the dishes. Vivien dried them, before setting up her new snakes and ladders game in the parlour. Wildly exciting time, thought Flora sardonically, sliding her counter down a snake.

Around teatime there was a hammering at the door and Flora hurried to open it, hoping Mike had managed to get away, but it was only a rosy-cheeked Hilda accompanied by Kevin Brown.

'Merry Christmas!' Hilda aimed a kiss at her sister's cheek. It landed on her ear. 'I bring you a gift.' She flourished a bottle of sherry. 'I bet you haven't got any drink in the house.'

'You guess right,' lied Flora, attempting to take the sherry only to have her sister snatch it back as she swayed on high wedged heels. 'In a minute, Flo. Say Happy Christmas to my fiancé, but don't overwhelm him with the Christmas spirit. He's mine, remember?'

Flora gave Kevin a quick look as she hauled her sister into the lobby. He stared back at her, with his beautiful dark eyes slightly out of focus. She had given him only the briefest of congratulations a few days ago. She nodded to him, releasing her hold on her sister's arm. Hilda swayed up the lobby.

'Come on in, Mr Brown,' said Flora with assumed friendliness. 'My father's inside so there's likely to be high jinks when he and Hilda meet.'

He stepped into the lobby, closing the door behind him, and caught her arm as she would have led the way. 'No seasonal kiss, Flo? We're going to be related now.' His fingers dug into her flesh, hurting, and she could smell rum on his breath. She offered him her cheek but he grabbed her chin and kissed her on the mouth with such force that he pressed her lower lip into her teeth and drew blood. It hurt, and unable to pull free, she ground her heel into his foot just above the edge of his brown polished shoe. She felt the shock of his recoil, and he released her abruptly. 'It's going to be like that, is it?' he said, breathing heavily as he brought his foot up and rubbed it. 'You're not very friendly.'

'That kiss wasn't either,' she responded in a flash.

She left him and went into the kitchen where the tea table was set, to be brought up short by the sight of Hilda wrestling with the sherry bottle and her father. 'Let go, you soft old bugger,' she was saying. 'I want to pour you a drink. The prodigal has returned. So let's have a party!'

'There'll be no party, yer daft bitch,' he grunted, his chest rising and falling as he managed to wrench the bottle from her, only to fall backwards into his chair.

Hilda shook her head at him. 'You meany, Father. Give it to Flo. It's for her and we'll all drink a toast. There's going to be a wedding, a lovely, lovely wedding,' she chanted.

Her father stared at her. 'A daughter of mine drunk! You oughter be ashamed.'

'Why? Men get drunk and they couldn't care less!' she exclaimed defiantly, clutching at the table. 'Don't be an ol' misery guts.' She caught sight of her sister. 'Flo! Get the jars out.'

'Sit down before you fall down,' said Flora, unable to prevent a laugh. Never had she imagined the meeting between the two of them would be like this. 'I'll get the glasses and we'll drink to good health and your coming marriage.'

'You shouldn't encourage her,' said her father, reluctantly handing her the bottle. 'Don't be giving me any of that. I wouldn't wash me insides out with it. A nice drop of Navy Rum is what I like.' His eyes almost crossed as he gazed at her fiercely.

'I've got some rum,' said Kevin from the doorway.

The old man switched his attention to him. 'And who are you? Come in and bring your rum, or go out and shut the door.'

Kevin advanced further into the room, pulled by Hilda who had hurried over to him. 'Father, dear Father,' she cried. 'This is my one true love. Will you give me away? His father was a Black Sir Knight — one of your Lodge crowd — Orange as King Billy himself, so you should be pleased with me.' She stood swaying in front of him, clinging to Kevin's arm.

The two men eyed each other carefully. Flora's father spoke first. 'A pretty boy, that's what you are. But I'll maybe let you have my daughter's hand, seeing as how you're on the right side. Now pour me some of that rum and I'll drink yer health.'

Kevin moved swiftly to comply with the old man's request,

filling the small glass that Flora handed to him. A toast was drunk, then in quick succession her father downed another two tots of rum.

A quarter of an hour later when Flora handed her father a salmon sandwich, he whispered almost with an air of triumph: 'I'm glad that one of me daughters tries to please her old father by bringing the right kind of man home. You take a lesson from your sister now, girl, and be shut of that Yank altogether.'

Flora said nothing. What was the use? Nothing would change her father's mind about Mike. She picked up her sherry glass and downed it in one go as she thought of him and his generosity, of his looks and that special something he had for her. She thought of Rosie, and would have given a lot to have had Christmas Day different. To have said yes to Mike, she thought defiantly, staring at her father. Perhaps she would next time she saw him.

On Boxing Day Flora and Vivien went for a walk in the park. George was out with several mates playing football. They were on their way home when they encountered the whole Murphy family excepting Little Paddy. The girls ran on ahead of them but Flora lingered, setting her pace to that of the heavily pregnant Carmel. They exchanged pleasantries, asking after the other's Christmas before discussing Carmel's pregnancy.

'I've told him it's the last I'll be givin' him,' said the Irishwoman, her broad features determined. 'Even if it's another girl — that's it!' Her lips compressed in a straight line. 'I've told Father O'Reilly too. It's all right for him to go on about the blessings of children but he doesn't have to have the "little innocents". I nearly bled to death last time.' There was a silence and Carmel looked at Flora as if waiting for her to say something, but she kept her mouth shut. Some people had a habit of instantly taking the other viewpoint if you agreed with them. 'And how are things with you, Flo? How's yer Yank? Still seeing him?'

'Not that much,' she said brightly. 'They're busy at the base with their aeroplanes.'

'Mike's a fine Catholic lad. Pleasantly spoken and has a lovely way with him.' She did not quite meet Flora's gaze.

237

'Mrs Jones said she thought she saw him coming out of your house the other morning.'

'And what morning would that be?' asked Flora, frowning as if in deep thought. 'Monday, Tuesday, Wednesday, Thursday or Friday?' Her voice tightened and she stopped abruptly. 'I'm certain she has her spyglass out every day just in case she misses anything to spread around.'

'Now Flo, girl! Don't be taking things the wrong way.' Carmel eyed her uneasily. 'I wouldn't be doing me duty as a good neighbour if I didn't tell you that you're getting yerself talked about.'

Flora tapped her foot on the pavement. 'Do you think I don't know that? Let them talk. I don't care.'

'You're vexed,' said Carmel, sighing heavily. 'I don't blame yer, girl. But think — what about George? He's old enough to be taking notice. And though most people wouldn't dream of saying anything directly to him, he's bound to hear the gossip sooner or later.'

Flora's irritation and discomfort simmered over. 'It's not what you all think!' she said in a hard voice. 'He stayed the night in Vivien's room due to the fog. He wants to marry me but I've said no so far.' She paused then added wickedly. 'Only because he's a nice Catholic boy and I don't want to be his ruin. Haven't you all noticed I'm painted scarlet!'

Carmel opened her mouth but Flora did not stay to hear what she said, walking on swiftly. Her emotions were in a tangle and she did not know what she was going to do. But Carmel's words about George had hit home and she knew that a decision was being forced upon her. Next time Mike came could be the last.

238

Chapter Nineteen

D'you think my hat looks all right?' Flora gazed doubtfully at her reflection and pushed a lock of glossy copper hair beneath the green felt hat which had artificial white gardenias under its brim. She wore a matching green dress and jacket.

'You look lovely' said Vivien, smiling at her own image. 'It's a pity it's not your wedding, Aunty Flo.'

Flora said nothing. It was over two weeks since she had seen Mike and she had almost made up her mind what to say to him when he did come. She cast another frowning glance at the mirror before moving away and seizing a wire brush to bring some order to Vivien's curls. 'I wish this was going to be a quiet affair but I reckon your mam's pulling out all the stops. There'll be piles of people we don't know.'

'She said it's her big day – that she's waited for it for a long time,' said Vivien seriously.

'I hope it goes well and she gets all she wants,' muttered Flora, adjusting the shoulders of the flower-sprigged pink frock that Vivien was wearing.

'She says that Uncle Kev's her Prince Charming.'

Flora raised her eyes heavenwards but kept her peace. 'Where's George? It's time we were going.' She whirled round, hoping he had not left the house and was mucking up the new jacket and trousers that she'd put herself in debt for. 'George!' she yelled.

'Here, Mam.' He came in from the back kitchen, his cheek bulging, and looking reasonably tidy for once. His tawny hair was slicked down with Brylcreem.

'Will you leave that jam pot alone,' she said severely. 'Lick your left cheek and brush the crumbs from your mouth.'

He hastily complied with her request. 'I hope there's some decent grub at this do.'

'There'll be plenty of cake, meat pies and sausage rolls. We were hard at it all yesterday.' A smile lit her face. 'Are you ready?'

He nodded. 'D'you think Grandad'll get to the right house on time?'

'If your Aunty Hilda's wants him there, she'll see to it. And I laid out all his clothes for him last night.'

'Clean socks and his best bowler?' He grinned.

'Yes. I hid his old cap.'

She straightened George's tie and found her handbag. 'Let's be having you then,' she said, pushing the door wide and ushering them out into the wintry sunshine.

'Dearly beloved, we are gathered together here in the sight of God, and in the face of this congregation, to join together this man and this woman in Holy Matrimony . . .'

Flora's gaze shifted from the face of the Vicar to Hilda's as the words of the marriage service started majestically. She looked like a princess out of a story and Kevin, the handsome hero. She watched the Vicar's lips moving, telling them what marriage was all about: for the procreation of children, to avoid fornication. The nerves in her stomach tightened. Fornication! What a strange sounding word for what she and Mike had been doing for months. How far she had fallen from her high standards of years ago. God forgive her!

Someone cleared a throat and Flora recognised the sound as belonging to Stephen. Her sister had not told her that he was going to be there. Why couldn't she have fancied Stephen more than Mike? It would have made life much simpler. Should she tell him that Viv could be Jimmy's daughter? Her mind was still undecided. Stephen might not want to believe it was true. The old jealousy of Jimmy could rear its ugly head just as it had with Tom so often in the past. Best to keep quiet for now.

The Vicar directed his attention on the bride and groom and Flora tried to relax. 'I require and charge you both, as ye

240

will answer at the dreadful day of judgment when the secrets of all hearts shall be disclosed, that if either of you know any impediment, why ye may not be lawfully joined together in Matrimony, ye do now confess it. For be ye well assured that so many as are coupled together otherwise than God's word doth allow are not joined together by God, neither is their Matrimony lawful.'

Lawfully joined together in Matrimony ... She and Mike had deliberately sinned. They hadn't just fallen into it but gone into it with eyes, and legs, open! She groaned inwardly. How could she make a joke of such a serious matter? It was all wrong. They really would have to stop it. Having come to that decision she gave her attention to the Service again.

'Kevin William, wilt thou have this Woman to thy Wedded wife?'

'I will.' He hurried over the response.

'Hilda Anne, wilt thou have this Man to thy wedded husband ... and forsaking all other, keep thee only unto him, so long as ye both shall live?'

'I will.' Her sister's voice was loud and clear.

'Who givest this woman?' Jack Preston limped forward slowly, and Flora smiled. His bowler was not sitting straight but set at a jaunty angle. Was that due to too much rum or her sister's hand? Flora could remember a younger Hilda placing another bowler on her head and doing a Charlie Chaplin impression. Was her sister ready for marriage? She was still pondering that question as the organ music swelled and the bride and groom processed up the aisle.

'It was a luverly wedding.' Maggie beamed at Flora as they stood in the crowded room about the Bakery sipping port and lemon. 'I'm awful glad that I was invited.'

'I'm glad you came.' Her eyes were warm. 'There's not many people I know here.'

'I wasn't sure whether to come.' Maggie's expression was suddenly downcast. 'I've had a few funny turns lately. I think it's me age, and Mr Brown does expect his pound of flesh. But I'll say this for your sister — she knows just how to get round him. As sweet as pie she is to him when I've seen them together, but she's saucy for all that.' She took another sip of her drink. 'She said that she might come to a gathering with me. That there's a couple of men that she'd like to have a word with. Wants to know what they meant by leaving her in the lurch the way they did.'

Flora stared at her. Was Hilda referring to Tom and Jimmy? It was possible. Her sister had a wicked sense of humour at times. 'I think she might be teasing you, Maggie.'

The older woman went pink and giggled. 'I did think she might be. She's a naughty one! That's why I thought I'd mention it to you. Because you know what Mr Brown's like over me getting in touch. He thinks it's a big joke.'

Flora's eyes strayed to where Kevin stood by the window that stretched almost floor to high moulded ceiling. He was talking to Stephen and even as Flora looked at them, Stephen turned his head and stared at her. Their gaze held a moment before he gave his full attention to Kevin once more. She continued to talk to Maggie a little longer before moving in the direction of the fireplace where George was perched on the arm of his grandad's chair. Before she reached them, Stephen came up to her, a smile on his craggy face.

'Hello, Floss. You look smashing.'

'Thank you.' Her voice was light. 'How have you been, Steve?'

'Busy. That's why you haven't seen much of me,' he said quickly. 'Haven't had much time for being sociable. There's a lot involved in running a business.'

'I'm sure there is. How's the Old Man?'

Stephen stroked his cheek with the edge of his glass, and seemed to be searching for words. 'Not too good. He gave me quite a fright a couple of weeks ago. Had a bit of a heart attack.'

'But he's all right now?' she asked, concerned.

'Oh, he's fine now!' A muscle twitched in his cheek. 'He's not getting any younger, of course. So one has to expect these things.'

'Poor ol' man,' said Flora softly, twisting her sherry glass between slender fingers. 'I've always been fond of him.'

'He was fond of you, Floss,' he said seriously. 'I'm sure he'd appreciate a visit from you. That's if you've got time, of course,' he added hastily. 'I know how busy you are, but I could always pick you up at your house.'

She hesitated. 'I'd like to – but I don't know whether I'll be able to or not. If I can fit it in, I'll let you know.'

They both fell silent and Flora was wondering how she could get away when Stephen said, 'Have you given any more thought to coming to work for me?'

'Not really,' she said hurriedly. 'Although I have been considering changing my job lately.'

Stephen's face brightened. 'Then why don't you come? I'd be real made up to have you, Floss, as you know.'

'Maybe.' She felt guilty for not feeling over-enthusiastic, but she had her reasons. Even so she was not keen at all on staying where she was. 'Perhaps I could let you know next week? I can't walk out on Mr Brown right now when he's taking a couple of days off for his honeymoon.'

'Of course not.' He squeezed her arm. 'I admire your loyalty, Floss. Can I get you another sherry?'

'Thanks.' She handed him her glass and watched him cross the room.

Vivien tugged at her sleeve. 'D'you think Uncle Steve would get me a lemonade if I asked him? I can't get anybody to take any notice of me.'

'I'm sure he would,' said Flora, considering that it might not be such a bad thing if Stephen and the girl made friends. 'You just go and ask him.'

Vivien pushed her way through the throng. Several people patted her head and made a path for her. She responded like a flower to the sun, lifting her face and smiling. She was an attractive child, thought Flora. Perhaps if she did go and see the Old Man, it might not be a bad idea if she took Vivien with her.

She sat down to await Stephen's return only to have him come back accompanied by Hilda, her white satiny skirts hushing on the polished wooden floor. 'Well, Flo! What do you think? Wasn't it a lovely wedding?'

'Lovely,' agreed Flora, smiling up at her. 'When will you be leaving for your honeymoon?'

'Soon. We're going to Blackpool – staying in a posh hotel. It should be fun. There'll be music, dancing.' Hilda's blue eyes sparkled. 'You'll have to come and wave us off. A taxi's coming at five o'clock. In the meantime I'll go and check that everybody's enjoying themselves.' She turned her attention momentarily on Stephen. 'Don't let her get away from you this time. She needs an upright, strong chap like you to keep her out of the hands of the riff raff of the new world,' she said with a mischievous twinkle. 'Flo's so easily led astray.' She fluttered away, a mothlike creature, thought Flora, attracted to the bright lights.

'Upright,' muttered Stephen. 'She makes me sound stuffy.' He tossed back his sherry in one go. 'What's she mean about the riff raff of the new world?'

'One of our Hilda's jokes,' murmured Flora, not prepared to tell him about Mike being a Yank.

'Oh!' He frowned. 'I'll take you home if you like. I've got the car.'

'You'll have to make room for Viv and George as well?'

He nodded. 'D'you want to go now?'

Flora shook her head. 'I'd like to see my sister off first.' He agreed and began to talk about how the firm was expanding.

It was less than an hour later when they all trooped downstairs and spilled out on to the pavement. Kevin and Hilda followed a couple of minutes later, the bride now clad in an airforce blue coat and matching hat with a wide brim. She carried her bouquet of white carnations and red roses.

She stood on the running board of the taxi. 'Who's going to be next?' she cried, her face alight.

'Me!' called a couple of girls. Hilda laughed, her eyes scanned the group, and the next moment the bouquet soared into the air in Flora's direction. Instinctively as it plummetted towards her she caught it.

'Well held!' cried Hilda, half in, half out of the taxi. 'I'll expect an invite, Flo.'

'Let's go,' said Kevin, his handsome face impatient as he dragged on her sleeve. Hilda waved and the next moment they were gone.

The group began to disperse except for those who were staying behind to clear up. Flora had not been asked to help so did not like to offer. Stephen was at her elbow. 'Are you ready, Floss?'

'As ready as I'll ever be,' she murmured, looking round for George who did not look too pleased when he was told who was taking them home. He brightened up however when Stephen said he would not come into the house as he wanted to pop into work and check something.

Sunday morning was quiet and uneventful in comparison, and Flora decided that she would go to the cemetery and put Hilda's flowers on the family grave while Vivien and George were at Sunday School. She was just walking down the step when Mike came up the street.

'Here comes the bride,' he drawled, pushing his cap to the back of his head.

Flora smiled faintly. 'I'm going the cemetery, and I've got to go now to be back for the kids.'

'I'll come with you,' he said resignedly. 'How's things been with you? How was Christmas?'

'Fine.' She lowered her eyes. 'Thanks for the presents.'

'My pleasure.'

'I haven't opened the champagne .' She pulled on his arm. 'Let's go up the entry. Mrs Jones has probably got her spyglass out.' She was feeling nervous and quickly changed the subject. 'Hilda got married yesterday. She looked lovely. It all went off very well.'

'Good!' he exclaimed, his eyes narrowing as he looked at her sidelong. 'Is there something new about Mrs Jones spying on people?'

Flora shrugged. 'Mrs Murphy's had words with me.' She tried to sound amused. 'You and me are *big news*. A clean living Catholic boy like you going out with a tarty piece like me! I'm leading you astray.'

He grimaced. 'You're hurt.'

'Yes,' she murmured. 'George could get to realise what's going on between us and I don't want that.'

He squeezed her hand against his side. 'You know the answer. Make an honest man of me.'

245

'Easier said than done.'

'There's always a way round things, Flora,' he said roughly.

'So you say.' She frowned. 'I didn't want to go straight at this as soon as I saw you. Where've you been the last couple of weeks?'

'You've missed me?'

'Do you need to ask that?' He was silent and suddenly she thought, maybe it was better that he doubted her love. The thought was painful. She took a deep breath. 'Mike, I can't go on as we are – *fornicating*. I went to church yesterday and waited for the thunderbolt. I felt terrible. I've lost people's respect and I don't like it. I've always done the proper thing before.'

'So what do we do if you won't marry me?' His voice was deep and intense. 'Keep two feet between us on the sofa and shake hands at the door?'

'We could try,' she said firmly, avoiding looking at him and taking her hand out of his arm.

He stopped and stared at her. 'You mean it!'

'Of course I mean it. You don't think I say that sort of thing for fun!'

He swore softly and carried on walking so fast that she had to run to keep up with him. They came to the main road. 'I know it's hard on you,' she said.

'Only on me?' He laughed. 'You're kidding yourself if you think it'll only be me that'll suffer.'

She flushed. 'I know. But I've done without before. There's more to life than – than –'

'Sex!' he yelled.

Several people looked in their direction and Flora wished herself anywhere but where she was. 'I could kill you,' she said through gritted teeth. 'Here's the tram and I'm getting on it. You can do what you like.' At the moment she did not care what he did.

He followed her on to the tram but instead of sitting next to her, he sat on the seat behind. Three stops later he hissed against her ear, 'It's impossible, Flo. The man-woman thing has to be going somewhere. That's progress. We can't just have a platonic friendship now.'

'You'd rather we stopped seeing each other?' Her voice was low. 'I can't see any other way out of this, Mike.'

'You refuse to see any other way,' he whispered. 'Marry me.'

'Stop saying that! I've told you I can't.'

'Won't.'

Flora got up and sat on another seat. A few minutes later Mike moved into the place beside her. 'How far is this cemetery anyway?' he said gloomily.

'Not far.' They sat silently until Stanley Park came into view, and then Flora got up. Mike followed suit, walking a little behind her until she crossed the road.

They entered the cemetery and Flora could feel the tension building up inside her. It was an impossible situation. She started when Mike spoke. 'Sweet Jesus, some of these died young.'

'Yes.' She read the inscription on the pink and white marble gravestone he was staring at and then walked on. 'You know what they say – only the good die young.'

'We should live forever then,' murmured Mike wickedly, before adding quietly, '"Father, I have sinned and fallen short –"'

'Don't,' she said with a passion that took them both by surprise. 'The wages of sin are death! Surely you know that one. I'm worked up about it all, Mike. I don't need reminding I've broken the rules.' Her fingers twisted agitatedly among the flowers in the bouquet.

He stared at her, a certain rigidity about his mouth. 'I would have married you from the word go. If you'd agreed then you wouldn't be torturing yourself like this. It makes me wonder how you ever came to suggest our making love that first time.'

'I thought I would never see you again,' she whispered, coming to a halt in front of the family plot. Resting on one knee, she removed the fading Christmas wreath. Without speaking she fetched water and placed the flowers in a container. She stayed there a while longer, gazing down at the grave, while Mike stood watching her.

Neither of them spoke till they moved away. 'If you loved me,' he said in a strong voice, 'you'd marry me. I respect your reasons yet I wonder why you aren't prepared to make sacrifices for me.'

She glanced at him. '*If* I loved you. What's that supposed to mean? You don't think I'd have gone to bed with you if I didn't.'

'I don't know,' he said with great deliberation. 'Perhaps you only wanted me for one thing.'

Colour flooded her face. 'You're suggesting that I've used you for sex,' she said tight-lipped. 'Well, I'll ask you this, Mike – would my behaviour be any worse than yours if I had? I've only ever been with Tom and you. How many women have you had?'

'That's in the past,' he said harshly. 'We're talking about now.'

'So we are!' Her hazel eyes flashed green. 'So how can you say I want you for your body when I'm suggesting a no strings friendship? And why is it you've talked about *me* making sacrifices?'

'Okay!' He held up a hand. 'You've made your point about my body. It seems you don't want it. But the other thing – a woman's always lived where her man does.'

'Oh yeah!' She laughed bitterly. 'What you're asking me to do is to say to hell with my father – to hell with my son's ambitions to play football for Liverpool – to hell with my faith – to hell with coming here and tending my daughter's grave. Who would do that if I wasn't here?' she asked in a furious voice.

'Oh, come on, Flora, I'm not saying it like that.' He kicked up a cloud of gravel. 'I admire you for wanting to do what's right but I want you as my wife. There would be gains, Flora, for you. A whole new life. A better life!'

'In America,' she said grimly.

'In America,' he reiterated.

'I won't do it,' she said, digging her hands deep into the pockets of her mustard and brown coat. 'I can't.'

'Won't,' he retorted harshly. 'You had it right the first time.' There was a silence.

'Then it's goodbye,' said Mike. 'We can't go on the way we are and we can't just be friends. I can't anyway. It's all or nothing, Flora.'

She felt sick inside. 'Then it's nothing,' she whispered.

They stared at each other and there seemed a peculiar stillness in the air.

'I'll see you home,' he said quietly.

She tilted her chin. 'You don't have to. I know the way.'

'I'll see you home.' His voice was a little louder.

'Mike, I'm not a child,' she snapped. 'Let's finish it here and now. It had to come sooner or later.' She thrust out a hand.

He took it and held it so long that she had to snatch it back. Then she turned and walked away.

Chapter Twenty

The next few days were difficult for Flora and the nights even harder. She did not kid herself that it was going to be any easier getting over Mike this time than it had been three years ago. She kept half-expecting to find him waiting on her doorstep when she arrived home but he was never there.

Hilda and Kevin came back from their honeymoon and a couple of days later, to Flora's surprise, her sister announced that she was going to work part time in the shop. 'It's Kevin's idea,' said Hilda brightly, breathing on her painted nails and polishing them on the overall she had donned. 'The Brown women, apparently, have always helped in the shop. It's a real family business.'

'I can understand that,' murmured Flora, wrapping a loaf in tissue paper for a customer. 'Not that I've ever seen any sign of his family in here.'

'You know what I mean, Flo.' Hilda pulled a face. 'The only problem is that Kev expects me to get up with him at some ungodly hour and cook his breakfast, and then help him in the back.'

'You can cook, can you?' said Flora drily. 'That's something new. Learned how in Paris, I suppose.'

'Very funny.' Hilda yawned as delicately as a cat. 'But making toast isn't that difficult — as long as you watch it. The trouble is I forgot about it because I was *that* tired.' She frowned and lowered her voice. 'The toast was only a bit black, but you'd think I'd committed all of the seven deadly sins. Anyway I got it right the next time so that was all right.'

Flora could not help being amused. 'What are you going to do for tea?'

Hilda wrinkled her nose. 'I can open a can — and boil some potatoes. There can't be anything hard about that.'

Flora raised her eyebrows. 'As long as you don't forget about them.'

'I'm not stupid,' said Hilda, moving away as Kevin came into the shop. She addressed the next customer cheerfully. 'What is it you want, mate?'

The customer responded with a smiling alacrity and Flora was aware that Kevin watched his wife for several minutes before shifting his attention to her. He gave her the briefest of unsmiling nods then went back into the bakeroom. She remembered her former resolution to find another job — but maybe she would give it a few more days. It would be interesting to see how her sister dealt with her husband and being a part time housewife and shop assistant.

'Flo! How d'you make rice pudding?' Hilda whispered furtively. It was a couple of days later and Flora and Maggie were already at work when Hilda came into the shop.

'Lucky you, having rice to make a pudding with,' said Flora, smiling.

'Aren't I just?' said Hilda impatiently. 'I don't know what he wants rice pudding for when we're surrounded by jam tarts and cakes. But he's bought a bag of the stuff and I suppose I'll at least have to have a go.'

'Yer can get sick of cake if yer lookin' at it all day,' said Maggie.

'I didn't ask you,' snapped Hilda, scowling as she watched Maggie opening the till.

The older woman reddened. 'I'm sorry, Mrs Brown.'

Flora nudged Hilda. 'Don't be so sharp with her. She's got a point, you know.'

Hilda tapped her foot on the floor. 'I didn't ask you, Flo, to give me lessons on how to handle the staff. Now are you going to tell me about this rice pudding or not?'

'If you keep a civil tongue in your head,' said Flora, her mouth tightening slightly.

'Oh, all right!' Hilda frowned. 'It's just this cooking lark. I always thought it was easy.'

'It is, once you get a bit of practice.' Some of Flora's irritation evaporated. 'Come on, Hilda. It's not that hard. An ovenproof dish — two tablespoons of rice, sugar, a knob of butter, a sprinkling of grated nutmeg, and a pint of milk or water, depending on what you can afford. You just bung them all together and in the oven on a low heat for a couple of hours.'

'It sounds simple enough,' said Hilda cautiously, nodding her head slowly. 'Thanks, Flo.' She breathed out with relief. 'You will bring Viv on Saturday, won't you?' Flora nodded and got on with her work.

That evening Stephen called. 'I've come to see if you've made up your mind about coming back to the firm,' he said, accepting the cup of tea she offered. 'Only Molly's left me high and dry and I have to get somebody in a hurry.'

Flora was surprised. 'It's not like Molly to let people down.'

'We had a tiff,' he said shortly and pursed his lips. 'She was always interfering and putting in her tupenny ha'penny worth. You know the way she is.'

Flora thought it wiser to say nothing and for a moment she hesitated before saying, 'When would you want me to start? You say you want someone in a hurry but I'd have to serve my notice.'

'I understand that.' His face brightened. 'You'll come then, Floss?'

'Yes. If we can agree that I only work till four everyday and no Saturdays,' she said decisively, feeling certain that there could be a thousand irritations with her sister if she stayed in the bakery.

'No problem. I need you.' He paused then added, 'Are you still seeing that Mike fella?'

'No,' she said shortly.

He smiled. 'That's all right then.'

Flora felt sure she knew what he meant and was uneasy. He began to talk about how business had really taken off, Hilda's wedding, and the latest film he had seen.

Vivien came in and made a fuss of him. Fortunately he left before George came home and disturbed the harmony of a fairly pleasant evening. All Flora had to do now was break the news of her departure to Kevin and Hilda, something she looked forward to with mixed feelings.

'You're giving notice! Why?' demanded Kevin, his face twisted with annoyance. 'Is it more money you want? Out with it if it is!'

'Money's only part of it,' said Flora, standing upright and composed in front of him in the untidy bakeroom. 'It's the hours mainly. I don't like working Saturdays.'

'That could be worked round.' He took off his cap and threw it on the table and lit a cigarette. 'Now that Hilda's working here, she could do Saturdays for you.'

'No thanks,' said Flora. 'I'm going back to my old job.'

'In the printing?' He drew deeply on his cigarette, leaning against the table. 'For that Stephen Martin your Hilda invited to the wedding?'

'Yes.'

There was a brief silence and he exhaled a cloud of smoke. 'Does he know about your Yank?'

Flora's eyelashes flickered. 'It's none of your business.'

'He's packed you in, has he?' he said with a slight smile.

'Have you finished poking your nose into my affairs, Mr Brown?' she said, more calmly than she felt. 'I'll get on with work if you have.'

He nodded and shooed her away with both arms.

Flora went into the shop carrying a tray of tin loaves, only to be brought up short by Hilda stopping in front of her. 'Why were you so long in the back with Kev?' Her eyes were narrowed suspiciously.

Flora smiled sweetly. 'I was giving in my notice. So now if you'll get out of my way? This bread's heavy.'

'Your notice! Why?' Hilda sounded bewildered. 'Is it working with me? I know we don't always see eye to eye —'

'No.' She began to place the loaves on the shelves. 'It's several things but the main one is that I don't like working Saturdays.' She glanced over her shoulder. 'You should be glad because you won't have to have Viv now.'

'But — but I like having Viv,' said Hilda quickly. 'I can still have her in the mornings. It'll give you a break, Flo.'

Flora stared at her. 'You surprise me, but okay. Thanks.'

'It's the least I can do to help you out.'

A small laugh escaped Flora. 'Could it be said that marriage is improving you?'

'It could.' Hilda smiled. 'But that depends on whether you believe I can be improved on.'

'Conceit!' Flora shook her head at her. 'How was the rice pudding?'

Hilda grimaced. 'He ate it – that's all I'll say.'

Flora's expression was one of puzzlement. 'What went wrong?'

Her sister shrugged. 'Two tablespoons of rice didn't look much in all that milk.'

'So you put more in.' Flora smiled.

'I kept putting more in,' said Hilda, giggling unexpectedly. 'And more. You could stand a spoon up in it in the end.'

'Rice swells,' said Flora.

'I know that *now*.' Hilda frowned at her. 'Where are you going when you leave?'

Flora hesitated, not wanting her sister to read things into what she was going to say. 'Stephen's place.'

'Oh! So you've taken your big sister's advice at last.' She looked towards Maggie and one of the new girls as the bell jangled and a couple of customers came in. 'What about Mike?'

'I decided to stop seeing him,' said Flora, and walked away before Hilda could ask any more questions; although she expected her sister to say more about Mike some other time.

To Flora's surprise, during the following week her sister remained unusually silent on the subject. Instead she seemed determined to make the other girls and Maggie realise that she was to be treated with the respect that her position as the boss's wife merited. Flora felt sorry for Maggie and when on her last day her friend said, 'I'm really gonna miss yer. Yer the only one I felt like I could talk to. These young ones are flighty,' she felt like a traitor, and realised that she was going to miss Maggie and her talks of the Other Side, as well as the smell of freshly baked bread. Printer's ink didn't have quite the same appeal.

Still Flora had made up her mind and she started at

Martin's, to be reminded almost instantly of Rosie as she entered the lobby that had been given its brighter coat of paint the day that her daughter had drowned. She brushed the sad memory aside and instead set her thoughts on her job. It was obvious that the firm was doing well. All the machines were in operation and there was a general air of prosperity about the place. There were quite a few new faces, and one other old face besides Molly's had gone — Johnny Foy's. She commented about it and received a curt answer from Stephen.

'I would have kept him on only he gave in his notice when my uncle packed in. Said he'd always had a yen to try his hand at a smallholding in Wales.' He raised his eyebrows. 'I'd never heard him mention it before, had you?' She shook her head. 'I ask you! To throw everything up at his age and gamble his savings.'

'He's all the more to be admired, don't you think?' said Flora. 'He's got guts.'

Stephen smiled. 'You always make excuses for people, Floss. That's what I like about you.' He squeezed her shoulder and walked away.

Flora wondered if it was true that she made excuses for people. She had only said what she had because she believed Mr Foy had left because he and the Old Man had been through a lot together and she doubted he would have liked Stephen's new regime.

She had not been back long before she realised that the girl who had taken her own place was not a quarter as good as Molly had been at the job, and not a half as good as herself. She relaxed a little. Perhaps Stephen's reasons for asking her back were purely business.

Then he asked her to go out with him. She made the children her excuse. Stephen could never take Mike's place and she would rather suffer the dreadful loneliness and deprivation of life without him. But Stephen was persistent, and in the end she said yes when he asked her to visit his uncle with him.

She was shocked by the change in him. He was agitated and fussed a lot and seemed unable to keep a conversation going. She felt that Stephen was to blame by retiring him too early but kept that to herself.

George was not too pleased about her renewed friendship with Stephen but her father rejoiced. 'You've come to your senses at last,' he crowed. Vivien was delighted, although she mourned Mike's no longer being on the scene.

It was on the tip of Flora's tongue several times in Stephen's company to bring up the matter of Jimmy and Hilda being friends years ago — and so work her way round to Vivien, and Hilda's confessing to who her father was. But some inner voice always prevented her from doing so, despite Hilda's encouragement.

Her sister was another one pleased about Flora's relationship with Stephen. 'Now you're showing sense, Flo. He's got enough money for you to be comfortable, and when that uncle of his snuffs it, you'll have a ready made home with garden and bathroom. Everything you want for yourself and Viv. Let's be honest — she has a right to all that. If Jimmy hadn't been killed, it would be me and Viv in your place.'

Flora was not convinced, and besides she had been talking to Vivien and had a bone to pick with her sister. 'Viv's been telling me that you've had her working for you in the flat,' she said tersely. 'If that's true then I think you should give her pocket money.'

Hilda stared at her, a picture of wide-eyed innocence. 'I don't see why I should. She's my daughter and she's glad to help me out.'

'Help out!' exclaimed Flora. 'From what she says she's doing more than helping out while you're putting on your nail varnish.'

'That's a lie,' said Hilda strongly. 'I'd nearly finished my nails by the time she arrived.'

'You'll pay her,' said Flora emphatically, her hands on her hips and her expression determined.

Hilda shrugged. 'I'll give her sixpence.'

'A shilling,' said Flora. 'You're not an invalid and you've given little enough to Viv in the last couple of years.'

A flush darkened Hilda's cheeks and an angry retort was on the tip of her tongue, only she remembered in time that Kevin did not like kids that much and Flora just might get awkward. 'Okay!' she murmured. 'It'll be worth it. You've trained her well, Flo. I'll give you that.'

'Thanks. Could you come and pick her up in future? Because I've been asked to go in the odd Saturday morning and it's likely that I won't know just which one till the night before.'

'Sure. That's fine with me.'

'And you'll see that she gets back safe?'

Hilda blew out a stream of smoke. 'Of course,' she said with a long suffering air. 'Now I'll have to be going.'

Hilda did come and pick Vivien up, and for that Flora was relieved. The only fault that Flora could find with her was that she lingered and went on about how strong and virile and like James Mason Kevin was — and that Flora really should think of marrying Stephen.

The weeks passed, heralding in spring and the expected arrival of the Murphys' baby. It was Kathleen who breathlessly brought them the news. 'I've got a brother! We're callin' him Brendan Patrick Edward Michael, and Mam said would yer like to be coming and seeing him?'

Flora flushed with pleasure. 'I would.' She had only passed the barest of times of day with Carmel since their exchange over Mike in the street.

'Can I come?' demanded Vivien.

'Yeah!' Kathleen's eyes sparkled. 'Mam wouldn't mind if the whole street comes. Dad's gone the boozer to wet the baby's head. I bet he's already halfway to being paralytic.'

So they went to see the Murphy boy and an exhausted Carmel lying in the front parlour. 'He's beautiful,' Flora said dishonestly, but expecting that Brendan Patrick Edward Michael would improve once he got over the shock of the birth.

'Nine pounds, ten ounces,' Carmel informed her weakly but proudly. 'He nearly killed me. Paddy says he. doesn't know where he came from being that big, and him so small an' all.'

'He's got Paddy's eyes and nose,' said Flora, gazing into the squashed features. 'As for size, Carmel, he must take after his mother. You're a fine figure of a woman,' she teased.

She smiled. 'It's good of you to say so, Flo. I'm glad we're speaking proper.' She lowered her voice so that the girls crooning over the baby in the drawer would not hear. 'I'm sorry if I hurt your feelings over Mike. I see he hasn't been around for a long time. I hope it wasn't – '

'It was, but – ' Flora forced a smile. 'I had to make the decision sooner or later as to where we were going. And there were too many things in the way for us to go anywhere in the end.'

Carmel moved her head wearily against the pillow. 'It's a pity, Flo, because you made a lovely couple.'

Flora shrugged. 'Our Hilda got married.'

'George told Kathleen. A lovely wedding, I believe.'

Flora raised her eyebrows. 'Did our George say that? I'm surprised.'

'No. It was Viv. She talks to the other girls. Been telling them about working for your sister.' She chuckled unexpectedly and the girls turned and looked at her.

Vivien said, 'Me and Mam have this game where I have to crawl under the bed and bring out Uncle Kev's socks and underwear.'

'Doesn't sound much fun,' said Flora drily.

'Mam said that about one of the new girls,' informed Vivien. 'She wants Uncle Kev to get rid of her.'

'Why? Which one is she?' asked Flora, unable to conceal her curiosity.

'Dark and smiley. She laughs a lot at things Uncle Kev says and he laughs with her. Mam says that what he's up to isn't funny. But I think it is funny when they laugh. Perhaps he tickles her. He tickles me sometimes then gives me a shilling. Mam had a row with him the other morning and threw a cup at him.'

'Did it break?' asked Kathleen with sudden interest.

Vivien nodded. 'I had to clean it up. It was one of the nice ones that had been Uncle Kev's Mam's – china with flowers on it. He wasn't half angry and gave me an extra sixpence for clearing it up before he told me to go on home.'

Flora grimaced. 'Do they often argue in front of you?'

Vivien shrugged. 'Not all the time. Mam says she likes a good argument – that it clears the air.'

'That's true,' said Flora, deciding it would be better to

drop the subject. She was vaguely worried about her sister but thought it better to keep her worries to herself. She began to talk confinements — a subject that she thought would take Carmel's mind off Hilda, herself and Mike. Although now he had been mentioned it was difficult for her not to dwell on the times they had spent together and to wonder what he was doing.

Despite all her good intentions, Flora had followed with almost greedy interest the reports in the local newspaper about the goings on at Burtonwood base, or Little Detroit as it was nicknamed. There had been a lot of changes in the lot of the servicemen. Living quarters had been improved and recreation halls built. There was a basketball team, the Burtonwood Bullets, whose record of wins was phenomenal. They even had a football team, the Burtonwood Eagles. Every week a ship sailed into Liverpool from America to stock up the base's shops with food special to the American palate, and consumer goods which were hard to come by in Britain. There was a dance hall and a theatre.

She read of records being broken in how many planes could be cleaned and maintained and sent back to carry on the air lift to the Western Sectors of Berlin. Of giant Globemasters landing at the airport. Flora wondered how long it could go on.

Then in May the Russians gave up the blockade and Flora stopped reading the papers, not wanting to know when the Yanks would move out of Burtonwood.

That same month Stephen's uncle died of a heart attack.

Flora went to the funeral, an occasion of mingled sadness and pleasure. It was good to see Molly there and to talk of old times. She realised that was a sign of her getting older. In June she would be thirty-one. Suddenly she remembered how Stephen had talked of birthdays and having years and years ahead of her. She had yelled at him, only able to think of the loneliness without Tom. Then Stephen had made her fight back, and at the same time roused her pity. She had liked that Stephen — but the new one? She watched him talking to Molly's husband. He had put on some weight and his jawline was blurred. Success was changing him. He looked over at her and waved a hand and suddenly she had a terrible sense of fatalism. He would persist and she would marry for Vivien's and comfort's sake, and that would be that. She was glad when the funeral tea was over.

A week or so later on the Whit bank holiday Flora was enjoying a day off work, although she was not having a day away from the boss. Stephen had said he would call later in the afternoon. George and Vivien were playing out and Flora was just about to have a cup of tea when the knocker sounded.

Hilda stood on the step, wearing a new waist-length jigger coat in scarlet. It had wide sleeves and deep cuffs and was fastened by a single button at the neck. Flora envied her it.

'Hello, Flo. I thought I'd come on a social visit.' Her voice sounded artificially bright.

'I'm flattered,' she responded with a smile. 'But aren't you and Kevin going out, seeing as how it's a holiday?'

Hilda pulled a face. 'He's working — and he expected me to work as well. I told him I'm sick of it!'

An old familiar feeling swept over Flora. 'You'd better come in,' she said, leading the way.

Hilda sat, pulling out the inevitable packet of cigarettes. Flora watched her light up, noticing that she had more make-up on than usual.

Her sister inhaled deeply and closed her eyes. 'That's better,' she murmured. 'It's been a hell of a day already because I told Kevin that I'm quitting the shop. I've been pulling my guts out in that bakery as well as trying to keep the flat clean and everything else.' The cat came and stropped its head against her ankles. She pushed it away with her foot, her expression taut. 'Well, I'm not doing it any more. Watching that girl going in and out of the back, and listening to her giggling drives me mad! She's been doing hardly any of what I'd call real work.'

'She's pretty, isn't she?' said Flora, unable to resist making a comment.

A spasm twisted her sister's face. 'I wouldn't say so. Flirty and fluffy more like! But Kevin can't see anything wrong with her. He says that I'm being ridiculous — that I'm jealous!

260

Me — jealous!' She gnawed at her lip. 'I know why he won't get rid of her, of course.'

'Why?'

'He's getting back at me because I threw away all his socks.'

Flora stared at her. 'What?'

Hilda smiled maliciously. 'I used to wash the smelly things in the early days, but I took all the skin off the back of my fingers.' She gazed down at her hands with their painted nails. 'I asked him for one of those new boiler type machines, but he refused to buy me one — so I refused to wash his socks. They mounted up and then when he couldn't find a clean pair and complained, I brought up about the machine again. He told me to go to hell — so I threw out all his socks.'

Flora had to struggle to keep a straight face. 'What did he say?'

Hilda raised delicately drawn-in eyebrows. 'What didn't he say? We had a helluva row and I'm sure he'd have liked to have throttled me.' The hand that raised the cigarette shook. 'He doesn't lift a cup, you know, Flo. He thinks that once his work has finished, that's it. He never hangs anything up and he throws his underwear under the bed. I'm sure he does that deliberately. I used to get it out but I've stopped that. When our Viv comes I send her under.'

'I know, she told me.'

Hilda shrugged. 'I suppose she told you about the fights we have, as well?'

'Only the odd one. Perhaps things'll be easier now that you're given up the bakery?'

Hilda shrugged. 'Kevin's not pleased about it. Slave labour, that's what I was in that shop. He wasn't paying me as much as Maggie and I'm his wife.' She puffed at her cigarette, her brows drawn together. 'I'm not being a slave for no man. You used to slave for Tom. I don't think I could be like you, Flo, not in a hundred years.'

'But you started well. You could change a little bit more if you wanted to.'

Hilda flicked ash into the fire. 'There you have it, Flo. I don't want to change any more. I wouldn't be me then.' She got up. 'I think I'll go into town and look in the shops.'

Flora stood as well. 'I was just thinking of going out when you came. Father's marching with the Lodges today. Why don't you come with me to watch?'

Hilda did not answer immediately. Slowly she picked up her jacket, staring at her reflection in the mirror as she put it on. Flora wondered what was going on in her mind, then she noticed the dark shadow on her cheekbone. Their glances caught and Hilda smiled brightly. 'I think I will come with you. We'll probably get caught up in the crowds but it'll be like old times when Mother used to take us.'

'Fine,' said Flora with forced cheerfulness, grabbing her two tone mustard coat. 'Let's go then.'

They picked up Vivien on the way and chattered about everything but nothing as they walked through Sheil Park to stand on the corner of Boaler Street among the noisy crowd. In the distance could be heard the deep tone of a single drum beat. The sound grew closer and closer and with it came files of marching men and women. Banners fluttered and flutes began to play. 'I hope we haven't missed Father,' whispered Flora against her sister's scented ear. 'Some have already gone into the park by the look of it.'

'Does it matter?' said Hilda, frowning.

It did to Flora but she said nothing, only watching as two girls dressed as William of Orange and his queen Mary, with their hair in long ringlets, led a procession of men in uniform, and women and children in peach satin dresses. Suddenly they burst into song and so did some of the people on the pavement. 'Sons of the sea, and we're all British Boys, Sailing the ocean . . .'

There was a sudden loud 'Coo hee!' a few feet away from Flora and Hilda, and the next moment they saw a woman dance into the road beside the marching men. She had her black skirts high revealing a pair of emerald green knickers.

A giggle burst from Flora, and Hilda's face lit up. 'If your mother comes from Ireland,' they sang.

The woman, who looked about forty, slanted them a roguish look before skipping along in an attempt to keep pace with the men who after hurried glances, acted as if she were not there.

262

Perhaps its was being ignored by them that drove her to act in a foolhardy fashion because she attempted to weave a dancing step between the men and caused several to stumble.

An angry murmur rippled through the ranks to be echoed in parts of the crowd. The intruder was seized by one of the marching women. A struggle began and both women were soon on the ground. Hair was being pulled, names called. Another peach-dressed woman joined the tussle. The green knickers seemed destined to be dragged in the gutter to hoots of derision. Then a policeman on a horse came charging up. Stones were thrown and the next minute there was a free for all as Orange and Green sides were taken.

'Let's get Viv out of here,' said Flora. Hilda nodded and without any further ado they linked arms and managed to force their way out of the crowd.

The two sisters paused to straighten their hats on the other side of the road. 'That was fun till it got nasty,' said Flora.

Hilda nodded. 'Orange and Green — they're just opposing sides in a game. Like Everton and Liverpool football teams.'

'And like football fans they have their heroes,' muttered Flora moodily. 'William of Orange! He wasn't even British. He crossed the Boyne in Ireland and defeated the Catholics. Now we're enemies because of some battle hundreds of years ago.'

'What's up with you?' said Hilda. 'We've always known that.'

'Yes, and it's daft. Christians are supposed to love each other.'

'Hmmm! Like green knickers and peach frock. It'll take some doing,' said Hilda. 'I wonder if she was drunk.'

'It took guts.' Flora suddenly smiled. 'She was probably tipsy. People do the daftest things when they drink.'

Hilda solemnly agreed. 'Where are you going now?'

'Might as well go the park and find Father there.'

Hilda pulled a face. 'I'll see you then. I'd better go home and see how his Lordship is. He just might enjoy the joke.'

Flora did not know exactly why but she was certain in that moment that the shadow on her sister's face was a bruise, and the reason for her wearing so much make-up. 'Take care of yourself,' she said, leaning forward and planting a kiss on her sister's cheek.

Hilda drew back, a slightly disdainful smile tugging at her mouth. 'What's up with you, little sister? I can take care of myself, don't you worry.' And with those parting words she walked away.

Flora stood a moment, staring after her. Then she took Vivien's hand and they went towards the park.

Chapter Twenty-One

'Did you like the house?'

'What?' Flora summoned her wandering attention and replied to Stephen as they walked home from the pictures.

'My uncle's house.' He squeezed her hand. 'It would do us for now, Floss.' His deep blue eyes were warm with confidence. 'The furniture's a bit old-fashioned but it's good stuff. Not like what they're making these days. Utility! I get sick of hearing that word.'

'I agree with you about the furniture,' she murmured. 'But I haven't said I'll marry you yet, Steve.'

'You will.' He smiled. 'You're a sensible woman, Floss. Look what I can give you. And things'll get better.'

'I can't be bought,' she said determinedly. 'I'm fond of you but I don't love you.'

He frowned. 'Tom's been dead five years.' He fingered the scar near his eye. 'You can't still be carrying a torch for him.'

'I'm not! Forget Tom, Steve. It's just that I don't want to be rushed.'

He smiled. 'All right, I understand that,' he said playfully. 'But I'm not giving up. I had a letter from France from a mate of mine. He married a French girl he met in Caen. Suggested I might go over and visit them sometime. It wouldn't be a bad idea.' He smiled at her. 'I thought perhaps we could go there for our honeymoon.'

Flora stared at him. 'When were you thinking of going?' Her voice was low and firmly under control despite the fact that her stomach was twisting itself into a reef knot.

'I think August would be the right time.'

'It's too soon!' The words burst out of her despite the control she thought she had over herself. 'And the children will be home from school. I couldn't possibly leave them with Father for a week or more during the school holidays.'

Stephen's mouth tightened. 'George is old enough now not to be any trouble to your father. He definitely seems to have more sense than he used to. And I don't see why your Hilda can't have the looking after of Viv. She's a nice kid but she's Hilda's after all. It's a ridiculous situation when your sister's got a husband of her own, who can afford to keep them both, and you're keeping her kid!'

Flora was tempted to say, 'But she's your brother's child and *your* responsibility in a way.' She did not, partly because she was not completely convinced that Jimmy was Viv's father. She still half believed that Vivien could be Tom's child. She also realised that Stephen might use the information as a lever to hurry her into marrying him. Time! She needed more time to get over Mike, 'I love Viv,' she said quietly. 'In a way she's taken Rosie's place in the family. I don't know what I would have done without her in those months after I lost Rosie.'

'I can understand that.' Stephen patted her hand. 'But you spend too much time worrying about others. You let people play on your good nature, Floss. Now you must get your priorities right and think of yourself, and us getting married.'

'I wasn't brought up to put myself first,' she murmured, irritated, feeling he was talking down to her.

'Of course you weren't. Your Aunt Beattie did a much better job on you than she did on your Hilda. Selfish, that's your sister! She always did like her own way. Wayward, Mam called her.'

Flora stared straight ahead, glad that the bottom of her street was in sight. 'She's my sister and marriage seems to be quietening her down so if you'll drop the subject, Steve, I'd be glad. You don't mind if I don't ask you in, do you? But I've got a splitting headache and want to get to bed as soon as I can.' She added wickedly, 'Besides, the neighbours do talk and I have my reputation to think about.'

266

'You're kidding me.' He shook his head at her. 'Your father's in your house. And besides the neighbours know me. Probably guessed that we'll be getting married.'

'Probably,' she said lightly. 'But let's keep them guessing, shall we?' She pulled her hand from his. 'Goodnight, Steve, see you tomorrow.' And before he could claim a goodnight kiss she walked swiftly up the street, praying that she was not going to have marriage and a honeymoon in France stuffed down her throat every time she saw him from now on.

Fortunately next day he was out on business. She was relieved, and found herself daydreaming about Mike.

He was still in her thoughts as she lit the fire and put a liver casserole in the oven that evening. On impulse she went over to the sideboard and took out the négligée he had bought her. What would Stephen say if he knew she had received such a gift? She rubbed the silky material against her cheek. Perhaps she would never get to wear it? It wouldn't be right to put it on for Stephen. Suddenly depressed she placed it back in its tissue paper and in the cupboard. Her hands felt the hard outline of the bottle of champagne. It seemed a waste not to drink it and she was in need of cheering up, but somehow it did not seem right to drink alone. She toyed with its foiled top, then put it in her shopping bag.

Brendan was sleeping in his pram on the step outside the Murphys' so Flora knew that Carmel was in. Besides the front door was ajar. She knocked and called up the lobby.

The next moment Carmel popped her head out of the kitchen doorway. 'Come in, Flo girl. My sister Mary's here. She was in the Wrens during the war but I think you've met, haven't you?'

'I don't want to intrude,' said Flora, suddenly thinking that her idea was crazy.

Carmel smiled. 'Don't be an idjit now. Come on in.'

Flora did as she was told, and smiled at Mary. She was an attractive girl with a heart-shaped, merry face, and short black curly hair. She was wearing the new longer look, having lengthened a shorter frock with a different piece of material. The effect was much more feminine than any frock Flora had seen for a long time. They talked about the weather before moving on to the local gossip. Then there was a lull in the conversation when Brendan woke and Carmel brought him in to put him to the breast. Flora thought it an appropriate time to bring out the bottle of champagne. Carmel's and Mary's eyes fixed on it and Flora cleared her throat. 'I was thinking,' she said, 'that I never got round to wetting the baby's head. And I've just found this bottle of champagne in my sideboard cupboard.'

Mary, much younger than Carmel, giggled. 'Just like that. D'you have any leprechauns in your house?'

Flora smiled, and her spirits lightened. 'Well, I got it from someone who had a touch of Irish in him.' She tore the foil off the bottle.

'Mike,' said Carmel, nudging her sister. 'I've told you about him.'

'Ah!' Mary's brown eyes twinkled. 'The charmer. I wish I'd met him if he hands out bottles of champagne.'

'He'd do you more good than that Protestant you've got yourself engaged to,' said Carmel, frowning her down.

Mary wriggled her shoulders uncomfortably. 'Reggie's a good man and he's prepared to go my way. He says I'll have the rearing of the kids, and it's up to me how I bring them up. So don't let's be having a row in front of Flo.'

'No, let's not,' said Flora, her gaze going from one to the other as she tossed the wire into the hearth and began to ease out the cork as she had seen it done in films. The popping sound the cork made as it shot out and hit the wall sounded loud in the small room and somehow filled her with excitement.

'Glasses, quick!' she cried to Carmel.

'Two beer mugs is all we've got,' said the older woman, panicking slightly as Flora tried to stop the fizzing wine with her thumb.

'Here!' said Mary, looping her finger through three cups and thrusting them beneath the bottle. Flora filled them to the brim.

'What shall we drink to?' said Mary, raising her cup.

'To Brendan,' said Flora. They all drank.

'Another toast,' said Carmel. 'To your wedding, Mary. That it'll go off without a hitch.'

'I'm sure it'll be like all weddings. His and hers and never the twain shall meet.' The level of the champagne in the cups dropped.

'The bubbles tickle.' Mary rubbed her nose, smiling. 'Another toast — everything should be done in threes. Let's drink to this Mike.'

'To be sure,' said Flora, whose own accent had taken on a definite Irish lilt, 'we wouldn't be drinking at all, at all, if it wurn't fur dear ol' Mike.'

'To Mike,' said Mary. 'Wherever he may be. Health, wealth and happiness.'

They all drank, but to Flora it suddenly didn't seem such a good idea after all. Did she really want Mike to be happy without her? Perhaps he'd found himself another girl, an all American girl, just as she had got Stephen. She blinked back unexpected tears and emptied the remains of the champagne into their cups.

The talk turned to weddings and which one of the uncles in the Murphy family could drink the rest under the table. The children came home from school and Flora knew she should be heading home. She got up, only to have Mary insist that she have a cup of tea before she went.

'Tea and sympathy,' said Mary, smiling gravely. 'You looked sad before, Flo. What's worrying you?'

'Nothing.' She peered into her tea cup. 'I wish I could see into the future.'

Mary stared at her, then smiled and took her cup, gazing down at the tea leaves. 'Let us see what the future holds,' she said in a deep voice.

'Don't be daft,' said Flora, trying to take the cup back. 'I was only joking! I don't believe in such things. And besides you shouldn't try to find out — it might be something awful.'

Mary snatched the cup out of her reach and moved back. 'I can't promise you a tall dark handsome stranger, but there's definitely going to be changes in your life. There is a man and water. Are you thinking about taking a trip over the water?'

Flora stared at her and laughed shortly. 'Perhaps I'm going on the ferry across the Mersey.'

Mary shook her dark curls at her. 'Don't mock, Flo. There's definitely a ship in the leaves.'

269

'Stranded, is it?' Then the laughter died in her face. 'France. Maybe I'll go there with Stephen after all,' she said slowly.

'Who's Stephen?' Mary looked at her sister for the information.

'The man in Flo's life now. A war hero, with a business an' a house with a big garden an' a bathroom.' She addressed Flora. 'Viv told our Kathleen about the house. She's quite taken with it.'

'Well, there you are then,' said Mary, winking at Flora. 'The leaves never lie.'

'I don't know how you can see a ship in the tea leaves,' said Flora, picking up the empty bottle in a rebellious mood. 'I think we're all a bit tipsy, but thanks for telling me about going on a journey. It sounds familiar.'

'Pleasure,' said Mary, smiling. 'Bring us a stick of rock from Paris.'

Flora fluttered her fingers in their direction and left, deep in thought. Men in boats ... It was stupid! But again she experienced that trapped feeling, a sense of time running out. She had no wish to go to France and she would tell Stephen so. Why should some tea leaves make her mind up for her?

Still in a decisive mood she told Stephen that she did not ever wish to go to France the next time they went for a walk in Sefton Park with Vivien.

'What's brought this on?' he said in a bewildered voice. 'I'm willing to postpone going, Floss, till after we get married.' They were standing by the bronze statue of Peter Pan.

'You might have to wait a long time,' she retorted. 'As long as this fella waited to grow up.'

'I don't think you want to marry me at all,' he said moodily.

'I haven't said that,' she murmured, not wanting to hurt him too much all at once. 'I don't feel it's right to talk marriage so soon after your uncle's died. And besides, George needs more time to get used to the idea.'

'George!' He scowled. 'You and that son of yours. I've a good mind to go to France on my own.'

Her spirits lifted. 'Do,' she responded with a smile. 'You could probably do with the break, and will enjoy being with your mate better without me.'

He muttered agreement, adding, 'Perhaps you'll miss me.'

'I probably will.' She kissed his cheek.

He went the last two weeks in August and Flora relaxed and caught up on all the jobs that hadn't been done for a long time, such as washing paintwork, clearing out cupboards and tidying her small garden.

Vivien came in one evening with the news that there was a fair in the park.

George, whom Flora was trying to ease into sitting for the thirteen plus, looked up from his book. 'A fair?' He smiled. 'That'd be fun.'

'The Murphys are going,' said Vivien, jiggling up and down, as if unable to keep still. 'I know we have to be careful with money, but we don't have to go on anything. Just being there in the dark is exciting.'

'I've got some money,' said George, slamming the book shut. Flora and Vivien stared at him. He raised his thick tawny eyebrows. 'You don't have to look at me like I've robbed the Bank of England. I collected jam jars through the holidays and took them to the rag yard. I was saving up for something, but — '

'Say no more.' Flora forced herself to her feet. 'If you're prepared to part with your lolly, I'm prepared to spend some of mine. We could all do with a bit of fun. Get your coats on.'

They met up with the Murphys crossing the road to the park. Kathleen and her sisters were skipping some distance in front of Carmel, who was pushing the enormous old pram with Brendan in it. 'Haven't seen much of you lately, Flo. Everything okay? Any sign of that trip overseas?'

'Stephen's gone to France. Strange, but I don't really believe in fortune telling.' Flora smiled, resting her hand on the handle of the pram as she gazed down at Brendan. She tickled his tummy and he chuckled. 'He's a gorgeous lad,' she said, laughing herself.

Carmel agreed vaguely, before adding, 'Perhaps you should

believe, Flo. Are my eyes playing tricks on me or is that really Mike coming along the road from the tram stop?'

Flora's head turned quickly. It was Mike. She could hardly believe it. But he halted a foot away from them and seemed substantial enough. 'Hi!' He smiled faintly. 'I couldn't believe it when I saw you walking along the road. Where are you off to?'

'There's a fair in the park,' said Flora, not looking directly at him after that first scrutiny. How was he still here? It was difficult to take in that they were talking normally as if they had not parted the way they had, and for as long as they had.

'Mind if I walk along with you?' His grey eyes looked uncertain. 'It's some time since I've been to a fair.'

'It's a free country,' she responded flatly.

Carmel looked at them both and hurried on after the children.

'How have you been?' said Mike, falling into step beside Flora.

'All right,' she said. 'How are things with you?'

'They've eased up a bit. You've probably seen the headlines in the paper. The Russians lifted the blockade months ago but we're still airlifting supplies to Berlin.'

'I didn't know you were still airlifting,' she said quickly. She dropped her eyes. 'I'd convinced myself that you'd already gone home.'

'It'll be coming to an end soon, and everything will wind down.'

'So you'll be going home then?' She lifted her head and stared at him, still barely able to believe he was there.

'It looks like it.' He buried his hands in his pockets. 'I didn't want to go, though, without seeing you.' His gaze searched her face. 'Without asking if there was any hope of your changing your mind. I still feel the same way about you, Flora.' His voice had deepened with emotion.

'Do you?' Her tone was muted.

'Yes. I'm sorry about all those things I said to you.'

She looked up at him then. 'We were both angry — not thinking straight. I must have seemed ungrateful to you. Hard. Unfeeling. But I'm not! Even so I can't see what

272

good you being here can do, Mike. Nothing's changed.'

He was silent a moment before saying, 'Nothing at all?'

'The same problems are there.' Regret and longing were overcoming her again, affecting her voice and making it wobble. 'Why can't you give up on me?'

His face darkened. 'Because I won't! I got to thinking about what you said that night just before Christmas. Remember the fog? Best friends, you said. I didn't act afterwards like I was your best friend.'

She was choked by tears and for several seconds could not speak. Then, 'I didn't act like yours either.'

Mike smiled. 'Perhaps we can try just being friends before I go back to the States? Have it like it was in the early days, just after the war.'

She was silent. They were walking on grass now with the darkness all around them but ahead the bright lights of the fairground could be seen. 'I suggested that once before and you said it was impossible.'

'Perhaps I was wrong.'

She shook her head. 'I think you were right. But if you want to go the fair — then there it is. Hear the music?'

'Sure.'

'Then let's not think further than tonight.'

In Mike's company the fair was fun. George greeted him like he had never been away, and Viv ran up to him. The jam jar money remained in George's pocket because Mike said everything was his treat.

Swinging boats, roundabouts, the ghost train — they went on them all, as well as the waltzer which left Flora's head spinning. Mike's arm, which went round her shoulders momentarily when she stepped off it, was a reminder of how it had been once upon a time. It did not stay there as they shied for coconuts, and sent hoops spinning in an attempt to win tawdry prizes.

He walked them back to their street but refused to go further than the lamp post. 'See you soon,' was all he said on leaving.

Just like that, thought Flora in a daze. It's starting all over again and I should stop it. But she couldn't.

There was a familiar yet subtly different pattern to their

relationship. One not lacking in sexual tension and excitement as they deliberately set out not to touch each other. A deed that was made easier if George or Vivien were with them.

Then Stephen came home. Flora perhaps welcomed him more warmly than she would have if she had not been seeing Mike. He talked a lot about his trip to Normandy and his visit to the war graves. She asked if he had seen Tom's. His reply was brief and he quickly moved on to another subject: marriage. Perhaps just before Christmas? Flora's reply was non-committal. How could she think of marrying Stephen when Mike was back on the scene?

Mike talked a lot too, but not of weddings. The shops and their goods at the Base, aeroplanes, films, America, sport. Mike had joined the Base soccer team and had played against Manchester All Stars in May.

There was more food on their table when Mike knocked on the back door and came to tea. Flora knew that she was not behaving fairly or sensibly, but the feeling of time running out was still strong within her.

One September evening she fobbed Stephen off with an excuse. Mike had arranged for the two of them to go alone to the theatre. Flora's father said he would keep his eye on the kids. She did not disillusion him when he assumed that she was seeing Stephen.

It was a long time since Flora had been to the theatre. She found the experience heady, and was still in a vague, unreal mood when they came out into a dusk that held a cold crispness that set her cheeks tingling.

'How about a drink?' suggested Mike.

'Fine,' said Flora, not resisting when he pulled her arm through his. They walked along Lime Street together in the direction of Lewis's.

He stopped in front of the imposing entrance of the Adelphi Hotel. Flora shot him a sidelong glance. 'You don't really intend going in there?' She gripped his arm tightly, nervously.

Mike laughed. 'What are you scared of? It's not a cage full of wild animals, Flora.'

'The rich might as well be,' she said frankly. 'I'm as different from them as a tiger is from me.'

The creases about his eyes deepened. 'It's only money that makes them different. And my money's just as good as theirs any day. Even better than some, probably.'

She frowned thoughtfully. 'It's not just money, Mike. It's class.'

'Sod class, Flora! That's the trouble with you English. Your class system.' His mouth set. 'There's been a war and I reckon things have changed and are going to carry on changing. I fancied a taste of luxury this morning so I reserved a room for the night – so if you don't want to be with the sort of people in the bars and restaurant we can have some food and drink sent up.' She stared at him. 'That's if you trust me, of course?'

'Can I?' Her voice was pensive. 'I know you've behaved like a perfect gentleman in the last few weeks, but –'

'It's your decision.' He smiled that smile that still made her feel warm inside. 'You can turn and walk out any time you like.'

'So you say.' She adjusted her green hat to a more jaunty angle and squared her shoulder in the rayon dress and jacket. Her expression was doubtful but she knew what she was doing. 'Right.' She took his arm and sauntered with him towards the entrance.

By the time they had managed to find their way through the revolving doors into an entrance hall with marble pillars and a polished cork floor, her heartbeat had settled down to a more sedate pace. She left everything to Mike and tried to look as haughty as some of the women in furs and long skirts. Everything was bustle with people coming and going and the porters were in great demand. She was expected to sign the register and saw that Mike had them down as Mr and Mrs O'Neill. For a moment she hesitated, staring at him. Her heart started to race again. He quirked his lips and she signed.

A pageboy took them up in a lift and along marble-lined corridors that seemed to stretch for miles.

Mike had a front-facing room that looked out over the war-damaged Lewis's store and across the city, hazy with smoke and light-spangled. Flora could hardly believe that view, or the splendours of the attached bathroom. 'It's beautiful,' she murmured. 'Really lovely.'

'Why don't you have a bath?' suggested Mike. 'While I order us some champagne.'

She turned quickly and looked at him. 'I don't know about the champagne. It might have a funny effect on me.'

He frowned at her. 'You drank the bottle I bought you?'

She nodded meekly. 'We wet Brendan's head with it – Carmel, her sister and me.'

'I thought you might have saved it for an extra special occasion – such as when you wave me goodbye. Will you do that, Flora?' he said, a little tight-lipped. 'Come down to the Prince's Landing Stage and send me on my way.'

'I don't like goodbyes,' she murmured, moving away from him to finger the gleaming bath taps.

'Do any of us?' he said quietly. 'Why don't you have a bath? You don't have to fill this one with a bucket,' he murmured. 'Just twiddle a couple of taps.'

'I've never been in a bathroom like this,' she said dreamily. 'If you get out, maybe I will have a bath.'

'Sure.' He smiled and went out, closing the door behind him.

She stared at the door for several seconds then began to run the water while she peeled off her jacket and undid the buttons on her frock.

Never had she been in a bath with water so hot. She lay partially submerged, realising that she had been right all along to doubt they could be just friends and they both knew it and had been playing a game the last few weeks.

When Mike opened the door and came in, she was not really surprised to see him clad in only a towel, carrying two glasses of champagne. 'Is it good?' he said quietly.

'You should have knocked.' She knew it was pointless trying to cover herself up now.

'I reckon it's good.' He came closer, and handed her a glass. 'Let's drink to both our countries, Flora. May they prosper.'

'I think you've already been drinking,' she said.

'Only one glass,' he murmured, sitting on the edge of the bath and gazing at her. 'You've still got a good figure, Flo.'

'You keep your eyes to yourself,' she said, but took the

glass from him. They made a toast and then he kissed her.

'You know what's going to happen next, don't you Flo?' His voice was quiet.

Her throat moved. 'I guess you're telling me that I can't trust you to keep your hands to yourself as well as your eyes.'

He said nothing, only filled her glass. She drank the wine quickly. She watched him put bottle and glasses down and drop his towel.

She was not quite prepared for what happened next. He got in the other end of the bath slowly and carefully, and she almost managed to get out. Only his hands slid over her feet and he pulled her towards him, kissing her ankles. Her fingers sought for a hold and she braced herself in the water. Her breathing seemed suspended as his mouth travelled up her legs kissing her so that she was all tingling sensation. She guessed then what he was going to do and was a little shocked. But his tongue's caressing of her secret places caused her to moan and melt in ecstasy.

He slid inside her and began to move. Desire soared. She wanted him to penetrate deeper and deeper, to possess every part of her, utterly. He kissed her where he could reach, small biting kisses that left marks, until once more pleasure overwhelmed her.

'You shouldn't have done that,' she whispered, as she lay, with his cheek resting on her breast, her arms holding him close. 'It's not right.'

'What wasn't right?' His voice was drowsy.

'You know! Kissing me where you did.'

'You didn't enjoy it?' He kissed the tip of her nose.

'Talk sense. But we shouldn't have done any of it. We said we wouldn't. And I'm going to be all spongy because I've never stayed in a bath so long.'

'You want us to get out?'

'We'd better.' She pushed him away. 'We'd better get out of here altogether before anything else happens.'

'You wouldn't like to spend the night here?'

'You're not thinking straight,' she murmured, dripping water all over the floor as she stepped out.

'I am.' He threw her a towel.

'Father's with the children.'

He pulled a face. 'We'll go and have a drink in the lounge downstairs.' He began to rub himself dry, his eyes on her body. 'You'll enjoy seeing it, Flora. You could fit the whole of your street in it.'

'I look a mess.' She frowned at her reflection in the mirror.

'You've never looked lovelier,' he whispered, and would have taken her into his arms again but she ducked and went into the bedroom.

At least three-quarters of the street could have fitted into the lounge, she thought. There were marble pillars, carpets and sparkling chandeliers. Mirrors the height of the walls reflected her dubious expression as Mike ordered more champagne. 'I didn't know you were so rich.' She surveyed the sparkling liquid in her glass.

'I thought you English thought all us Yanks rich.'

'I'm not our Hilda,' she said, taking a cautious sip.

'No,' he murmured. 'We would have been married by now if you were. She would have dumped the kids on your father and thought, what the hell, it's my life.'

'Is that what you'd like me to do, Mike?' she said with a touch of anger, tossing off the rest of the champagne.

'I respect you for the kind of person you are, and I love you,' was his reply.

She could think of nothing to say in answer to that. Life was so difficult at times. Her head was definitely light and she felt deeply unhappy and guilty. She was breaking the rules again — and why, why couldn't she want to do what she'd done with Stephen? Marrying him would be so sensible. Marrying Mike would never be dull. She watched her glass being filled again and did not demur. From somewhere came the sound of music. 'Cinderella is at the ball.' A sharp laugh escaped her.

'I never fancied Cinderella myself,' said Mike, his eyes serious. 'Have you ever noticed that she never did anything for herself? The fairy godmother did all the magic. She only obeyed. Even when the prince came round with the slipper, she was waiting at home. I much prefer Beauty and the Beast — she was more your caring woman, who had

278

compassion on the Beast and cared for him so much that she took a chance.'

'I've already taken a chance tonight, my love,' she said, slurring her words slightly. 'It's not something that I'd like to make a habit of.' There was a pleading expression on her flushed face. 'I should be going home.'

He toyed with the stem of his glass. 'I'd like you to stay here with me for the night. One night, Flo,' he said urgently. 'I'll be leaving soon. Couldn't you pretend for once that there's only us?'

'You want the impossible!' She pulled a face. "If you were the only boy in the world and I was the only girl." Life's not a song! It's hard — it's disappointing! It's hell saying goodbye all over again. But at least I'm not kidding myself that life could really be like this for me.' She looked about her and up at the elaborate moulded ceiling and chandeliers. 'Anyway, I don't think I'd like it.'

'How d'you know?'

'Because I do. It's not real.'

'It tastes real.' He held a mouthful of champagne against his tongue before swallowing.

'You're drunk, and so am I. I knew what would happen and I shouldn't have let it. There's no happy endings in life. Not forever anyway. When I said that about Cinderella — it's because I feel like her in a way. Maybe she was glad when the clock struck twelve and she could get the hell out of that palace. And maybe she didn't go looking for the prince because she felt safer where she was in the kitchen. It must take a heck of a lot of know how to run a palace. It takes nerve to begin a whole new life.' She stared thoughtfully into her empty glass, and added, 'I'd really like to have a go. It'd be an adventure. But perhaps after all I'm a coward because part of me is scared of going to America.'

He hesitated before saying, 'There'd be nothing to be afraid of, Flo. I'd look after you.'

She stared at him. 'I know. But who'd look after Father? And Rosie's grave? What about the religious thing? We're back to the beginning again.'

His fingers twisted round hers. 'There's no easy answer, Flo. It's a matter of choices.'

279

She grimaced. 'Right! I'll make one choice, Mike, and be content with that.'

'What?' he questioned with a slight smile.

'Let's live for now, have some food and then go to bed.'

He was silent. 'I should say no. It's not really the answer I want.'

'No,' she said sadly. 'But it's the best I can give you. So what d'you say?'

He kissed each of her fingers slowly. 'I never could resist you, Flora.'

The sun had not long risen and their room was still in shadow. Flora, always an early riser, was standing by the window, gazing out over the city. Her city, her home town. She was aware in that moment of how much she really cared for the place. Poor Liverpool — it was going to be a struggle to rebuild over the damage that Hitler's Luftwaffe inflicted despite its having been scheduled as a development area — despite the scheme to reconstruct the docks — despite its having been chosen as one of the sites for the Festival of Britain planned two years hence. It could never be the same Liverpool — but there would always be Liverpudlians. She would always be a Liverpudlian.

'What are you thinking?' Mike's voice at her shoulder caused her to start. 'You've been staring out of the window for ages.'

'I was thinking that although I told Father not to wait up for me — that I'd be late in — he'll be having a fit if he goes looking for me in the bedroom and finds out I didn't come home.'

'Cut yourself free, Flo.' His arm went about her waist and he kissed the top of her head. 'You're a big girl now. We could have our own home, rear a family, and be happy in every way.'

'Don't,' she said softly, leaning against him. 'Slow, slow, quick, quick, slow,' she whispered as if in a trance.

He sighed. 'You almost spoilt it by giggling. You kept saying how important it was to keep in step.'

'That must have been the champagne.'

'Not just the champagne, I hope.' He pressed her hard

against him. 'It was more like the Gay Gordons by the time we finished making love.'

A tiny smile lifted her mouth. 'What a thing to say, Mike. The Gay Gordons is all wild and mad with kilts swinging.'

'Exactly.' He paused. 'Look over there, Flo, towards the river. Over the horizon is the Irish sea and the Emerald Isle. Beyond that the Atlantic and home.'

The spurt of happiness drained out of her and she felt terribly tired. 'I wish I could,' she said strongly. 'Maybe if it was in ten years time I could say yes. Father's getting old. George is growing up. Time heals. But right now I can't.'

There was a long silence and neither of them moved.

At last Mike said, 'I'll see you home.'

She shook her head. 'We've been through this so many times. It won't make it easier. Let's say tarrah outside.'

His mouth tightened. 'No goodbyes, Flora. We'll just walk away from each other.'

She nodded and they both went and got dressed.

Chapter Twenty-Two

It was quiet in the house when she arrived, and for five minutes she believed that she would escape a telling off from her father. But she had just poured out a cup of tea when he came in from the yard.

She could feel the frost from feet away as he stopped short and stared at her, his bristling brows meeting above his hooked nose. 'And what time's this to be coming home?'

She glanced at the clock, and was tempted to say, 'Ten o'clock.' Instead she murmured, 'Sorry, Father. I told you I'd be late.'

'You didn't tell me you'd be this late. Or that you were seeing that Yank again,' he rasped, reaching for his pipe on top of the wireless. 'What's happened to your brains, girl? You've got a good upright bloke in Stephen and you're messing around with a bloody Yank, staying out all night! Where's your sense of decency? You used to be a good sensible lass, but you're going from bad to worse.'

'Yes, Father. I'm sorry, Father.' Her tone was meek as she watched him take out his tobacco pouch.

He scowled at her. 'Don't be thinking you're deceiving me with your "Yes, Father. Sorry, Father." You're not a bit sorry.'

'No, Father.' She could not prevent a slight smile.

'Don't be grinning all over your face,' he snapped. 'You ought to be ashamed of yourself.'

'I am,' she insisted, putting down her cup. 'Believe me!'

He grunted, pressing tobacco into the bowl of his pipe. 'I don't know what's got into you. Look at your sister. She's settled down. Surprised me — but there it is. Not a bad bloke Kevin, for all he's too handsome. Been giving me a loaf regular.' He shot a glance at Flora. 'I know where I'll be leaving all me money, girl, if you don't pull your socks up.'

Flora shrugged and took a sip of her tea. 'I didn't know you had much to leave. Anyway, what I've ever done for you is because you're my father and nothing to do with any money you've got. So you can't blackmail me.'

He turned his back on her and got a light from the fire for his pipe. There was a silence while he got his pipe going nicely. Flora waited, certain that he had not finished with her. She would get through it all right if she kept calm, although the thought of Kevin and Hilda being tops with her father irritated her when she considered all the years that she had gone back and forth to his house, shopping and cleaning for him.

He faced her again and she squared her shoulders. 'You're not setting a good example for the kids.'

'They know I've been out all night then?' She was dismayed. 'You've told them?'

'I said you were up early and gone on a message. They're out playing somewhere.' His yellowed teeth clenched on the stem of his pipe. 'I don't like telling lies to kids. So we'll be having no more of this staying out all night, girl.'

She nodded and said huskily, 'Perish the thought. I won't be doing it again.'

Flora had seen little of Hilda and wondered how she was really getting on now with Kevin. On Saturday mornings, her sister seemed disinclined to linger or talk much. But one morning she did not immediately rush off but delayed on the doorstep, a frown marring her pretty features. 'Did you ever mention about you and me and Mike to Kevin?' she asked unexpectedly.

Flora raised her eyebrows. 'You're joking! Me and your Kevin were never on those terms, whatever you might think. Why?'

'Someone has.'

'Well, it wasn't me.'

283

Hilda nodded slowly, and gingerly felt her upper arm. 'It's not funny how the word Yanks affects British men.'

'It can made them react passionately,' murmured Flora.

'Violently passionate,' said Hilda, her expression vague as she dropped her hand. 'They're dead jealous, I suppose.' Her eyes shifted to Vivien waiting at the bottom of the step. 'Perhaps Viv? Kevin plays with her. And he's made up with any excuse to get back at me. He's got a nerve when he's always flirting with the little tart downstairs.' She frowned and hurried down the step before Flora could say anything.

Flora tried not to worry about Hilda, but her words niggled as did the way she had felt her arm.

That evening Stephen came. 'Come and see over the house again, Floss.' His expression was bright with anticipation. 'I thought you might want to make some changes.'

She went, taking Vivien with them which didn't seem to please Stephen. He kept looking at the girl and tightening his mouth as the car sped down Rocky Lane.

It was a nice house, bigger than Flora's, with a good-sized hall, a parlour, kitchen, back kitchen and scullery. There was a bathroom and two large bedrooms and a box room upstairs. The back garden was huge with a couple of apple trees at its far end.

'Can I have the bedroom overlooking the back garden, please?' asked Vivien eagerly, her nose pressed against the leadened window.

Stephen exchanged a quick look with Flora, and she felt sure that he was going to say something different to what he actually did. 'The boy'll have to have that. He's the elder.'

Vivien looked disappointed but nodded. Stephen began to discuss bedding and cookers with Flora. Vivien began to fidget with the blind cord and received a sharp rebuke from Stephen. She wandered out of the room and Stephen said to Flora, 'She should really be with your Hilda. What about a kid of our own? We'll need the extra room.'

Flora gazed at him, her hands dug deep into the pockets of the mustard coat. The room was cold but that was not the reason for the shiver that passed through her. 'We don't have to get married, Steve,' she said in a tense voice.

'Don't be silly,' he said sharply. 'Everybody knows we're going out together. They'll all be expecting us to get married soon. Just because I've said what needs saying about Viv, there's no need to get in a huff.'

'I'm not in a huff.' Her voice was quiet. 'But you knew the score when we first started going out, and you were prepared to have Viv then.'

'That was before your Hilda got married and settled down. It changes things, Flo.' He sat on the double bed and patted the space beside him. 'Come and sit down and let's talk this over sensibly,' he coaxed.

Slowly Flora walked over to him and sat. His arms went about her and he kissed her. She responded as best she could but when he opened her coat and fondled her breasts and his kisses grew wilder, she wondered what was wrong with her that she was allowing it when she loved Mike. She pushed his hand away when he would have undone her cardigan. 'Viv might come, and it was her we were supposed to be talking about.'

'Damn Viv,' he muttered. 'I want you, Floss. I've wanted you for years. Since we were adolescents and you were going out with Tom. God, how I wanted you then!'

She looked at him in surprise. 'You never acted like you wanted me.'

'I knew Tom would get you, that's why.' His mouth twisted. 'Tom always got what he wanted and I was too shy to fight for you.' His voice sounded strained as he added, 'But he hasn't got you now and I'll have the last laugh.'

'Don't!' Flora stood. 'I don't like it when you talk about Tom the way you do. There's nothing you need fear from him now.' She shivered again and buttoned her coat hurriedly. 'Let's go downstairs to the fire.'

He nodded, grinning. 'I've got some crumpets. We can toast them and have tea.'

'Okay.' She forced a smile and they went downstairs, the matter of Vivien living with them shelved for the moment.

The following Saturday Flora hurried to the front door in response to a frantic hammering on her knocker. She was certain it was Hilda, impatient to be let in, and she was right.

'Hell, Flo,' said her sister, stumping into the lobby. 'What kept you? You'd think I had all day to wait on that step.'

'I was in the back kitchen doing some washing.'

'You want to get a machine like I've got.' Her smile flashed for a second. 'Or get that manfriend of yours to buy one. No! On second thoughts he's probably too tight-fisted, like Kevin.'

Flora stared at her. 'What are you talking about? You've just said you've got a machine.'

'Only because I went and bought it myself.' Hilda walked up the lobby. 'You'd think I'd been seeing another man the fuss Kevin made. The mean swine! He's cut my housekeeping to put the money back in his hoard and moved it to a different hiding place.' She flung herself into a chair, crossed her knees, and jerked one leg up and down. Her fingers fumbled for her cigarettes. She lit up before saying, 'Where's Viv?'

'Upstairs getting ready.'

Hilda nodded slowly. 'Stephen came to see me about her last evening.'

'What!'

The sisters' eyes met. 'You heard me,' said Hilda, her mouth tightening as the cigarette burnt between her fingers. 'I guess you know why?'

'Yes!' Flora sat abruptly. 'What did you say to him?'

'I said what you should have said ages ago. That she was their Jimmy's child.' She paused, frowning.

'And?' prodded Flora.

'And he nearly dropped in his tracks.' Hilda smiled and inhaled deeply, holding in the smoke for several seconds before exhaling. 'Then he said he didn't believe me. And I told him to go to hell.'

'And?' asked Flora, certain that there was more.

'And then he slagged my morals, so I told him to get out. So he went.'

Flora made tea, anger seething inside her because Stephen had gone behind her back to speak to her sister. 'What did Kevin have to say about it?'

'Nothing, because he wasn't there. And I didn't tell him because we're not speaking.'

'Oh, Hilda! Are you still arguing – or not arguing should I say?' She handed her sister a cup of tea.

A small laugh issued from between Hilda's rouged lips. 'Don't you be worrying about me. I'll work something out.' She sipped her tea. 'Anyway I think me and our Viv'll go to town. I could do with a new frock to cheer meself up.'

'Money?' Flora looked at her.

Hilda smiled. 'Sausage and chips he'll be getting after tomorrow for the next three days.'

Flora could not help admiring her nerve as she called Vivien down.

After they had gone Flora wondered how long it would be before Stephen turned up to tell her what he had done about Vivien.

When he came that afternoon she was ready for him as she opened the door. He had hardly set foot in the lobby.

'How dare you go behind my back and talk to our Hilda about taking Viv?'

His mouth tightened and his ears went red. 'I thought she'd come and tell you. Typical of her! Not prepared one iota to accept responsibility for her own child.'

'You didn't have to slag her off. And besides, I've accepted responsibility for Viv. And don't you think if she's Jimmy's child, you owe her something for his sake?'

'If!' He frowned at her. 'Why didn't you tell me that Viv's supposed to be Jimmy's child?'

Their eyes met, and Flora pulled a face. 'For exactly the reason you gave Hilda: I didn't think you would believe she was his. But they were close, and your aunt Molly told me that she'd seen them together in town the November before Viv was born. It fits.'

'Hmmm, perhaps.' He frowned. 'It still wouldn't surprise me if she was a Yankee bastard.'

'Steve, what a thing to say!' Even in her own ears she sounded terribly shocked.

'Sorry,' he said hastily, seizing her shoulders. 'It's just such a surprise, Floss. Give me some time to think about it.'

'I don't see what there is to think about. But if you need time, that suits me.'

He nodded vaguely. 'I wonder if Kevin ...'

Flora pulled herself out of his grasp. 'Don't, Steve, if you're thinking what I think you're thinking.'

He shrugged. 'Let's forget about it for now. Are you ready to go out?'

'No,' she said promptly. 'I'm not in the mood.' His expression fell and she sighed. 'All right then. I suppose your reaction is natural. Let's go the pictures. George's waiting in for Father and he's looking after the kids.'

He was obviously relieved at her change of heart and was chatty as they walked along the road. Flora was in a completely different mood to his, but she hid it, and allowed his words to go over her head.

Flora's period was almost three weeks late and she felt sick. With anxiety, she assured herself as she put down the heavy shopping.

If Viv had been with her, she would have helped her carry everything and also distracted her from the single thought which zig-zagged like some primary colour in a kaleidoscope in the forefront of her mind.

Weariness overwhelmed her almost as completely as nausea. A cup of tea and a plain biscuit would help; so would putting up her feet. She would not think that her sickness could be due to anything else but an upset stomach. It was six weeks since she had seen Mike and she knew that already some of the G.I.s had left Burtonwood and sailed for home.

Best not to think of him. His smile, and the way his grey eyes spoke of loving her without him saying a word. She pressed her eyelids tightly shut and opened them again, but still he was in her mind.

She began to unpack her shopping, and tried to concentrate on Stephen. Him she could marry. She felt certain of it, whatever decision he came to about Vivien. And a baby could be started on a wedding night – could come before full term. She hated herself for thinking in such a way.

Still the idea stayed with her in the following days when she was sick every morning.

On Wednesday Stephen called her into his office.

She stood in front of his desk, her fingers looped behind her back, watching him fiddle with a pencil on his desk for what seemed ages. She wondered why he was taking so long to speak. Perhaps she had made a bad mistake at work which had cost him money and he couldn't bring himself to say so, she thought wryly. Or maybe it was about Vivien. She doubted it because he normally kept working hours strictly for business.

After what seemed an age he looked up. 'Is it true that you and your Hilda fell out over some Yank during the war?' he said unevenly.

She was taken by surprise. 'Certainly not!' She paused. 'It was after the war, and not a bit like you make it sound.' Her voice was steady and light. 'She was going to marry a Yank, but hadn't told him about Viv. When he found out, he broke the engagement off. She believed it was my fault that he found out.'

Stephen stared at her, gnawing at his bottom lip. 'You didn't go out with a Yank yourself?'

Flora hesitated. 'For a short while,' she said carefully, lacing her fingers together. 'It was a time when everything was dark, after Tom was killed. Hilda introduced him to me. He went back to America after the war.'

He rat-tatted the pencil on the desk. 'You didn't – ?' he began.

'What?' she said coldly, drawing herself up to her full height.

'Nothing.' The pencil dropped to the desk and he stared down at it. 'I went to see Kevin about Viv and he mentioned about this Yank. He also said that that fella Mike you were going out with was a Yank. Is that true, Flora?'

'Yes, it's true.' Her voice was quiet. 'Why did you have to go and see Kevin? I particularly wanted you not to. I don't like the man.'

'Perhaps it's because he knows too much about you.' His ears had reddened and he picked up the pencil again. 'He says that your Hilda said that you and this Mike were serious.'

Anger hardened inside her. 'And if we were? I honestly don't see what that has to do with you or Kevin,' she said passionately.

'We are getting married, Floss.' His voice rose. 'I have every right to know. The thought of you with a Yank sickens me. We all know what they're like.'

Flora's eyes sparkled and she rested her hands on the desk

and leaned towards him. 'Do you? How many have you met? How many do you really know?'

'I met quite a few during the war. The way they talked about girls and sex —' The pencil snapped between his fingers and a muscle tightened next to his mouth.

'The British soldiers never talked about it? You mean you never had a girl, never went with one just for a bit of comfort when you were all keyed up waiting to go and fight?' she demanded.

'Floss! Of course not. You shouldn't talk like that.' He wriggled his shoulders uncomfortably. 'It's not nice to hear from a woman. Especially the woman I'm going to marry.'

She stared at him and thought of being married to him, of waiting on him hand and foot. Because that's what he'd expect. Of sleeping with him. Of foisting Mike's child on to him. Then she knew that she could not do it. 'I'm not going to marry you, Steve. I'm sorry, but I can't.'

'What?' He got to his feet quickly. 'It's because I went to Kevin, isn't it? Well, you don't have to worry. He won't have Vivien living with him. Says he won't have another man's child. But I'll have her, Floss. I mean, she *could* be our Jimmy's.'

'Thanks, Steve, but no. After all she mightn't be your brother's and I wouldn't want to foist three other men's children on you,' she said quite calmly.

'What?' He stared at her.

'I'm handing in my notice.' She forced her smile. 'It'll be much too embarrassing for you if I stayed.'

'What — what d'you mean?' he stammered.

'I'm having a Yankee bastard,' she said, and walked out.

Flora told George and Vivien that she would not be seeing Stephen any more. 'Hallelujah!' said George, grinning.

'I'll miss him,' sighed Vivien. 'I'd have liked a dad.'

'Hard luck,' said George, squeezing her shoulder. 'It's a pity Mike was a Yank,' he added, addressing his mother. Then he picked up his football and went out.

Flora almost agreed with him, knowing just what he meant by that, and wondered how she was going to tell the children about the baby when her condition merited it. The thought of abortion briefly passed through her mind but was quickly set aside. Too dangerous, and besides she did not want to destroy Mike's child.

On Saturday Flora returned from shopping to find that the post had been. She turned a letter over and stilled as she recognised Mike's handwriting. She dumped her basket and ripped the letter open eagerly. 'Has time changed anything? Meet me – the Prince's Landing Stage, 7 p.m. Sunday. *California Star*.'

'Oh God, what do I do?' Flora's knees shook. It was like a miracle in a way. But what was she to do? There was still Father, and Rosie's grave, and the religious thing. And how would George and Vivien feel about going to America? She did realise that it was unlikely that Mike intended her to go with him tomorrow evening because he knew that she would not be able to go just like that, but maybe he intended her following him out to America.

Suddenly she felt wild with relief, and also quite faint as she staggered up the lobby with the shopping. Collapsing in a chair in front of the slumbering fire, she sat for a long while, staring into the glowing embers, thinking. 'Has time changed anything?' Mike knew or hoped, she felt certain of that as a smile lit her face. At least, thank God, she had the chance of telling him about the baby. Kevin and Hilda were well in with her father. They could take care of him. She squashed any qualms she had about their marriage. Dear God, would she have to become a Catholic or would Mike let her have her way like Mary's bloke did her?

She jumped as the knocker sounded, and got up to open the door thinking without any good reason that it was going to be Mike.

Vivien fell into the lobby. Her cheeks were flushed and her breath came in great gasps. 'Mam wants you! She's had an accident. You're not to go through the shop, though, but straight to the flat door. Mam's given me the key.'

Flora stared at her fixedly, hardly able to take in what she was saying. 'What kind of accident?'

'She looks terrible! But she wouldn't tell me what happened. Just said I was to get you!'

'But why me? What about your uncle Kevin? Isn't he there? Or Maggie? Wouldn't she do?'

'She had her accident days ago, Aunty Flo,' informed Vivien, her breathing steadying. 'They know about it. She's in bed and doesn't look very pretty any more. She said she wanted you but you've got to be quiet.'

Flora stilled in the act of putting her purse in her pocket and her heart bumped uncomfortably inside her chest. 'Quiet? I don't understand.'

'Just come!' ordered Vivien, seizing hold of her arm and dragging on it. 'Come! She's all worked up and wants you! Only you.'

'All right, all right,' muttered Flora, brushing the girl's hand off her sleeve. 'Let's go then. She must be bad if she wants me.'

'She said that you're her sister and that's that,' said Vivien, and pushed the door wide. Flora went out, a sinking feeling in the pit of her stomach.

'Thank God you've come, Flo,' said Hilda in a relieved voice. A cigarette smouldered between her fingers as she lay propped against a couple of pillows and surrounded by disorder. There were magazines, papers, sweet wrappers, a dirty cup and plate, and a saucer spilling ash.

'I came as soon as I could,' said Flora quietly, attempting to conceal the shock she felt at the sight of her sister's face. It was swollen and bruised all down one side and she had a black eye that was turning yellow. 'How did all this happen?'

'I think you can guess.' Her mouth quivered. She took a deep drag of her cigarette and glanced at Vivien. 'I caught Kevin doing you know what with that floosie downstairs a few days ago.'

'What!' Flora licked her lips. 'What happened?'

'I hit her and pulled her out of bed. She beat it but Kevin had the nerve to tell me to keep out of his business, and called me a shrew, a tart and a lazy cow! I told him that it was my business and flew at him.' She fell silent, staring at a far wall.

'And?' pressed Flora, covering her sister's hand with hers.

Hilda stared at her. 'What d'you think?'

Flora touched her bruised swollen face and scowled. 'He did this to you.'

'Guessed it in one, Flo.' A bitter laugh escaped her. 'You warned me ages ago about him, didn't you?' Flora said nothing and Hilda continued: 'He slapped me about so hard that I fell down the stairs. I frightened the life out of him because I kept quiet and still — not just because I was stunned but I thought that way he'd stop hitting me.' She swallowed. 'When I opened my eyes he acted like he was all sorry then — that he hadn't meant to knock me down the stairs. Perhaps he didn't — but bloody hell, Flo, I'm not putting up with him belting me like that! He was all as sweet as pie and carried me upstairs. I hurt my ankle and it's still a bit swollen but I've been making out that it's worse than it is, because I've been waiting for our Viv to come. I knew you'd help me, Flo.'

Flora squeezed her fingers gently. 'I'll get the police.'

'No!' Hilda's expression darkened. 'They won't believe me. They're men — they'll take his side.'

'What d'you want me to do?'

Hilda's eyes glinted. 'I'm going to leave him and I want you to help me. I can walk, and by tomorrow I'll walk even better. I thought you might let me come to your place tonight and tomorrow I'll get out of Liverpool.'

Flora sighed. 'What'll you do for money? I haven't got much.'

Hilda pushed back the covers, sending the saucer flying and spilling ash. The rest of the paraphernalia on the bed slid to the floor. 'He thinks he's so smart — that I don't know where he's put his money now.' Her voice was harsh. 'But I'm not as daft as he thinks I am.' She stumbled over to the unlit fireplace, and pushing back her sleeve she thrust her arm up the chimney until her searching fingers found a tiny ledge. She brought out a black cloth bag. 'See!' There was jubilation in her voice.

Flora said nothing, only watching her unfasten the bag and take out a fistful of notes. 'He's not going to let you get away with this, Hilda,' she murmured uneasily. 'And our house is the first he'll try.'

'No, it isn't. He'll try Doris's.' Hilda's expression was set as she stuffed the notes down the front of her brassiere. 'He believes that there's no love lost between us. He doesn't realise how true it is about blood being thicker than water.'

'I think you're wrong but get yourself dressed,' she said in a resigned tone. 'He could come up here any moment.'

'Not at this time of day,' replied Hilda, starting to dress. 'I'm already packed. My case is under the bed. I didn't dress properly because he sometimes comes up when he knows Viv's around. He puts on an act of being nice and caring and fusses her, wheedling information out of her, but I made sure he knew when she left earlier.'

'Just hurry up then,' said Flora, getting on her knees and searching for the case. She humped it out, and eased herself up to see Hilda pressing on face powder. 'Are you crazy?' she muttered. 'You haven't got time for that! Let's go. If he comes up, your little escapade is finished.' Her sister nodded and did what Flora ordered.

Flora's hands were unsteady as she shot the bolts at the top and the bottom of the front door that night. She had no illusions about how Kevin would behave if he came looking for his missing wife and money. For tonight they should be safe. It was midnight and all was quiet. Hilda was in Vivien's room and the girl was in Flora's bed. She went upstairs.

She found it difficult to sleep, starting awake at the least sound outside or in. She tried to concentrate her thoughts on seeing Mike, and eventually she slept, to dream an old dream that she was the Statue of Liberty and Mike was scaling her.

She awoke with a start to find that the light was still grey in the bedroom and that someone was calling outside. For a moment it was as if she was back in the days when she had her early morning job and the van was outside. Vivien was awake and staring at her, bleary-eyed. For a further second Flora was reminded of the morning when Rosie had been wakened, and she experienced the old dull pain of loss. Then Vivien spoke.

'I think it's Uncle Kevin,' she whispered. 'Shall I go and see?'

Flora shook her head and went across the room to gaze

out of the window on to a foggy morning. Kevin was shouting Hilda's name fit to wake the whole street, but nobody was stirring on such a dismal Sunday. She drew back quickly before he could see her and went back to bed, glancing at the clock as she did so. It was later than she had thought — gone ten. 'It is your Uncle Kevin. We'll ignore him. With a bit of luck he'll go away.'

'He's come for Mam, hasn't he?' Vivien's brown eyes looked seriously into hers. 'You're not going to hand her over to him, are you?'

'Don't be daft. You saw what he did to her.'

'How can he be so wicked?' The girl's expression was puzzled. 'He was so nice to me, Aunty Flo. Was it all pretend?'

'Probably not. I don't understand men like him, Viv. I know his mam committed suicide — perhaps that changed him. That and the war. It gave some people a taste for violence.' She smoothed back a stray curl and hugged the girl. 'But it's cold outside and it's likely that he'll soon get fed up and go home.'

'I hope so,' said Vivien forlornly.

Kevin did not get fed up. Eventually, considering the neighbours, Flora went over to the window and opened it, letting in swirling fingers of smoky fog. It was very cold. 'Is that you, Mr Brown?' she called in feigned surprise.

'Don't be pretending you don't know it's me,' he shouted, his face twisting with anger. 'Hilda's in there so you just bloody tell her to get herself down here now.'

'I don't know what you're talking about,' said Flora in icy tones. 'If you don't go away I'll have to get the police because you're creating a disturbance.'

He swore at her. 'You've got a nerve, mentioning the police, you bitch. It's me who'll get them to break this door in.'

'You just try it and you'll be in trouble.'

He swore at her and she withdrew her head. As she went to close the window, Kevin shouted up: 'Tell Hilda if she comes out now with all the money I'll forgive her and take her back.'

'Generous of you,' called Flora, watching him fumble in

his pocket. 'But I told you that she's not here.' She slammed the window down.

Vivien's eyes were confused. 'Shall I tell Mam he's here? Maybe he's really sorry.'

A tired laugh escaped Flora. 'I bet he is! But for how long?'She reached for her clothes. 'But you go and tell your mam. It's her decision what to do.'

Flora went downstairs and was glad that she was not feeling so nauseous that morning. They were late, and gazing out of the window into the yard she could barely make out the gas lamp on the corner of the yard wall. There would be no Sunday School this morning for Vivien and George.

When Hilda came down there was determination and just a hint of satisfaction in her expression. 'Is he good and mad?'

'I'd say so.' Flora turned over the bread she was toasting. 'He says that he'll forgive you and take you back. Maybe he'll turn over a new leaf?' she said hopefully, considering her own plans.

'And maybe pigs'll fly.' Hilda sprawled in the armchair by the fire. 'I'm not going back to him. I hope he's freezing to death out there.'

'He probably is. You know how fog goes right through you.' Flora handed the toast to Vivien to spread dripping on, and forked another slice of bread. 'What are you going to do?'

Hilda smiled. 'I don't fancy going out into that fog – though I suppose it's the best time for me to vanish.' She laughed. '*The Lady Vanishes*. Remember that film?'

'Yes,' groaned Flora. 'Just like I remember *The Wicked Lady*.'

The laughter disappeared from Hilda's face. 'Don't remind me, Floss. I don't know why I ever wanted to get married to Kevin. It was pure slave labour. I must have been mad.'

'I did warn you,' said Flora mildly.

'You did.' Hilda toyed with her nails, her expression pensive. 'I liked Mike, you know.'

Flora stared at her. 'Forget Mike. I'm going to marry him. He was never yours and he never will be.'

'Who sez?' Hilda laughed. 'You've got a nerve, Flo. You

haven't had anything to do with him for ages. Viv told me he stopped coming.'

'You shouldn't believe everything that Viv tells you. Take it from me, I'm going to marry him,' she said confidently.

'Good God!' Her sister stared at her. 'I think you mean it.'

'I do.' She smiled.

Hilda shook her head, a puzzled expression on her face. 'You've no objection to my going to America, I hope?' she said, a little disgruntled. 'I was just thinking Kevin's money might just be enough. There's ships leaving Liverpool every week.'

Flora's heart sank. What about her father now? 'You're a married woman,' she said quickly. 'You haven't got a passport – and what about a visa?'

'I know, I know,' murmured Hilda. Her eyes twinkled. 'But I *have* got a passport. In my maiden name. I could sell my wedding ring – and *voilà*! I'm Hilda Preston again. Kevin can sue me for divorce, that'll suit me.' Her expression was suddenly dreamy. 'Imagine America. New York! Hollywood! California here I come! Has Mike any brothers?'

Flora shook her head at her. 'You've got to get out of this house yet, big sister.'

'There's a back way.'

'Kevin's not daft.' Flora turned to George. 'Go and look out of the parlour window and see where Mr Brown is.'

He was back in a minute. 'He's hiding up the entry, Mam. We'll have to lure him away if Aunty Hilda's going to escape.'

The sisters looked at each other. Then Vivien spoke. 'You and Mam could wear each other's coats. You're not that different from the back if you both wear scarves over your hair.'

'She's got something, Mam,' said George. 'If we can trick him into following you instead of Aunty Hilda, then we've licked it.'

'We'll give it a whirl,' said Flora. The sooner her sister was out of the way, the sooner Kevin would leave, and the sooner she could make her arrangements to meet Mike.

Hilda nodded. 'Let him freeze a bit longer while we work it all out.' She wandered over to the sideboard.

'What about Mam's suitcase,' said Vivien. 'Who'll carry that?'

'I will,' said George, determined not to miss out on the adventure.

'Isn't there anything I can do?' demanded Vivien. 'I don't want to miss out on the fun.'

'Fun!' Flora stared at her and shook her head. 'You'll stay out of it.'

Hilda nodded. 'We don't want you getting in the way,' she said absently, staring down at a sheet of paper. 'What's this, Flo?'

Flora looked at the paper and snatched it out of her hand quickly. 'Never you mind. It's got nothing to do with you.' She pocketed Mike's message.

When it actually came to the parting of their ways, it was not as easy as Flora had thought. 'Well, take care of yourself.' Her throat was unexpectedly tight with tears. 'You'll write this time?'

Hilda nodded, and her eyes were moist. 'It's not goodbye for good, Flo,' she said roughly. 'We're both going to America, remember?'

'Sure,' said Flora.

They stared at each other, hazel eyes meeting blue.

Hilda smiled brightly, and scrubbed a hand across her eyes. 'Dammit! I bet I look a worse mess now. Let's get on with it, Flo.' And she pushed her sister out of the kitchen.

George nodded to Hilda, who waved to Flora standing in the lobby. Then he went into the yard and climbed on the bin, dragging himself up on to the wall, making as much noise as possible. He sent a sidelong glance along the entry and was glad to see Kevin walking towards him. 'Hello, Uncle Kev! Mam said would you like a cup of tea? You must be freezing waiting there. The wind doesn't half nip up this entry.'

'Surprisingly generous of your mam all of a sudden, isn't it?' sneered Kevin, dropping his cigarette end and grinding it into the cobbles with his heel.

'My mam is generous,' retorted George. 'And if you wait here, I'll let you have that cup of tea.'

'Wait here!' exclaimed Kevin incredulously. 'You must be joking!' His expression was suddenly that of an alerted animal and without another word he turned and ran up the entry.

George caught the flicker of scarlet as his mam sped past the far end of the entry. He watched a moment before dropping from the wall and sliding the bolt on the back gate. Hilda was beside him in seconds and he took the case from her and began to race up the entry in the opposite direction to Kevin. Hilda hurried after him as best she could in heels that kept slipping on the cobbles. Vivien stared forlornly after them.

Flora fled through the fog with Kevin not far behind her. She could hear the hollow thud of his footsteps, but on glancing behind could barely make out his shape. How long would it take Hilda to get to the tram stop in the other main road? She had no watch so could not time herself, but worked out that if she headed in the opposite direction and took a tram for one stop and walked back that should be enough. As long as Kevin did not realise he was chasing the wrong woman.

The fog lifted a moment and she could see several yards ahead, before it came down again and she was running blind. She hoped that she would not fall even as she experienced a feeling of exuberance that surprised her. Then she realised it was because it felt good to be tricking Kevin. Every time she thought of her sister's lovely face, bruised and battered, she felt angry.

Suddenly she heard the clanging of a tram and saw the glimmer of lights. She had reached the main road. Without hesitating she shot across it and managed to board the tram. It moved away just as Kevin reached it. He and Flora stared at each other through the window and she knew that he had recognised her. He shook his fist before turning and crossing back over the road. Weak with relief, Flora sat down, hoping that her sister was well away.

Kevin was blazing mad as he ran across the road and back up the long street that led eventually to Flora's house. He did not really believe that he would find Hilda there but he considered that George could easily be a substitute for his wife. He would murder him when he got his hands on him. The bloody little swine, tricking him like that!

He paused to get his breath back and took out the flask he had been sipping from for the last few hours. He drained it. The fog was beginning to lift. He ran on, thinking that he would climb that back yard gate if he had to, and get inside the house even if he had to smash a window. Then he would give George the hiding of his life.

To Kevin's surprise the back gate was open. He kicked it wide, just for the pleasure of hearing it smash against the wall. He strode through the back kitchen and sat down to wait. His fingers drummed on the arm of the chair and he began to sing a soldier's song. He was on his third when he saw Vivien's feet under the table. He laughed, and getting up he dragged her out. 'Now, if it isn't you, little sweetheart,' he muttered.

'Mam's not here, Uncle Kevin,' she stammered. 'But perhaps if you ran, you might catch her.'

Fury flashed in his face. 'Little liar.' He hit her with a force that sent her head back and she began to whimper. The sound did something to him. He changed tack as he gazed down into the face so like Hilda's. It was marred by red weals. 'Me and you used to be friends, kid. You enjoyed it when we played together, didn't you?' His voice softened. 'Shall we play now?' Vivien made no answer, staring at him with tear-filled eyes. 'Tickle-ickle,' he murmured, tickling her. 'Laugh, Viv.'

'I don't want to,' she cried, attempting to wriggle away from him, but he pinned her down with his knees. 'Come on, kid, laugh!' He tickled her until she shrieked.

'Go away!' She tried to push him but his fingers dug into her the harder, then suddenly he stopped.

'Give your Uncle Kev a kiss. You're a prettily littily thing now. Better than your mam!' An ugly look twisted his mouth. 'She's a slut!'

Tears rolled down Vivien's cheeks. 'Go away − leave me alone! You're horrible. Aunty Flo will shout at you.'

His eyes narrowed. 'Fond of her, aren't you, kid? And she loves you. She shouldn't have left you.' He shoved her down and pushed up her skirts, holding her down with one hand while he fumbled with his trouser buttons. Vivien screamed. Neither of them heard Flora coming in.

'What the hell d'you think you're doing?' Her furious voice cut the air like a knife and she rushed to her niece's side, giving Kevin a violent push that sent him sprawling sideways. His hand whacked the table leg.

'Bitch!' He spat the word at her as he stumbled to his feet, and swung a fist at her. The blow caught the side of her head and sent her flying, knocking a dining chair over. He was on her swiftly.

Vivien, suddenly fearful for her aunt, stared wildly about her for a weapon and saw the poker in the fire. She picked up the knitted holder, wrapped it round the handle and pulled the poker out. 'You leave my aunty Flo alone,' she yelled.

Kevin looked up and swore. He automatically parried the blow as Vivien brought the poker down. Its white-hot end burned through his sleeve. He yelped as the metal touched him, but his arm swung with such force that he knocked the poker out of Vivien's hand and it fell on the rug, which began to smoulder. He staggered to his feet and hit her. She crumpled in a heap on the floor.

Horrified at the way matters had turned, Flora tried to rise. Her face was throbbing and she felt dizzy. Kevin turned and grabbed her wrist. He twisted her arm up behind her back and forced her down on her knees, smiling as he did so. A scream escaped her as he shoved hard and she overbalanced, landing on the rug. She felt heat and smelt singeing, and forced herself to roll out of the way, patting her head with frantic hands to stop her hair burning. The rug was on fire.

Kevin seized her, and another scream rose in her throat but she had no chance to utter it because his weight was crushing her, wedging her under the table. 'Fire,' she managed to whisper. 'Fire, you bloody fool.'

He lifted off her slightly but made no move to do anything about the fire. Instead he tore at the buttons on Hilda's coat. Overwhelming fear and panic seized her as he tried to force up her skirts. The smoke was in her nostrils and she wondered dizzily how he could ignore it. She struggled violently, clawed at his arms and screamed and screamed.

'Shut up! Shut up!' he yelled, and slapped her across the face.

Then, unexpectedly, footsteps sounded in the lobby, above

301

the hissing of the burning linoleum. Her head turned quickly in the direction of the door as George entered. 'Oh, thank God,' she sobbed. 'George, George, help me!'

But there had been no need for her to speak. He took in the situation quickly, his heart hammering madly as Kevin jerked back on his heels. The boy's eyes searched for a weapon, and he picked up a tin of peas from the sideboard. He did not hesitate but lunged forward and brought it down on Kevin's head with tremendous force.

Flora flung herself to one side as Kevin toppled forward. Her eyes were watering and she began to cough as George hoisted her to her feet. 'Get Viv,' she croaked. 'Get out of here quickly, both of you.' The flames were running fast along the floor now.

'And you, Mam,' he said in a rising panicky voice, his face pale as he pulled on her arm, rubbing at his streaming eyes with the other hand.

'I'm coming! I'm coming in a sec!' She dragged her arm free and pushed him towards Vivien, who was gasping and trying to rise. He did as he was told and lifted his cousin to her feet, hustling her into the lobby and outside.

Flora bent over Kevin and shook him, but he did not move. Her throat closed and a spasm of coughing overtook her. She hurried towards the lobby then stopped – to pull open the sideboard door with shaking hands. She dragged out her handbag and a green tissue-wrapped parcel. Without further delay she ran down the lobby and out into the still misty, cold air.

George was coming to meet her, having dumped Vivien on the pavement. 'What'll we do, Mam?' he stammered. 'What about him?'

'You can't do anything for him. You're not going back in there again. The whole kitchen's in flames.' Her voice broke on a sob. She took a deep breath and tried to gain control of herself.

George put his arm round her and walked her down the step. 'We're all right, Mam. We got out. Keep your chin up.' His voice kept breaking however hard he tried to keep it steady. He felt the shudder go through her and her head fell against his shoulder. 'Best knock on next door and tell them,' she whispered. 'And you'll have to phone the fire brigade.'

'Yes, Mam.' He left her sitting on the pavement next to Vivien while he ran to the corner shop to phone.

The whole of the ground floor was a mass of flames, and smoke issued from the bay window upstairs. A crowd had gathered and their next door neighbour was screaming at her kids to bring out the furniture and clothes in case her place caught fire. Several people went to her aid.

Flora, George and Viv were sitting on chairs on the pavement opposite with Mrs Jones's blankets round their shoulders. Tears made streaks in their smoke dirtied faces.

'There now, Flo girl, you take it easy.' Carmel pressed a cup of tea into her hand. 'Drink that while it's nice and hot.' Obediently Flora did. Vivien was clinging to her skirt and George had a hand on her shoulder. They needed her with them.

By the time the fire brigade clanged down the street and the ambulance arrived, the upper storey was well alight. Flora knew that there was no hope of Kevin's being alive. There would be questions asked and answers required and time was ticking away.

Chapter Twenty-Three

Bearing in mind what Hilda had said about policemen being men, Flora did not tell it exactly as it was to the constable on the beat. Her brother-in-law had had a tiff with her sister, she said, and he had come to her house looking for her. She wouldn't believe she wasn't there and turned quite nasty. He had been drinking. Got violent. No, she wasn't sure how the fire started exactly.

Tears started in her eyes at this point and the policeman changed tack. 'Do you have any idea where your sister is?'

'No,' said Flora honestly, dabbing at her eyes with her sleeve, and realised that it was Hilda's coat she had on. She only hoped that none of the neighbours who knew her sister would think to comment on it.

'We could put a message out over the wireless,' the policeman muttered, putting away his notebook. 'If I draw a blank at her friend's house.'

'Perhaps if a report of the fire is put in the *Echo*?' suggested Flora.

The policeman eased the strap under his chin. 'I don't doubt it'll be in tomorrow's paper. The newshounds are already on the scene. Have you got some relative you can stay with tonight, Mrs Cooke?'

'My father.'

He stilled. 'Your sister wouldn't go to him?'

'Oh no,' said Flora positively. 'They don't get on.'

'A bit of a tartar is she, your sister?' he said drily.

Flora smiled slightly. 'You could say that.'

'You'll be all right then?'

'Yes.' She wanted to get rid of him as quickly as possible. 'Thank you, constable.' She forced a smile. 'Can you tell me the time?'

He looked at the large watch on his wrist. 'Five-thirty-eight precisely.'

Her nerves jumped. 'Thanks.' He saluted her and walked away.

Flora watched him cross the road to speak to the chief fireman standing on her littered front step, then she rose quickly from the chair. 'Where are you going?' Vivien came up with her, still clinging to her skirt.

'Grandad's. We'll have to go to there,' she informed the girl, hurriedly folding the blanket. 'Kathleen, thank your mother for the tea and tell her where we've gone.'

The girl nodded, watching as George got to his feet. 'What'll yer do, Mrs Cooke? Where'll yer live now?'

Flora opened her mouth to speak but George was before her. 'America. Me mam's going to marry Mike,' he said roughly, kicking at a stone.

Kathleen's mouth fell open and she said shakily, 'Yer not goin' to America, George, are yer?'

George looked at his mother and shrugged his shoulders. 'I could live with me grandad,' he said in a hard voice, and turned away and began to walk up the street.

'I'll go to America with you, Aunty Flo,' said Vivien eagerly, perking up.

Flora made no response, only seizing the girl's hand and following in George's wake. She caught up with him, 'George Cooke! We are a family and we stay together,' she said emphatically. 'I haven't got to America yet, and you're not to mention any of this to your grandad. I'll tell him when the time's ripe.'

'He still thinks you're going to marry Stephen Martin,' he muttered.

'Well, neither of you is to tell him I'm not.' Her gaze went from one to the other. 'I've got to meet Mike at seven tonight. I haven't got much time and if I start trying to explain even part of what's happened to your grandad, I won't make it.' She hurried them along.

'You mean — we've got to tell fibs?' demanded Vivien. 'What about the fire?'

Flora gnawed at her lower lip. 'Perhaps it'll be best if I don't come in. Just see you to the door. He's bound to delay me. You can tell him anything you want. It's probably better to stick to the truth.'

George sighed heavily. 'Why d'you have to meet him tonight?'

'Because he's leaving,' she cried impatiently. 'And I'll have to be getting the tram soon to the Pierhead or I might never see him again. He doesn't know I'm marrying him yet!'

'He doesn't?' George stopped and stared at her, realising how it would be if she did not reach Mike in time, and had a moment's struggle with himself. At least he preferred Mike to Stephen. A long sigh escaped him. 'You'd better just see us across the main road, Mam. We don't want you missing the boat. Me and Viv know the way to Grandad's.'

Flora was so touched she could not speak. When they came to the main road, she kissed Vivien. 'You will be coming back for us?' said the girl anxiously.

'Yes,' said Flora. Then she turned to George. 'Thanks, son.' She hugged him.

'Get going, Mam,' he said roughly, freeing himself. His brown eyes were moist. 'There's a tram coming.'

'Across the road with you first, then, while I'm watching,' she said.

They ran, pausing to wave on the other side, and then they raced up the road. She wasted a few seconds watching them, then legged it to the stop.

Once on the tram Flora was aware of a couple of curious glances, and pulled her scarf further forward. Delving in her handbag she took a small oblong mirror out of the pocket and looked at her reflection. She touched the swelling on her face; already it was purpling. There was no face powder in her bag but there was the tiny phial of *Evening in Paris* perfume that Mike had tied on the Christmas tree. She dabbed it behind her ears, determinedly concentrating on the happy times and not the horrors of the day.

As the tram went down into the city Flora did what she had done a long time ago when she had gone to meet Mike in town. Her fingers rubbed a clear patch in the condensation on the window. It was dark and still a bit foggy and she imagined the pilot boat waiting on the Mersey — the tugs, the ocean liner *California Star*. Her stomach flipped over. What if Mike had meant it was sailing at 7 p.m.? Dear God! She sent up a prayer that it was not so. Time and tide waited for no man. Corny but true. She took out his letter. Why couldn't he have written more? Perhaps she was assuming too much? Maybe he wouldn't want her when she told him about the baby? He couldn't be blamed if he was fed up with her. Hurry up tram!

The Liver Building clock read a misty 6.45 p.m. when Flora stepped off the tram. Quickly she headed for the covered passengerway in company with a group of people. The tide was in, which meant the gangway sloped steeply upwards. By the time she came on to the floating landing stage, her legs were aching. The ferry from Birkenhead had just come in and she was jostled by a couple hurrying for it. She whirled to her right and began to run. Her scarf began to slide and she dragged it off and stuffed it in her pocket.

A fog horn sounded mournfully on the river. Her heart was pounding and there was a pain in her side. Her foot slipped on the wet wood but she caught herself up and went on, past where the Isle of Man boats berthed, and on. She felt quite sick. Then she saw the ship and people milling around. Her pace slowed to a walk, and her head turned this way and that as she tried to spot Mike, but she could not see any man dressed in the uniform of an American airman. She could not believe that she had come too late and her eyes turned automatically to the Liver clock, but it was lost in the fog at this distance. She hurried and drew closer to the ship. Now she could read its name, and with a sickening jolt of disappointment discovered that it was not the *California Star*.

Panic drove her on.

Then she heard her name being called. Abruptly she stopped, not quite sure where the voice had come from, but she looked up at the next ship. Again she heard her name, and recognised Mike's voice. The relief was overwhelming. She turned and saw him hurrying towards her in the familiar uniform of drab green. 'Mike!' she croaked and ran to meet him.

She fell into his arms, hugging and squeezing him. 'I thought you'd gone! I thought you'd gone!'

'And I thought you weren't coming!' His voice was muffled against her hair. 'You went right past me and I didn't recognise you at first in this coat. But you were running and I thought — you look familiar.'

'It's Hilda's,' she gasped. 'It's a long story and I won't have time to tell you it. I'll write, though. You do still want to marry me, don't you?'

'What d'you think that note was about, babe!' He kissed her.

'Thank God,' she said weakly, as his mouth lifted. 'I'm pregnant.'

'I thought you might be.' His cheek rested against hers.

'You did it deliberately.'

'You let it happen.'

'Yes. I think there's madness in our family.'

'I love you.'

'I love you too. When d'you have to go?'

He drew away from her, and taking her cold hand, placed it with his in his pocket. 'I have a choice, but before I could make a decision I felt I had to shock you into making a choice too, Flora.'

She stared at him and he quirked an eyebrow. There was a long silence. 'I got very puffed,' she said crossly. 'It's not good for a woman in my condition to be rushing through Liverpool. You've no idea of the kind of day I've had.'

'You can tell me all about it.' His voice was warm and soothing. 'But will it make you feel any better if I tell you that Burtonwood isn't closing down? With the way the situation is in Europe, the powers in charge think there's still a need for it. We could stay on here for a while if that would make life easier for you.'

It took Flora only a few seconds to take in what he was saying. 'Yes,' she said in a low voice, squeezing his hand. 'Thank you, Mike.'

'They call the base Little America,' he murmured. 'It'll give you a taste of the American way of life.'

'In Warrington?' A chuckle escaped her. 'Our Hilda wouldn't fancy that.'

'No. It wouldn't suit Hilda.' He smiled at her. 'It's too down to earth. Not a bit like the movies. What's this about you wearing her coat?'

'I'll explain.' Flora took a deep breath and began to talk.

She was still telling her story as they came to the passengerway. Mike's expression was grim and he hugged her close. 'You could have died in that fire. As it is, it looks like Hilda got away scot-free again,' he said bitterly.

'Not quite,' she said softly, pausing and staring unseeingly out towards the estuary. 'You didn't see her face.' There was a brief silence, then Flora murmured, 'She said that she's going to go to America with Kevin's money.'

'Hell!'

'From what I've heard it's a big country — big enough for us to stay out of each other's way.' But Flora did not believe it would be that way. Not really. Her sister had a habit . . .

'Yeah! But — God help America,' groaned Mike.

Flora laughed, and as they began to walk down the passengerway, she said, 'Hollywood! That's where she'll go. It's the place of her dreams. Now I prefer reality.'

'A house by the ocean?' He grinned at her.

'One day,' she said dreamily. 'One day, Mike, my dream will come true.'

'Sure it will. Didn't I say that I'd build you that house. But now, Flora? Anywhere you want to go? Anything you want to do?

She was silent a moment, but as they came out of the passageway she looked up at the Liver Building. Her eyes could just about make out the Liver bird hovering in the swirling fog. For a brief second Tom flashed through her thoughts, then he was gone.

She turned and smiled at him. 'You have a choice. Do we face my father straightaway or go to the Adelphi for food and — ?'

'A bath? You sure need one, honey.'

Mike whirled Flora into his arms and danced her across the cobbles.

No more needed to be said.

A SELECTED LIST OF FINE TITLES
AVAILABLE FROM BANTAM BOOKS

THE PRICES SHOWN BELOW WERE CORRECT AT THE TIME OF GOING TO
PRESS. HOWEVER TRANSWORLD PUBLISHERS RESERVE THE RIGHT TO
SHOW NEW RETAIL PRICES ON COVERS WHICH MAY DIFFER FROM THOSE
PREVIOUSLY ADVERTISED IN THE TEXT OR ELSEWHERE.

☐	40163 7	THE BUSINESS	*Charlotte Bingham*	£4.99
☐	17635 8	TO HEAR A NIGHTINGALE	*Charlotte Bingham*	£4.99
☐	40427 X	BELGRAVIA	*Charlotte Bingham*	£3.99
☐	40172 6	A WORLD OF DIFFERENCE	*Leona Blair*	£4.99
☐	40321 4	AN INCONVENIENT WOMAN	*Dominic Dunne*	£4.99
☐	17676 5	PEOPLE LIKE US	*Dominic Dunne*	£3.99
☐	17189 5	THE TWO MRS GRENVILLES	*Dominic Dunne*	£3.50
☐	40230 7	STOLEN DREAMS	*Barbara Harrison*	£4.50
☐	17151 8	SCENTS	*Johanna Kingsley*	£4.99
☐	40206 4	FAST FRIENDS	*Gill Mansell*	£3.99
☐	40360 5	SOLO	*Gill Mansell*	£3.99
☐	40363 X	RICH MAN'S FLOWERS	*Madeleine Polland*	£4.99
☐	17209 3	THE CLASS	*Erich Segal*	£2.95
☐	17630 7	DOCTORS	*Erich Segal*	£3.99
☐	40261 7	THE VILLAGE	*Sarah Shears*	£3.99
☐	40262 5	FAMILY FORTUNES	*Sarah Shears*	£3.99
☐	17659 5	THE SLIPPER	*Jennifer Wilde*	£3.99

*All Corgi/Bantam Books are available at your bookshop or newsagent, or can be ordered from the
following address:*

Corgi/Bantam Books,
Cash Sales Department,
P.O. Box 11, Falmouth, Cornwall TR10 9EN

UK and B.F.P.O. customers please send a cheque or postal order (no currency) and allow £1.00
for postage and packing for the first book plus 50p for the second book and 30p for each
additional book to a maximum charge of £3.00 (7 books plus).

Overseas customers, including Eire, please allow £2.00 for postage and packing for the first
book, £1.00 for the second book, and 50p for each subsequent title ordered.

NAME (Block Letters) ....

ADDRESS ....

....